DAVID ELLIS
THE HIDDEN MAN

ALSO BY DAVID ELLIS

Eye of the Beholder
In the Company of Liars
Jury of One
Life Sentence
Line of Vision

DAVID ELLIS

THE HIDDEN MAN

Quercus

First published in Great Britain in 2009 by

Quercus
21 Bloomsbury Square
London
WC1A 2NS

A CIP catalogue record for this book is available
from the British Library

ISBN (HB) 978 1 84724 878 7
ISBN (TPB) 978 1 84724 879 4

Printed and bound in Great Britain by Clays Ltd, St Ives Plc

10 9 8 7 6 5 4 3 2 1

For my beautiful Abigail

SUMMER 1980

ACT NORMAL, whatever that means. Normal. Like everyone else. Not different. Not like a freak. Just another person at the park.

It was a beautiful day, a glorious weekend in June, so bright you had to squint, so mild you didn't feel the air. The playground was a perfect chaos, abuzz with children's high-pitched squeals and whining pleas, parents calling after them in scolding voices, various playground contraptions in full animation, like busy turbines propelling the jubilant park.

Audrey. That was the name they called her. A surge of vicarious joy, watching her, her purity, her unadulterated innocence before the world turns cruel.

I feel like you sometimes. Like a child still. A child trapped in a grown-up's body.

Audrey. She wore pink overalls and a bonnet with polka dots. Her tiny forehead crinkled in concentration as she gathered the sand in her hands and watched, fascinated, as it dissipated through her fingers.

I know we have a connection, Audrey. I know we do.

Audrey. She looked around her, up at the sky, at the other children in the sandbox, at her mother, a range of emotions crossing her tiny little face as the toddler slowly discovered the world around her.

"Audrey." Saying the name aloud was dangerous. Someone might hear.

Don't dare get close. Her mother isn't far away. They'll know. They'll read it on my face, what I feel for you.

"C'mon, sweetheart." Her mother scooped her up in her arms. "Sammy! Jason! Jason, get Sammy. C'mon, guys." The boys, older by a few years, were over on the swing set. They jumped off the swings and landed with a flourish. The mother led the boys, still holding Audrey—Audrey—as she walked away.

I will follow you, Audrey. I will see you soon.

2

MARY CUTLER'S HEAD jerked off the pillow. A mother's reflex. She'd been a light sleeper since Sammy was born seven years ago. Probably some shift in the pressure in the house, some break in equilibrium, had stirred her. Probably that was all.

Her eyes drifted to the clock by the bed. It was ten past two. Frank must just be getting home, probably reeking of alcohol and cigarettes, maybe even perfume. A brief surge of rage penetrated her sleepy haze. She wondered if she would have the energy to raise the issue.

Her eyes closed again as she surrendered to exhaustion, one maternal ear open to external sounds as her face fit into a cool, comfortable space in a pillow, as her conscious mind spiraled away—

Her eyes popped open. Her body stiffened. Something dark and uneasy filled her chest. Her legs slid out of the bed. She stepped past her slippers and moved across the carpet in her bare feet. An unknowing feeling of dread reached her throat as she moved down the hall and pushed the bedroom door open, where her boy, Sammy, slept over the covers of his bed.

She crossed the kitchen toward Audrey's bedroom and felt a breeze reach her. She picked up her pace to a jog. Before she saw the empty bed, with the covers pulled back, she saw the open window, a window that had been closed when she had put her daughter down hours ago.

She didn't hear herself scream.

———————

AS HE NAVIGATED the corner in his sedan, Detective Vic Carruthers groaned. A small crowd of neighbors had already gathered around a squad car that had just pulled up outside the house. Was it idle curiosity surrounding the police presence? Or had word leaked out?

It had been five hours since two-year-old Audrey Cutler had been abducted from her home—snatched out of her bed at two in the morning. An insomniac neighbor, three doors down, had seen someone running down the street from the Cutler house. *It looked like they were carrying something*, the neighbor had said, with a trace of after-the-fact apology.

The trail had gone cold. The description was next to nothing. Medium height, baseball cap—best the neighbor could do from a distance of a football field, with the lighting weak at best. Nothing telltale from the scene. No fingerprints, no shoe prints, nothing.

Until they had run a check on prior offenders. Griffin Perlini, age twenty-eight, lived a quarter mile from the Cutler home. He had a kiddie sheet. And not just minors: He liked them young.

The arrests had been for sexual contact, but one had been dropped, the other convicted on the lesser charge of indecent exposure. Griffin Perlini had lured a four-year-old into the woods by a playground in a downstate town. The state had apparently decided it couldn't prove the sexual touching, but they convicted on eyewitness testimony that Perlini had been seen pulling up his pants as the witness approached him.

"Got a feeling about this," Carruthers told his partner, Joe Gooden.

They got out at the curb. Carruthers nodded at the uniform who followed in step behind the senior officers. Carruthers did a once-over. It was a ranch, like many of the places on the block. Old place with vinyl siding. Cobblestone steps leading from the driveway to the small porch. The lawn had seen better times. No vehicle in the driveway. A one-car attached garage.

Only seven in the morning, but already sticky-hot. Gooden had a sheen across his forehead.

Carruthers rang the doorbell and stepped back, keeping an angle that allowed him to look for movement near the windows. It came quickly, a stirring of a curtain on the east side front.

"He's got five seconds," Carruthers said. If his gut was right on this, he wasn't going to give Perlini time to dispose of evidence—or a little girl.

He heard a small pop at the door—the deadbolt releasing—then a face that resembled a mug shot he'd recently seen, staring at him through a torn screen door.

"Mr. Perlini?"

The man didn't answer.

"Detective Carruthers. This is Detective Gooden."

Carruthers stopped there. Curious about the response he'd get.

Perlini's eyes dropped. Pedophiles were like that. Wouldn't look adults in the eye.

"Yeah?" Perlini said.

"We're looking for a little girl, Mr. Perlini. She wandered off from her house. We think she walked this way, and we were wondering if anyone took her in. Y'know, to take care of her, until her parents showed."

The first order of business here was to get that little girl back home safe. Didn't matter how. He was giving Perlini an out, the opportunity to pretend that the child had simply wandered off, that Perlini had done what any good citizen might do. From Perlini's perspective, it was a way to stop this right now, with the possibility of avoiding a criminal charge.

Perlini didn't answer.

"She's real young," Carruthers elaborated. "Probably too young to even say her name. So we figured, maybe someone was hanging on to her. To be safe."

It was going to work now or never. The suspect couldn't hesitate on the answer. Either he had her or he didn't. If he had her, and he was going to buy this out Carruthers was offering, he'd have to purchase that ticket now.

"I was just sleepin'." Perlini scratched his head, gathered a bunch of his thick red hair in his hand.

Well, you answered the door pretty damn fast for being asleep.

"How 'bout we step inside and talk a minute." Carruthers wasn't asking.

Perlini scratched his head again and looked back over his shoulder. He had a small frame. He was skinny and below-average height. The neighbor's description wasn't much, but it generally fit this guy.

"What do ya say, Griffin? A quick talk."

"Um—well—my lawyer is Reggie Lionel."

His lawyer. Carruthers felt a rush.

Perlini pointed behind him. "I could call him, but it's early—"

"Your lawyer needs his beauty sleep, Griffin." Carruthers grabbed the handle to the screen door, but it wouldn't move.

Perlini's eyes moved up to the detective's, reading pure fear.

"You'll need to unlock this door, Griffin. Right now. *Right* now."

"O—okay. Okay." He pushed the door open.

Carruthers took the door handle. "Take two steps back, please."

Carruthers, Gooden, and the uniform stepped in. Perlini suddenly looked lost in his own house, unsure of what to do, where to stand or where to go. Carruthers thought he'd let Perlini make the call. Surely, Perlini would try to direct them away from anything telltale.

The detective's pulse was racing. She might be here in the house. She might still be alive. Behind him, Detective Gooden was strolling casually beyond the foyer, looking for anything in plain view.

"Is anyone else in this house, Griffin?"

Perlini shook his head, no.

"Griffin, you know a girl named Audrey Cutler?"

Perlini's eyes were once again downcast, in anticipation of unwanted questioning, like a child expecting a scolding. On mention of the girl's name, his eyes froze. His posture stiffened.

The answer was yes.

"No," Perlini said.

"Griffin," Gooden called out, "you don't mind I look around a little?"

He did mind; it was all over his face. But pedophiles, they didn't have a spine, not with adults. It wasn't exactly textbook consent, but Perlini hadn't said no. Carruthers was pretty sure he'd be able to reflect back on this moment and remember Perlini nodding his head.

"Eyes up, Griffin. Look at me." Carruthers gestured to his own eyes, his fingers forked in a peace sign.

Perlini did the best he could, his eyes sweeping back and forth past Carruthers like a searchlight.

"If there was a misunderstanding here, Griffin—if maybe you thought about doing something but changed your mind—hey, let's get that girl back home. No harm, no foul—"

"No. No." Perlini shook his head, the insolent child, and gripped his tomato-red hair in two fists.

Carruthers heard a noise outside. A voice, yelling. He looked through the door and saw a man pointing at the house, talking to a gathering crowd. Something about a child molester.

The detective turned back to Perlini, who was beginning to dissolve. He was shaking his head with a childlike fury, tears forming in his eyes.

"This won't get any better, Griffin," Carruthers told him. "Every minute you stiff-arm me, it gets worse."

"*Vic!*"

Gooden's voice sounded distant.

"Take that seat over there, Griffin." He pointed to a small living room, a beat-up love seat with a torn cushion. He nodded to the officer, who clearly understood his direction to keep an eye on the suspect.

Carruthers moved quickly down a small tiled hallway, turned into a carpeted room with a television and fireplace, and found the back door to the place ajar. He stepped outside, into a yard of neglected grass and some old lawn furniture.

"Vic!"

His partner was calling from the detached garage behind the house. No—it wasn't a garage at all, just a small coach house within the fenced property.

"I'm here," Carruthers said, opening the door. "Jesus Christ."

The room was filled with black-and-white photos on the walls and hung from clotheslines. Children. Toddlers. Dozens of them, looked to be ages two or three at best. Some of them were taken indoors—maybe a shopping mall, probably the one a couple miles away. Most of them were photos from a park.

Gooden walked along one of the clotheslines and fingered a series of photos taken of a small girl in a sandbox. Carruthers had seen the face very recently. For confirmation he did not need, he removed the photograph of Audrey Cutler from his jacket pocket, her innocent serenity lighting a deepening rage within him.

He marched into the main house, his body on fire, his hands balled in fists. He thought of Mary Cutler, hours ago, clutching her seven-year-old son Sammy in her arms, bursting out words breathlessly as she gave a physical description of Audrey.

He thought of that little boy, Sammy Cutler, the confused expression on his tiny face, not comprehending the situation entirely but understanding, on some level, that something bad had happened to his baby sister.

Griffin Perlini sat motionless in the chair, his head in his hands. The officer snapped to attention when he saw Carruthers, the officer's expression confirming the look on Carruthers's face.

Carruthers brushed past the officer. He grabbed Griffin Perlini by the shoulders and pushed him hard against the back cushion.

"You tell me where she is," he said in a controlled whisper, "before I rip your throat out."

Twenty-six
Years Later
September 2006

3

"PACK A MARLBORO LIGHTS, box. Make it two." Sammy Cutler fished a crumpled twenty out of his pocket. He threw a container of Tic-Tacs onto the conveyer as well, joining a couple of frozen dinners. The grocery store clerk, a young Latina woman with soft skin and hair as dark as coal, looked as bored and tired as Sammy felt. Sammy had just finished a double shift on the new highway being built. He figured he had another month, tops, of good weather before the construction trade shut down for the long winter. He didn't have a back-up plan at the moment. Employers weren't knocking down the door for ex-cons.

He slipped one pack of cigarettes into the pocket of his flannel shirt, the other in his leather jacket. He noticed his hands, big and rough and hairy and swollen from another day of manual labor.

"Where the hell is Manny?"

Sammy glanced at the complaining man, standing in the next grocery line over, wearing a starched white shirt and a name tag that indicated some authority. Top grocery guy. He grabbed a plastic bag and began packing groceries that were piling up in the area past the register.

"Griffin," the man said. "Griffin!"

Sammy felt his body go cold.

"—your change, mister."

Sammy looked down at the green bills and silver coins placed into his hands. Then back up, at a man who entered his sight line, approaching the grocery store manager. The man was small, hunched, with small green eyes and cropped hair, grayed at the sides but mostly a dark red.

"Work this aisle, Griffin. Where is Manny?"

"*I* don't know."

Sammy bristled at hearing the voice. He'd never heard the man speak. Never even laid eyes on the man. He'd been so young.

Griffin.

And surely there were other people with the name, however unusual it may be.

But he looked the part. Sammy had served with some of them, the ones who liked little kids. You could spot them from a mile away. Meek and squirrelly. Like they carried an inner shame that never left them.

Yes. This was the man that had killed his sister twenty-six years ago.

Sammy felt himself move, his focus on the grocery clerk named *Griffin* shifting from front to profile.

"Don't forget your groceries, mister."

Sammy's trembling hand reached out. His grip closed over the plastic handle of the bag.

"Don't worry," he said slowly. "I haven't forgotten."

ONE YEAR LATER
OCTOBER 2007

4

HE CALLED an hour ahead for an appointment, and he called himself Mr. Smith. Over the phone to my assistant, he didn't specify the reason for the visit other than saying he had a "legal matter," which distinguished him from absolutely no one else who entered my law office.

From the moment my assistant Marie showed him in, he felt wrong. He presented, frankly, better than most potential clients. He was thin, precisely dressed in an Italian wool suit, a deep dimple in his shiny blue tie, gray hair immaculately combed. It was clear that whatever he wanted from me, he'd be able to afford the freight. So far, so good.

But still—wrong. His hand was moist when I shook it, and he didn't make eye contact. As I retreated behind my desk, he closed the office door behind him. It wasn't uncommon for visitors to want discretion with their lawyer, but still—it was my office, not his. It was a power move, establishment of control.

"Mr. Smith," I said, wondering if that was his real name. I was assuming this was a criminal matter, and I like to guess the crime before the client tells me. A slick guy like him made me think of financial crimes or pedophilia. If it was the latter, this was going to be a very short conversation.

Smith didn't seem too impressed with the surroundings. I wasn't, either. I had a couple of diplomas on the walls and some pieces of art picked up at an estate sale and some bookcases filled with law books I never use. My brother had given me a couch that I put near the back of my office, though I wasn't sure if that made the place look too cramped.

In his thousand-dollar suit, Smith looked like a fish out of water. He had one of those pocket squares that matched his tie. I never owned a pocket square in my life. I hate pocket squares.

"We'll require your services, Mr. Kolarich. Can you tell me your hourly fee?"

In my recent reincarnation as a solo practitioner, I find that I have three categories of clients. Category one is a flat fee to handle a small criminal matter, like a DUI or misdemeanor. Category two pays me by the hour, with an up-front retainer. Category three is the client who promises to pay but stiffs me instead.

My hourly fee, where applicable, is usually a buck fifty. But I decided, then and there, that it was time to have an escalating fee schedule, depending on whether my client wears a pocket square.

"Three hundred," I answered. It felt nice just saying it.

Smith seemed amused. Well-bred as he was—or was trying to appear— he stifled any comment. He was getting a mark-up, and he wanted me to know that he knew.

It usually took me a full half hour to dislike someone, but this guy was narrowing that window considerably.

"Three hundred an hour would be acceptable," said he.

Then again, maybe I was being too hard on the guy.

"You're young," Smith said to me. "Young for a case like this."

"Mozart composed a symphony before the age of ten."

"I see." I didn't get the impression that Smith was placing me in the same category as the prodigy Amadeus.

"You came to me, friend," I reminded him.

He didn't offer a response, but I could see that he wasn't here by choice. Why, then, *was* he here?

"The man you'll be representing is charged with first-degree murder, Mr. Kolarich."

That sounded like something important, so I reached for my pen and notepad. I wrote, *pocket square = big fee.*

"The man he killed was a sexual predator," Smith told me.

My would-be client killed a pedophile? Well, if you're going to pick a victim, there's none better.

"And who are you to this guy?" I asked Smith.

He thought about that for a while. It didn't seem like a hard question to me.

Typically, if it's not the defendant himself reaching out for counsel, it's a family member on his behalf. I didn't get the sense that Smith fell into that category.

"As you can imagine," Smith finally said, "sex offenders usually count their victims in the multiple, not the singular."

Right, but he was being vague. Talking around the subject. I do that all the time, but I don't trust people who remind me of myself.

It didn't feel like Smith, or someone he loved, had been victimized by this pedophile, which was what he was suggesting. He wasn't carrying that emotion. I like to think I can read a guy, and his face wasn't registering that kind of pain. I was getting disdain, though it seemed to be directed more at me than anything else.

"You'll take the case at three hundred dollars an hour," he informed me. "Or someone else will gladly handle it."

With that, Smith pushed himself out of the chair and remained standing before me. I'm not a big fan of ultimatums, unless I'm the one giving them. It's been said that I have a problem with people telling me what to do. I think I was the one who said that.

Smith checked his watch. He'd obviously figured that I would jump at the chance for a case like this, but I hadn't. In his mind, I was either stubborn or stupid.

But, I noted, he hadn't walked away. He didn't like bidding against himself, but for some reason he was set on hiring me for this case, and he knew he needed to give me more.

"When was he arrested?" I asked.

"September," he said. "Of last year."

"September—of '06?" If this were a single-defendant case, as it seemed to be, that meant the trial couldn't be far away.

"Four weeks from today," Smith informed me.

"Well." I waved a hand. "We'll have to get the trial date kicked."

"That won't work."

Sometimes I smile when I'm getting really annoyed with someone. I smile and count to ten. After reaching the count of six, I said, "We need to be clear on a few things, Smith. If you want to pay me, that's fine. I don't care who's doing the paying as long as the money is there. Right? But you don't decide what will work. My client and I make those decisions. You're not my client, nor are you even related to this client. So you have no say. You're an ATM machine to me and nothing more. And I'm not taking a first-degree on one-month's notice."

Smith nodded at me, but he wasn't agreeing with me. Kind of like how I smile when I'm pissed off. "You'll consult with your client on that," he said.

"I'll tell this client what I just told you, and if he doesn't like it, he won't be my client."

Smith considered me. I wanted to wipe the smug expression off his face. Maybe I'd use his pocket square to do it. Finally, the briefest hint of a smile appeared.

"The client is an old friend of yours," he said. "The client is Sam Cutler."

Sammy. It came at me at once, a tidal wave of images, sights and sounds and smells from so long ago. So this was why Smith had picked me.

"Audrey," I said. "Sammy killed the pedophile who killed his sister, Audrey?"

"Correct." Smith nodded. "Griffin Perlini, you'll recall."

Even now, I physically shuddered at the name. The bogeyman to a seven-year-old. I could attribute many sleepless nights, and many burned-out lightbulbs, to that name. The man who single-handedly laid wreck to the Cutler family.

"There are those of us who believe that Mr. Cutler should not be punished for that act," Smith said.

Of all the images that might stick, for some reason it was this: Audrey Cutler, a year and a half old, staggering around on a toddler's legs in the grass backyard, Sammy hovering behind her to catch her fall. One of the other kids made a joke about how Audrey walked—*she looks retarded* or something like that. Sammy didn't say anything at the time; he only looked at me. When Sammy's mother called for Audrey to come in,

Sammy carried her inside. By the time he returned to the backyard a few minutes later, I was already holding the kid down, and Sammy and I made sure he never had anything but compliments about Audrey's walking ability in the future.

I didn't know how to feel about all of this. Since Talia and Emily, most of my emotions had atrophied. I felt tension and panic begin to flex their muscles.

Sammy, obviously, had asked for me. That stood to reason, I guess. I wondered how closely he had followed the course of my life. I hadn't spoken to Sammy Cutler in almost twenty years. I had no idea what had become of him, which made me feel uneasy with myself.

"The money will not be a problem," Smith informed me. "I will have a healthy retainer delivered to you no later than tomorrow. I trust you'll have time in your schedule to visit Mr. Cutler this afternoon?"

I nodded absently, as the wave of memories poured forth, a young boy who'd lost his sister, a devastated mother, the picture of an open window into Audrey Cutler's bedroom on a haunted summer night.

TALIA PUSHES OUR DAUGHTER, Emily, in the stroller through the city's zoo, stopping at the sea lion pool as Emily squeals with delight. Emily wants out. Talia lifts her in her arms and approaches the gate, where the sea lions pop out of the water to the delight of the children, proudly thrusting their black snouts in the air.

"Seals," Emily says.

"Sea lions." Not that Talia knows the difference. She smiles at her daughter.

Talia always loved the city. The daughter of Italian immigrants, she was born and raised out east but moved to the city for college and never left. She loves the vitality, the pace, the diversity, the theater and dining and culture. She wants Emily to grow up here.

"Seals," Emily says. But after ten minutes, her attention span is spent, and she is saying, "Hippos."

"Okay, sweetheart." Talia musses Em's hair and kisses her forehead. Emily doesn't want the stroller and she doesn't want to walk, leaving Talia to carry our daughter while pushing the stroller.

"Where's Daddy?" Emily asks.

"He has that case he's working on, honey." But Emily has already moved on, distracted as they pass by the next exhibit, otters. She forgets her question and struggles with the word. "Ott-oh," she manages, clapping her hands in self-applause.

Talia's face lights up, as it always does when our daughter is happy. Funny how those tiny details can make such a difference.

Talia kisses the top of Emily's head. "I love you, sweetheart," she says.

I love you, too. I love you both.

I WAS A LITTLE EARLY to the detention center where Sammy Cutler was held. The center, next to the criminal courthouse, was shiny new, but with the new construction came additional security as well. It no longer mattered if you had a bar card; attorney or not, they ran you through the metal detector and inspected your bag. I didn't mind because I wasn't in a hurry. I wasn't ready to concentrate on what Sammy would tell me. I was thinking about Emily, the first time she reached out to grab my nose, though her little wrinkled hand couldn't yet form a fist. I remembered that baby smell, the feel of that warm, tiny body in the cradle of my forearm, those wondrous, innocent eyes—

I took a ridiculously long drink from the water fountain, used the bathroom, splashed cold water on my face, and looked at myself in the mirror. I was always in a foul mood after lunch, but still I kept that daily appointment, notwithstanding the fierce come-down, the growing resentment with each passing day, wondering when it would get better, if it would get better, why it would get better.

The only thing I knew was I was still a mess, still mired in a combination of self-pity, bitterness, and hopelessness. I was a lawyer, but I would be of no use to Sammy Cutler.

Sammy. Many different snapshots filtered through: The skinny little kid with the big ears and flyaway hair, scampering through the rushing water of an open fire hydrant. The ten-year-old with a buzz cut, a growing solemnity in his expression. The teenager, hardened, solving problems with his fists. Differing portraits as time moved forward, I realized now more than I had as a child.

I didn't notice him until he approached the door with the security escort. We made eye contact, an awkward moment, as we appraised each other with the mild surprise that accompanies any encounter following decades of separation, no matter how you try to make adjustments for maturity, for hard breaks along the way. I'd done that time-adjusted analysis and come up short, way off. He wasn't what I expected. He looked, in fact, much more like the clients I'd been defending for the last six weeks.

Sammy was thick in the torso with meaty arms, a blotchy complexion, oily hair pulled back in a ponytail. His nose was crooked, with dried, crusty skin around his nostrils. His eyes were the only sign of life, large blue eyes that searched me with the hope I've seen many times from clients.

So many things came back so quickly, but seeing him in manacles brought back the most logical, the most obvious vision. Age sixteen, Sammy in handcuffs, his head down inside the police interview room.

Better me than you, he'd said to me then.

"You don't need to do that," I told the prison guard, who had seated Sammy in the chair and was locking his handcuffs to a metal clip on the table. The guard locked him down anyway, before leaving attorney and client to their own devices.

Sammy smiled nervously, almost apologetically. From his perspective, this had to be incredibly difficult, a reunion while in a prison jumpsuit. With some effort, given the manacles connecting his hands, he fished out cigarettes and lit up.

We were eleven when we first did that, stole a smoke from his mother and ran to the park, vainly attempting to light the damn thing by striking a match on a rock, then coughing as the smoke burned our throats and chests. Sammy never really stopped after that time, and neither did I until the day Coach Fox realized that I had some speed and could catch a football.

"Jason," he said.

Even that simple greeting felt wrong, painful. I don't recall Sammy ever addressing me by my first name. It was never Jason. It was *Koke,* short for *Koka-Kolarich,* a play off my last name.

"Some place for a reunion, huh?" he added.

Right, and one of those awkward ones where nobody wants to talk about their past. Most reunions would start with a rundown on immediate family. There wouldn't be much of that here. For starters, his sister, Audrey, was abducted when Sammy was seven.

His father, Frank Cutler, a plumber who drank more often than he worked, left only a few weeks later. Way I heard it, Sammy's mother had allowed no shortage of blame for Audrey's abduction to fall on Frank, who had been out on a bender that evening.

Sammy's mother, Mary, died about nine years later from kidney failure, some rare genetic thing, leaving him with no immediate family. By then, Sammy was already serving time in a juvenile detention facility. When he got out, he had no mother, father, or sister.

I knew, only from reading the file Smith had given me, that Sammy later did two stints in the penitentiary, one for possession with intent, the other for aggravated battery. The truth was, I'd barely spoken to Sammy after that day the cops had taken him away.

Better me than you, he'd said to me then. *Better me than you.*

"So you're like a big-time lawyer, huh?" He said it like he approved. That was how I remembered Sammy. He was rough around the edges, but he never intended anyone harm. "Saw you on TV a while back about some big case."

That was back at my old firm. I'd second-chaired the defense of a state senator on federal corruption charges. It was a fourteen-week trial, in which the feds had prosecuted a sitting state senator, Hector Almundo, on eleven counts, running the gamut from taking bribes to extortion. The trial began exactly two weeks after Talia gave birth to Emily.

"That seemed like a pretty big deal," Sammy said.

It was, especially for me. I had joined Shaker, Riley and Flemming only about a year earlier, after being a county prosecutor. The pay jump was tremendous, and Paul Riley's law firm was the place to be. When Paul tapped me to assist on the *Almundo* defense, and then we somehow managed to pull out a not-guilty, I was established. I was in. I was set, at the finest litigation shop in the city.

My family was a different story. Talia had had a rough pregnancy, especially near the end, and then delivered Emily as we were on the cusp of trial. Talia wasn't deaf to my need to establish myself in my career, but still, it was hard to sell the trial to a first-time mother trying to care for a newborn by herself day and night.

Therein was the irony. It was after I was left with an empty house, and basically fell apart, that I left the law firm that had cost me such precious time with my wife and daughter.

"I mean, there we was, watching the news, and I see you on there, and I told everyone, I knew that guy, we were—we used to be—"

Sammy didn't complete the sentence. We both sensed the awkwardness. *Used to be.* Used to spend every waking moment together. Used to be so close that we called each other brother.

"So—how's Pete?" he asked, changing the subject.

My brother Pete, five years my junior, lives in the city like me. He's hit a bump or two along the way, struggled with drugs a little, but he's a good egg, and I think he's on a straight course right now. Then again, I'm not exactly one to judge.

"You know my mom passed," I said.

"Yeah, heard that. Heard that." He gestured at me without looking in my direction. "Jack's still"—he gestured with his head—"y'know—"

"Inside, yeah." He was talking about my father. Sammy and I referred to Jack by his first name behind his back, a minor rebellion. My father's fourth strike came about three years ago. He should probably be good for parole within the next few years, but I haven't done the math and don't plan to do so.

"You married?" he asked me. He smiled. "Bet you got a hot wife, right?"

"*Had* one," I said. It wasn't fun to acknowledge it, but in an odd way it felt good to pass on some misfortune of my own to the man who had spent much of his adult life in prison, and who could well be on the way to many more years at the same address. Maybe it leveled the field ever so slightly.

Sammy stubbed out his cigarette and grew quiet. I thought to ask him why he took so long to contact me—he'd been arrested almost a year ago and he waited until a month out from trial to get in touch with me. But it wasn't hard to imagine his reluctance. Sammy was always fiercely proud, and it was probably killing him to come to me for help.

"This is the guy who killed Audrey," Sammy said. "You know that, right?"

"I know, Sam."

"This asshole deserved to die. Right?"

"Right," I agreed. It felt like he was looking for justification, which meant that he was acknowledging that he had killed Griffin Perlini. But I didn't push the subject. Defense attorneys never do. And I was his attorney first, friend second—if I'd be his attorney at all.

"So," Sammy said, "can you help me?"

It was a question I literally couldn't answer, which, I suppose, was an answer in itself. I'd been back on my feet for six weeks, and I'd gotten some good results for some clients, but this was a first-degree homicide with all kinds of complications and little time to prepare. The cases I'd handled were mostly bench trials with only a witness or two, and the truth was, I was mostly winging it, hoping to take advantage of less experienced prosecutors and looking for a lucky break here or there with a missing witness or lost documents. I could do that. That was easy. This case would require dedication, consistency, and full work days, and the price of fucking it up would be my old friend Sammy Cutler spending his life in jail.

So of course I said, "Sure, Sammy," and shook his hand.

6

HALF PAST THREE in the morning. We navigated the bar, my brother and I, a place that opened six months ago, a series of rooms belowground, like a trendy coal mine, everything bathed in artificial blue light, the bass thumping like a migraine through the club, smoke and cologne and alcohol reaching a gag in my throat as beautiful people glided past us, trying their best to look intriguing and glamorous.

Pete wasn't as drunk as I was because he actually gave a shit about making an impression. He was looking to meet someone, which put him in company with the other five hundred people crammed into this fire-code violation. Pete was five years younger; he drew the longer straw in the charm and looks department, while I got the athleticism and ambition.

"Two o'clock," he said, turning back to me in what passed for a whisper among the pandemonium, which meant it was just short of screaming into my ear.

I started to correct him when I realized he wasn't informing me of the hour but directing me through the stampede to a gaggle of young ladies sitting around a small circular high table. I stifled an objection, because I could hardly expect Pete not to be looking. He was young, handsome, and single. Why the hell shouldn't he be hitting on women?

And what had remained unspoken these last few months was that, while Pete was on the make and I was anything but, it was actually my idea to kill most of these nights out at the clubs. I still hadn't grown comfortable spending time in the house where Talia and Emily and I lived together, nor could I bring myself to sell the place.

So I found myself playing wingman as Pete made his approach. By the time I was close enough to hear what little brother was saying, two gals were already laughing. The kid had a gift for it, something he got from our dad. Then again, these women seemed like their inhibitions had been loosened by alcohol a good three or four hours ago. There were four of them, young and shapely, in revealing outfits, their hair done up. Two were white, one Asian and one African American. They looked like they came out of a sitcom on NBC.

"Which one of you is Phoebe?" I asked, but none of them could hear me.

"This is Jason," Pete said. "My brother."

They seemed to think that was cute, at least the Asian one did. They seemed generally interested in Pete's banter, though their eyes moved about the room, too, scoping the place for other men. Or maybe women. I know if I were a female, I'd be a lesbian.

"Be right back," Pete said. "Gotta take a leak."

I gave Pete a look. I didn't typically inquire of my brother's scatological needs, but Pete had a history here. Before I could say anything to him, things turned even worse: the music changed to that song by Fergie, not the Dutchess of York, but the one who is booty-licious or something like that. And I didn't think I could feel worse.

"What do *you* do?"

The good thing about intoxication is I can get lost for a while, but the downside is that Talia always finds me again, and this is when it's the worst, when the defenses are down, the emotions the rawest. I heard, in my head, that little vocalization Emily used to make, once she hit three months, something between a moan and a squeal, capping off at a delightful, high-pitched squeak—

"What do you do?"

I directed back to one of the white girls, who was leaning over the table at me. Based on her outfit and posture, it seemed important to her that I take note of her cleavage, so I made a point of not doing so.

"I'm a fortune-teller," I answered.

"You are not."

"I knew you were going to say that."

I caught eyes with a woman up near the bar, a woman in a green dress, the Lady in Green, who broke eye contact in an easy way, as if she hadn't been looking at me. I suppose I should have been flattered but it made me feel uneasy, for some reason. Or maybe it was the five vodkas I had drunk. I pondered for the twentieth time tonight what I was still doing here, why I had come here to begin with, why I still feared God.

I also wondered who had hired me to defend Sammy Cutler.

"—a doctor or a lawyer or something."

I watched the Lady in Green's eyes tour the bar again as she waited for her drink. She had a narrow, sculpted face. Her head angled upward, revealing a vulnerability that belied her confident appearance.

"I'm a police detective," I told the lady trying to converse with me. I say *trying* because she'd had more to drink than I had.

"A *cop*." She said it like a cuss word. Lot of people feel that way about our city's finest. Sometimes I'm one of them.

Now I had the attention of the entire tribe of women at the table. What kinds of cases did I handle? Did I ever shoot someone?

"You don't seem like a cop. You seem like a Wall Street banker." This from the black woman, or I guess I'm supposed to say African American, but she had a British accent so did that make her English American? African British? I thought of asking her but I would need a bullhorn to communicate with her across the table, and no matter how I tried to phrase the question it would probably sound politically incorrect. Why bother? Why bother with any of this?

"When I was a boy," I said, "my parents were killed in front of me by an armed robber. I swore, that day, that I would devote my life to fighting crime."

Pete returned from the bathroom, wearing an enthusiastic grin, rejoining the conversation with renewed vigor. I doubted that taking a piss could have put him in that good a mood. I trained my stare on him and he knew it, but he avoided my look and the question it raised.

"Jason's a lawyer," Pete chimed in. "One of the best in the city."

"That explains how he lies so easily."

I laughed, for the only time that night. I looked back at the Lady in Green who, yes, was checking me out again. The logical part of my brain, when it was functioning, told me that at some point in my life I would be interested in women again, but it seemed beyond comprehension thus far.

I watched Pete work the ladies. The kid had been through some rough patches. He got it a lot worse at home than I did, growing up. My father could look you in the eye and convince you he was heir to the British throne, but in his soul he was not an enlightened man. He was bitter and temperamental and opted, instead of a psychiatrist's couch, to relieve tension by taking swats at his boys. I went through a pretty good spell of it myself, though I spent more time working up a sweat dodging my father's punches than actually receiving them. I would juke right, fake left, hit the floor, anything to make him miss, only heightening his drunken rage, but in the end usually exhausting him, until he finally turned his ire on an inanimate object like my bedroom door, sometimes a chair. The wall of my bedroom looked like a Beirut stronghold.

Looking back, it was probably comical, my father swatting at air, cursing me out, while I danced around him or crawled beneath him. I probably should have hung one of those punching bags in my room. My dad could have gotten in a pretty good workout, maybe even turned pro on the welterweight circuit. But he wouldn't have enjoyed people hitting back.

Once I sprouted up in height, and especially once I started making a name for myself on the gridiron, my dad basically left me alone. Something in the acclaim I received on the football field, and throughout the community, gave me immunity within the confines of our house. I figure, my father couldn't put me down when everybody else was propping me up, so he gave it a rest.

Either that or he paid attention that one night when I actually swung back. I always wondered if he had even remembered the punch the next day, waking up with a hangover and a shiner under his left eye, which he rightly could have chalked up to another night at the office in his line of work. That was right around the time the abuse stopped, as it happened, but I never really knew if he remembered his kid popping him, and it didn't seem like polite dinner conversation. One of the many unspoken things that festered among our family.

There was something ironic in the ability I had to make defensive backs miss in the open field, each of them my drunken father lunging at me and finding air. I have a distinct memory, my junior year of high school, taking a screen pass sixty yards or so for a touchdown, dodging two or three defenders in the process, then standing in the end zone and looking up in the stands at my family. My mother and Pete were there, as always, but that particular time so was my father, though I don't remember him clapping. What I do remember is wondering, at that moment, looking up into the stadium lights on a cool Friday night, several hundred fans screaming with enthusiasm, what my father was thinking and having no idea. My best guess was that my father resented me at that moment.

In any event, when I was no longer a convenient target, Pete bore the brunt of our father's abuse. He was younger but also smaller and more docile. He wasn't a fighter, and he wouldn't avoid my father. He took it, every time. I would listen to it, lying awake, my head inches off the pillow, the sickening sound of open-handed slaps and closed-fist punches, Pete's muted groans. I did nothing to stop it. To this day, I can't put my finger on why. No matter how much I hated him, no matter how much I disrespected him, and even when I stopped fearing him, he was still my father.

Pete and I never really discussed it. I broached the topic a time or two, but he always deflected it. As a child myself, I took it as survival instinct, a coping mechanism, but as an adult I can't imagine what it did to him. I do know he's had trouble committing to an occupation (three jobs in four years, currently in pharmaceutical sales) and to a woman (three in four months), and he gambles and parties way too much. It doesn't take Freud to see a connection.

It pained me to watch him at work here, reminding me as he did of our father. A part of me wanted to shake him, because he had all the charm of our dear daddy but none of the underlying malice. He could put up an impressive front, no question, especially in a setting like this, entertaining a flock of women. And it wasn't insincere. There was a big heart in there. This guy basically rescued me after everything happened with Talia and Emily. Maybe it helped him, in a way, looking out for me instead of the other way around, over these last few months.

Now, here he was, back to sneaking cocaine in the bathroom of a nightclub. He'd never been an addict, per se, at least as far as I knew, but how far removed from addiction could he be? I hadn't been in a position to know, not these last few months.

I felt a surge of nausea, thanks to the vodka and the mixture of smoke and expensive perfume in the air. I excused myself for the bathroom. I made several wrong turns through the mosh pit of people, then I felt nauseated again and decided to get some fresh air. I didn't see the point in entertaining these women any longer, assuming they had been amused at any point. I certainly wasn't entertaining myself.

On the other hand, I wasn't in a hurry to get home, and I only lived twenty minutes away, so I decided to hoof it. I like the city in predawn, the world in transition, decelerating from the night's sins, the first glimmer of orange-red warming the sky after the city has recharged its batteries. Plus the streets are pretty much empty, so I don't have to talk to anyone.

I was thinking about Pete, and about Talia and Emily, when I passed the window of an all-night diner populated with drunken revelers and college kids and law students taking a break during all-night cramming sessions. Good times. *Don't grow up*, I silently warned them.

As I stopped at the diner's window, I felt something subtle change, not so much a sound but the absence of one, a shift in the cacophony of white noise behind me. Nothing I could pinpoint, just a sense that as I had stopped walking, someone behind me had stopped, too.

I tried to use the window's reflection, looking at an angle to the street behind me, but it was hard to make out anything more than a solitary figure. I was mildly curious, sure, but mostly I just wanted to make sure nobody was closing the distance. I wasn't in the mood for a fight, and I didn't feel like canceling all my credit cards and getting a new driver's license, or breaking my hand on someone's face.

I started onward again toward my house, listening intently, trying to soften my own footfalls so I could hear those of someone else, but not looking behind me again. From what I could tell, I was being followed, but whoever it was had no intention of making a move on me. I didn't know if this was someone looking for an easy mark but ultimately deciding I didn't fit the bill, or someone who never had any intention of approaching, who was following me for some other reason. If I'd had anything left to fear in this world, I might have let it keep me up at night. As it was, I made sure to lock my door, set the house alarm, and let the whole thing bother me for a good thirty seconds, until exhaustion and intoxication allowed me a couple hours of sleep in a cold, empty bed.

7

I WOKE UP at eight o'clock and stared at the ceiling of my bedroom for about half an hour. This constituted tremendous progress, as there was a time when I'd required at least two hours' examination of the plaster and that one stain on the ceiling from a champagne cork when Talia and I celebrated our third anniversary, before leaving the bed.

Things to do, I had things to do. I had a client coming and I had to get started on Sammy's case. This would be the second day in a row that I would take a shower.

I got to my office at ten. I share space with an old friend, Shauna Tasker. We have a corner space and double up on a secretary/receptionist. We are, technically, two separate law firms, but we help each other out whenever need be.

Shauna was sitting in our conference room as I passed. We've been friends since back in high school. She was a prosecutor for a couple years, like me, but she left the office sooner, moving to a silk-stocking law firm until she got tired of the senior partner putting his hand on her knee.

I put my hand on her knee a time or two, myself, back in high school, but that was a long time ago. We became pals afterward, and at State— where she went on merit and graduated cum laude, while I went on an athletic scholarship—she became one of my closest friends. She's petite and shapely, on the surface a real *feminina*, but she could always drink me under the table, and when you got her going, she could cuss like a truck driver.

After everything happened with Talia and Emily, and I quit my law firm and spent almost three months holed up in my house, Shauna cajoled me into renting space from her and hanging a shingle of my own. I thought of putting ENTER AT YOUR OWN RISK on that sign but settled on LAW OFFICES OF JASON KOLARICH.

"Hey." Shauna had her feet up on the long walnut desk, reading over some complicated transaction. Shauna still did trial work but when she'd left her law firm, she took with her a client that shoots her transactional work, too. When you're a solo practitioner, you become a jack-of-all-trades, and Shauna was a fast learner. "Get any sleep, dear?"

I hadn't exactly been keeping regular hours lately. Many of those nights had been spent out with Pete, who seemed to have boundless energy when it came to bars and women. Occasionally, Shauna would hang out with me, too, which was a different kind of sport because I got to watch a lot of sloppy-drunk idiots make a play for her.

"Smitty and Dom want to grab lunch today," she told me, not even looking up from her case file. "Wanna come?"

Her request was deliberately casual. She didn't know, specifically, how I spent my lunches but probably had a good idea. She'd been trying to pull me out of my funk for the past four months. Still, she hadn't pushed, and she wasn't pushing now.

"Can't do it, m'lady," I told her.

She looked up, training those loving but disapproving blue eyes on me for only a moment before looking back into her file. She hasn't known how to handle this thing with me. I was a train wreck there for a while, holed up in my house, feeling sorry for myself, and the best she could figure was that it was better for her to be around than not. She probably understands me better than anyone I know, so she knows that I'm a loner at heart.

"Marie said something about a murder case?"

"Trial starts in four weeks."

"Oh, well—four whole weeks." That's what I like about Shauna. She doesn't get emotional about very many things. Even when that senior partner started sexually harassing her at her old firm, she simply responded with a counteroffer: She'd contact the EEOC, and his wife, if he didn't give her a generous severance package and let her steal a client or two. "How'd that come about?"

I told her the name of my client.

"Sammy Cutler?" The name wasn't registering with her, but she knew it should. "Sammy—" Her feet came off the table. "From BonBons?" she asked, meaning Bonaventure High School. "That freaky guy who wore the army jackets and got stoned all the time?"

Her reaction made me feel worse than I already did, only highlighting the divide that grew between Sammy and me after I became a jock. Shauna didn't even know that Sammy and I had been friends. It was a painful and embarrassing reminder of how much distance I had put between us once I became a member of the high school elite, a varsity athlete in my sophomore year.

"Sammy was my guy growing up," I said, allowing enough tone in my voice to call for a little respect on this topic. Shauna grew up about two miles away from Sammy and me, which to us was a different neighborhood altogether, a middle-class area that also fed into BonBons. "My next-door neighbor."

"And he killed someone?"

Sammy hadn't come out and confessed to me, but I certainly assumed so. "He killed the guy who killed his sister," I said, which of course forced me to unload the entire story on her. Shauna, like me, would have been seven years old when it happened, and she might have heard something about it—no doubt her parents did—but it wouldn't have registered in the way it did with me, naturally.

After listening to all of this, she exhaled dramatically. "Well, Mr. Kolarich, that's one heck of a case ya got there. You need help?"

"I might," I said. I tapped the door and left before she could engage me in further conversation.

"You notice," she called after me, "I didn't ask you if he had any money."

I have accused Shauna, in my haughtier moments, of placing too high a premium on receiving prompt payment from customers. "You're a true humanitarian, Tasker."

"Come to lunch with Dom and Smitty, Jason! I'm serious! Smitty'll buy."

I ignored her, though I appreciated the gesture. I had my regular lunch appointment.

"When did Shauna become a humanitarian?" This from Marie, our assistant, without even looking up. Marie is a fair-haired young woman only three years out of college, who reminds us constantly that she has a degree in archaeology and will leave us, without notice, as soon as (a) she finds a job in that vocation, which seems unlikely given that we live in the Midwest and the only things to be found underground are the bodies of mafia informants, or (b) she gets tired of taking our abuse, which in truth she actually enjoys.

When I walked into my office, a shiny new, brown leather briefcase was resting on one of the chairs opposite my desk. Marie informed me that my new friend, Smith, had dropped it off first thing this morning. I opened the gold clasp and counted out ten thousand dollars in cash. A healthy retainer, indeed, but it was rare to get this kind of money in cash. Smith, apparently, was not inclined to reveal aspects of his personal information that a check would disclose.

I fell into my chair and checked my watch. A client was due to arrive shortly, for a second tour of duty. Ronnie Dice was the second client I represented in my ill-conceived reincarnation as a solo practitioner. He was, as far as I knew, a fairly small-time crook. He'd grown up as a pickpocket, lifting wallets on buses, that sort of thing, but when he came to see me, it was on a gun charge. Ronnie had been around, but not part of, a scuffle on the south side. When two patrol cars showed to break it up, Ronnie had suddenly discovered his legs and decided to *adios* in a hurry. Headlong flight is not usually an activity in which innocent people partake, so one of the patrol officers, not surprisingly, decided he'd like to inquire of Mr. Dice and gave chase.

Here's a good rule of thumb if a cop is somewhere nearby: Don't run. He'll notice.

Ronnie was caught and found with an unregistered firearm. They charged it on the state level, not federal. I tried to suppress the evidence of the gun, saying the cops lacked probable cause. I lost. At trial, I argued that the gun was planted by the white cops on the black defendant. I had two jurors in mind in making that argument. They ended up hanging 8-4, which meant I actually got four jurors toward reasonable doubt.

The state said they'd retry but the judge let the prosecutor know that she wasn't favorably disposed to that idea, which was a polite way of saying she didn't want to take up three more days of her docket on a bullshit case. I felt lucky to get four jurors the first time and didn't think Ronnie would fare so well the second go-round. So I told the judge that, after the testimony of the officers at trial, I thought I had new grounds to argue for suppression of the evidence. I also proposed, in lieu of a retrial, a misdemeanor plea. The judge said she'd be willing to reconsider my suppression argument if the state retried and basically forced the misdemeanor plea down the prosecutor's throat.

You'd think Ronnie had received the electric chair, the way he fussed and moaned, but I think he realized the thing had turned out pretty well, all things considered. Especially because he stiffed me on the bill. Ronnie Dice, to whom we now affectionately refer as No-Dice, taught me the single most important rule of a criminal defense attorney: Get your money up front.

At a quarter to eleven, Ronnie Dice walked into my office. I told him he was late and he acted like I'd just made a joke. Ronnie was dressed the same as the first time he paid me a visit, in a gray hooded sweatshirt, ratty jeans, and canvas high-tops. He had a painfully youthful look about his eyes that made me think, as I did so often with my clients, that things should have turned out differently for him.

"Jason Kolarich the man," he said, getting comfortable in the chair across from me.

"Ronald Dice the deadbeat."

He ignored that, launching into the story of his latest brush with the law, a story that, with minor variations, I'd heard many times. As a warm-up, he informed me that the whole thing had been a giant misunderstanding. Apparently he had no idea that there was dope in the bag he was carrying from one lowlife to another. He tried to explain the communication breakdown to the friendly neighborhood policeman, but alas, the officer was less than receptive to his plea.

Part of being a criminal defense attorney is being an editor. Clients tell you all sorts of things that have nothing to do with the case. Ronnie seemed to think that, in addition to me clearing him of all criminal charges, we would have one whale of a civil-rights case against the cops because Ronnie's forehead got in the way of the car door when he was being helped into the backseat.

"Ronnie, if memory serves, a month ago I hung a jury and pleaded you down to a misdemeanor when you were looking at eighteen months. But when I sent you the bill, you told me to go fuck myself."

"Nah, boss, you should've gotten that payment."

Interesting how he put that. "I agree, Ronnie, I *should* have."

"I don't know what coulda happened."

Another misunderstanding, apparently. "You're lucky I'm in a good mood."

"This is you in a good mood?" He laughed, overcompensating. He gave me the details, including the date of the prelim, the names of a couple of witnesses, and a sincere promise to have twenty-five hundred dollars in my hand by close of business tomorrow.

"Try to get the money legally," I suggested, prompting more laughter. He was laughing because the odds of my ever receiving payment were longer than the odds of Ronnie Dice becoming a figure skater with the Ice Capades.

TODAY, lunch is a picnic in the park. Talia lays out a checked cloth blanket—part of a picnic set, a wedding present—while little Emily runs around in circles, her arms out straight, emulating an airplane.

Talia has the food—her wonderful chicken salad, new potatoes, and coleslaw—set out on a couple of plates, a lunch for two. She opens a bottle of Evian and calls out to our daughter. "C'mon, honey, let's eat," she says.

Emily, still playing the airplane, circles the picnic table and comes in for a safe landing. She picks up one of the small triangles of sandwich her mother has cut and crinkles her nose. "I don't like it," she says.

"You like chicken salad, Em. You liked it last week."

Emily sets the food down and frowns. "I don't want it."

Talia puts her hand on Emily's head of blond curls, her only physical feature owing to me. "You want peanut butter and jelly?" Talia brought an extra sandwich just in case.

Emily looks up into the sun, squinting as the rays beat down on her face. "Is Daddy coming today?"

Talia reaches down and gives our daughter a kiss. "Not today, sweetheart," she says. "We'll see him soon."

You will. You'll see me soon.

8

HIS NAME WASN'T SMITH, though that was the name he had given to the lawyer, Jason Kolarich. He didn't expect Kolarich to buy it, but he guessed—correctly—that Kolarich wouldn't worry too much about the identity of his benefactor, not when that benefactor was offering three hundred dollars an hour, and not when the client was an old friend.

Smith fondled a cuff link as he waited in his client's office. The office was spacious but simple, the office of a man who paid no heed to the finer details, who freely delegated and expected compliance.

He stood as his client entered from a side door.

"Hello, Carlo," Smith said.

Carlo dropped his large frame in a plush leather high-back and fixed on Smith. "Tell me about the lawyer," he said.

"His name is Jason Kolarich. He grew up with Sammy Cutler. Next-door neighbors. Near Forty-seventh and Graynor, Leland Park—well, you know the neighborhood. Mother was a housewife. Father was a grifter. Mostly small-time stuff, card games, and petty rips. He's doing eight inside now for a mortgage-fraud scam he ran."

"Where?" Carlo asked. "Where's he inside?"

Smith thought for a moment. "Marymount."

Carlo was silent. Smith figured Carlo was thinking about how he could reach someone inside Marymount Penitentiary. Surely, there was a way.

"I don't know how much Kolarich cares about his dad," he told Carlo.

Carlo gave Smith a hard glare. He didn't appreciate the suggestion in Smith's comment.

"Continue," Carlo said.

Smith nodded dutifully. "He has a younger brother named Pete. Had some scrapes himself but nothing major. Looks like maybe the apple didn't fall far from the tree with Pete. He lives here in the city. He likes to engage in the occasional recreational drug."

Carlo seemed to take note of that.

Smith knew the notes by heart. "Jason Kolarich was a football player, a real good one. A wide receiver. He played ball at State on scholarship for two years. Then he was kicked off the team when he got into a fight with one of his teammates. Put the guy in the hospital."

"The hospital." Carlo chuckled, allowed a tight smile. "A fighter."

"Stayed in school, though," Smith went on. "Put himself through the last two years, then went to law school. He was a prosecutor for a few years. A pretty good one, from what they say. He was doing felony cases at the criminal courthouse until he went into the private sector. He worked at a law firm called Shaker, Riley and Flemming, which is a very well-established firm in the city. He defended that state senator who was charged with extortion. He won that case."

"He beat the feds?"

"He beat the feds."

Carlo seemed impressed. "What about his family? Wife? Kids?"

Smith shook his head. "Kolarich's wife, Talia, and their baby daughter, Emily, were killed in a car accident four months ago. Their car went off the embankment on a county road heading downstate."

"Jesus." Carlo winced. Even Carlo, Smith knew, would be sympathetic. "That's gotta fuck a guy up pretty bad."

"Of course," Smith agreed. "Every day, at lunch, he drives to the cemetery and sits by their graves. He just sits there for an hour, then gets up and goes back to work."

"Yeah, well—yeah." Carlo got out of his chair and paced the large room. A guy like Carlo wasn't comfortable with these kinds of emotions, and predictably, they evolved into anger. "Well, Jesus Christ, what are we getting with this guy? A violent guy who just lost his wife and daughter?"

Smith wasn't sure of the answer. "He was a rising star at a blue-chip law firm before this all happened. After his wife and daughter died, he dropped off the map, left the law firm, and didn't reemerge for three months. When he did, he opened up a one-man shop, sharing office space with an old high school friend and handling small-time cases. From what I've been able to tell, Kolarich is only halfway back. He works sporadically. Some days, he never leaves his house. Much of the time, he stays out at bars all night but doesn't make a play for anyone; he just gets drunk and then goes home." Smith took a minute. "This guy Kolarich will not be reliable, Carlo, but he's the guy Cutler wanted. He wouldn't take our people. He wanted Kolarich. And we're going to do all the heavy lifting, anyway. All he'll really have to do is show up in court. Hopefully, even he can handle that."

Carlo was silent for a long while. He walked over to the single picture window in the office and stared, motionless. Finally, he turned his head in Smith's direction. "And he still has that brother, right?"

"Right."

"And they're close? I mean, he gives a flying fuck about this brother? Pete, you said."

"He seems to, yes."

Carlo turned back toward the window. He breathed out deeply and cast a hand over his face. "Good," he said.

9

THEY WEREN'T THE FIRST, the state trooper tells you, as if that were any consolation, as you stand together near the police barricade, artificial light illuminating the otherwise dark county road past four in the morning. It was a sharp turn, a blind curve on a county road along the bluffs, accompanied by a warning sign that, for some reason, Talia must have missed. Her Bronco had busted through the guardrail and toppled over a hundred feet into the river.

You'd done the drive with Talia dozens of times, part of the route downstate to her parents' place. But you, not Talia, had always been the driver.

She was visiting her folks? the trooper asks you. You don't recall answering, but you must have said yes. What you surely didn't answer was whether your wife was going for a visit, or whether she was leaving you for good.

I was supposed to go, you tell the trooper, defending your position, though it isn't under attack. And it's the truth. You've been planning this weekend trip, but you were tied up, as always, with an emergency at work. You were following a last-ditch lead on the case with Senator Almundo, as the prosecution was preparing its rebuttal case and you were working on one last witness, a final nail in the coffin on a case that you were beginning to realize you actually might win.

I'm doing this for us, you kept telling yourself, working well into the morning hours consistently on the *Almundo* defense. *We win this case, we pull this rabbit out of a hat, and I'm in. I'm set. We'll be on easy street. Emily will have everything she ever wanted. Talia will have everything she deserves.* Yet you can't deny that you are also doing this for yourself, the ego boost, the utter high of the high-profile trial, navigating through reporters on a daily basis and seeing your name in the *Watch*.

When the call came, you'd been waiting by the phone in your office for your informant, the guy who might be able to give you the final lead, the home run in your case. Ernesto Ramirez, a high-ranking ex-member of a street gang—the Latin Lords—to which your client, Senator Almundo, had been connected, was going to deliver the message to you that day. The government's theory was that Senator Almundo had led an extortion ring that terrorized the city's west side, resulting, among other things, in the death of a local businessman, who was unwilling to pay the obligatory protection money. You'd found Ernesto Ramirez on your own, some extracurricular due diligence on your part, and hit a potential gold mine: Ernesto was going to offer you proof that the storekeeper hadn't been murdered by the Columbus Street Cannibals but, rather, by a rival street gang, the Latin Lords. The revelation would shatter the underlying premise of the government's case.

Day had turned into night, which had forced you to cancel with Talia, who decided to take Emily and go anyway. By ten o'clock that evening, you were in a real mood, wondering whether you had missed a weekend with your family over a red herring. When your office phone rang, it hadn't even occurred to you that Ernesto always called on your cell, not at the office.

Mr. Kolarich, I'm Lieutenant Ryan with the State Troopers. I'm afraid I have some bad news, sir.

I drove back from the cemetery with the windows down, breathing in the earthy, foul smell of the autumn air, the deadening leaves and mold, the crisp air whispering across me in a crosscurrent, wondering why I still made this daily trip to Talia's and Emily's graves but unable to stop. It was my one hour a day, my break, but it only made reality all the more gut-wrenching.

I closed my eyes as I pulled up to a traffic light outside the cemetery, trying to squeeze the sights and sounds from my mind, knowing that I could push them away but not wanting to.

Looks like they died on impact, the state trooper tells you. You accept the statement without question, wanting to believe it was a painless death, knowing that an infant child in a car seat probably would have survived the impact but unable to fathom the possibility, the probability, that neither of them had died on impact, that both of them had drowned.

"You're in a special place now," I said aloud, cursing a God that would have let this happen but needing now, more than ever, to believe in His heaven. "You're in a special place and it doesn't matter what happened." A horn honked behind me and I opened my eyes, a considerable distance having opened between my car and the one in front of me, the light green. I gripped the wheel with white knuckles and took deep breaths, my heart rattling against my chest, my arms trembling.

You were supposed to live. You were supposed to have a childhood full of happiness and then become an artist or a doctor or a—you were supposed to fall in love with someone and have children of your own and be compassionate and warm and loving and happy and I—I wasn't—I wasn't there when you needed me. I wasn't there ever. Not ever.

I slammed on the brakes and stopped just short of the SUV idling at a light in front of me, two children in the backseat turning their heads. I wiped thick, greasy sweat from my forehead and struggled to breathe. This happened, from time to time, when I let it get the better of me. I would calm in a few minutes, and it would wash away to my default mode.

That's what happens to those of us who get to live. We fight through, grit it out, and move on to something better. It's the dead who have to settle for what they had.

10

I MADE IT to the detention center by two o'clock, having calmed down from my lunch appointment. I had to get my act together for Sammy's sake. And I was pretty sure I could do it. If there is one thing I took from my father, it was that ability to compartmentalize. He was a bitter, insecure asshole who could charm a rattlesnake when he turned it on. My version came in a different flavor—I was about as charming *as* a rattlesnake—but I could focus when the need arose.

I wondered, briefly, how Sammy would feel about his lawyer being *pretty sure* he could handle his case, but by then a guard was showing me back to the glass conference rooms. You get to know these guards, who are usually your typical robotic public servants, and it always pays to get on their good side. That's always been my instinct, being nice to the staff, because they can make your life easier, though I wasn't really sure what good it was having a prison guard on my side. Either way, for some reason entirely unknown to me, prison guards are not big fans of defense lawyers. And most of them, I've seen more humor in a hungry alligator. This guy pushed the door open like he didn't want anything to do with me and pointed at the table where I was to sit.

"This is great, thanks," I said to the guard. "I'll start with a shrimp cocktail, and maybe I can see a wine list?"

The guard didn't see the humor. "You being smart?"

"That was my first mistake. I'll talk slower next time." I opened the small file that Smith had given me on Sammy's case. Sammy and I hadn't discussed the details of the case yesterday. It was enough for us, yesterday, to simply reconnect after a long separation.

The case file was relatively small, but sufficient to tell me that the state had a pretty decent case against Sammy.

Griffin Perlini had answered his door on the evening of September 21 at about nine o'clock, whereupon he was greeted with a bullet from a .38 special through the forehead. A neighbor saw a man in a brown bomber jacket and green stocking cap running down the hallway. A married couple, strolling the sidewalk outside, positively ID'd Cutler as the man they saw passing them at a sprint, coming from the apartment building where Perlini lived. And a security camera from a convenience store down the street caught Sammy's eight-year-old Chevy parked outside.

I'd reviewed a copy of that tape, typically grainy footage with a real-time clock running in the corner of the screen. The camera was positioned in the store's back corner, providing an overview of the entire shop, including the front register, and continuing to a small area outside the store. At the time of 8:34 P.M., a beat-up Chevy sedan pulled up next to the convenience store, parking mostly out of the camera's sightline but, alas, the rear end of the car was in full view—including the rear license plate, which confirmed it was *Sammy's* beat-up Chevy. The car remained there until 9:08 P.M., at which time it drove away, out of the camera's view. The time frame matched up perfectly with someone who drove to Perlini's apartment, got in and killed him, and left. The only silver lining was that the camera could not, at any point in time, show the front of the car, or who got in or out—but Jesus, it wasn't exactly a quantum leap here.

Once the police visited his house to inquire, Sammy didn't exactly acquit himself well. He was asking for a lawyer before he had the door open. Then he changed his mind, at the police station, and unleashed a tirade against Griffin Perlini before they even mentioned why they were questioning him. He never outright confessed but that's like saying Custer never outright surrendered.

I reviewed the list I had made:

1. Neighbor witness—saw man in brown jacket, green cap fleeing
2. Married couple—ID'd Cutler running from apartment building
3. Security video—Cutler's car parked down street
4. Police interview—Cutler brought up Perlini's name spontaneously

The case against Sammy looked pretty solid. Eyes at the scene, his car on camera at the scene, and a statement tantamount to a confession. But what was missing from all of this was what, in my opinion, was the most obvious element of the defense.

Sammy had pleaded a straight not-guilty. What he should have pleaded was a diminished-capacity defense, probably temporary insanity. He should admit he killed Griffin Perlini and tell the jury why—because Griffin Perlini was a child sex offender who had preyed on Sammy's sister, Audrey. No jury would convict Sammy on those facts. Hadn't his public defender explained that to him?

Sammy walked in, deputy escort in tow, and remained silent until the guard had locked him to the table and left the room. He had darker circles under his eyes than yesterday, and those eyes fixed on me with none of the curiosity and tolerance from our first meeting. He nodded without enthusiasm at the case file in front of me as he reached for his cigarettes. "So you know everything?"

You never know everything from a cold file. "They have you at his apartment building at the time of the murder," I said. "You got any valid reason to have been in that neighborhood?"

He shook his head. "Nope."

"You own a thirty-eight special?"

"Nope."

The cops didn't recover the gun, which was something, at least. Nor did they recover the brown bomber jacket or green stocking cap from Sammy's place. Obviously the theory would be that Sammy tossed the gun and clothes, but at least plausible deniability was an option.

"Anyone ever borrow your car?"

Sammy stared at me with a sour expression. "Yeah, there's this guy who goes around killing child molesters who wanted to borrow my car that night. You think that might be important? Should I have mentioned that before?"

He was in a real mood. What did he think, I wouldn't ask him any questions? But I played along. "This vigilante, did he own a brown jacket and green stocking cap?"

He didn't seem to like my return volley. He was pissed off about something. Maybe it was my questions, which reminded him of how tight the state's case was. Maybe it was the fact that he was looking at life in the pen. It felt like something more personal.

"Sammy, your public defender ever mention a diminished-capacity defense?"

He blew out smoke with disgust. "What's that? You mean the insanity shit?"

That's what I meant. Temporary insanity, irresistible impulse—the idea that Sammy was so overcome with rage after seeing his sister's killer that he lost all ability to act with reason.

"Yeah, he mentioned it, and I said no." Sammy leaned forward, banging his manacles on the table, eyeing me. "I'm not saying I was nuts. I may not have a fancy law degree, but I ain't nuts."

Okay, so it *was* directed at me. But I didn't have time for it. Sammy needed to see the big picture here. I silently cursed his public defender for not helping him do so. Diminished capacity was the obvious play here.

I said it quietly, trying to defuse the hostility. "Listen, Sam—all you'd be saying is that your act was legally justified. You get to tell the jury *why* you killed that piece of shit. And the jury would go along with that, Sam. If you say you didn't do it, then everything that Griffin Perlini did in his past, to Audrey, to others—none of that is relevant. It's not relevant because you're saying you didn't kill him. My guess is the judge wouldn't even let the jury hear about all the sex crimes Perlini committed. So you go to trial on this murder beef, and you and I know what Griffin Perlini did—we know all the shit he's done—but the jury has no idea. You get me?"

"Yeah," he said evenly. "Even without a college degree, I get you."

I sighed. My take was that Sammy had thought about things last night, how things had turned out for the two of us, and he was figuring that he'd drawn the short straw. "Listen, your best defense is to say, yes, you killed him, but here's why—because that scumbag killed your sister. I think the jury would walk you, Sam. That's more important than some damn principle. You get your life back. Let's tell the jury what he did to your sister."

By now, Sammy had broken eye contact. He was being stubborn but, I thought, also had trouble, to this day, thinking about what happened to his sister. I was hoping my plea had sunk into his logic. "And how do we prove what he did to my sister?" he asked me.

Well, now, he had a point. The police couldn't stick anything against Griffin Perlini back then. They had a pedophile with a history, they had photographs of Audrey—and many other girls—found all over his coach house, but they never found Audrey's body and couldn't get a confession out of him. That was the extent of my knowledge of the case, from the perspective of a seven-year-old boy. The cops couldn't prove their case. But now I'd have to revisit all of this. I would have to find a way to prove that Griffin Perlini killed Audrey Cutler.

"Maybe—maybe look at other people he hurt," said Sammy. "Other families had a beef with this guy, right? Audrey wasn't the only one."

It was an obvious thought, a good one. But Sammy didn't seem to be rushing forth to proclaim his innocence, so I doubted that pointing the finger at another father or brother or victim of Griffin Perlini's crimes would ultimately get me anywhere.

"I'll do that," I promised. "But I need more than a month to prepare, Sam. I need *six* months, minimum."

Sammy shook his head. "No. No more time. I want out of here."

"If you make me go to trial in four weeks, you'll never get out of here."

"I said no."

I sat back in my chair. I understood that he'd want out of this place, but trading a couple months for a lifetime in the pen was an easy call. What was the problem here?

"Let me do this the right way, Sam. The jury will see a child killer. They'll see the anguished brother. We'll have a fighting chance."

Sammy remained motionless, but I could sense violence welling up within him. His hands were balled in fists, his arms and shoulders trembling. A shade of crimson colored his rugged face. I didn't blame the guy, but I didn't see what the problem was. I was right, and we both knew it.

I decided to change topics. "Tell me about Smith. What's his story?"

It took him some time to decompress. His only bodily movement was a faint shrug of his shoulders. "Guy says he represents some interested parties or shit."

"Other victims? Their families?"

"You're the guy went to college."

"Shit, Sammy, what the fuck do *I* know about this guy? I don't even know his real name."

Sammy took out some frustration on his cigarette, stubbing it into oblivion. "Guy says people wanna help me. They got money. They can get me some fancy lawyers to spring me. I say, you gonna get me a fancy lawyer, I want Kolarich. He says he can get me someone better. I say it's gotta be someone I—"

He stopped there, emotion choking his throat. *Someone I trust*, he was going to say. Sammy probably hadn't received sparkling representation in his previous forays into the criminal justice process. He was counting on an old friend.

"You should've called me day one, Sammy. I don't care about money."

"Well, you're here now, and you're gettin' your money, so win this fuckin' case. I've been sitting in here for a year and I ain't waitin' more than four weeks, and I sure as shit ain't gonna say I was crazy. This guy Smith, he'll give you what you want. So win this case, all right, varsity athlete?"

With that, Sammy pushed himself out of his chair, though he couldn't move from his position with the manacles. He nodded to the guard, who walked to the glass room and opened the door. "You owe me, Koke," he said. The guard unlocked him from the table and led him out.

"I know," I answered, after he'd left the room.

11

"YEAH, that Sammy's one piece a work."

Patrick Oleari, the public defender assigned to Sammy Cutler, parked himself in a chair in the diner located in the criminal courthouse basement. All around us, defense lawyers and prosecutors negotiated plea deals and traded war stories over weak coffee and crappy deli sandwiches. I'd caught up with Oleari after court, just after four. He'd been in a hearing all day and was having a very late lunch, the life of a trial lawyer. Oleari had been out of law school for five years, compared to my nine, but he had plenty of experience as one of the state-provided defense attorneys to the lowest of the low.

I remember being this guy, though as a prosecutor, not a PD, grinding through the intermediate levels of the county attorney's office—traffic, juvie, misdemeanors, the three-days-on, three-days-off of felony review—waiting for the Show, the felony courtroom. It was a noble endeavor, to be sure, putting away the bad guys, but in truth it felt more like selfish fulfillment. I was like most of them; I would never be a "lifer." I wasn't a true believer, but I relished the sport of the thing and dreamed of a payoff in the private sector one day.

"Anyway." Oleari wiped at his mouth. "They have eyes on Cutler leaving the house. They have a store vid of his car parked outside the vic's apartment building. And Sammy didn't exactly distinguish himself in the interview." Oleari shook his head. "I mean, this thing has 'diminished capacity' written all over it. But try telling him that."

I did. Apparently Oleari had struck out on that score, too.

"Did Sammy tell you he killed Perlini?" I asked.

Oleari made a face. "No, but the evidence did."

Right. I said, "I have to get Perlini's past in front of the jury. If they know who they're dealing with, they'll acquit *anyone* the prosecution puts in front of them."

"I know it. I know it." Oleari gave up on his soggy roast beef sandwich and wiped his hands with a napkin. "Judge already ruled on that, y'know."

I didn't know. I didn't have the entire file yet.

"Judge Poker said Griffin Perlini's priors for child molestation are irrelevant."

I was afraid of that. As long as Sammy was claiming he didn't kill Perlini, it made no difference whether Griffin Perlini was the pope, the CEO of General Motors, or a two-bit child predator. I would have made the same ruling if I were the judge. The murder victim's history makes no difference if the defendant is merely claiming that he didn't do it.

But Sammy wouldn't plead diminished capacity. He wouldn't claim he temporarily lost control. That left me with a case that looked pretty damn strong for the prosecution.

"There's one guy." Oleari was using a toothpick. "One guy who says he saw some black guy running from the apartment building at around that same time."

A black guy fleeing the scene. As a defense attorney, I wasn't above stereotypes, and white jurors might be willing to buy into the idea.

"Was he wearing a brown jacket and green stocking cap?"

Oleari smiled, then shrugged. The truth, I figured, was that he didn't know the answer. The interview had probably been conducted by one of the PD's investigators, and a trial that was four weeks away, in the chaotic life of a public defender, might as well be four *years* away. "So you got a nice elderly couple that ID'd Cutler, you got a neighbor that saw the same guy with the bomber jacket and ski cap just outside the vic's apartment, plus the store vids, plus Cutler's incriminating statements to the cops—"

"And on the other side, I have one guy who saw a black man running."

"Right. So unless you got a jury from Simi Valley, you better talk Sammy into a temporary insanity defense."

By the tone of his voice, it was clear that Oleari didn't expect me to have any more success than he did in that area. But a lightbulb went on. I still had a couple of synapses firing in my brain. "You got Griffin Perlini's criminal history in your file?"

"Sure. Yeah. We'll get the whole thing over to you tomorrow, after the judge lets you in."

Tomorrow, I would appear before Judge Kathleen Poker and formally substitute into the case for Patrick Oleari. I was looking forward to a closer inspection of the entire file.

"Hey, not for nothin'." Oleari nodded at me. "This is a long way from defending politicians in federal court."

Apparently, Oleari had followed the *Almundo* case, too. The federal government doesn't lose too often, and a lot of people took note. He probably figured I was still at my former, blue-chip law firm. I didn't have the stomach to correct him and explain myself. Oleari was wondering what in the name of Clarence Darrow I was doing representing Sammy Cutler.

"We have history, Sammy and me," I explained. I thanked him and left.

I had an idea about how I would get Griffin Perlini's sordid life before the jury. It was a long shot, and I only had four weeks to pull it off, but it was the only chance we had.

I would need help. I would need a private investigator. A prayer wouldn't hurt, either, if I still believed in that crap.

I drove back to my office in silence. I thought about old times, back in the day, Leland Park. I don't remember life before Sammy. He was my first friend and my best friend. Both of our mothers worked part-time and they switched off baby-sitting chores, so whether it was my house or his, we were together from the time we were infants with one of the moms watching us. I made little distinction between his house and mine. If we couldn't find a toy or a sock or a pack of Crayolas, the first order of business was not a search of my bedroom but a trip next door. I ate half my meals next door. I shit in half my diapers next door.

Sammy and I against the world, it felt like, though it was unspoken. People put us together, Fric and Frac, whatever we did, as if we were twins. My first fight, in kindergarten no less, I didn't even throw the first punch; Sammy did, coming out of nowhere and popping Joe Kinzley in the kisser after he'd pushed me.

We were never apart, and it felt like we'd never *be* apart.

No one would have mistaken Sammy Cutler and Jason Kolarich for Boy Scouts. We were poor, and we took some liberties with the law. Shoplifting was our favored method, from candy bars and baseball cards to jewelry and clothes at department stores that we would boost with our friendly neighborhood fence, a drop-out named Ice who paid fifty cents on the dollar. We started smoking dope when we were thirteen and then started selling it, too, which supplemented our jobs at the grocery store. Man, were we punks. We had no respect for anything or anyone. We committed petty offenses just for the hell of it, tossing rocks through windows, spray-painting garage doors, keying nice cars that made the mistake of parking in our neighborhood. We were scraping for whatever we could, causing a little unnecessary ruckus for fun, and surviving life at home.

When I was a freshman at Bonaventure, I was on the road to nowhere. I was able to discern, by that stage of my life, that I had something going for me in the brains department, but I saw no reason to apply myself. College wasn't a consideration. Maybe I had listened too closely to my father, who didn't have a favorable opinion of my present or future. It was in gym class, of all places, that my life turned around, a wayward pass thrown in a flag football game that, for some reason, I felt the urge to chase down, ultimately grabbing the ball with one hand outstretched, catching not only the pigskin but the attention of the varsity football coach. It was like something out of a movie. *What's your name, kid?* he asked me. I knew who he was. Everyone knew Coach Fox. If you were me, if you were one of the kids who didn't fit in, who smoked weed off-campus and blew off homework and generally avoided any school-sponsored event, you thought Coach Emory Fox was the Antichrist.

Payton, I told him. *Walter Payton.*

Yeah, okay, Walter Payton. I want you right here, on the practice field, after school.

I don't know why I complied. It would have been more in character for a smart guy like me to blow it off. But I showed up, and he put me through the paces. I stood there, with the varsity quarterback, Patrick Gillis, directing me to run patterns and hurling the ball at me while one of the defensive backs tried vainly to shadow me. It felt as natural as breathing, hunting that football through the air, feeling it into my hands, tucking it in and running away from everything.

Sammy laughed when I told him where I'd been. *They want me to come out*, I told him. *He said he wants me to play on varsity.* Sammy searched my face, seemingly waiting for the punch line. *You're gonna play on the fucking* football *team, Koke?*

I read something in his eyes, disappointment, in some sense a feeling of betrayal, when I told him that yes, I was going out for the football team.

YOU OWE ME, Koke. Sammy's words to me a couple of hours ago, words he'd never said back then.

I rubbed my eyes and sighed. I had four weeks to pay my debt. I had four weeks to prove that Griffin Perlini did, in fact, abduct and murder Sammy's sister, Audrey.

This week, for the first time in twenty years, I would go home.

12

THE PROSECUTOR on the *Cutler* case was Lester Mapp. I didn't know him, but I'd looked him up on the Internet last night. He'd been a federal prosecutor for six years and then went into private practice with Howser, Gregg, a predominantly African-American law firm that practiced criminal defense. Two years back, he'd been recruited by the newly elected county attorney, a black alderman named Damien Sands. Sands had elevated a number of African Americans to prominent positions in the office. I'd heard some old-timers around the office throw around words like *affirmative action*, but I didn't buy it, personally. I had little doubt that a number of minorities had been denied rightful promotion over the years, and besides, in my mind, to the victor went the spoils. You work in an office run by elected politicos, don't expect fair. You don't like it, there's the door.

Besides, I didn't have much time for the racial thing. I dislike everyone equally.

The judge on our case was the honorable Kathleen Poker. She'd assumed the bench after a career as a prosecutor—find me a criminal court judge who hadn't—and was generally considered tough but fair. I'd never had a case in front of her but, based on her reputation, she was a relatively good draw.

I sat in the courtroom among the myriad of criminal defense attorneys waiting for the call. It was not, by and large, an impressive bunch.

These are not the lawyers you see on television, the thousand-dollar suits and trendy haircuts, the passionate crusaders. These are guys and gals who work for a living. They take their money up front. If they're good, they only lose about ninety percent of the time. They don't like their clients and they have trained themselves not to care too much, else they will never again enjoy a decent night's sleep. And when the money runs out, so do they, or they'd go broke. They do not have the benefit of an armada of young lawyers performing research and investigation. They have the cards stacked overwhelmingly against them and they know it. They know how to cross-examine a witness but have far less experience in directing their own clients on the stand, because most of their clients take Five. They drink their Maalox from the bottle and tell themselves, every day, that they are playing a necessary role in the criminal justice system.

Other than that, it's a great job.

We got called near the beginning, because our motion was routine. Judge Poker, looking rather austere with gray-brushed hair, peered over her glasses down at me. "Mr. Kolarich, you are aware of the October 29 trial date? Less than a month away?"

"I am, Judge. We'll be ready."

She held her look on me a long moment, then looked over at the prosecutor, Lester Mapp.

"No objection," Mapp said. He was probably thrilled that I'd be playing catch-up. Presumably, he'd expected me to ask for an additional six months.

She smirked at the prosecutor's feigned graciousness, delivered a little too eagerly. I decided then that I liked her, and I could make her like me, if I were so inclined. "Granted," she said, and two minutes later, Mapp and I were leaving the courtroom together.

It was my first chance to size him up. He dressed like a guy who'd spent some time in the high-end private sector, dressed in an Italian suit with a stylish yellow silk tie. All in all, he was an impressive-looking chap and, from the way he carried himself, I figured it might be the one thing that he and I would agree on.

He shook my hand and gave me a wide smile. "Great to see ya," he said, though we'd never met previously. He was way too polished for my liking, but I suspected he would be formidable in court. "You got everything from the PD?"

"He's sending it over today," I said.

We stopped at the elevator.

"Ready for trial, are you?" His tone suggested that he didn't buy it.

I figured I'd help him down the road he was already traveling. "Hey, I told Cutler, he's crazy if he's going to trial on this."

He smiled again, predatory eyes appraising me. I wanted him to think that I was planning on pleading this out. I wanted him complacent, sure of himself. I wanted to be the farthest thing from a threat to him.

"Well, hey, you always got that black guy running from the building," he said, palming my arm before heading into the elevator.

YOU DON'T INQUIRE, not when you're a self-absorbed, seven-year-old kid. Something wakes you up, a familiar noise. Then you pinpoint the sound, a window frame sliding up. A moment of terror, filling your chest with dread, until you open your eyes and look at your own window on the second floor and realize it's not yours. You look through your own open window, through the screen, and you listen, but you don't inquire. You hear some more noises, rustling. Maybe you could identify that sound, too, but you don't try; you just hear things happening. Later you will realize it, of course, the sound of someone crawling through a window. The sounds subside, you're lost in your own world, suffused with drowsiness, and your face eases back into the cool pillow. Maybe you drift off a moment until you hear it again, those same rustling sounds, but then there is urgency to the movements, and that sound— the sound of footsteps running on grass—you have no trouble identifying.

But you're a kid. You don't place it in context. It feels wrong, yes, but you don't confront it. Finally, you get out of bed, tentatively, and move to your window. It's probably no accident that you waited until the running footsteps have faded before you look. You look down into the window next door, into the bedroom of Audrey Cutler, Sammy's sister, where the window is open, the curtain is dancing in the light wind.

You return to bed. It feels like you have drifted off to sleep. You lose

track of time again, because it doesn't register at first; it takes you a
moment before your head jerks up again, at the sound of Sammy's
mother wailing out, a horrifying shriek.

Later, you will say you didn't hear anything, that you were asleep. No
one expects anything different of you. It's not like you could help them
out, anyway. You didn't see the man who abducted Audrey. Still, you
always wonder: Could you have done something?

I felt my heartbeat kick up a gear as I saw the sign for Leland Park. The
old neighborhood looked just that—old. I had to attribute that, in part,
to the mere fact of my own maturity, returning to your roots, but Leland
Park looked a lot worse for the wear. I had expected change, something
different, and found surprise in the absence of change. The houses were
the same, aged a couple of decades, well-worn bungalows and the occasional board-up. This wasn't one of the neighborhoods in the city that
was attracting new construction; this was a neighborhood people were
leaving.

I turned onto my old street, braking for a young black kid who chased
a rubber football into the street. Now that was different. My neighborhood had been all-white; the folks had an unwritten rule about it: You
didn't sell your house to blacks. I'd heard of a lawsuit filed about ten years
ago, a claim of racial steering brought against the real estate agents and
some of the residents, which apparently had succeeded.

I pulled up to the fourth house from the corner of Graynor and 47th.
The house I grew up in was a two-story house with siding, a small porch
of rock and a gravel driveway. All of that was still true, but the siding was
torn on each side and now there was a porch swing. The half-acre lot
looked smaller than I'd remembered it.

I didn't feel anything. I saw my mother on the front porch, calling me
in for dinner; my father drinking a Coors while he fussed over his Chevy
on the driveway; my brother Pete running around in circles on our small
front yard; Sammy coming to my front door for the walk to school. But it
didn't register in any way. Nothing. My emotions had run daily mara-
thons for months and needed a rest.

Next door was Sammy's old house. A German shepherd was barking at
me from a chain-link fence in the backyard. I looked at the window on

the side of the house and pictured Griffin Perlini carrying little Audrey out of the house. Our neighbor down the street, Mrs. Thomas, had seen it happen from her bedroom window, watched them run down Graynor, turning right down 47th. Other than Perlini, Mrs. Thomas was the last to see Audrey Cutler. She hadn't known what she was watching, of course. She was a middle-aged widow looking down the street, the distance of a football field, at a figure running awkwardly, hunched over, without pumping his arms. She hadn't realized that the reason he couldn't use his arms was that he was carrying a two-year-old girl.

I remember the next morning, Mrs. Thomas hugging Sammy's mother, trembling uncontrollably, apologizing for not having done more. What could she have done?

I wondered if Mrs. Thomas was still alive. It was possible. It was less possible that I was going to prove that Griffin Perlini killed Audrey Cutler.

I drove on, turning on 47th and heading six blocks west, then three blocks south, then two more blocks west. The house was in the middle of the street, a ranch-style with a roof that was openly suffering, old vinyl siding, and a neglected lawn. I'd passed the house several times, more as a curiosity than anything else. I'd never gone in or thought of going in. I'd thought of a few other things, like putting a few bullet holes through the windows, but as a teen I never did anything more than pass by the home of Griffin Perlini and stare.

An elderly woman stepped out onto the porch and took the mail from the slot. I found myself getting out of my car and approaching. I caught the woman's attention, and she didn't seem concerned. This wasn't a nice neighborhood, but I was in courtroom attire and I didn't pose any visible threat to her.

"Mrs. Perlini?" I asked, taking a wild shot. Griffin Perlini hadn't lived with his mother at the time of Audrey's abduction, and I had no idea what had happened to the house afterward.

The woman didn't respond, but she opened herself up toward me, receptive to my question. Had Griffin Perlini's mother moved into this home after he left?

"Mrs. Perlini?" I asked again, as I slowly approached the porch.

"Can I help you?" Her voice was weak, befitting her small frame. She was wearing a light sweater and gray pants that perfectly matched her long hair.

Wow. I'd lucked out. This woman was Griffin Perlini's mother.

"Mrs. Perlini." I stopped short of the porch. "My name is Jason Kolarich." I gestured behind me. "I grew up around here."

"Oh." Her voice softened, but she didn't smile. "You knew—did you know—"

"Griffin? No, ma'am. I mean—no. But that *is* why I'm here."

Her face moved into a full-scale frown. She kept her composure, watching me and letting silence fill in the blanks.

"I'm a lawyer, Mrs. Perlini. I'm defending Sammy Cutler."

She nodded, as if somehow she suspected as much. I could have predicted any number of reactions, but she seemed to accept me as if I'd said I was selling something she knew she had to buy but didn't particularly want to.

She lowered her head, as if she was speaking in confidence. "You knew the Cutlers?"

"I lived next door."

"I see." Her gaze drifted off, over my head, beyond me. I couldn't imagine what it must have been like for her, everything her son became, everything he'd done.

"You'll want to come in, then." Mrs. Perlini walked into her house. I took the steps up and opened a flimsy screen door. I didn't know what I was doing or what I was hoping to accomplish. This whole thing had been a lark, and now I was about to have a conversation with Griffin Perlini's mother.

I sat down on a flimsy couch while I listened to her toil in the kitchen. The clinking sounds told me she was making coffee. I didn't want coffee, but I wanted anything that would elongate this conversation.

The place was drab but well-kept. The walls were painted lime green and were covered with photographs, in some of which I recognized Griffin, but it was clear that there were several children in the family. A good-sized crucifix was prominently centered.

Five minutes later, Mrs. Perlini was placing a cup of weak-smelling coffee in front of me. She sat in a rocking chair across from where I sat and held her cup of coffee in her lap. She didn't seem in a hurry to take the lead, but as soon as I cleared my throat and started up, she chimed in.

She asked me, "Do you think what he did was justified?"

I assumed she was referring to what Sammy did, killing her son. "Do you want me to answer that?"

"I suppose not." She studied her coffee cup but didn't drink it.

"Do *you*?" I asked.

"Do I think it was justified?" She thought about that a moment. "I suppose from his perspective—" She struggled with her answer. "Your first instinct is to protect your children."

"Sure."

"But when your child's sickness hurts other people—innocent children—well, it allows you to see more than one perspective."

I looked again at the gold crucifix on the wall. This woman must have spent a good deal of time conversing with the Almighty. You chalk it up to a sickness, I imagine, like she'd said. *It's not my fault. It's nothing I did. My son was ill.* But do you believe that? Is there a part of you that thinks back, that second-guesses, that wonders if you'd done something differently—

"I have to prove that your son killed Audrey Cutler," I said. "And I'm wondering if you can help me with that."

She closed her eyes and whispered something to herself. I had the sense she was praying. For some reason, I felt a rush of anger. I'd had a few go-rounds with the Almighty myself, but it hadn't helped any. I tried cursing Him for what happened to Talia and Emily, but the conversation always ended with the blame stopping at my doorstep. I surely didn't blame God for their deaths. But I didn't find comfort, either, and I found myself back to my childhood bouts with religion and logic. Faith, by definition, is the absence of proof, and as a logician, a lawyer trained in linear thinking, I struggled to make sense of a line of logic that had no end.

My family was dead, and there was nothing upstairs that could explain why. The truth was, I was afraid *not* to believe, afraid of being left off the guest list when my time came, but if push came to shove, if I really challenged myself with a focused question, I didn't have an answer. I didn't know if I believed or not. Maybe that, itself, was an answer.

"I just want the truth," I said, interrupting her reflection. "Surely God wouldn't want you to lie."

She opened her eyes. I didn't like what I saw in them. She wasn't angry so much as concerned. "I wasn't asking for advice," she told me. "I was asking for strength."

I decided to remain quiet. I didn't want to insult her further and I didn't want a sermon, either. I just wanted an answer.

"He never told me he kidnapped that poor girl, if that's what you're asking, Mr. Kolarich. He told me the opposite, in fact. Now, I may be a lot of things, but I'm not ignorant. I know my son. I know he did things." She drank from her cup and let the liquid play in her mouth. I suddenly felt very small.

"He was always troubled," she went on. "Always. He never bothered much with girls, but I just thought he was slow to develop that interest. Growing up, he was so introverted, so tortured, but I never knew him to act on any of the impulses that he obviously had. I never knew. Does that sound odd? A mother didn't know her son had this horrible sickness."

She drank from the cup again and nodded to herself. "About a year before—before his first arrest—that was when I first discovered something about his—his preferences." She shrugged. "I honestly had no idea before that time."

I knew, vaguely, that her son had a criminal record before Audrey was abducted, which was the reason the police had focused on him so quickly.

"What happened?" I asked her.

"Oh, well, Griffin—he injured his knee very seriously. He tore the—his anterior something-or-other?"

"The anterior cruciate ligament," I said. It was a common injury in football. A buddy of mine at State tore his ACL and never played ball again.

"That's it," she said. "He was off his feet for weeks. It's not like we had the money for surgery. He was all but immobile. So I stayed here with Griffin, while he was recuperating. One day, I was just trying to clean up. He was so messy, that boy." She sighed, relishing a momentary memory of her son that did not include his sexual affliction, before she darkened again. "I saw some—some photo—"

"You saw some disturbing photographs," I gathered.

"That's right." She touched her eyes. "I—I talked to him about it. He told me it was just some joke that a friend had sent him." She looked at me. "Of course I should have known better. I make no excuses, but—a mother wants to believe, doesn't she?"

"Of course she does."

"And then, later, there were those few incidents in Summit. And Griffin told me they were misunderstandings, he swore to me he would *never* touch a child. Can you imagine how much a mother would want to believe that?"

She was referring to Griffin's first brushes with the law in a town downstate, one ending in a *nolle* and one in a conviction for indecent exposure.

"And then," she said softly, "there was little Audrey."

Her eyes welled up. I imagine, by now, it took a lot to make the tears fall. I realized now why she had made Griffin's home her own. It was penance. She was punishing herself for the sins of her son by immersing herself in the memory.

"I told him, Mr. Kolarich, I did. I said, 'Griffin, if you did something to that little girl, you have to tell them.' But he wouldn't admit it."

He wouldn't admit it. Different than saying he denied it.

"Do I think he did something to that little girl, Audrey? Well, the answer is yes."

I nodded. "Can you help me at all?"

Fresh tears spilled down her face. I sensed that it was more than mere generalized grief. She was struggling. She had something to tell me.

I was about to burst, but I had to let this play out naturally. I would beg and plead if necessary, but it felt right to let her make the next move.

She took a while, a good cry, wiping her face, blowing her nose, mumbling to herself, before she finally heaved a heavy sigh.

"I guess there's no sense trying to protect him anymore," she said.

13

AREA THREE HEADQUARTERS was no more than half a mile from where I grew up, a place where I'd spent a very uncomfortable evening in the summer before my junior year at Bonaventure. I still remembered the taste of sweat on my upper lip, the thick cologne of the police detective who stood over me, the whack from the heel of Coach Fox's hand across my face. I didn't remember the name of the cop, but it wasn't Vic Carruthers.

Carruthers looked to be near retirement, a broad guy with an extra chin and a face that looked like a map of interstate highways. He sat back in his chair and looked crosswise at me, a guy who was reminding him of a case that hadn't gone so well for him.

"Perlini's dead," he repeated back to me. "And Audrey's brother is the one that killed him."

"He's charged with that murder, yes."

"And her son being dead, that accounts for the mother's change of heart. She figures there's no reason to keep it a secret anymore."

"Right."

"She didn't"—he came forward, leaned into me, his jaw clenched, a fire to his eyes—"she didn't feel the need to help out that girl back then."

"I don't think she knew," I said. "And she didn't want to believe it. She still doesn't know for sure. But she suspects."

"She suspects. She suspects." Carruthers ran a large hand across his face. "I don't even know where this school is, I don't think. Fifty-seventh and Hudson?"

I nodded. Hardigan Elementary School had a large hill behind it that supplied a good toboggan slide in the winter, and a hangout for recreational drug users in the warm weather, when I was a kid. The hill crested down sharply into a thick set of trees, in front of which was a large fence that formed the boundary of the schoolyard.

Mrs. Perlini had no way to be sure, she'd told me, but she knew that Griffin had continued to visit the site as an adult. There would be one obvious reason for someone of Griffin's sexual inclinations to want a bird's-eye view into an elementary school yard, but Mrs. Perlini could never shake the notion that Griffin had used the cover of the thick trees for another purpose.

"She thinks it's a burial site," Carruthers said. "She found muddy shoes and a shovel in his garage one day? That's it?" His anger was rising, bringing color to his jowls, but I imagined the source was the reminder of this unsolved case, his inability to nail the man who killed a little girl on his watch.

"It was a place he went," I said. "She thinks it's where he would have put her. I happen to think she might be on to something."

"*You* happen to think. You score a few touchdowns for Bonaventure and that makes you a police detective."

I didn't bother to fight. He was doing a pretty good job battling himself. He didn't speak for a long time, scratching at his face and, it seemed, reliving the investigation. From what I knew, Carruthers had gotten a little rough with Griffin Perlini while they searched for Audrey, but that hadn't been the problem. The problem was that Griffin Perlini had never said a damn thing to the police, not a word, once they trained on him. No little girl's body, no incriminating statement.

Carruthers opened a drawer on his cluttered desk and removed a photo. It was Audrey, frozen in time as a child.

"You don't forget a case like that," he said. "Not ever. Not a day goes by . . ."

I knew a little something about regret, and I didn't want to be reminded.

"The girl's dead and her killer's dead," Carruthers said.

"Yeah, but her brother's not." I gathered my things and stood up. "Sammy Cutler is entitled to know." I looked at the photograph of Audrey, clutched in the detective's hand. "And so are you."

YOU'RE DUMB TEENAGERS, you and your buddy Sammy, careless with your side business, the one you work between shifts at the grocery store. Careless because you never consider the consequences. You tell yourself, it's only pot, it's just you and your buddies getting stoned, it's not addictive, no one's getting hurt, and you're just making a couple of bucks.

You don't think much about the guy who sells you the stuff, Ice, the twenty-year-old who sells out of his house and who, you later learn, is into a lot more than just marijuana, and who has attracted the attention of the police.

So you drive up to his house like you're visiting a friend. You keep your stash in the trunk of the car. Turns out, you're in the wrong place at the wrong time. Sammy sees it first—*Look*, he says, pointing at the window of Ice's house, through which you see a man in the living room with a badge hanging around his neck.

You stop on the driveway, turn and run, just as the front door bursts open, people shouting after you, just like how it goes on television, *Freeze—police*, and some instinct causes you and Sammy to separate, Sammy running south, you running north. You've spent a year on the football squad by now; you've honed your physical skills. You can run like lightning and you do, full force, never looking back, using all the advantages of a boy on foot, cutting through alleys and over backyard fences, maximizing the difficulty of anyone giving chase by car. You don't stop until you're far beyond your neighborhood, a good five miles at least.

Sammy. You don't know. He can't run like you. You think about it and you hope, you pray. Yes, you've abandoned your car across the street from Ice's house, and you know what's in the trunk. Still, it's possible, all of it: It's possible Sammy got away; it's possible the cops don't know it's your car; it's possible Ice hasn't given you and Sammy up—after all, the police weren't after small-timers like you. They're after the higher-ups in the chain, right?

The next hours, the late afternoon and early evening, are agonizing. You walk aimlessly, slowly circling back toward your neighborhood. You're hesitant to make it home that night, wondering if a police car is awaiting you on the driveway. You approach your house tentatively, scanning up and down the street. When you walk through the front door, your sweat-drenched hair stuck to your forehead, your pulse rattling, your mother is sitting at the kitchen table with your brother, Pete.

Sammy's at the police station, she tells you.

I DROVE BACK from the police station, thinking about Sammy in his cell, thinking about Mrs. Perlini and the denial she lived with, and thinking about the blue Chevy that had kept a pretty safe distance from me since I first drove back to my old neighborhood earlier today. I could only assume that this was the same friend I'd made a couple nights back, leaving that club. I was being followed, no question.

I called Pete on my cell. He wanted to head out tonight and I said I'd think about it. He sounded okay on the phone, but I was still thinking about the other night at the club. I was pretty sure he'd been using drugs, and for all I knew, he'd been back using for quite some time. I'd been in such a funk for the last four months that it had probably escaped my attention.

"We gotta talk, little brother," I told him.

He laughed. "'We gotta talk?' What does *that* mean?" He was being defensive. From what I knew, Pete had never been more than a casual user, but the slope, as they say, was a slippery one.

I didn't respond to him because he knew what I meant. I didn't have any right to tell him what to do, and I had no real desire to do so. Add to that, Pete had done a pretty good job watching over me these last few months, so it felt a little weird preaching to him. Still, I couldn't just let it go.

"Just—we'll talk tonight," I said, after tiring of his moaning.

"Forget about tonight," he said. "Save your sermon for someone else. And hey—it's nice to see you're back to form, telling me how to live my life."

I drove home with the music down, keeping an eye on the Chevy following me, memorizing the license plate, though I assumed that a trace wouldn't get me anything. I thought about screwing with the guy, hitting the brakes, maybe letting him pass me, waving hello to him or tailing him, but I didn't see any advantage in any of that. Better he should think he's a world-class expert in surveillance, until I could figure out what I needed to do with him.

14

I SPENT THE NIGHT IN, staring at the walls of my bedroom, watching the television with the sound low. I was beyond the point of self-torture. I no longer played the CDs that Talia loved, Morrissey and Sarah McLachlan and Tracy Chapman. I no longer obsessed over our wedding album. I no longer so much as set foot in Emily's room, the nursery, which Talia had done out in pink and green with a Beatrix Potter theme, cute little bunnies prancing among soft pastel colors.

Nor did I drink, at least not for the purpose of drowning my sorrows. Alcohol didn't work for me that way; it heightened the pain, unleashed emotion. When you're drowning, you already feel out of control. You don't need intoxication to feel unstable.

No, the only thing for me was frivolous diversion, the most innocuous sitcom or infomercial I could find on the tube, the easiest beach-read paperbacks I could buy. I couldn't handle extremes, so I was reaching for the soft middle.

In some ways, it's better now, but in most ways it's worse. The death of a loved one is unfathomable initially, this amazingly horrible thing that can't have really happened, and then you're immediately assigned to the rather mundane tasks of notifying people, arrangements with the cemetery, planning a funeral. And then everyone you care about is surrounding you, delivering food in Tupperware and lingering about for a required length of time. After a couple of weeks, everything returns to normal, and that's when you realize that *normal* has a new meaning. That's when you realize that this is your life now, that you own a three-bedroom, two-bath home with a nursery done up specially for a daughter you don't have, sleeping in a bed for two when there's only one.

I fell asleep watching syndicated reruns, sitting up in bed with my clothes on, probably some time around two in the morning. I had a dream, the contents of which evaporated from my memory when my eyes popped open; the only thing I recalled was the sound that had awakened me—the sound of Emily crying out, as she had so many times in the depth of night, a whimper that slowly grew into a wail.

It was dawn. I was desperately tired but unable to sleep. I got out of bed and went to the bathroom, getting the toilet lid open just in time to vomit. I sat on the floor of the bathroom, taking deep breaths, scolding myself to no avail. I threw up again and then took a shower.

At nine, I got in my car and drove to see Tommy Butcher, the one witness in Sammy's case who could actually help us. From what I had read in the report he gave to the police, on the night of Griffin Perlini's murder at the approximate time of the murder, Tommy Butcher was leaving a bar called Downey's Pub when a black man came running out of Perlini's apartment building. Being someone who, like most people, prefers to mind his own business, Butcher thought nothing of it and went on with his life.

Butcher gave his statement to the police only three weeks ago, after reading about the case in the newspaper—meaning that by that point, the police had long ago arrested Sammy and fixed their focus on him as the murderer. Once the police decide they have their man, it's game over for them. I knew that the prosecution would go to great lengths to discount Tommy Butcher's testimony and, if possible, discredit him personally.

For starters, Butcher's statement to the police came roughly a year after the murder, which would make someone wonder how he could be so sure about the precise date that he saw the black-guy-fleeing-the-scene. And undoubtedly, Butcher's memory would be expected to be faulty, after he'd spent a night in a bar. But maybe something had stood out that made him remember the event particularly well. Maybe the black-guy-fleeing-the-scene had said *I just killed Griffin Perlini* as he sprinted by.

He'd asked to meet at a coffee shop near 87th and Pershing, which was near a job Butcher was working. Tommy Butcher was a principal at Butcher Construction Company, a family-owned construction firm that had offices in the city and in a large downstate town called Maryville, principally known as the home of Marymount Penitentiary. Butcher Construction had built the addition to the prison and did some other work in that area, but mostly the company did public construction jobs here in the city. Fair or not, you think of big city contracts, you think connections. You think corruption.

Butcher looked like a guy with a lifetime in the trade, a wide guy with half a head of hair; a rough, tan complexion; and a meaty hand that engulfed mine when he greeted me. He sized me up and didn't seem too disappointed, though I couldn't guess what criteria he was using. Having had some experience with contractors when Talia and I did some renovation work on our home, I generally put the integrity of construction types right up there with politicians and car salesmen.

"Doing the new park district building over at Deemer Park," he told me, as we waited for coffee. "City's throwing a shit-fit because we're two weeks behind schedule."

I thought he was trying to tell me that he didn't have much time for me, so I got right to asking him what happened.

"I'm over at Downey's," he began. "Having a few drinks. I left about ten, maybe, something like that. I'm walking east, I guess—yeah, east on Liberty and I'm going by this building. It's got a walk-up, a staircase, up to the front door. Looks like a real fleabag place, so it fits right in with the surroundings, right?"

"Right."

"Right. So anyway, this black guy comes out of the door real fast, right? And he's flying down those stairs. His jacket's flying open kind of, while he's running and all, and I see this guy has a gun stuffed in his pants. So me, I don't want no part of this guy, right? So he goes running past me, and I'm not getting in this brother's way, right? Guy flies right past me and that's about it."

I nodded. I was scribbling some notes.

"And so, yeah, I guess it sure seemed like this guy wasn't running away because he'd done something good. But what am *I* gonna do? I didn't do nothing. What am I gonna do, call the cops and say I saw a guy running?"

"Nothing for you to report," I agreed.

The coffee arrived, and he filled it with cream. "Nothing to report. Right? Am I wrong?"

I'd already answered that question. There's no crime in running out of a building, and Butcher hadn't known that someone had been shot.

"So then, okay, I'm reading about this guy who's been shot at this building, and I'm thinking back, and then I check my calendar and yeah, I was pretty sure that was the night I was at Downey's, and I call my brother Jake and we think about it and then we're sure. It was that Thursday, September 21. And I'm thinking, holy Christ, I gotta tell someone."

It sounded plausible. It would be a lot better if I could come up with a black suspect, and even better if Butcher could ID that suspect. But I didn't have anyone, not yet, at least.

"Can anyone confirm you were at Downey's that night?" I asked. "You mentioned your brother."

"Yeah, Jake, my brother. He could say."

"Who else?"

He shook his head. "Just me and Jake."

I asked him for brother Jake's contact information. He gave me a cell phone number.

"You pay with a credit card?" I asked.

"I don't think so. Why, someone's gonna say I wasn't *there*?" He didn't seem happy about the prospect. I figured Tommy Butcher was used to being in charge and didn't appreciate dissent.

"It won't be me. I'm on your side." I thought that last point was worth making. I wanted it to be us against them. I wanted to harden his resolve for the inevitable doubts that would be forthcoming.

"Do you remember what he was wearing, this black guy?" I asked.

"I remember the gun, mostly." That stood to reason. Most witnesses, when they see a gun, don't remember much else. They find themselves predominantly concerned with whether that weapon might be pointed at them in the immediate future.

"The man seen leaving Griffin Perlini's apartment was wearing a brown leather bomber jacket and a green stocking cap," I said. It was simply a harmless, innocuous observation, not a blatant attempt to coach the witness.

He thought about that for a minute. "Coulda been," he said. "Coulda been." His fingers played on the table. Then he nodded at me. "Your guy got a chance to win this case?"

I shrugged.

"I mean," Butcher continued, "paper said this douche bag got killed, this guy Perlini, right? They said he killed your guy's sister. So I guess that gives your guy a pretty good reason to do what he did."

"If he did it," I answered.

He exhaled out of his nose, a wry smile, like I'd just made a joke. I thought he was suggesting to me that a jury wouldn't convict a guy avenging his sister's murder. He was thinking, perhaps, that I had a pretty good case. I needed him to understand otherwise. I needed him to understand his importance to my case.

"Problem is," I said, "Perlini was never convicted of killing my client's sister. They couldn't make a case against him. He walked. So I can't get up and say that to the jury. I can't say Sammy was doing this for his sister, because there's no proof of it."

My explanation seemed to trouble Tommy Butcher, which was precisely my intention. "I mean, we all know Perlini killed her," I said. "I just can't prove it. Not yet, that is."

Butcher repeated my words. "Not yet."

"Not yet. I'm trying. But digging up an almost thirty-year-old case—and I'm not a cop, I don't have an arsenal of investigators or anything. I'm trying, but it's going to be hard. And I don't have much time. So you're the best I have, Tom."

Butcher thought about that, his lips pursed. "You're gonna try to solve an old case like that?"

It wasn't typically my practice to share my strategy with a witness. But he seemed genuinely sympathetic to Sammy's plight, and we were forming some kind of weird bond. I didn't want to freeze him out and kill the soft, warm chemistry.

"I'm going to try, yes. Because it's all I have, Tom. I mean, all you can say is there was this black guy, which is great, but you can't even say what he was wearing. So what can I do? The best I can do is a one-man investigation into what happened way back when, and hope I can come up with something." I shook my head. "Because if I can't, I've got you against about ten witnesses."

It wasn't quite ten. I was laying it on a little thick. But I was also finding that, as much as I was snowing this guy, I was speaking the essential truth.

"Listen." He knifed his hand down on the table. "Look. This is, like, privileged, right?"

Wrong. This guy had no privilege with me. But I wanted to hear what he had to say, so I didn't rush to disabuse him.

He leaned forward and lowered his voice. "I don't know any of these people from Adam, right? But if someone said I shot someone, and it turned out there was this brother running away from the scene with a gun—I mean, right? I'd want someone to come forward. Know what I'm saying?"

It was the second time he'd referred to a black guy as a "brother." He was saying there was something self-evident about a black man running from the scene. I wasn't going to be president of this guy's fan club, but I needed him—Sammy needed him—and I wasn't here to heal a racial divide in our society, at least not this week.

And I'd told him the truth: As of this moment, he was the best I had.

"You have a sister?" I asked.

"I sure as hell do." His jaw clenched, the reaction I wanted, imagining what he'd do to someone who hurt his sister. I considered laying it on even thicker, but I didn't think I needed to.

Butcher leaned back again, looked around the place awhile. I took a drink of the coffee, which was terrible. I didn't do or say anything, because I felt the momentum.

"Leather bomber jacket," he said. "Green stocking cap? Yeah, now that I'm thinking back, I mean, really focusing on that particular aspect and whatnot—that sounds about right."

15

YOU'RE TREMBLING when you enter the police station with your mother. *Sammy's at the police station*, was all your mother had said, and you'd played dumb. You had no idea why. You forgot to mention to your mother that you and Sammy had run from the police outside a drug dealer's house earlier that day.

You see Sammy's mother, who is inside pacing until she sees you. Your mom and Sammy's hug. Mrs. Cutler is crying. She says they found drugs in Sammy's car. *Sammy's* car, which is technically true because he bought it, the title is in his name, but both mothers know that you drive it, too.

Your mother looks at you, a long, hard glare, but she doesn't ask the question. So you don't answer. You don't know what you're going to say.

A cop walks out, an athletically built guy in a dress shirt and badge. He takes one look at you and he says your name. *Jason Kolarich?*

Your legs go weak. Your mother takes hold of your arm. *I'm Jason's mother*, she says, defensively.

The cop waves his hand in a dismissive manner. *It's not like that*, he says. *We just want to talk to him. Sammy wants to talk to him.*

It's okay, Mom, you hear yourself say. And then you are following this man through a door, and then down a hall. He doesn't speak to you. You're not sure you'll be able to find your voice again.

Class of '78, he says to you. You don't catch his meaning. You don't say anything.

He stops at a door with frosted glass bearing the number 2. When the door opens, you see Coach Fox standing in the room, his back to you. He turns around and stares at you.

What the fuck are you doing, Kolarich? he asks you. *Sit the fuck down.*

You sit. Coach Fox points to the cop and tells you, *Detective Brady here, he was an outside linebacker when we went to sectionals in '78. He worked his ass off,* he tells you, *went to college afterward and became a cop.*

I didn't have the talent you have, the cop says to you. *So why the hell are you gonna squander it? Getting messed up with this kid Cutler?*

Sammy. It comes back to Sammy. *He's my best friend,* you tell the room. *This is my fault, too.*

They don't like it. Coach Fox spits out a curse. *This year was nothing,* he says to you. *We're winning state next year, Kolarich, if you don't fuck it up for us.*

You hear yourself again, saying the words: *It was me and Sammy together. It was both of us,* you tell them.

Coach Fox goes quiet. He turns away, as if he can pretend he didn't hear it. The cop, Brady, leans in so he's close to your face.

That's not how Sammy tells it, he says.

I LEFT the coffee shop not particularly pleased with myself but happy to have at least one fairly solid witness for Sammy. Tommy Butcher didn't have the first damn memory of what the black-guy-fleeing-the-scene had been wearing and I'd handed it to him. I was sure, at this point, between his racial leanings and his sense of rough justice, that Butcher would testify very clearly that the black-guy-fleeing-the-scene was, beyond any doubt, wearing a brown leather bomber jacket and green stocking cap.

You owe me, Koke. Maybe that truth allowed me so easily to suggest a memory to Butcher. As a prosecutor, I was obsessive about ethics to the point of a rebuke, on more than one occasion, from my division chief. One of my apprehensions upon joining the defense bar was a fear that the standard was diminished on the other side of the aisle—most prosecutors viewed most defense attorneys as corner-cutters, cheaters, sometimes downright liars. I'd been grateful to learn otherwise, under the tutelage of Paul Riley. Paul had been steadfast on the *Almundo* case, when the senator had suggested how certain witnesses might be cooperative. *That's not how it works, Hector,* Paul had told him. *At least not with me.* And not with me, either.

Maybe it was Talia's and Emily's deaths that gave me a more universal perspective, allowing the ends to more liberally justify the means. Either way, I owed Sammy, like he said. But that conversation with Tommy Butcher would stay with me awhile.

I checked my cell phone and found that I had a message. I played it while I drove.

> *This is Detective Vic Carruthers. I'm sending over copies of the files like you asked. And I wanted you to know, we're going to do the dig. And if I find that little girl's bones on the side of that hill, I'm going to rip Perlini out of his grave and beat the ever lovin' shit out of him.*

Good. Progress, at least. Maybe I'd be able to conclusively pin Audrey's murder on Perlini. That just left me with the small task of convincing the judge that it was relevant to the case, even if Sammy was continuing to claim that he didn't kill Perlini.

I had my usual lunchtime stop to make, and then I'd go visit Mrs. Thomas, my old neighbor.

WHEN THE CURTAIN PARTS, a number of kids are lying on the stage, curled up in the fetal position, feigning sleep. Behind them, a row of children move awkwardly, side by side, across the stage, wearing cardboard across their waists that are supposed to represent clouds. Talia and I, sitting in the third row, perk up, because we know the sun is about to shine.

Emily, with the golden-orange cardboard sun across her chest, slowly rises from a crouch. "Riiiise and shi-innnne," she says.

I train the camcorder on our daughter as many in the audience coo with delight. Clearly they understand that Emily Kolarich is the most adorable child in the play.

"'Time to wake up, everyone,'" Talia whispers, a line she worked on with our daughter all of last night.

"Time to wake up, everyone!" Emily calls out.

Talia finds my free hand and locks her fingers with mine.

"She's so beautiful," I say to her. "God, Talia, she is so beautiful."

AFTER LEAVING THE CEMETERY, I drove down to the city's south side, to the nursing home where Delilah Thomas was spending her elderly years, no more than five miles from our old neighborhood in Leland Park. The all-brick front along a busy Cardaman Avenue made the place look more like a condo complex, which I suppose wasn't altogether inaccurate. The place was called the St. Joseph's Center for Assisted Living. Mrs. Thomas, like everyone else on our block, was a card-carrying Catholic.

I had called yesterday to set up the appointment, because I figured these places were pretty rigid in their structure. They were expecting me when I walked into a spacious reception area decorated in light purple.

A black guy in white escorted me to an elevator and hit the button for six. "You were all Lilly could talk about last night, after you called," he told me.

Mrs. Thomas had been widowed in her fifties—I was young then, and I struggled now to recall her husband's cause of death. I'd always remembered Mrs. Thomas in her backyard, tending to her garden, always the first to church. She and her husband had never had children. I could only imagine her loneliness now, but then, I guess, it didn't hurt surrounding herself with seniors.

"How is she?" I asked the guy, whose name tag said Darrell.

"Oh, Lilly?" His face lit up. "She's a peach. She does real good. Real good. Real spry little thing."

We got off at six, and I was, indeed, in what was basically a condo complex. The hallway was dimly lit, the walls white with that light-purple color again, a horizontal stripe along the center. A woman, moving slowly down the hall with a walker, stopped and watched Darrell and me. Darrell said something cheerful to her, and she seemed to react favorably but didn't smile.

Darrell knocked on the door at 607 and called out for Lilly, surprising me with the volume of his voice. We waited awhile before the door opened.

Mrs. Thomas had to be in her late eighties. I recognized her by her eyes and the way she held her head slightly angled. Otherwise, I could have passed her on the street without recognition. It was like a layer of skin had been overlaid on her face. Still, at first glance, she seemed to be holding up well, slightly stooped but thin, and her eyes were vibrant.

She put her hands to her face, and her small mouth opened. "Jason, Jason," she said softly. "Oh, look at you."

I took her hands in mine, and then her arms came around me for a hug. I held her delicately as she repeated my name a few more times. She smelled like flowers. The whole place smelled like flowers.

She took my wrist and led me into her small apartment, where a spread of finger sandwiches and desserts lay on a tray on a coffee table. She'd always been a cook. I remember holidays, particularly, when Mrs. Thomas would bring over cakes and cookies of all assortments and it would strike me, within the narrow confines of a child's observations, that she had no one else to bake for.

I felt that weird symphony of happiness and sympathy, poignant childhood memories fusing with the pain of realizing they're gone, that life marches onward, trampling everything in its path. Mrs. Thomas was at that stage where hope meant something new and different. I startled myself with the recognition that hope had meant something different to me, too, four months ago.

I played defense to her questioning for a good hour, like I used to when I'd come home from school and my mother would interrogate me. It was annoying at the time, though I wonder how it would have felt had she not inquired. You know you're a good parent when your child takes you for granted.

I bobbed and weaved, though I tried to fill in as much of the blanks as I could to satiate Mrs. Thomas, who kept insisting that I call her "Lilly" but I couldn't, I just couldn't. She knew my mother had died and she notably did not raise the subject of my father, currently serving time in prison, so we talked much about Pete—I left out the part about him having a couple of drug-related scrapes with the law, or his inability to find a direction to his life—and mostly about me.

There, too, I edited, letting her take joy in my brief turn as a celebrity athlete, and my scholarship to State. She didn't seem to be aware—or she'd forgotten—that I'd been kicked off the team for fighting with a teammate, after I'd used up all of my goodwill, even in a sport where violence is prized. She knew about law school and asked me about my law practice. She didn't know the details beyond that, and when she hit the real sore spot, I decided it best to just tell her that "No one's tied me down yet," rather than burden her mind with my misfortune, particularly when I was about to raise another tragedy. She beat me to it, asking after Sammy, and however old she may be, her eyes still worked behind those substantial bifocals, and she knew she'd hit on something dark and messy.

She listened carefully, her facial expressions deteriorating further into sadness with each new development I laid on her, a quick intake of air with each twist to the plot. It's never fun to hear of a murder, even if it was a scumbag child predator like Griffin Perlini. It's even worse to think of a sweet, if troubled, young boy from the neighborhood pulling the trigger.

"Oh, my." Her small frame seemed to turn into itself, as if trying to shield her from the memory of what happened to Audrey Cutler. "You know, Jason, every day I pray for forgiveness that I didn't say something. That I didn't call out after that man or call your mother or Mary right away."

"You had no way of knowing." It was, in fact, much like the conversation I'd had with Tommy Butcher—there's no crime against running. That was all she'd seen that night that Audrey was abducted.

Mrs. Thomas nibbled at a couple of fingernails, her haunted expression telling me she was reliving the whole thing. "If I could have been more sure," she said. "I—I just couldn't be sure. And Lord help me, I couldn't say something if I wasn't sure."

She was talking about the identification. As the only witness to the abduction, Mrs. Thomas had been asked to identify Griffin Perlini in a lineup. And obviously, she'd been unable to do so, or Griffin Perlini might have stood trial. In her mind, then, she'd failed the Cutlers a second time.

"It would have been almost impossible for you to identify him," I told her. From my trip back to the neighborhood, I'd estimated that Mrs. Thomas was looking at someone running with his back to her, in the middle of the night, from the distance of maybe half a football field.

Detective Carruthers had sent over copies of his files on Audrey's abduction for my review. I hadn't had the chance to look through them save for the file on Mrs. Thomas, so I would know what she'd said back then before this visit. In those files was a lineup report indicating that Mrs. Thomas "could not conclusively identify" Griffin Perlini as the man who had taken Audrey.

From my years as both a prosecutor and defense attorney, I knew that cops had a way of taking literary license with their view of events. *Could not conclusively identify* left an amount of interpretation that could fill an airplane hangar.

"Can you tell me how that happened?" I asked. "The police lineup?"

Mrs. Thomas gathered her sweater, currently around her shoulders, as if to stifle a chill in a room that was anything but drafty.

"I know it's hard to remember—"

Her eyes shot to mine, surprising me in their swiftness. "Oh, Jason, it's not hard to remember *that*. No, no, no."

She laid it out like I would expect. A couple of suits—a prosecutor and Griffin Perlini's lawyer—a couple of cops, and Mrs. Thomas, looking through a window into a lineup of, in this case, six male Caucasians holding numbered cards. "I—I told them I didn't know," she said. "I couldn't be sure. He was number two."

"Griffin Perlini was number two." I could only imagine how she'd known that. My guess was, Detective Carruthers had scratched his face with two fingers, or maybe crossed his arms and rested a peace sign on his bicep for her to see—something that would escape the notice of Perlini's defense lawyer. Prosecutors don't like to think about how witnesses can be coached.

She shook her head, but not in response to me. "He was so—such a small man," she said.

Perlini was about five-seven and scrawny. So she was right, but I didn't catch the significance. Or maybe the problem was, I did.

"*Too* small?" I asked.

My question seemed to snap her out of the memory. She was silent for a long time. I hated the fact that I was taking this sweet elderly woman back to that time, but I hated even more that I'd pulled her away now. Finally, she looked at me. "I don't fool myself that my memory is strong enough now," she said. "A man—a figure—running very fast. I honestly have trouble remembering what I saw."

I nodded. Accurately summoning memories is tricky, far more difficult than most people realize. It's not that you don't recall a vision, it's that the vision is probably not what you actually saw at the time.

"But you remember what you *felt*," I said.

She nodded solemnly.

Could not conclusively identify. "What did you tell the police, Mrs. Thomas?"

"Oh, Jason." She crossed a leg with some difficulty, turning her body slightly away from me, a classic defensive response. "The man was running so fast, and he was—he was—"

She leaned forward slightly. She didn't want to come out and acknowledge the horrible truth that he was cradling little Audrey in his arms, but I got the point.

"He was running fast and he was hunched over," I said.

"So you can see why it would be hard for me to know."

Sure. But I didn't have an answer yet. "Please tell me what you told the police," I said.

Mrs. Thomas stared out the window of her apartment, her expression now a forced stoicism. "Please tell Peter that I'd love to see him some time, Jason," she said. "And please, take some of this food with you. I swear I'll never eat it all."

16

THE COP, BRADY, walks you down the hall to the room where they have Sammy. You find him inside, sitting in a chair in handcuffs, his head hung low.

Hey, you say, trying to be encouraging.

He shakes his head.

Hey, you repeat.

You don't want no part of this, Koke.

But we're—it was both—

What's the point? He gestures in your direction. *Better me than you. You got your whole football thing and all. What do I got?*

It hits you hard, the distance Sammy has suddenly put between the two of you.

You got me, you say.

Tears well in his eyes, but he shakes his head. *Go*, he says, his voice growing hoarser.

You admit it to yourself, a sense of relief accompanied by resulting shame. You don't want to get arrested. You want to survive this.

Go! he shouts. He still won't look up, but you see his eyes nonetheless, filled with fire and pain.

The cop walks into the room and takes your arm. Sammy drops his head again. *C'mon*, the cop says to you. You turn one last time, as the door is closing, to see that Sammy is watching you leave.

———

I STOPPED at a pub a few blocks from my house and ate dinner. The restaurants within a two-mile radius of my house were probably the only ones that benefited from the death of my wife and daughter. I wasn't much of a cook so I either ordered in or ate out almost every night. This night, I read through the newspaper and ate a cheeseburger. I called Pete on his cell, but he didn't answer. Five minutes later I got a text message from him saying: *No sermons.*

He was still being defensive, which meant I was on to something. He was telling himself, no doubt, that his use of drugs was recreational, ignoring how easy the slide would be to addiction, not to mention the danger of onetime use alone.

It hadn't helped Pete that we grew up poor, or that our old man put Pete down every chance he got, but he didn't have much of an example from his older brother, either. Pete knew that Sammy and I sold weed, and he knew that the only thing that got me off the wrong track and onto the right one—football—was not available to him. He was like me—the screwup—but minus the athletic ability. It had left him free, I guess, to justify his own foray into drugs.

A Ford Taurus had been following me today, from my trip to see the witness, Tommy Butcher, to my visit with Mrs. Thomas, but I didn't see it now. They probably figured I was eating close to home and then heading there for the night. I thought I might find the car on the block where I lived, but I didn't. I went inside and ran on the treadmill for about half an hour before picking up a paperback mystery. By page fifty-six, I had figured out that the serial killer was the priest, and by ten o'clock I had confirmed as much.

At half past midnight, I fell asleep to an episode of *MacGyver*, the one where our hero finds himself in a jam and uses his knowledge of science to extricate himself. At three in the morning, I woke up to Emily's phantom cry. I stopped shaking at about four; then I liberated my stomach of all of its contents in the bathroom and went back to bed. At five, I tried one of my mental games, imagining Talia and Emily living happily ever after, but it didn't work for some reason. I read another paperback until eleven, showered, went to the cemetery, came back home and slept until dinner. I ordered in a pizza but lost my appetite, so I walked it down the street to the park and gave it to a homeless guy. Having done my good deed for the day, I retired for the evening and read some more until I fell asleep to a rerun of *Hogan's Heroes,* the one where our indefatigable hero manages to sneak several American POWs to safety under the nose of the hapless *commandante* and to the bewilderment of the incompetent sergeant.

I awoke at half past three from the dream I'd had many times since Talia's and Emily's deaths. When I'm awake, I constantly replay the events in such a way that I am driving them to Talia's parents' house that night, and everything turns out fine—we are still together. In my dream, too, I am behind the wheel, but I miss the curve just like Talia did. I lace my hands with Talia's as we come upon the dark, slick curve along the bluffs, and my eyes pop open as the SUV crashes through the guardrail.

I took a moment to orient myself: It was Friday, October 5. The trial would start in twenty-four days. I had a lot of work ahead, but my brain was fuzzy, my heartbeat slowly decelerating from my dream. I finished a mystery paperback by about ten in the morning and dozed off. I woke up again to the phone ringing. I looked at the caller ID but it was blocked so I answered it.

"This is Vic Carruthers. We did the dig, like you said."

"Okay?" I sat up in bed.

"We found some bodies," he said.

I COULDN'T GET anywhere near the burial site behind Hardigan Elementary School. The media had caught wind, so trucks had lined up all around the barricades, with news copters flying overhead. I parked on Hudson, about three blocks away, and walked as far as I could go. I wasn't accomplishing anything by being here, but I thought if I could catch Detective Carruthers, he might give me some skinny.

Bodies, he'd said. Plural. A cemetery of toddlers behind a school. Griffin Perlini had taken a lot of secrets with him to the grave.

Around me, it was bedlam. Beautiful women and average-looking men were posing before cameras and speaking with urgency into microphones. Parents were parking wherever they could find an open space and hustling into the school to pick up their children. Law enforcement—local cops, sheriff's deputies, technical-unit agents—were scurrying about.

One of those *bodies*, no doubt, was Audrey Cutler. I didn't know how to feel about that. She was dead, of course, long gone, but maybe now whatever remained of her could be laid to rest next to her mother. Maybe it would give some closure to Sammy, though I couldn't imagine why—I just knew it was true. Families always want to find the physical remains, as if that earthly need to collect the tangible body has any relevance after death.

My cell phone rang, a blocked call.

"Four bodies," Carruthers told me, slightly out of breath, probably a combination of exertion and excitement. "Four children."

"I'm here," I said.

"Go back to work. There's nothing for you here now. I'll be in touch."

I hadn't come from work, but it seemed like a good idea to go there now. It seemed like a good time to wake up.

As I worked my way slowly through the ever-expanding population of people who rushed to the school to witness the carnage, I thought about this development. Four children, presumably molested and definitely murdered by Griffin Perlini. I hoped at that moment for a God, which meant a Satan, too. Like my overall belief in the Almighty, I struggled as a child with the idea of the pearly gates and the devil. The whole thing seemed far too black-and-white for me. I remember lobbing questions at the priests: *What if you were on your way to confession when you got hit by a truck? You don't get into Heaven? What if you think you did the right thing but God doesn't? Are you supposed to repent anyway?* Those priests, who preferred black-and-white to gray, really loved having me in class. Me, I was still waiting for answers to those questions.

YOU SEE HER for the first time wrapped in a pink blanket with a tiny bow somehow fastened to the scant hair that covers her tiny, egg-shaped head. Her skin is a slight yellow—*jaundiced*, they say—and the only sounds that escape her mouth are throaty cries. She cries, she feeds from her mother, and she poops and pees. The adults let you close to her—*Don't touch her*, they say—and you put your face close to hers. Her eyes are not focused. She smells like lotion. They say she looks like Mary— Mrs. Cutler—but you think she looks more like a shrunken old man.

Hello, Audrey, you say with mock formality. *Nice to meet you.*

Sammy isn't outside as much that summer. He spends a good deal of time with her. By July, Audrey is eating food. You watch Sammy feed her, putting one hand delicately behind her tiny, bobbing head and inserting a lime-colored spoon full of food into her mouth. *There you go*, he says, mimicking his mother's words and tone. It's not exactly the same between you and Sammy now. He reserves a part of himself for his little sister. He measures himself in her presence, keeping a watchful eye, springing forth at her cry, or if she loses balance and falls to the side.

You're like my little sister, too, you tell her that winter. She makes a noise—*eh-bah*—and grabs a handful of your hair and pulls hard. You don't mind. You laugh. *She doesn't mean to hurt you*, Sammy tells you. You know that. You know you're special to Audrey, too. She is still too young to appreciate strangers. She breaks into a cry around anyone other than the Cutlers and your family. She lets go of your hair and you get your face up close to hers. She breaks into a big smile, and you feel something light up inside you. The word "beautiful" comes to mind and you think you have found a new definition of that word.

I GOT TO my car and navigated the escalating traffic as the hordes continued to flock toward Hardigan Elementary School. This would be all over the news, and Sammy probably would learn of it, so I needed to pay him a visit.

Sammy. He needed his lawyer. As the duly appointed same, my first concern was how quickly they could identify the remains. DNA testing could take months, especially for bodies that had probably been buried for years. There would be no sense of urgency, no crime to solve when the perpetrator was already dead. This would not go to the front of the line. I would need to see what I could do about that.

I had to admit it—after talking with Mrs. Thomas and Perlini's mother, I'd had some doubts about Perlini as Audrey's killer. One of the things that had bothered me was that pedophilia and murder were very different things, and Perlini hadn't had any history of killing little girls. Or so we'd thought, before today.

So much of solving crimes is luck. Nobody would have bothered to question Griffin Perlini's mother *after* his death, yet it was precisely *because* he was gone—because there was no need to protect him anymore—that his mother gave me the tip about the hill behind this school. Now, there was no doubt that Griffin Perlini had escalated several of his crimes.

"Audrey," I said aloud. My voice cracked, betraying emotion I hadn't acknowledged. There is something unspeakable about a child's death under any circumstances; I didn't know if the time would ever come that I could fully comprehend the loss of Emily. But the murder of a child exposes something so hideous that anger is not even the appropriate response. We despair. We lose hope. We lose faith.

Audrey Cutler had a plot of land in the Catholic cemetery, next to which her mother, Mary, was buried. We would have a proper funeral, I decided. Sammy and I would bury his sister.

I picked up my cell phone, dialed the number, and got voice mail. "Pete," I said into the phone. "Pete, I—I—just give me a call when you can."

17

YOUR LAST GOOD MEMORY of her, the weekend before she was abducted, the picnic held after the successful construction of the new wing to the university library. You are with the Cutlers, trying to throw a Frisbee with Sammy, while little Audrey tries to partake, tries in vain to intercept the flying disk. *My turn*, she keeps saying.

Let her have her turn. Mrs. Cutler is happy today. She is wearing a sundress, and the wind is playing with her bangs. Mr. Cutler is off drinking beers with some of the other guys involved in the construction. He does that a lot, always with a beer in his hand at home. You heard Sammy's mom describe the work at the library as "good work," saying it to Mr. Cutler—you thought they were fighting about that, about how many absences were allowed by the union before you were kicked off the job. Mr. Cutler is a plumber, but he only works sometimes; you don't know why or when. Some days, Mr. Cutler just stays home, drinking beer and yelling at the television.

Audrey has tired of Frisbee and wants candy. They are passing it out, the company that sponsored the picnic, M&M's candies with the company name, Emerson, on them. *They're Emerson M&M's*, Sammy says to Audrey. She tries to say it back but it ties her tongue. Something like *Em-o-son-em's* comes out, and you and Sammy laugh. She keeps trying and you keep laughing, until Sammy tells her it's okay, she did a good job, and he picks her up and puts her on his shoulders. He runs around as Audrey yells, *Em-o-son-em's* and squeals with delight.

I SPENT the afternoon in my office, going through the files in Sammy's case. Included in those files was the criminal history of Griffin Perlini. That gave me a list of people whose daughters had been victimized in some way by Perlini. It felt indecent, morosely ironic, that this list of victimized families was, for my purposes, a list of potential suspects.

It wasn't much of a list, really. Two girls were part of his initial foray into sexual predation, which as far as anyone could tell did not reach the level of sexual contact with the children. Perlini had been convicted only of exposing himself to these children.

The other two girls had been part of the case that put Perlini in prison until 2005. Over one summer, while working at a park district, Perlini had abused these girls, who had enrolled in a summer program. The case had gone to trial, which presumably meant the children had to testify. These would not be fun conversations, both because of the obviously uncomfortable subject matter and because I might have to argue, at trial, that one of these sets of parents should be suspects in Griffin Perlini's murder. I wasn't sure I had the stomach to do it, to throw salt on already gaping wounds, but it would be irresponsible not to explore it. That's the kind of thing that makes the general public hate lawyers, especially the criminal defense bar. Much of what we do, to a layperson, is counterintuitive. A guy gets caught with a kilo of cocaine in his basement and the first thing we argue is that the evidence should *not* be admitted, because of a Fourth Amendment violation. A guy confesses to a crime and the first thing we argue is that the jury *shouldn't* hear the confession, courtesy of the Fifth Amendment. We try shaky defenses like temporary insanity or play the race card, anything plausible to free our client. People will carp and moan about every single attorney on the face of the earth except for one—their own, if they ever need one, in which case their view of the Bill of Rights becomes infinitely more expansive.

I was tired, and thinking about a cup of coffee from the shop downstairs, when my intercom buzzed. Marie, through the speaker: *"Mr. Smith to see you."*

Smith. The last person I felt like seeing. But something inside me told me that I wanted to take this meeting.

My door, which I'd uncharacteristically closed, opened, and Smith walked in. "Afternoon, Jason." He looked as polished as last time, a gray double-breasted suit with a charcoal tie, hair sharply parted. But as he moved across my small office, seating himself in front of my desk, I sensed that he was less tentative, more self-assured, than he was at our last meeting.

"Tell me your name," I said. "Your real name."

"I was hoping for an update on the case," he said, not answering my question.

"Hope is a dangerous thing."

He forced a smile. "You're being paid well. Very well."

"So are you. Who's paying you? Maybe we can share information."

At this point, it seemed clear that Smith was representing a family that had been subject to Griffin Perlini's predatory appetites in some way or another. I could understand the desire for discretion, and really, Smith wasn't my problem. I didn't care who was paying. My loyalty was to Sammy only, and if someone else wanted to bankroll the defense while cloaked in anonymity, I wasn't sure I cared.

On the other hand, I'd assumed that the people tailing me since the day Smith first appeared in my office were connected to him. On the scale of things I cared about, that issue rated a few notches higher. He was keeping tabs on me, and I didn't know why.

"There are four aspects to Mr. Cutler's case," Smith graciously informed me.

At least he was capable of counting. The four areas of concern were the eyewitnesses who had Sammy running from the scene of the crime; the convenience store videotape that caught his car parked down the street from Perlini's apartment; the black-guy-fleeing-the-scene; and Sammy's statement to the police.

"From what little I've been able to gather," said Smith, "it sounds as if you have one potentially favorable witness. I don't recall the name. Butler, was it?"

Butcher, actually. Tommy Butcher. Again, no need to help him with information.

"Apparently a black man was spotted near the crime scene," he continued. "Has Mr. Butler given you a description of this man beyond that?"

As luck would have it, after I had applied a healthy dose of sympathetic grease, Butcher had seemed willing to go along with the brown-jacket-green-cap story I had pitched him. But Smith didn't know that, and I wasn't going to illuminate him. I shook my head and opened my hands.

"I'm going to help you with that, Jason. The empty chair."

Someone to point the finger at, he meant. Someone who was not sitting in the courtroom, who didn't have a lawyer to defend himself, who didn't have any constitutional protections. And he was right, of course. If I could place at the scene of the crime a black guy who had any hint of a motive or criminal background, I might have something to show the jury.

"You're going to find me the black-guy-fleeing-the-scene, Smith?"

His head inclined ever so slightly. "I am, yes."

"Oh," I said. "Thanks. And what about the eyewitnesses? Perlini's neighbor, and the elderly couple that ID'd Sammy running from the building?"

"Don't worry about them," he answered.

I didn't like the sound of that, neither the words nor his icy delivery. "Explain that."

"Don't worry about the eyewitnesses. They're my problem." He could read the expression on my face, no doubt, so he elaborated. "It's not what you're thinking, Jason. It's just that—memories are a funny thing. Sometimes, if you think back, it wasn't the way you thought it was. Right?"

"You're just going to help them with their memory." Even as I said the words, careful to show my disapproval, it occurred to me that I had just done the very same thing with Tommy Butcher. I'd fed him all sorts of information to bathe my client in a sympathetic light and then spoon-fed him a description of the black-guy-fleeing-the-scene.

But that was a little different, I gathered, from what Smith had in mind for the other eyewitnesses. "If any harm comes to any of them, Smith, you're going to answer to me."

He stared at me, losing any trace of a smile. "Don't ever threaten me, son."

"Don't think I'm going to sit idly by while you murder witnesses."

He regarded me for a moment, then a chuckle escaped his throat. "There are ways short of physical force, my friend. Everyone has a pressure point. Everyone. Including you."

"And you," I volleyed.

He slowly nodded. "Believe me when I say, you don't want to find it."

I didn't answer.

"Jason, one of your best friends is on trial for murder, and I'm gift-wrapping an acquittal for you. I'll find you a scapegoat, and I'll help you with the eyewitnesses. The only things that remain are the videotape placing Mr. Cutler's car at the scene, and the statement Cutler gave to the police. Those are the only things that require your help. You'll need to find a way to finesse Cutler's incriminating statement, and you and I will have to come up with an innocent reason that Cutler's car was in the vicinity at the time. Those two things are your only assignments. Anything beyond that is a waste of time and a distraction."

I nodded. I thought I understood now. "You've been watching the news today."

"I have, and I don't see what you can possibly gain from the discovery of bodies behind a school. What do you intend to prove? That Griffin Perlini killed Cutler's sister? The judge has already ruled that evidence off-limits."

"For now," I said.

"For now. For now." He fell back in the chair. "Don't make this harder than it is. The trial is only about three weeks away. There is no time for red herrings. This will end in an acquittal if you follow my directions. If you start playing Lone Ranger, you could screw everything up." He held up two fingers. "Two items, Jason. Cutler's incriminating statement and a reason why he would have been near the scene of the crime. The confession and an alibi. You're expected to give us explanations on those two items and nothing more. Nothing," he repeated, "more."

Smith let his speech sink in for me. He was probably wondering why I hadn't taken notes. This guy, I could see, was accustomed to giving out orders and having people follow them. He shot his cuff links and fixed his tie and said, "Good. We have an understanding."

I watched Smith walk to the door before I answered.

"With just one caveat," I said. "You will shove your retainer up your ass and go crawl under a rock. I will do whatever I think is best for Sammy and we'll never talk again."

Smith's face dissolved into a frown.

"Tell me your real name, whom you represent, and why," I said. "Or you're out of the picture as of right now."

My mysterious benefactor thought for a while, weighing the pros and cons, before answering. The fact that he was even considering responding meant something, I just wasn't entirely sure what.

"Obviously, Jason, my clients are a family, or families, who have a particular interest in seeing that Mr. Perlini's murder go unpunished."

"Someone whom Perlini assaulted. Or her parents, or family."

He waved a hand.

"Victims who testified against him in court?" I asked. "Or victims the police never knew about?" Smith didn't answer, so I added to my question: "Victims who were buried behind Hardigan Elementary School?"

It had occurred to me, but never so keenly as now: Smith might be representing someone who killed Griffin Perlini, for the same motive Sammy had—a bitter parent, or sibling, of a child Perlini molested or even killed.

Was Smith here to steer me away from the real killer?

Was Sammy *innocent*?

"I strongly urge you to stick to the script," said Smith.

"I strongly urge you to go fuck yourself."

Smith played that around on his lips. "You're making a mistake," he said. "When you change your mind, I'll be in touch."

I detected a hint of a smile cross his lips.

"*When* I've changed my mind?" I asked.

He nodded at me. "When," he said, as he walked out the door.

18

MY OFFICE MATE, Shauna Tasker, stuck her head in around six o'clock. She mentioned dinner, and I soon found myself at one of the new trendy restaurants in town, a Spanish place called Cena. We ordered a couple of tapas—dates wrapped in bacon and an omelet of potato and onions—after which Shauna ate a pork chop stuffed with goat cheese, while I pushed a piece of black grouper around the plate and avoided the mushrooms, which I hate and didn't realize were part of the dish.

I'd had a few vodkas and sensed danger. I didn't use alcohol to escape so much as to change the landscape, to alter something. Maybe there was no difference. But I felt my emotions destabilize, and I also sensed something hanging between Shauna and me.

Shauna seemed to be appraising me, which I didn't particularly enjoy, but she had her subtle ways of doing so that made it hard for me to be angry. She had a gift for that sort of thing. She could operate in any circle, the wealthy client or the poor, men or women. She had delicate features combined with silky blond hair that might be described as pretty, but not in a threatening way. Other women liked her and most men both liked her and lusted after her. She knew all of this and thrived accordingly. On the surface she was generally regarded as sincere, open, trustworthy, sometimes passionate. But those pretty blue eyes were skeptical. She had an internal barometer that cautioned against intimacy, that generally distrusted others. She was the best judge of character I'd ever known, which is what made me uneasy when she trained that judgment on me.

She asked me what I'd been doing yesterday, when I was once again AWOL from the office. The truth was there were still many days when I just couldn't function, when I was no use to anyone, when I couldn't stand the pity, when I couldn't concentrate, when I just didn't give a shit about anything. I simply told her I'd been "reading at home," which was true if you counted paperback novels. She didn't seem to think much of the answer.

"You talk to Pete lately?" I asked her. She hadn't known Pete particularly well. Shauna was my age, so she didn't go to high school with Pete, who was a freshman when we graduated. But she'd gotten to know him a bit after Talia and Emily died, when they tag-teamed on the Jason Kolarich Sympathy Tour, taking turns making sure I had company while I was nursing my wounds.

"Not recently," she said. "Why?"

I shook my head. "I think he's back to his old tricks. Scoring."

"Cocaine? No, I don't know about that. I'm not sure I *would* know."

"Yeah, Pete's pretty good at keeping it under wraps."

"Is this serious? Or is it just when he's out partying?"

I didn't know. "I'm not sure I make that distinction," I said. "Sometimes it's hard to keep recreational from becoming addictive." I lifted my empty glass of vodka to the waitress, signaling for another. Shauna was still working on a glass of wine and shook her head. "I've had my back turned, Shauna. I've been so caught up in myself—first that *Almundo* trial and then Talia and Emily—I haven't been watching that kid. I feel like I've—"

"Please don't finish that sentence." Shauna raised a hand. "Just—please don't say that you've let your brother down."

She went quiet. I didn't know what to make of the hostility, which she took out on the remaining piece of pork on her plate, shaking her head in disgust as she did so.

"The hell is *your* problem?" I asked.

"No problem here, Kolarich. Not a care in the world." She finished the rest of the pork chop, and I tired of focusing on the fish I had no intention of eating. The waitress brought me a fresh vodka and Shauna watched me.

"Say something," I said.

"Say something?"

"Yeah, say some goddamn thing."

"Okay. Okay." She wiped his mouth with her napkin. "Get off your ass, Jason."

"Come again?"

"Snap out of it. Get off your ass."

"Oh, wait. Is this the get-busy-living-or-get-busy-dying speech? My wife and child died, but I didn't? They'd want me to get on with my life? That about cover it?"

Shauna looked away, that expression of distaste that she used effectively. "I haven't said anything for—what—four months now. Four months, I've watched you beat yourself up. Blaming yourself for Talia and Emily. Not *pitying* yourself. *That*, I could understand. But you've managed to rewrite the script so that everything is your fault."

I took a healthy drink of the Stoli that the waitress placed before me. It went down harsh, a burn in the back of my throat.

"And now you're doing the same thing with your brother, who, last I checked, is nearly thirty years old, which I believe puts him in the category of adult."

"I see."

"Don't belittle what I'm saying. Don't do that." As she spoke, the sleeve of her shirt dipped into some sauce on her plate. "Look, I know you feel bad about getting caught up in that trial when Emily was born. I know it was hard on Talia, and I could sense that you guys were having a few problems. The timing was terrible. Your baby's born just as you're second-chairing a monster trial that could make your whole career. Okay. So the trial comes first. It has to. You were doing this for your family."

"Was I?"

She drew back. "Of course you were. What, you're gonna tell me you enjoyed it, too? You got an ego boost? You were enjoying the thrill of a headline case? You got off on seeing your name in the paper? Is that supposed to be a crime? You liked what you were doing, Jason. That's allowed."

"Tell that—"

"—to Talia, and Emily. I know. I get it. I've heard it fifty times now. You would have made it up to them, Jason. I know you. I *know* you would have. But you never got to, because something really tragic happened. But that doesn't make it your fault. See the difference there? So when you go the cemetery every *single* day at lunch to talk to your wife and daughter—"

I recoiled.

"Yes," she continued, "I followed you once, and I really don't care if you don't like it. When you go visit them every day, you can tell them how much you love them and how much you miss them. You can tell them that you were planning to make up for lost time if you'd had the chance, but *do not* take responsibility for their deaths. Okay?"

At the neighboring table, a woman was having a birthday. The waitress delivered a piece of fried custard with a single candle on it as the table broke into song. Everyone seemed to enjoy making a big spectacle of it.

Talia's birthday is next week.

I gestured to Shauna. "You dragged your sleeve through your plate."

"I know and it sucks. I just bought this." She dabbed her napkin into her glass of water and we both laughed.

I TOOK A CAB HOME. My head was a little foggy from the vodka. I had some of the case file at home with me, but I wasn't in the shape or the state of mind to focus on it.

I walked into Emily's room. My heart did a small leap as I flicked on the light, a fancy little chandelier Talia had purchased for the room. The whole nursery was pink and green, from the wallpaper and paint to the crib, even a custom rocking chair Talia had ordered. I sat in the chair and rocked, my eyes dancing when I closed them. I thought I could still smell her, the baby lotion we used, the cream we used on her tush. I had a distinct image of her face, her eyes alighting when I lifted her into the air.

I opened my eyes and shook my head fiercely. My chest filled with emotion, heavy, suffocating. Love, for me, was always suffused with pain, with vulnerability, the accompanying fear of losing what you love even as you immerse yourself in it. But now they were dead, so there was no fear of loss, only the love that remained, now unadulterated, pure, over-powering.

I got out of the chair, turned off the light, and left her room. I stripped my clothes and got into bed. Sleep did not come immediately. I stared at the ceiling and thought about what Shauna had said. To some extent, she was right. I was merging two things, my guilt for time lost with my family because of work, and remorse for their loss, but letting the former over-power the latter, making myself to blame for their deaths.

Still, I couldn't let go of one very clear fact: I was supposed to go with Talia and Emily downstate that weekend. I'd cleared it with the boss, with the client. We were nearing the end of the trial, the defense was about to rest its case, and I'd completed the witnesses I was assigned. *Go spend time with your family*, Paul had told me. *That's a direct order*. But I had to be the hotshot. I'd caught a lead. I'd found Ernesto Ramirez, the ex-Latin Lord, who had information that could blow up the government's case, who could pin the murder of the neighborhood businessman on a rival street gang, not the gang whom the government had tied to Senator Hector Almundo. *The government has the wrong street gang*, we would have told the jury.

It had been my decision, and mine alone, to stay back and follow up on this lead instead of spending the weekend downstate with my family. If I could tie the business owner's murder to the Lords and not the Columbus Street Cannibals, the government's premise for the case would be undermined. Devastated. Though Senator Hector Almundo was charged under a multiple-count indictment, the charges related to that murder had been the centerpiece of the case.

I chose being a hero over taking my wife to see her parents, over taking my baby to see her grandparents. I was supposed to be driving the car that night.

Somewhere in those thoughts, I drifted off. When I opened my eyes again, eyeing the clock, which read just after three in the morning, it wasn't the sound of Emily's cry that had stirred me. It was the telephone ringing at the side of my bed.

It was my brother, Pete.

"Jason," he said breathlessly, "I'm in big trouble."

19

THIS ONE HAS ALWAYS stayed with you: a family dinner, itself an unusual occurrence. The old man is usually away in the evening, plying his trade at poker games or bars, petty hustles that might pay the groceries next week if he doesn't blow it on booze. Not tonight. A tension in the room, typical in his presence. Mom has brought the pot roast, potatoes, and carrots to the table in silence. The old man—Jack, you call him, but not to his face—is reading the paper and mumbling under his breath.

He doesn't intimidate you, not anymore. That one thing, your ability to catch a piece of pigskin and break away from defenders, has given you immunity in the confines of your house. But the other two, Pete and your mother, are a different story. Pete is looking at Jack while he slowly eats, and you're trying to figure out if it's love or fear in his eyes, and you decide it's both.

"How was practice?" your mom asks you.

"Fine," I say. "I pulled a hamstring. I'll have to sit out this week to be ready for Saturday."

"So you'll only score *two* touchdowns," says Pete.

God, Pete looks just like Jack. It's painful to make that connection. He is docile, like Mom, but with the face and build and maturing voice of our father.

"I was thinking about next year," Pete says cautiously. Next year Pete will be a freshman at Bonaventure, while you'll be off to whatever university whose scholarship you accept.

"What about next year, honey?" Mom asks.

"Next year," you say, "there will be high school girls calling this house every night."

Mom smiles and looks at Pete. "What about next year, Pete?"

Pete shrugs. "I was thinking, maybe—maybe I'd try out for the football team."

"*You?*" This from Jack, his eyes looking over the paper, one word followed by a disapproving grunt.

You? A single word that deflates Pete, returns his focus to his plate of food, his face now ashen. You look at your mother, who is frozen, too, unwilling to cross the line that Jack has laid down.

"Yeah, prob'ly—prob'ly a dumb idea," Pete mumbles.

"I think it's a great idea," you say, catching the eyes of your father. "I think you should give it a shot, Pete." But you are talking to the old man as much as to your brother. You have locked eyes now, and you realize it now more than ever, that you want to get as far away from this house as possible.

I MADE IT to the police station within an hour of receiving Pete's call. Never a happy place, the station house was particularly grim at four in the morning. A few family members, tired and disappointed and worried, awaited the release of their loved ones. Otherwise, the place was empty, the cheap tile floors showing the dirt, the air thick with sweat and body odor. I found the desk sergeant behind a plate of bulletproof glass and showed him my credentials, which he did not receive warmly.

They buzzed me in and a cop with sandy hair and deep-set eyes was waiting behind the door. "Denny DePrizio," he said to me, not offering his hand but turning toward his desk, assuming I would follow. He actually took me past the desks to an interview room, where I took a seat across from him.

"Drugs and weapons," he said to me. "Over a ticket of uncut rock and unregistered firearms."

A kilo of rock cocaine and guns? "You got the wrong guy," I said.

"He's definitely wrong, I'll give you that."

"My brother's a lot of things," I continued. "He's not much for the nine-to-five job. Sometimes he's a shithead. But he doesn't run guns and he doesn't sell rock. C'mon, Detective. Take a look at the guy. He was scoring some powder, because he's an idiot, and he wasn't careful where he bought it. He was in the wrong place at the wrong time."

He liked that, treated it like I was joking. "These guys come in all shapes and sizes, Counselor. Hell, we busted a grandmother a few weeks back, selling rock off her back porch. A grandmother."

"I'm not saying walk him. I'm saying, simple possession."

He laughed out loud. "Wasn't how it looked to me," he said. "Baby brother didn't look like he was making a small purchase."

"Bullshit."

His smile wavered, then disappeared. "See, this is where you'd be trying my patience, Counselor. I see this kid selling a crate full of weapons, there's a couple tickets of uncut rock as a nice throw-in, and now I got his brother telling me to skate him on a simple possession? You got some big-ass stones, my friend."

I wasn't getting anywhere with this guy, not that I'd expected to. I wasn't even sure I'd convinced myself. As much I fought it, I couldn't deny the possibility that Pete was guilty as hell, that he'd royally messed up.

I did the calculations in my mind, though I'd need to look up the sentencing statutes to be sure. With priors for simple possession, assuming here a possession with intent and gun charges, Pete could be looking at ten years inside.

"What you should be worried about," DePrizio said, "is a federal transfer."

That was worse. Federal prosecutors had a real hard-on for guns these days. A federal conviction would be a minimum of ten years, and federal time was hard time, not day-for-a-day like in state court; at least eighty-five percent of the sentence had to be served in a federal prison.

But this guy wasn't raising the specter of a federal transfer just to pass the time.

"Unless," I said.

The detective nodded at me. "Right, unless."

Unless he cooperated, DePrizio meant. Traded up the chain. Was Pete part of a chain? Was he really selling cocaine? I couldn't believe it, which is to say, I was literally incapable of putting together a set of facts that had my little brother selling drugs and running guns.

"Maybe we should talk about that," I said.

"Maybe we should. But not tonight." The detective checked his watch. "I'm on in four hours. I'm going home. You want to see your brother?"

To be continued. I didn't know what kind of hand I had to play yet, anyway.

"Please," I said. I followed a uniform down to the basement. I was buzzed past two sets of barred doors, and he directed me to the final cell, with cinder-block walls and metal benches bolted to the floor. There were over a dozen people inside. Most of them were black, and most of them looked like it wasn't their first time in a cell. A guy in the corner, a white kid strung out and in the midst of obvious withdrawal, had recently thrown up, and the others were either heckling him or yelling at him to clean it up.

Pete was sitting on the floor, against the wall, his arms wrapped around his knees. He was keeping his eyes straight forward, an obvious attempt to avoid any confrontation. He was wound as tight as I'd ever seen him.

Jesus, I thought. Pete couldn't hold up for one week in a penitentiary.

When I stopped at the cell bars, some of the attention turned my way. I caught a couple of hoots and hollers. More than one of them was hoping, I gathered, that I was here for them, that their family had hired them a private attorney to handle their case.

"I gotta take a piss!" one of them said.

"Lawyer man, you comin' to set me free?" another called out.

At that, Pete looked up and saw me. His eyes were blood-red, his hair matted, all standing in stark contrast to the lively blue shirt and khakis and polished loafers he was sporting.

"Motherfucker white boy gets the lawyer."

Pete approached the bars tentatively. I raised a hand, to keep his voice down, to keep it cool while he was sharing a cell with anyone.

"Jason, I swear . . ."

I took his hand and gripped it. Tears welled up in his eyes, and I struggled not to return the favor. My little brother. I was supposed to protect you.

"We'll figure this out," I promised. I leaned against the bars, so that we were almost nose to nose. "Pete, listen to me. Don't you say a word to anyone in here, okay? These guys trade on that sort of thing all the time. Don't be telling your story to anyone, right?"

He closed his eyes, swallowed hard, and nodded.

I leaned in closer. "Who were you arrested with?"

Pete shook his head and answered in a whisper. "I was with two people," he said. "I think one of them got away. The other guy, I don't know him."

"Is he here?" I whispered.

He shrugged his shoulders. "No."

I looked behind Pete at the occupants again. Most of these guys were bigger than Pete, and all of them were meaner. Three guys in particular caught my attention, looked like Tenth Street muscle, but I'd have to see their bicep to know for sure. These guys were the ones to watch. They would be calling the shots. Two of them had their hair done up high and were calling after the junkie who had vomited, but the guy in the middle, the bald guy with arms that bulged out of his sweatshirt, eyed the others in the cell without comment. He was the leader.

"Okay," I said gently. "One step at a time, Pete. We'll figure this out. I will figure this out." I gripped his hand as tight as I could, trying to shake him out of what looked, to me, like the first signs of my brother completely falling apart. "You stay tough tonight, and I'll get you out of here within twenty-four hours. We can talk about your case then."

He took a minute with that, squeezing my hand back. He wanted to hold on to my hand for the next twenty-four hours but knew that he couldn't. "God, Jase, I'm sorry," he whispered. "You gotta know, what happened here isn't—"

"Later," I said. "Later, Pete."

I looked past him again to the guy I made for Tenth Street, the big bald guy. Most people eventually catch on when they're being eyeballed, and soon enough he turned in my direction. I nodded to him. "You got a lawyer?" I asked him.

He looked at me like I'd asked him if he was enjoying the surroundings. I removed a business card from my pocket and held it, with two fingers, through the bars.

He took a long time with that before speaking. "Ain't gettin' no lawyer."

He wasn't planning on a private attorney, he meant. "Have I got a deal for you," I said.

I could see that this guy wanted to dismiss me, but he was interested. He decided to make me wait, but finally he got off the bench and approached me. He got within a few feet of the bars and looked down at my business card without taking it.

"What-choo sayin' now?"

"You want a lawyer who gets paid by the same people who pay the prosecutor and the judge?" I asked. "Or do you want me?"

"I ain't got it."

The money, he meant. "What's the collar?"

"Dime bag."

I nodded. "Not your first?"

He shook his head, no.

"I'll take your case," I said. "No cash. Just one favor."

He cocked his head. I pointed to Pete. "My guy here gets through processing clean. Not a hair out of place. Okay?"

This guy took my card and read it. "Kola-rich. Kolarich." He wagged the card in his hand. "Hey, boss, can't nobody make *that* kinda guarantee."

"You can," I said. "If you say so, they'll listen. Right?"

He acknowledged as much and seemed to appreciate the respect. This whole batch of prisoners would be together for the rest of today, from this cell to transport to the basement of the courthouse to bond court. It was the courthouse basement that troubled me the most—that was where the county guards were known, on occasion, to look the other way—and I could only hope that, with this guy's say-so, Pete would be okay.

"What's your name?" I asked.

"Cameron," he said.

"We got a deal, Cameron?"

He stared at me a long time, then at Pete, who seemed to shrink in the glare. "Yeah, lawyer-man, okay," he said. "White boy stays clean and I got me a law-yer."

I took some information from him—family members, job, the kinds of things I'd need to know to try to secure him bond later today—and shook his hand. When he returned to the bench, muttering something to his buddies, I was alone with Pete again. I repeated my earlier admonitions—mouth closed, eyes down—and struggled to pull myself away from that cell, secure in the knowledge, at least, that he'd be okay until I could spring him later today.

If I could spring him.

20

I DROVE HOME on empty roads as the sun came up. I took a shower and threw on a suit, hoping bond court for Pete would be today, a single thought repeating itself as I did so: This was wrong. Though I'd been posturing for the cop at the station, I'd spoken the essential truth. I couldn't believe Pete would be involved in this. But the longer I played it out, the more my mental defenses dissolved. Once you started with the proposition that Pete was using cocaine recreationally, the rest became a familiar tale. Recreational usage becomes addiction. An addict can't hold down reliable work, while at the same time more and more of his money, discretionary or otherwise, goes into that sweet nectar that increasingly becomes his sole focus. Suddenly he is out of money and looking for any way to come up with funds for the next score. Next thing he knows, his supplier decides that Pete might be useful for his purposes, that maybe he could introduce him to a new group of clients.

I'd handled hundreds of drug cases as a prosecutor, big and small, and I knew all of this well. During my stint on felony review—assigned to a police station to interrogate suspects and approve charges—I'd seen guys arrested for possession with intent who looked more like the addicts who bought the stuff than the guys who sold it to them.

And I had to acknowledge, as I had last night with Shauna, that from being swamped by the *Almundo* trial, to being a new father, to falling into a funk after losing Talia and Emily, I hadn't been keeping a watchful eye on my little brother. This could have been building up for the better part of a year, and the whole thing eluded me.

I went to the office at nine. I needed to make some calls to some old friends at the county attorney's office, hoping to call in some favors for Pete, which would be a minor challenge on a Saturday. I also needed to do some Internet transactions to have money liquid in case I needed to bond him out. He'd get bond of some kind or another for a nonviolent, though guns weren't far from violence and the judges treated them seriously.

When I walked into my office, the front page of our city newspaper, the *Watch*, was sitting on my chair. GRAVE SITE FOUND ON SOUTH SIDE, said the headline, including an old photograph of Griffin Perlini and a sky-view photograph of the hill behind Hardigan Elementary School, complete with law enforcement swarming the area and a crane lifting dirt. "At least four" children found buried, said one smaller story. MOLESTER MURDERED LAST YEAR; VICTIM'S BROTHER ACCUSED, read another, with side-by-side photographs of Audrey and Sammy Cutler.

This, of course, was a residual benefit I'd always hoped for. I wanted to prove Perlini killed Audrey to help my case, but I also wanted Perlini's name to become infamous in the minds of potential jurors. I wanted a county full of potential jurors who knew, full well, that Griffin Perlini was a child molester and a murderer.

I imagined the look on the face of Lester Mapp, the smug prosecutor, as he read this very public account of Griffin Perlini's misdeeds. This was not a good development for him.

But it was hard to focus on Sammy's case, concerned as I was for my brother. There was nothing I could do for Pete yet. I didn't know anything about the case. Pete had told me that he was with two people when the police came down on them, and he thought one of them got away. The other guy wasn't with Pete in the holding cell, which made me wonder.

And what had the cop, DePrizio, said? *I'm on in four hours.*

I went to bond court early to try to hook up with the prosecutors. The courtroom was fairly empty and the judge wasn't present, so I cornered a young assistant county attorney named Warren and made my pitch for a low bond. He listened patiently to my spiel, which included a few dropped names, and told me he couldn't go below a hundred. I wasn't surprised. Too much rock, and guns, to boot. That meant I had to come up with ten thousand. I'd transferred enough money in my checking account to cover that and more.

By the time the judge was ready to assume the bench, the courtroom was full of family members hoping that their loved ones would get I-bonds—allowing them to leave of their own recognizance, meaning no cash down—or at least something low that they could afford. The judge assumed the bench without fanfare, without a call to order by the bailiff. The Honorable Alexander Lotus—Lex Lotus—was a former prosecutor who'd come to office in the last election. He was about my age but graying, a solemn man who looked displeased at his assignment to bond court.

He started with the outstanding warrants for people who had missed court appearances. With each of the roughly twenty men who came before him, he listened to both sides and casually said, usually without looking up from his papers, "Warrant to stand," after which the people were scooped—taken back into custody.

I settled in when Judge Lotus then turned to the misdemeanors, because that meant Pete's case—felony charges—would be last. That was the standard protocol for these judges, starting with the small stuff before handling the felonies.

Every person, upon arrest, is entitled to a *Gerstein* hearing, where the judge determines that probable cause exists to detain. In theory, this determination might consist of a searching review of the records, maybe even the calling of witnesses, but in bond court in a big city, the judge usually had the words "Probable cause to detain" out of his mouth before the defendant reached the bench.

After the *Gerstein* finding, the judge would turn to the question of bond, which could take a bit longer unless the prosecutor and defense attorney had agreed on the amount. The judge can choose an I-bond, which lets the defendant walk and only pay the bond if he fails to appear later, or a D-bond, which requires a deposit of ten percent of the money before release.

"Probable cause to detain, circumstances?" The judge would then listen to the attorneys discuss bond before announcing, "Ten-thousand-D, or "One-thousand-I," never deviating much from formula. If any one case took more than five minutes, the judge wasn't doing his job.

Prisoners were shuffled in through a side door and lined up in the area that, in other courtrooms, would be reserved for the jury. Sometimes there were benches or chairs, but not in this courtroom. Prisoners stood, manacled, looking through Plexiglas at the profile of the judge, hearing what went on in the courtroom through a speaker, until their case was called.

A fresh batch of prisoners shuffled in, and I saw Pete. My heart sank at the sight. He clearly hadn't slept, which was a smart move, but I saw nothing to indicate he'd been treated roughly. His shirt and pants were badly wrinkled and his hair was oily and flat. His eyes searched the courtroom until they found mine, and I nodded to him. He blinked twice, then nodded back.

The words finally came from the clerk: "Kolarich, Peter."

"Jason Kolarich for the defendant," I said from the front row, before I'd even approached, hoping the name might register with the judge. Our time as prosecutors had overlapped, though we'd never met.

"Prob—" The judge's eyes lifted off the papers before him. He straightened his posture. "Counsel," he said to me. A lightbulb had gone on.

"Good afternoon, Your Honor."

He nodded to me, then glanced in Pete's direction. "This is a relation, I take it?"

"This is my brother, Your Honor."

He took a deep breath. "Well, Mr. Kolarich, I think at this stage I would find probable cause to detain."

"I understand that, Your Honor." There was absolutely no possibility of my convincing him otherwise, so I showed him some courtesy back, hoping for another return from him for the bigger question.

"Circumstances, Mr. Warren," the judge said quietly to the prosecutor.

"Officer complainant," Warren answered, meaning that a cop—DePrizio—was an eyewitness to the crime, as opposed to a layperson. "One point seven kilos of uncut rock cocaine and over thirty handguns. The defendant has two priors for—"

"I see his history, Counsel," the judge said, waving a hand. Another courtesy, sparing Pete from having his criminal history—two possession busts—being stated publicly.

"People request one-hundred-thousand-D, Judge."

The judge ran a hand over his mouth. "Mr. Kolarich, sir?"

"Judge, I would request an I-bond. Judge, my brother isn't going anywhere. He's gainfully employed, and he's not going to run from this. If he does, he should be more worried about me than you."

The judge thought about it a moment, then said, "Three-hundred-thousand-I."

I breathed out. He was releasing Pete on his own recognizance, making the usual judicial trade-off—stiffening the amount but not requiring anything up front. If Pete skipped a court appearance, he'd be on the hook for three hundred thousand dollars.

"I'll see you back at processing," I told Pete. He nodded but didn't answer as he was led back to the holding area.

I waited around because I had to cover another bond hearing, for Cameron Bates, the guy who watched Pete's back for the last twenty-four hours. The judge gave him ten-thousand-D, meaning he had to cough up only a thousand dollars for release, which I intended to pay to get him out. The judge, seeing me step up again for a guy who was obviously held along with Pete, probably figured what I'd done and gave me yet another courtesy, kicking down Cameron's bond by about half.

About two hours later, I walked out of the same police station where Pete had been jailed, with my younger brother quietly by my side. He was continuing to heed my admonition about keeping his mouth shut, even staying silent in the parking lot, as if the police had wired up the overhead lights to listen to confessions.

When the car doors slammed shut, before I could even turn the key in the ignition, Pete turned to me.

"Jason," he said, "I think I was set up."

21

CAN'T MAKE IT, your brother tells you. *Got an algebra test Monday.*

An algebra test. It doesn't sell with you. Your brother's made every home football game, all six your freshman year at State and the four, so far, your sophomore year.

Everything okay? you ask, but you know you won't get an answer. And you know, with a sinking feeling, what the answer is.

I just have a damn test, don't make it a big frickin' deal, he snaps.

You don't push it. You don't know—you can't know—what it's like for him now, since you've left the house. You haven't bothered to ask because you know he wouldn't say anything anyway. Pete has always kept his distance that way.

The conversation echoes in your head through Friday and Saturday, even during the game, looking up into the packed stands that seem empty without him there.

The game, a mid-afternoon start, goes well. You don't score but you have nine catches for over a hundred yards by the third quarter. Your finest moment comes next, not even a pass, a running play, a sweep right. You cut back on an angle and make a beeline for the middle linebacker, who is shuffling to his left. You feel the momentum build with your speed. You want it; you can taste it. He sees you, but it's too late. You plow into him, the top of your helmet connecting just under his face mask, your shoulders pads barreling into his chest. You knock him off his feet, driving his body backward. You land on him with a force, but you're not done, you keep driving your feet even as he's on the ground beneath you, your helmet forcing up his face mask, almost taking his helmet off his head. He pushes you off and you slam your fist into his face mask as the whistle blows but you keep throwing punches at him until someone grabs you and lifts you off.

What the hell are you doing, Kolarich? your teammate shouts at you, as the referee picks up his yellow flag and points at you.

Fifteen yards, personal foul, another fifteen for unsportsmanlike conduct, and you're out of the game. On the sidelines, the coach is furious, but you don't even hear him. You walk past him, past your teammates, and off the field.

You throw off your pads in the locker room and don't even shower. You find your car in the parking lot by the dorm, your piece-of-shit Ford, and you drive the ninety miles home. You're surprised by your calm, the icy deliberation. When you get home, the house seems empty. Both cars are gone. *Pete!* you call out. He comes out of his room, surprised to see you, still with the black paint under your eyes, in your sweats.

What's going on? he asks, before he realizes exactly what's going on. He immediately turns his head to the left, but you've already seen the shiner, the swelling and bruising beneath his left eye.

He did that? you ask.

No, I—I fell—

It's even worse to hear the denial, the covering up for an abusive father. It means Pete's not only been beaten physically but mentally. You leave the house, return to your car, and drive. You don't know where Jack is— he could be working, hustling somebody, but he has a couple of familiar haunts and you find his car at one of them, a dive off the highway called, of all things, "Pete's."

You wait. He won't be there forever. Not because he'll stop drinking, but because he'll run out of money.

At ten o'clock, he stumbles out with another guy, but they separate. Jack Kolarich staggers over the gravel rock of the parking lot, unaware of you. When he reaches his Chevy, he stops and then, as if he senses your presence, turns and looks down the way, four cars down. His eyes squint in the darkness, looking at you like you're an apparition.

You walk slowly toward him, watching the expression on his face take a tour of emotions from confusion to anger to apprehension, but back to anger. Always back to anger.

Superstar, he says to you.

You close the distance swiftly, and it is clear that he knows why you're here. He takes a step back, draws in his shoulders, a proud man unaccustomed to backing down to one of his boys but realizing his physical disadvantage here. You got the height and build from your mother's side of the family. You have a good four inches and thirty pounds on your father.

Go back to school, he says, as you swing and hit the side of his skull, a miss, but with enough force to send him against the trunk of his car, off balance. He covers up and you start swinging, both hands raining down blows on him until he slides off the trunk and falls to the ground. You turn him over and continue the onslaught, blood spurting from his battered face, your anger cresting now, and you feel the tears on your face as you keep pummeling your father until his screams subside and he is barely conscious, his face broken, swollen and beet-red, soon to be purple.

Never again, Jack, you say. *Or I'll kill you.*

PETE AND I hit a drive-through for some burgers, and then we stopped at his place so he could get a few changes of clothes and some toiletries together. For the next week or so, the plan was, Pete would stay at my place with me. I felt the need to keep my brother close.

I took him to my house, ordered him to shower and get some sleep, and then we'd talk.

He was set up, he'd said. You hear all kinds of similar stories from defendants. Usually it's portrayed as a misunderstanding, but sometimes the paranoia rises to an allegation of intentional police misconduct. Like anyone would care enough to take the time to frame some asshole small-time criminal.

Still, I'd watched Pete closely from the time I picked him up at the station until he was at my house, throwing his clothes into a dresser and preparing to shower. If he was an addict, he'd be what the prison guards would call "dope-sick," feeling withdrawal pains. His stomach would be churning. He'd have the shakes. Pete was run-down from the ordeal and clearly terrified, but he wasn't in withdrawal.

So my gut told me that Pete wasn't an addict, and that, to me, was the first crack in the foundation. If he was merely a recreational user, then turning to crime would be more a conscious decision than a desperate need, and I just couldn't see Pete taking that plunge.

I sat on the sofa in my living room, my head fallen back on the cushion, staring at the ceiling, trying to think through the situation. When it rained, it poured. I was up to my ears just keeping up with Sammy's case and his mysterious benefactor, Smith. Now my little brother was jammed up in a big way. I didn't know if there was enough of me to go around.

I heard Pete coming down the stairs. He walked into the living room in sweats and bare feet, his hair still wet but combed, smelling fresh and clean again.

"You need sleep," I said.

"No, I need to tell you that I was set up." He took a seat in a soft brown leather recliner that Talia conceded for me, even though it didn't particularly match the green and yellow décor of this room. It was the best spot on the planet to watch a college football game.

I rested my elbows on my knees. "Start from the start," I said.

"Look, I'm an idiot. I know that. I was buying some coke. Same guy I always buy from." He seemed to catch himself—the *always* part suggested more prior usage than he'd wanted to concede.

"Just tell me," I said, weary. "Start with his name."

"John Dixon," he said. "J.D. He's a pretty reliable guy, real discreet."

"How does it work with you two?"

He shrugged. "I'd call his cell phone and he'd find me."

"How much would you buy? Typically."

Pete grimaced. "Why does this matter—"

"You let me decide what matters. Answer me."

"Well, 'whatever' is the answer. Sometimes, just a gram or two. Sometimes more, if some of us are gonna party."

"Eight-ball? Something like that?"

He nodded. "So I called him on his cell phone last night. He tells me to meet him at this spot over on the near-west side, this warehouse out past Dell. He says it's that or nothing."

"And what time was this?"

"Like, I don't know—one in the morning?"

"You had to have a score at one in the—"

"We were partying, Jason. What do you want from me? A bunch of us."

"But you went alone."

He shrugged again. "Yeah, I always do. J.D. doesn't like crowds."

"Okay, so you're at this warehouse."

"Right. And J.D.'s there with this guy he calls Mace. He says Mace, he's an associate or something. I don't really care, I'm just there to—y'know, to buy. And before I know it, this cop is running in, yelling at us, his gun's out, nobody move, that kind of thing. He points his gun right at me and I freeze. I put my hands up and I don't move. J.D., he took off and—I don't know, I guess he got away." Pete threw his hands up. "Then there's a couple other cops, and me and that guy Mace got handcuffed. They put me in a car, drive me to the station, and they're talking about 'uncut rock' and 'weapons.'"

Pete went quiet. His hands were trembling, but it wasn't withdrawal. It was horror. "Look, I didn't say anything to them. That's what you'd want, right? I didn't say anything."

"Right," I said. "Good." We were quiet for a while. I wanted to reach over and smack the kid, but he needed a lawyer right now. "So," I finally said, "where do you get that you were set up?"

"I don't know," he said. He looked up at the ceiling. "They put me up against a wall, and this guy Mace was a little ways down, and I hear him say 'Easy,' or 'Easy, now,' something like that. But, like, in a tone that he knew the cops. He was calm, y'know? I mean, I was freaking out, and this guy was like, 'Take it easy' to the cops, under his breath."

I closed my eyes. I could see it now. Pete *was* set up, in a sense, but not in any illegal way. It was a classic "spider web." This guy Mace was working for the police, attracting buyers to his lair so they could be scooped up. Only Mace had to be picked up, too, as if he were under arrest as well, to maintain his cover. That was why Mace wasn't in lockup, along with Pete. They pretended to go through the motions of an arrest but probably released him as soon as they drove Pete off. He keeps his cover; he works for them again the next night.

"You talked to J.D. on your cell phone?" I asked.

He nodded.

"Do you remember the conversation?"

"Yeah, I remember. I said, 'Where are you?' He told me where he was, and I met him there. Not much to remember."

"And this Mace? Did you guys talk about anything?"

"Just hey, how-ya-doing."

"That's it?"

Pete opened his hands. "Yes, Jason, that was it."

"Was J.D. into guns?" I asked. It wasn't your everyday guy who came in to purchase a bag of handguns. Drugs was one thing, weapons was another, especially since the feds here had such a hard-on for gun crimes these days. A lot of gang-bangers now carry blades only, precisely because they don't want the ten-year pinch for a federal gun charge.

Pete shook his head. "I really don't know if he was into guns or not."

Okay, so that was probably it. J.D. was probably into guns. J.D. was the bait. But then he got a call from Pete, and suddenly it would be two flies snared in the web, not one. The cops, and a snitch like Mace, would be smart enough to wait for Pete to join the party before closing the deal. Mace was probably earning points after having been collared himself, and two was always better than one.

"Were the guns showing?" I asked. "Did you see guns? Or uncut—"

"*Christ*, no. I was only expecting J.D., and he's with this guy Mace, and before I know it, I'm under arrest."

Pete ran his fingers through his wet hair and moaned. "I am fucked," he said. "I am so totally fucked."

Maybe, but I wasn't ready to concede. Something about this felt wrong. I couldn't put my finger on it. But I knew that the first order of business was finding Pete's supplier, John Dixon. I had a few questions for him.

"You're going to take a week off that sales job," I said. "You're going to stay here with me, get some rest, and we'll figure this out." I walked over and put my hand on his shoulder. "We'll get through this, Pete. I promise." I was calm and resolute as I spoke, so at least one of us would believe what I was saying.

22

THE NEXT MORNING, I left Pete some bacon in a pan and a note, advising him not to leave the house for any reason and to call me when he awoke.

I had to see Sammy. I'd meant to do so yesterday, after the news broke all over the city about the discovery of the bodies behind Hardigan Elementary, but I'd been caught up with Pete's arrest and bond hearing.

It was Sunday morning, October seventh. Twenty-two days until Sammy's trial. It dawned on me, on my drive to the detention center, that the water line was reaching my nose. A reasonable person might inquire as to my fitness to handle Sammy's murder case, under the circumstances, and now I was juggling Pete's problem, too. It probably said something about my mental condition that I was able to make this observation with a cool detachment—an outsider looking in. I had absolutely no business being calm about things. A man I once called my best friend, my brother for all practical purposes, was facing a life sentence, and my real brother was in quite the pickle himself. I was never one to panic, to let my nerves overtake me, but that was because I refocused that adrenaline to enhance my performance. Now, I wasn't panicking because there wasn't any adrenaline, period.

What the hell was I doing handling Sammy's case?

I waited in the same glass room at the detention center, drumming my fingers, alternately thinking about Sammy's case and Pete's. Time was, I wouldn't have distinguished between the two people—brothers, each of them. I'd left Sammy behind, moving on to bigger and better things, and I suppose in some sense I'd left Pete behind, too.

They walked Sammy in and chained him down to the table, as always. His eyes were bloodshot, and he had a hint of a shiner. I didn't even want to know the underlying story.

"Did they find Audrey, Koke?" he asked, measuring the words delicately. Inmates have access to newspapers, and someone must have pushed this article in front of him. I scolded myself for not coming yesterday, when the news broke, but with everything going on with Pete, I didn't have a chance.

"Sam, they found a number of bodies buried behind that school. Bodies of young children. They think Griffin Perlini murdered those children. But they haven't identified the victims yet."

Sammy didn't react, save for his lips parting. He struggled to find words. The blood drained from his face.

Neither of us spoke for a solid twenty minutes. Sammy's a big, burly guy, and those are the ones who look particularly infantile when they lose their composure. Sammy was moving in that direction. He didn't know how to react. He'd lost his sister decades ago. He'd hardly known her. Truth was, he probably struggled to retain a mental image of her. And he knew she was dead. Still, she'd never been found, and this news was a catalyst for emotions long suppressed.

I busied myself with my notepad, then paced around the room, anything to give the guy a modicum of space and privacy.

"Why—why now?" Sammy mumbled.

I told him how I'd visited the old neighborhood, how I'd driven past Griffin Perlini's house on a lark, met Mrs. Perlini, and gotten the tip about the hill behind the grade school.

"We need to get DNA testing done right away to confirm it's Audrey," I said. "We need to hire someone on our own and get a court order. The jury needs to know what he did to your sister."

I looked at Sammy for the first time since I'd given him the news. His eyes were still wet, but his face was set hard. He was long-accustomed to digesting difficult news with a stony front. Prisons, Sammy's home for much of his adult life, were not places for hand-holding and group hugs. Long ago, Sammy had learned to distill his pain with anger.

"If it's Audrey," I told him, "we'll make sure she has a proper burial, Sam. We'll bury her next to your mother."

Sammy covered his face with his hands and nodded. A rush of emotion gripped my throat. It felt like we were kids again, covering each other's backs. It was that feeling that held me back from what I'd intended to tell Sammy—that I had to bow out as his lawyer, that I wasn't ready to do this. On many obvious levels it was absolutely the right thing to do, but something deep within me said otherwise, that I was the only one who'd be willing to take whatever steps necessary to help my friend, that it would be obscene for me to turn my back on Sammy now, no matter how ill-equipped I was.

YOU COME UP the ramp in your sweats, your hair still wet from the fresh shower, your soiled football uniform in a bag over your shoulder. You see Pete, beaming, nodding at you with approval. You enjoy it, the way he looks up to you, and today was special—you've had your best game so far of your high school career. You don't know the official stats, but Coach was saying you had over a hundred fifty yards receiving, and the two scores.

Where's Ma? you ask Pete.

Pete's smile vanishes. *She went to see Mary*, he says. *It's getting bad.*

You drive Pete to the hospital, where Sammy's mother, Mary Cutler, has returned. She's been in and out of the hospital for over a year now, since she was diagnosed with a genetic kidney disease. She's been in the hospital two weeks now, but apparently things have taken a turn for the worse.

It's not good, your mother whispers, pressing her body against yours, in the hallway outside Mary's room. *It's not good.*

Out of Mary's room walks Sammy, ashen, his eyes lifelessly following the floor. Your heart skips a beat. You haven't seen Sammy in almost a year—God, a year. Sammy was initially sentenced to one year in the youth detention center on the drug charges, but the judge had extended his sentence when Sammy seriously injured another kid in a fight.

He looks so different, you think. His hair is tightly cropped—a require-ment—replacing his previously long, red locks. He has lost a significant amount of weight, too. But there is something beyond the physical.

He sees you. His eyes run up and down you, your sweats, your jock look. Then he looks away with disinterest.

It's just the situation, you tell yourself. His mother is dying. Cut him some slack.

Hey, you say.

Hey. He doesn't look at you. His tone indicates he isn't interested in conversation, not with you. He doesn't seem interested in much of any-thing.

Different. Sammy was a troublemaker, sure, but not in a malicious sense. He had a tremendous heart, a real spirit. That's it, you think to yourself. He has lost more than his long hair and fifteen pounds in that detention center.

Your mother and Pete go into Mary's room. You find Sammy down the hall in a lounge area, sitting alone on a long couch. You stand, silent, for a long moment, waiting for any response. You take a seat next to your old friend. His head rises slightly, the barest of acknowledgments, but he doesn't speak.

You start and stop many times. Nothing you want to say feels right. It's never been like this before. There was never any effort.

It's not just awkwardness you feel. There is an element of danger in Sammy's carriage, as if he's poised, ready at any moment to unleash something evil.

Sammy, you say, but nothing follows.

When he turns to look at you, his expression is severe, intense eyes probing you as if he's never met you before. Different, you realize. Every-thing is different.

Tonight you will be flown out east, to one of a dozen schools offering you official recruiting visits as they dangle a scholarship before you. It's become a full-time chore in your junior year, weekly visits from repre-sentatives advocating the merits of their respective universities. Heady stuff, no question. You are a celebrity. They write about you weekly in the newspapers. The teachers pretend not to cut you any slack but their rev-erence is unmistakable. And the girls? It's like a buffet.

Two weeks from tonight, you will announce that you'll be staying close to home, accepting a scholarship at State. You will dream of the ultimate—turning pro—ignoring the reverse stereotype about white kids. You will keep your grades up, chase women, but otherwise have a singular focus on the sport of football.

The following week, Mary Cutler will die. Sammy will attend the funeral, dressed in an ill-fitting suit, and then return the next day to his detention center. After the funeral, you will lose track of Sammy. He will become a memory, part of your childhood, a piece of your life you have put behind you.

23

I DROVE BACK to the office, thinking about Sammy and Pete, two people for whom, at one time or another, I had reserved the most exclusive space in my heart. Drive and ambition, in different forms, had separated me from each of them. Shauna had probably been right about my assuming too much responsibility for the fate of others. But the facts were there, with both of them. I couldn't feel guilty about having athletic ability or for using it to get an education, but I didn't need to forget about a childhood bond in the process. There was nothing wrong with diving into my job and family, but it didn't mean I had to ignore Pete's struggles.

Still, I was left with the reality that I couldn't change what had happened, only what would happen going forward. I was given a second chance now, with each of them.

I drafted a motion in Pete's case for *Brady* discovery—asking the prosecution to turn over all evidence against Pete. Included in that information, I expected, would be the full name of, and contact information for "Mace," the police snitch who helped the cops snare Pete. The prosecution was obligated to give me that information even without my asking, but I didn't want to wait around until the next status hearing. I wanted it now. I wanted to see what I could do to nip this thing in the bud.

My intercom buzzed. *"Smith on 4407."*

Smith. Again. I didn't think I'd be hearing from him so soon, if ever.

He'd given me explicit instructions on what I was and was not allowed to do on Sammy's case, and I'd given him explicit instructions to shove his demands up his ass. What had he said?

When you change your mind, I'll be in touch.

When.

I did a slow burn. Adrenaline filled my limbs. I reached for the phone tentatively, pausing a moment, doubting it, but then sure of it. It was not a coincidence that Smith was calling me the day after Pete had been arrested.

"Smith," I hissed through clenched teeth.

"I heard your brother had a spot of bad luck."

Pressure points, he'd said last time. *Everyone has one.*

I rubbed my eyes, rage filling my throat.

"Don't say I didn't warn you. But I can help with that, Jason. I can make sure your brother never spends another night in a cell. I'll help you if *you* help *me*."

I was set up, Pete had told me. I hadn't believed him, at least not in the way he'd meant it.

"If you haven't noticed, the people I represent have the ability to make a number of things happen, or *not* happen," he continued. "You were a prosecutor. You know there are plenty of ways a case can collapse. I'll make that happen for Pete. As long as you follow directions on the Cutler matter."

My mind was racing, trying to imagine how Smith had manufactured this case against Pete. There were many possibilities, but I couldn't be sure of anything. And now was not the time. *Listen and learn*, I'd been trained. *The less you say, the more they say, the more you learn.*

"I laid out your assignment the other day, at your office. I'll find you a scapegoat, an empty chair. And I'll handle the eyewitnesses. You work on the confession and a reason Cutler was parked near the murder scene. You do your part—you stick to your role and we get Cutler off those charges—then your brother walks. If not, he's looking at ten years, I'd suspect. I thought I was being pretty goddamn clear last time we talked, Counselor. Am I being clear now?"

I didn't speak. I wasn't sure I was capable of doing so.

"You forced my hand, Jason. But I can walk this back. Just do as I say.

And listen, if this all works out, there'll be a bonus on the back end. We'll give your brother twenty-five grand for his troubles. Not too shabby for a guy who has trouble holding down a job."

He was offering me a light at the end of the tunnel. He was playing hard, but he was trying to appear accommodating, too. He wanted me to believe that this could all turn out okay.

"Isn't this the part where you tell me not to call the cops?" I said.

He laughed. "You wouldn't be that stupid. We'd just let Pete go down. Who'd believe you?"

He was right. The prisons of this state were full of people who claimed they'd been set up.

I tried to play it out. I had time on my side. Pete's case wouldn't go to trial any time soon, not if I didn't want it to. He had a noose around my neck, but it was a long rope.

I said, "I'll withdraw from Sammy's case. I'm out as his lawyer. So I'm not a problem for you. The second you get my brother's case kicked, I withdraw."

I wasn't sure if I meant it. Would I drop Sammy to save Pete? More than anything, I just wanted to hear Smith's response.

"Quit fucking around," Smith said. "Cutler wants you. It sure as hell wasn't my idea. His case is going to trial in three weeks with you as the lawyer. I'm doing most of the work, so I don't see where this is going to be too hard for you. You try to withdraw and it's your brother who suffers. No continuances. No withdrawals."

Right. Smith had told me that, at our first meeting—I'd wanted a continuance and he'd objected. It made me valuable. It gave me leverage.

I said, "Then you do what you have to do to get Pete's case dropped before Sammy goes to trial. That's the deal. First Pete, then Sammy. Otherwise, I have no guarantee that you'll step up for Pete. I'd hate for you to forget about me and my brother after you get what you want."

Smith was silent for a long time. He probably didn't expect a counter-offer. "No," he said. "You do your part; then we'll do ours."

"No deal," I said.

"You're not thinking this through, Jason. Pete gets us what we want. Once we get that, we want to rid ourselves of you. The way to do that is to clear Pete, and give him some sorry-for-your-trouble cash. We'll do that."

There was some sense to that, I had to concede. "No deal," I said.

"This can get worse, son. You don't want to find out how much."

"Neither do you." We were fighting for control. This was, in many ways, just another negotiation. It was hard for me to tell who had more leverage. Only Smith knew that answer. For now, all I could do was trust my gut.

"No deal," I said. "And Smith, you better sleep with the light on."

With that, I hung up the phone. I backed away from it, like it was radioactive, my heart ricocheting against my chest. I grabbed my cell phone and made a call.

24

I SPENT THE NEXT HOUR dissecting that conversation with Smith, trying to ignore the escalating guilt I was feeling toward my little brother. He was in the soup because of me. Pete had been duped into a serious criminal charge because of my stubbornness.

But it was done. There was little I could do to reverse it. I couldn't drop Sammy's case. The die was cast, as Smith had said. I was counsel of record now, and any change of counsel would likely require the case to be continued. That, apparently, was unacceptable to Smith.

I had three weeks to win this case for Sammy and hope that Smith would do his part for Pete. Alternatively, I realized, I had three weeks to figure out who Smith was.

At four-thirty, I went down to the sixth floor, to the building's conference room that any tenant can reserve, and which was obviously open on a Sunday. I had a meeting scheduled, and something told me not to have that meeting in my office. I was trying not to indulge in paranoia, but Smith clearly had someone following me, and I didn't know the extent of his surveillance. I couldn't rule out the possibility that he had bugged my office.

A few minutes later, Joel Lightner strolled into the conference room. Joel was the private investigator we used in Senator Almundo's trial. There was no one better.

Lightner threw his jacket over a chair and took a seat. He was a former cop, the guy who solved the Terry Burgos murders on the southwest side with Paul Riley. He still had that sideways look a detective can shoot you, but he had obviously polished up over the years spent in the private sector. He was wearing a plaid button-down and jeans, the most casual I'd ever seen him. Then again, it was a Sunday afternoon.

"How ya been, buddy?" Joel and I hadn't been particularly close, having just met when I was added to the *Almundo* defense team. But you get to spend a decent amount of time with a guy in the heat of trial, and Joel was one of those who could command a room with his stories. Many a late night, prepping for tomorrow's day of trial, Lightner would have us in stitches.

He'd come to Talia's and Emily's funeral and even called one time a month after, asking about lunch. But it didn't happen, and we hadn't talked since.

"Riley told me you resurfaced at your own shop. He was sorry to see you go. You didn't have to, you know. I mean, after *Almundo*? You were a rock star at that firm."

I shrugged my shoulders. "Change of scenery, I guess." There were times when I second-guessed my decision to leave Shaker, Riley. I hadn't been around to hear the verdict in the case but I have no doubt that Paul Riley took many a victory lap through the office. How often does a public official beat the rap on federal corruption charges? But I couldn't imagine working within those walls again. It would be a constant reminder of old failings.

I paced around the conference room, trying to find the proper introduction to the tale I had to tell.

"Try the beginning," Lightner suggested.

"Okay." I exhaled a long, nervous breath. "You're never going to believe this."

"About five years back," he said. "We're tailing a cheating spouse. One of my guys is working it, but he's sick, so I cover for him. I see the guy with the woman. They're in the kitchen of this lady's house. I've got the telephoto lens and I'm snapping away. Then the guy drops down, disappears out of camera shot. I'm figuring, okay, this is something kinky, maybe he's sucking her toes or something, because she's just standing there shouting something at him." He shook his head. "He wasn't sucking her toes. He was eating dog food out of a bowl."

I took another breath. "There are some people—a guy named Smith, not his real name—who are very interested in the outcome of a murder trial I'm handling. So interested, Joel, that they set up my brother for an arrest on gun and drug charges, and now they're holding it over my head. They say if I don't do what I'm told, my brother goes down. If I behave, they'll find a way to clear him."

Lightner, who had begun writing, stood perfectly still. "Okay, that beats the Puppy Chow story."

I laid it all out for him, from Audrey Cutler's abduction to Griffin Perlini, to Sammy's arrest, to my visit to Mrs. Perlini and the discovery of the bodies, to my visit with my old neighbor, Mrs. Thomas, to everything I knew about Smith, to Pete's arrest.

Joel was a good listener. It was his job. He didn't interrupt, only jotting notes on his pad to save for the end. *Listen and learn*, a quality he knew well. When I was finally done, over an hour later, Joel leafed through his notes.

"Best bet, Smith is representing one of Perlini's victims. Someone who's very happy that Perlini got what was coming to him and doesn't want Sammy Cutler to pay the price."

I nodded. "Maybe a victim we know, maybe not. We know of four people who complained against him, and Audrey Cutler makes five victims. But there are obviously more—the four kids buried behind that school. And he's a pedophile, so he probably had a continuous stream of victims."

"Bottom line, it's one of his victims, or their families, but we don't know who. Okay." Joel scribbled something on his pad. He seemed to be enjoying the mental exercise. If he didn't, he was in the wrong business. "So here's a question, Jason. If these guys are so interested in the outcome of this case—"

"Then why did they wait until one month before his trial to show up? And why are they so concerned about this trial happening on schedule? So much so that they're willing to go to such drastic measures. I mean, this is bizarre, Joel."

"Right. Right. Timing. Timing is a question."

It was *the* question. These guys took their sweet time in getting involved, but suddenly time was of the essence, even if it deprived Sammy's lawyer of sufficient time to prepare.

Joel said, "It makes me wonder—"

"If maybe they *don't* want him acquitted."

Joel looked at me. "It makes me wonder if you're going to stop finishing my sentences."

I laughed. "Sorry, man. I'm bouncing off the walls here."

"No problem. But you're right, Jason. If they're willing to bankroll a defense and apparently do whatever it takes to help Sammy, why be sticklers about timing?"

It brought me back to a previous thought. "I'm wondering if Smith is representing the person who killed Perlini, and they want to control the defense to make sure nobody discovers who that is. They offer to help me, and maybe they mean it. They don't care if Sammy can beat the case—they just want to make sure they're not implicated. The more time I have, the more likely I'll figure it out. So they hand this to me at the last minute and dole out assignments to make sure I'm not looking under certain rocks."

"That works." Joel popped a mint in his mouth. "Fine with them if Sammy beats the rap, but the principal concern is that they're not discovered." He nodded at me. "So, Counselor, does that mean you have an innocent client?"

Sammy hadn't directly told me one way or the other, I told Joel, but he'd certainly implied that he'd killed Griffin Perlini. I'd followed the tried-and-true path of the criminal defense attorney who doesn't ask the million-dollar question.

"Maybe you should," Lightner suggested.

He was right. Sammy and I would need to have a heart-to-heart.

"So tell me about Smith," Lightner said.

"I think he's a lawyer," I ventured. "The way he talked."

"He said a lot of words that don't mean anything? Lied to your face?"

I was in no mood to trade wisecracks, but I felt reassurance amid Lightner's calm.

"Well, he's obviously intelligent," I said, "so I ruled out a cop."

Lightner winked at me. It felt good, some humor in the face of every-thing.

"The way he talked," I explained. "From day one. He talked about 'noticing up a motion,' and 'presenting' a motion, and the 'empty chair.' Phrases lawyers use. And he seems to have a pretty good handle on how to engineer a criminal defense."

"Okay, so Smith is a lawyer. That it?"

So far, it was. If I could figure out how to find this guy, I was a long way to where I needed to be.

"Then let's talk about your brother."

"John Dixon—J.D.—is the guy who'd sell to Pete," I said. "I need his record, his address, anything you can get. Then there's this other guy, 'Mace.' Only know the nickname."

"J.D., I can handle. Mace will be tough." Lightner made a note. "Espe-cially if he's this cop's CI."

"Yeah, but how confidential can he be?" I asked. "They're going to have to disclose his name to me in discovery."

"Yeah, that's right." Lightner thought about that. "So why do you need me? You'll get his info, and J.D.'s info, too. If you want it now, do a *Brady* motion."

Joel was right. The defense had the absolute right to receive all relevant information from the prosecution. I already had drafted the motion requesting it. But I'd decided against filing it, at least for the time being.

Joel was also right to wonder why I wanted this information before-hand—before I officially requested it. He was putting one and one together, and it was looking a lot like two: He was concerned that I might be seeking this information about J.D. under the radar because I had plans for that gentleman that exceeded the boundaries of the law.

"Listen, Jason. You lost your family, and now your brother's ass is on the line, too. You're scared, justifiably so. But you should let someone else handle the case for your brother, and you should let go of it completely. Don't try to play hero for your brother."

"He needs a hero," I said.

"Then someone else can do it. Hell, ask Riley. I'll bet he'd be happy to help you out with Pete."

He was right, of course. Under the best of circumstances, I should think twice about handling a case for Sammy, much less my brother. And these were not exactly the best circumstances.

"I need names, addresses, and criminal backgrounds," I said again. "Please, Joel."

Lightner thought about further protest but ultimately conceded. "How do you know Smith isn't bluffing? He sees your brother get pinched; he decides to take credit for it."

I'd considered that possibility. But the timing made me think otherwise. "He comes into my office issuing ultimatums, I tell him to go scratch, he tells me I'll change my mind, and the next night my brother's being accused of selling uncut rock cocaine and running guns?"

"I guess." Lightner couldn't argue with the logic. "I'll take a look at this cop, DePrizio. Maybe he's with them. Or maybe it's just the CI, Mace."

Right. It could have worked either way. If somehow Smith's people owned a cop, the whole thing would be easy. If not, they could get hold of someone like Mace, who would contact DePrizio and tell him he had a buyer. DePrizio could have thought the whole thing was legit. I didn't know. But I could try to find out.

"These guys are following me, Joel. That's why we're not meeting in my office. We need to keep our communications under the radar."

Lightner looked concerned. I ignored his look, but Joel isn't one to hold back. "I can help you out however you need, Jason, but look. It's bad enough you're representing an old friend. But your brother, too? It can skew your priorities, is all I'm saying. You've got a long career ahead of you, and whenever you feel the urge, you could have a dozen law firms vying for your services. After *Almundo*? You're a star. I'd hate to see you throw it all away."

I waved Joel off, but we both knew he was making sense. I obviously wanted information on the people involved with Pete's case without making a formal, official request. I wanted maximum flexibility in how I dealt with these customers. I wasn't planning on letting legal boundaries limit my actions. I needed Joel Lightner's covert assistance, but I couldn't let him get too close to what I was doing.

"You own a gun, Jason?"

I laughed. "You think I need one?"

He didn't answer. Maybe that was part of the reason he asked, a concern for my ability to defend myself if things got hairy. But I suspected there was another reason, too, and it was that other reason that prompted his frown. It was a serious question that deserved, but would not receive, a serious answer.

The answer was yes, I did own a gun. And no, I'd never used it. But yes, I knew how. I'd taken some training along with some other ACAs when I was a prosecutor.

And yes, I'd be willing to use it, but I didn't mention that to Lightner.

25

I TURNED TO MY COMPUTER and finished drafting a motion
I would file in Sammy's case. It was a motion for expedited DNA testing of the four bodies found behind Hardigan Elementary School. In the
alternative to expedited testing, I would ask for a continuance of the trial
until DNA testing could be completed. That continuance, any veteran
attorney like Smith would know, could last up to six months, maybe even
a year. This ran directly against Smith's adamant desire that the trial pro-
ceed as scheduled.

Then I ran through the list of Griffin Perlini's known victims, in particular the two for whom Perlini went to prison. I made a couple of calls
to set up meetings. This, too, ran counter to Smith's instructions.

I wasn't wasting any time testing the limits of my leverage.

I noticed that Shauna was in, which wasn't unusual for a late Sunday
afternoon. As a one-person shop, she had to handle the business end of
things, too, and she often came in on the weekend to handle payroll, rev-
enue projections, and other nonlegal tasks. I walked down the hall to her
office and poked my head in. She was on the phone, so I waited, as Shauna
spoke authoritatively to a client, assuring them that she was giving it hard
to the "idiots" on the other side of the litigation. Clients like it when you
call the other side disparaging names. It shows an attorney's investment
in the case.

When she got off the phone, I closed the door behind me.

"I need your help, Shauna," I said.

I SPENT the evening at home with Pete. We ordered in pizza and drank cheap beer. Pete was wearing one of my sweatshirts, too large for him, and a haggard expression. His sleepy, bloodshot eyes kept drifting off, maybe thinking back to the arrest, or thinking forward to many years in the pen.

I was kicking around what to tell him. He'd told me he thought he'd been set up, and now I had information that he was probably right. What good would it do to tell him what I knew? On the other hand, he had a right to know.

We ate mostly in silence, Pete enjoying the comfort of my house, contrasted with the jail cell. He was placing his faith in me. He was making the assumption that I'd come to his rescue, the big brother with the Midas touch, not realizing that I was probably the reason for his problems in the first place.

I'd never been comfortable in that position—the hero, the celebrity. I'd always felt like an imposter. People give you a status based on a physical accomplishment, something you do in a game. Plenty of women flocked to the athletes in high school, and even more so at State. I was no priest. I freely accepted the accoutrements. But I never mistook it for reality. The truth was, it was a lonely existence, questioning the motives of everyone around you—the coaches, the boosters, the women—not trusting anyone with your feelings. State used me and I used State, getting a college degree and heading to law school.

Talia was not one for idol worship. Nor did she know the first thing about football. We'd met in the last year of college, and she couldn't have cared less about sports. That, I assumed, was one of the many things that drew me to her. She'd listen with interest to the accounts of my accomplishments, but it seemed more of an information-gathering process, just another piece of a puzzle that was Jason Kolarich.

I never knew, precisely, what that puzzle looked like with all the pieces in place. The only thing I knew for sure was that, whatever it used to look like, it would never be the same. I would never fully recover from the loss of Talia and Emily. The raw, gaping wounds would close but they'd always be sensitive to the touch.

I watched Pete, boyish in his messy hair and oversized sweatshirt, drink one beer too many. I watched his expression occasionally deteriorate as he pondered what lay before him. I watched him, and I knew that I would stop at nothing now.

I wasn't a football player at heart, and I sure as hell wasn't a team player. I was a competitor. I wanted to win and I enjoyed the thrill of the battle.

But now it was personal. Smith and his friends had invaded what was left of my family. I would make sure he'd regret that decision.

MONDAY MORNING—twenty-one days until trial—I was in the office by nine. Marie buzzed me just as I was opening some files to review. *"Arrelius Jackson from Reynard Penitentiary?"*

I didn't know the name. An inmate, obviously, doing state time.

"Take a message," I said.

A moment later, Marie buzzed again. *"He says it's urgent. He says Mr. Smith referred him?"*

I felt my blood go cold. "I'll take it." I punched the lit button. "Jason Kolarich."

"Yeah, I need to talk to you." There was heavy background noise. An inmate using a pay phone.

"So talk."

"Nah. Face to face, man."

"I'm busy."

"Not too busy for this, man. You know where Reynard is?"

"I know where it is," I said. "I sent a lot of people there."

I thought he laughed. "You better come, man, you know what's smart."

The line went dead. I stared at the phone, as if it could give me some answers. I had a pretty good idea what this was about.

Smith, it seemed, wasn't taking no for an answer.

My cell phone buzzed. I looked at the face and it was Joel Lightner. I took a moment to decelerate from my conversation with Mr. Arrelius Jackson and answered.

"I've got something on John Dixon. Ready?"

"When you are," I said.

"Black kid, age twenty-eight. Seven pops, all drug-related. Three of them dismissed, three pleaded down, some community service, one stint inside. He was affiliated for a time, a Warlord, but as you know, the Warlords don't have much going on anymore. Anyway, he's a Lone Ranger now, he lives down south in Marion Park and works as a courier for an investment banking firm."

"A courier."

"Yeah, ain't that rich? He probably has half his clientele right in that damn firm. Anyway, 4554 West Elvira is the addy. He's single but has a kid that lives with the mother. The firm he works at is McHenry Stern, downtown. The Hartz Building."

"Sure." I continued to scribble. "Awesome, Joel. You're a peach."

"You want a tail?"

"I don't think it would look good on me."

"Hey, smart guy? What's it gonna be? Do I tail him? Interview him?"

"Let me think about it," I said.

"Yeah? You're making me nervous, kid."

"Any luck on this 'Mace'?"

Joel used silence to express his disapproval. Hell, he found people for a living. Why would he assume the worst about *my* intentions?

"No luck," he finally said. "Nickname isn't much to go on, right? And cops don't usually advertise their CI's."

Fair enough. John Dixon was the one I wanted, anyway.

26

REYNARD PENITENTIARY was a maximum-security prison out in rural country, a good fifty miles northwest of the city. It took me more than an hour to get there, which put me at about half past one. Visiting hours began at two, if memory served, though as a prosecutor we could get access to inmates whenever need be. I'd been out here a few times in my stint as an assistant county attorney, usually flipping witnesses through a combination of sticks and carrots.

The place was a brick fortress with several acres surrounding it on all sides, covered with the usual barbed-wire fencing and in-ground sensors. I was stopped no less than three times on my way in, always checking my identification against the visitor sheet. Arrelius Jackson had put me down as an "A" visit—meaning an attorney-client visit, which entitled us to special rooms where, allegedly, we could speak in confidence. I say "allegedly" because the Department of Corrections, on occasion, had been known to overlook this special privilege and eavesdrop on attorney-client conversations, too. There had been a scandal about five years ago with a downstate penitentiary, resulting in a handful of resignations and typical reactionary reforms.

I didn't really care. I didn't have the slightest impression that Arrelius Jackson was looking for a lawyer. I'd done a search on him back at my office. Age thirty-four, African American, unmarried, a sheet starting when he was seventeen. Mr. Jackson was serving consecutive life sentences for a triple homicide in the city about a decade ago. His appeals had long dried up.

I was searched, seized, X-rayed, poked and prodded. I gave my autograph a couple of times and passed through two metal gates before I was finally ensconced in a small room of concrete walls, painted green, and a metal table at which I sat. The single door to the room popped open with a hydraulic *whoosh* and in walked the man of the hour, none other than Mr. Arrelius Jackson, in an orange body suit, accompanied by two of Reynard Penitentiary's finest.

Inmates used the phrase *stone cold* to describe the nastiest, scariest of the prison population. The term was typically reserved for the sexual predators and the enforcers. I didn't know if Jackson was either of those but I figured if I looked up the phrase in the dictionary, I would find a picture of the man now standing before me.

Jackson had several scars on his forehead, followed by braided hair pulled tightly over his skull. Uneven facial hair straggled along his jaw line. His eyes were small and cold, and fixed on me from the moment he walked in the room.

One guard—unarmed—bolted Jackson's handcuffs to the metal clip on the table while another armed guard observed from a safe distance. The protocol had been established a couple of decades ago, after a manacled inmate managed to lift the handgun out of a guard's holster during this very process. The guards left us, closing the thick metal door. They could monitor us from a camera posted in the corner of the room but they couldn't listen—allegedly.

Throughout this entire process, Jackson never took his eyes off me, not showing a trace of emotion. He had raped and killed. He had no hope for release. His life would be spent in this Darwinian hellhole, where the only hope for survival was to be meaner and tougher than everyone else.

Arrelius Jackson hated me. He hated every man associated in any marginal way with the criminal justice system, with authority, a cop, a lawyer, a judge, the people who felt entitled to lock him in a cage. Undoubtedly he hated his own lawyer, part of the same system, in his mind probably equally corrupted, in cahoots with the prosecution all along. Given the chance, he would come over the table right now and pummel me, smash every tooth in my mouth, use my skull for a punching bag, probably piss on my dead corpse.

Usually that didn't happen until people got to know me.

I leaned back in my uncomfortable chair and stared back at him. I wasn't going to speak first. It was his dime. His call.

"Bitch," he said, then he chuckled to himself, amused.

That cleared up any minute possibility that he was seeking my legal assistance. He was here to intimidate me. Smith had reached this guy. I had a pretty good idea of his sales pitch from here on out.

"Is that what your mama used to call you?" I asked.

"Say again?"

"I mean, Arrelius—that's a girl's name, right? Did your mama dress you up in pretty pink doll outfits and call you 'bitch'?"

He didn't engage. His face balled up in rage, then eased. His mouth was a tight, straight line.

"Your brother," he said. "Nice white boy like that. Nice little bitch. Be *my* bitch, he come here. Don't matter where, man. Be someone's bitch. We'll be sure a that. Time we're done, he be *beggin'* for the blade." He made a motion, a finger tracing across his throat. "We gonna slice that white boy wide open," he said.

I had expected this. I'd prepared for this. Still, it was all I could do—it took every mental muscle I could flex—to look disinterested, bored, unaffected, as this lifer inmate threatened to commit every conceivable felony on my brother. Smith was telling me he had a wide reach. He could get to Pete inside. Pete would never make it out of the penitentiary, and his time inside, while still alive, would be worse than death.

I bottled the rage, ignored the hammering inside my brain, and slowly nodded at Arrelius Jackson. "Is that it? Anything else?"

He took a moment, then smiled at me. "I'll keep a spot warm for him, man."

I got up and picked up my briefcase. I walked past Jackson and stopped behind him, positioning myself so that, chained as his hands were to the table, he could not reach me. I leaned into him and whispered into his ear.

"Redgrave Park," I said. "That's where your brother lives, right? Arrelius, one thing happens to *my* brother, I'll castrate yours. And I'll send you a picture."

I left him, straining against his restraints, unsure of whether I was bluffing or telling the truth.

I drove away from Reynard Penitentiary with electricity flowing through my limbs. I told myself to focus on solving the problem but couldn't stifle unimaginable images, courtesy of Arrelius Jackson. As a prosecutor, you hear that prison rape happens but not as often as they say. Still, a scrawny, good-looking white boy like Pete? He wouldn't stand a chance.

Solve the problem.

Smith's people had connections, all right. He'd managed to frame Pete and to get an inmate to threaten Pete's well-being inside. He was flexing his muscle for me, and it was working.

"McHenry Stern on South Walter," I said to the automated voice. I was driving back to my office, calling information on my cell phone. "Connect me," I answered when the robot asked me my preference. I was all for technological advancement, but Christ, can't I get a human being on the phone once in a while?

A woman answered the phone and spoke so quickly, I wasn't even sure I had the right number. "I'm looking for John Dixon," I said. "He works in the mail room."

"Please hold for the mail room."

Apparently the mail room was in another country, because it took a painfully long period of time to connect me, to the point that I was about to hang up, call information again, and start over with the speed-talking receptionist, when a gruff male voice answered. "Yeah."

"Looking for John Dixon," I said.

"He's—hang on." The man moved the phone from his mouth and called out behind him, but I had no trouble hearing him. *"J.D.'s off this week, right?"*

"—be off for a while—"

"—visit his family or something—"

"He's not here," the man said, returning to me. That was a bit more succinct than the dialogue I'd just overheard.

"Do you know when you expect him back?"

"No."

"Will he call in for messages?"

"I don't know."

"Can I leave a message with you?"

"Um—we don't really do that."

"You've been a tremendous help." I closed the cell phone.

So J.D. had taken a powder from work for the time being. Maybe this had been some time off he'd been planning, but I'm not a big believer in coincidences.

The Buick came back into my focus, several car lengths behind me. I drove to my parking garage, across the street from my office building, where I have a monthly pass. I approached the entry gate, which popped up when its sensor clicked with the module attached to my dashboard, and found a place to park on the fourth floor. I took the elevator down and slowly walked across the street to my building—slow enough for anyone watching to see me. I didn't actually see the Buick or its occupant and didn't want to be obvious in looking. I had to assume that they didn't know I was on to them.

The building has a north and south exit. I figured they had someone on each side, should I choose to move on foot, with the Buick positioned to be near the parking garage if I were to travel by car.

In my building, I took an elevator, but it was an elevator down. Shauna, who had rented space in this building for a few years now, had become eligible for in-building parking, meaning she got to park her car underground. I found her fancy foreign car where she'd described it to me and used the spare key she'd lent me. From my briefcase, I removed a baseball cap and windbreaker. I replaced my suit coat with the jacket and threw on the cap. None of Smith's people would be looking for a two-door Lexus, but the light cover gear would help in the event they happened to glance at the car, anyway.

It seemed like I made it out of the building, up the ramp, and toward the highway without incident. I had to be prepared for the possibility that Smith's people were following me now. In the end, while I preferred to conduct my investigation without his knowledge, I was going to do it either way. I agreed with Joel Lightner—I couldn't assume that Smith wanted Sammy to win his case. I had to make it happen on my own.

Griffin Perlini had been convicted of molesting two girls in the summer of 1988, crimes which had landed him in the penitentiary until 2005. The girls had enrolled in a summer program run by the city's park district. The two families were from a south-side neighborhood. According to my files, one of the families still lived in the same house and the other had moved to a nearby suburb.

I started with the people who hadn't moved. Robert and Sarah Drury lived in a modest home in the middle of a very clean, well-kept, middle-class neighborhood. It was dusk by the time I reached the house, and the temperatures had fallen sharply with a promise of snow. The cold and early darkness of winter lent an appropriate cast to this visit. I was going to talk to these people about the man who molested their daughter some twenty years ago.

Robert answered the door in a sweater vest, khakis, and loafers. My gut told me this late-fifties guy was more likely to host a bingo game at a church fund-raiser than kill a pedophile. Then again, I'd prosecuted harmless-looking people who raped and murdered.

He showed me in and I met his wife, who was possibly a tad younger than him, somewhat overweight and graying. They didn't know why I was here. I'd only told them I was an attorney.

I trust my gut, my first impression, and what I'd hoped to do with these people was inform them of Griffin Perlini's death and monitor the reaction. But the news accounts of the bodies found behind Hardigan Elementary had stolen my best line. They obviously would have heard the news.

"I'm representing Sammy Cutler," I said.

It only took a beat before Robert's genial expression hardened. He lifted his chin slowly. "Yes, all right."

Sarah looked at her husband, then at me. "How is he?"

"As good as someone can be, staring at life in prison." I looked at each of them, alternatively. "You know Sammy?"

"We talked once," Robert said. "Before the trial started." He meant Perlini's trial, for molesting his daughter. "We knew about his sister, and—I guess I can't say why—we wanted to meet him."

That wasn't uncommon. Victims of a common perpetrator often form bonds.

"You want us to testify?" asked Sarah.

That wasn't why I was here. I was auditioning them for the part of Griffin Perlini's killers, someone to show the jury. So far, the only audition for which they could compete would be as the parents in a 1950s sitcom. I began to hear the musical theme to *Leave It to Beaver*.

"I'm trying to get some background," I explained. "I'm painting a picture here."

The husband's eyes narrowed. "Char was five when it happened," he said. "She was scared and confused while it was happening. She thought she was doing something wrong. Later, after we discovered what had happened and that man was arrested, Char seemed moody, prone to anger. But she developed into a very ambitious and successful student and woman. Is she still scarred by what happened? Probably. But she's moved on. She's getting a master's at Oregon State."

"Great."

"*We've* moved on," said Robert. "And we'd prefer to keep it that way. But if we have to testify to help Sammy Cutler, then we'll do it."

"Did you ever have contact with Perlini after his conviction?"

"No, of course not."

"Did you testify at Perlini's parole hearing in 2005?" I asked.

"No." He shook his head. "I mentioned it to Char, but she was in Oregon, and she didn't want to come back. And I wrote a letter but never sent it." He looked at his wife. "I think Archie might have testified."

"I think he did," she agreed.

They were talking about Archie Novotny, father of the other victim in that park district summer program. Perlini was convicted of crimes against both the Drury and Novotny daughters in the same trial. Archie was next on my list.

"I know of five victims, not counting the bodies discovered at the school," I said. "There was Sammy's sister, though he wasn't convicted of that crime. Your daughter and Jody Novotny were the two involving actual—actual contact. There were two girls earlier in time, in the late seventies, but as I understand it, it was just lewd exposure. There was no physical contact."

"That's my understanding as well," said Robert.

And those victims—well, their families had had plenty of opportunities to kill Griffin Perlini before he was charged with the Drury and Novotny abuse. I could think of no particular reason that those two families would suddenly seek vengeance, so much later in time, when they didn't feel the need earlier.

And I didn't see the Drurys as plausible suspects. No chance.

That left me with only one other possibility—my next stop, Archie Novotny.

27

SOMEWHERE IN TIME after his daughter was molested by Griffin Perlini, Archie Novotny had moved to Marion Park, a southwest suburb. As I drove through MP, I noted the difference in the town since I'd last visited during my childhood. The Latino influence, nearly nonexistent during my youth, was obvious from the storefront signs and billboards. The gangs had moved in, too, something I knew full well from my time as a prosecutor. The rise in crime notwithstanding, what remained of the middle class still found Marion Park a nice enclave just outside the city proper.

Archie Novotny lived in the older part of town, the smaller homes bunched together on streets bordered by cul-de-sacs. The realtors would say that the circular blocks of concrete at the end of each block promoted slower vehicles, safer for children to ride their bikes and play in their streets. The truth was, their purpose was to discourage drive-by shootings.

It was near six o'clock now, and I needed to get back to the office with Shauna's car, so she could leave work, and so I could leave in my own car. The later in the day it got, the more Smith's people might come to realize they'd been blown off. It was important that they think their surveillance was working just fine.

I rang the doorbell and stood, bouncing on my toes, on the front porch.

"Door's open!" called a voice from inside.

It felt like old times, a different era, when people kept their doors unlocked and invited people in, sight unseen.

I opened the door and stood at the threshold on a dingy black-and-white tile floor. "Mr. Novotny, it's Jason Kolarich." I closed the door behind me. To my left was a winding staircase. Straight ahead were a hallway and a small room. To my right was a coat closet, open, with a full rack of coats and windbreakers, caps and mittens and scarves on a top shelf, boots and shoes on the floor.

"Call me Archie," said the voice.

Okay, Archie, but I wasn't going to head upstairs without an invitation.

I waited a good five minutes, enjoying the comparative warmth of the home. Finally, a man bounced down a few stairs into my view.

"Come on up, Jason."

My first take on the guy, wearing a flannel and cords, was Paul Bunyan on Social Security. I made it up the stairs to the second level—the living room and kitchen, finished hardwood, green furniture, and small windows—and found Novotny in the corner of the room, unplugging a floor sander.

"Put in the hardwood last week," he told me, brushing dust from his hands. "Got a little extra time on my hands these days." Novotny was a union guy, a painter with the electric utility.

"Hard finding work?"

"Has been, lately. Yeah. Working at Home Depot in between jobs." He nodded to the corner. "They let me steal the sander for the week."

I took a seat across from him and adjusted my initial impression. He had an outdoorsman's face, weathered and rugged, matching his large hands. I figured mid-fifties. He looked like a guy who used to be powerful and who had finally softened physically but not mentally. He looked me square in the eye, a hint of amusement in his expression.

"Can I do you for?" he asked. "A lawyer wants to talk to you, your mind runs wild."

"Sure, sure." I raised a hand. "Archie, I represent Sammy Cutler."

He didn't look surprised. "Sure, Sammy. Heard about what happened. He gonna be okay, you think?"

"I hope. I'm doing everything I can."

He seemed to be sizing me up. "Including talking to me."

I smiled at him.

"Why?" he asked. "You want me to tell the jury that Griffin Perlini was a sick, low-life piece of garbage? That he deserved what he got?"

Everything about him changed in an instant, the heat to his face, the clenched fists, the stiffening of his shoulders. My radar was inconclusive at this point. If a guy had molested my daughter, I don't care how much time had passed, it would light a fire in me.

"Name the time and the place, if that's what you want," he said.

This felt promising. Something made me think I needed to prompt him.

"You testified at the parole hearing," I said. I wasn't sure about that but the Drurys had thought so, and it seemed a better idea to state it as a fact. A trick we learned as prosecutors, when interrogating witnesses.

"I sure as hell did. They gave him twenty-five and he shoulda *served* twenty-five."

I'd need to get a transcript of that parole board hearing. Again, for now, I'd bluff.

"You spoke in very strong terms," I said.

He played with that for a while, rubbing his hands together, clenching his jaw. "My daughter cried herself to sleep for years afterward. You know what that's like? Jody couldn't sleep in the dark. Ten years later, she was still having nightmares. You know what you do as a parent? Are you a parent?"

I choked on that one. I went with "No."

"Well, you will be. Your job is to protect the innocence of your child for as long as you can. And this man—this monster—he stole her innocence at the age of seven. She never got a childhood."

"I under—"

"My wife died, three years after this happened. Did you know that?"

"No," I said.

"Jody was having night terrors, she couldn't make friends, she was always crying, and my wife died thinking that this was all Jody would become."

I didn't answer. I was trying to keep this on a clinical level. I was trying to see if this was my guy. I'd come to one conclusion already—I might be able to sell him as a suspect to the jury. But I hadn't yet decided if I could take the route, adding insult to deep, deep injury.

Was this guy working with Smith?

"Hey," he said.

I looked up at him.

"Why you asking about me testifying before the parole board?"

I shrugged my shoulders. "Trying to get my arms around the entire landscape here."

"That sounds like something a lawyer would say when he doesn't want to answer the question. The landscape." He leaned in toward me. "You investigating *me*?"

"Should I be?" I always loved that question. But it moved the conversation in a different direction. Now I was confronting him.

He squinted at me. He had a pretty good poker face. He didn't reveal much of anything. I figured he was running through his options. He could tell me to take a leap and kick me out of his house, but he was smart enough to realize that such a response would only pique my interest. More likely, he would take the common route of anyone cornered—he'd try to talk his way out of it. That's an option I always encouraged as a prosecutor and strongly discouraged as a defense lawyer. It's the human impulse to defend yourself, but often you just dig a deeper hole.

All of this assumed that Archie Novotny had something to hide. But the longer he stared at me through those narrow slants, the more I thought I'd stumbled onto something.

"I was at a guitar lesson that night," he said. "I've had guitar lessons every Thursday night for three years." He nodded presumptively. "I was playing guitar."

Interesting that he had an alibi at the ready. I wanted to explore this. And I wanted to seem nonchalant in doing so. But that effort typically backfires; in fact it has the opposite effect, trying too hard to seem unaffected, and then you've emphasized the importance of the question still further by trying to be underhanded about it. I wanted to know more about this alibi, and there was no way to ask about it in a casual manner.

I was instantly sorry that I hadn't brought a "prover"—somebody who could verify the contents of this conversation in court. I couldn't testify, obviously, as I was counsel, and it had been an oversight on my part not to bring Joel Lightner or anyone else along with me. I'd been so focused on sneaking out of my building without Smith's guys seeing me that I hadn't taken this elementary precaution. It was another reminder to me that I wasn't bringing my "A" game to this case, that I probably wasn't capable of doing so, that I quite possibly was in over my head as I tried to help my childhood friend escape a first-degree murder charge. The usual physical symptoms of minor panic showed themselves—my chest tightened, my throat constricted—but I had no way out at this point and there was simply nothing I could do but motor forward and play out this string. I took a deep breath and refocused.

"Who said Griffin Perlini was murdered on a Thursday, Archie?"

He drew back. "Wasn't he?"

He was. September 21, 2006, was a Thursday. But how did he know that?

"I heard about it," he explained, rather vaguely.

"When did you hear about it?" I asked. "How did you hear about it?"

"*I* don't know." He shrugged his shoulders. "Hell, I heard about it, is all."

If this were a game show, a buzzer would have gone off. People don't remember details of most things that happened in their lives, even last week, but they typically remember quite accurately the wheres and hows of memorable events. I remember exactly where I was when President Reagan was shot; when I learned my mother had had a stroke; when the second plane hit the World Trade Center.

The significance of Griffin Perlini's death would have been tantamount to 9/11 to Archie Novotny.

I tried to control my reaction. This conversation, this line of questioning, was precisely why I was here, but I realized, now, that I hadn't expected this to happen. Sammy Cutler had not asked me to believe in his innocence. His comments had essentially suggested his guilt.

Did Archie Novotny kill Griffin Perlini?

"Where do you take guitar lessons?" I asked.

Novotny shook his head, his eyes cast off toward the window. Things had turned decidedly adverse now, and he was rethinking his strategy. Again, I considered, and rejected, the idea of downplaying things, telling him I was just dotting i's and crossing t's. This guy's feet were on the fire, and I needed to let this play out.

After a long pause, he seemed to calm, his crimson face settling in tension, a clenched jaw and the narrow squint. "She still has nightmares, you know. And she won't admit it to me, but she still thinks, on some level, that it was all her fault." His eyes, still focused on the window, grew shiny with tears. "Perlini told her, you know—he told her that Mommy and Daddy said it was okay. He told her that we *knew* what he was doing to her and it was okay with us."

I knew a little something about self-torture and guilt, and it was everything I could do to keep a clinical perspective. If this guy killed Griffin Perlini, I would offer to defend him, free of charge. But I had to know. And this guy had *motive* written all over him.

And if he was working with Smith, if he had engineered a criminal case against my brother for leverage, I couldn't let my sympathy for his plight get in my way.

"When we found out about this monster—when the Drurys came forward about their Charlene—we asked Jody about it. Just like every parent who had a child in that park district program. And I remember thinking, then, that Jody had become really moody that summer, she was wetting the bed, she wasn't eating—it all dawned on me, and I remember thinking to myself, How could you not have noticed? How could you have missed it?"

I didn't dare speak. My heart was rattling against my chest.

"And when we asked her—when we sat her down and talked to her about it, you know what she said to me? To me and my wife? You know what she said? She said, 'I'm sorry.' She—*she*—apologized to *us*."

My eyes dropped to the floor. I felt like an eavesdropper, a witness to something intensely private, which I had no right to observe.

"This man has haunted our home for twenty years," he continued. "He doesn't get to haunt us anymore." I looked up just as he turned to me, a sharp frown, a snarl, on an otherwise emotionless face. "So you don't get to ask me these questions. Okay, *Jason*? You want to try to pin his death on me, you go right ahead. You'll get no help from me."

He was kicking me out. I wasn't ready to go. I tried the only words I could imagine that would avoid a violent reaction, a complete shut-off of the valve.

"Sammy Cutler," I said. "He knows a thing or two about being haunted. He lost his sister for good, Archie."

Novotny placed his hands on his knees and pushed himself off the couch. "Music Emporium," he said. "Greenway and Thirty-ninth. Every Thursday night, eight to nine. Guy who teaches me is Nick Trillo. Be on your way, now, Jason."

He didn't wait for me to leave. He returned to the corner of the room and plugged in the sander. I took the stairs back down, finding myself back at the front door. I reached for the doorknob but pulled back. Overhead, I heard the high-pitched whirr of the floor sander.

My eyes drifted to the coat closet. I pulled the string for the single light bulb and did a quick inventory of the hanging ware. There were a couple of windbreakers, a baseball jersey, a heavy coat, and—yes—a brown leather bomber jacket.

I raised up on the balls of my feet and looked at the top shelf. There were four baseball caps, all with union labels, a ski mask, and yes, there it was.

A green stocking cap.

28

WHEN I LEFT Archie Novotny's place, I kept driving west. I was already in Marion Park, so there was no reason why I couldn't stop by another address in that town, the home of John Dixon—J.D., Pete's supplier. I'd already called his place of employment, McHenry Stern, and it sounded like he'd taken a leave of absence of some kind. If I was right, and he'd decided to lay low while my brother Pete was out on a limb, then it stood to reason that J.D. would not be lounging around his home, either.

The address Lightner had given me was 4554 West Elvira. It was a three-story walk-up, which Joel hadn't mentioned. The signs on the buzzers showed J.D. as occupying the garden apartment, his front door just a short walk down a few steps, but protected by a gate ten feet high. It looked like there was no one home at *Chez* Dixon, but I buzzed for good measure.

No answer, but it was dinnertime, so I tried another buzzer, beside the name WILLIS. After a long wait, I noticed in my peripheral vision a stirring of a curtain on the second floor, presumably checking me out. Shortly thereafter, a voice cackled through an intercom.

"Hello?"

"Hi, I'm sorry to bother you. I'm looking for John Dixon."

"He's not around. I think he's gone for a few weeks."

"Okay. Shoot. Well, thanks." I walked away before I'd have to explain myself to J.D.'s neighbor.

So J.D. had taken off work and he'd left his home, too. He was in the wind, on the order of whoever had hired Smith. J.D. had been part of the setup. I needed to find him. And I thought I knew how.

I dialed up Joel Lightner again and made the arrangements. Then I explained to him what I had just learned at Archie Novotny's house.

"Brown bomber jacket and green cap," Lightner said. "Wow. Hard to argue with that. You got a shot of it?"

I did. I'd taken a photo of the jacket and the green cap in Archie Novotny's closet using the camera on my cell phone. Again, it would have been preferable to have a prover with me, someone who could authenticate the photograph in court. For the time being, the only people who could attest to the accuracy of the photo were Novotny and me.

Joel asked, "You think he's our killer?"

"Don't know. Don't know. Leather jackets aren't all that rare."

"But green stocking caps?"

"Yeah, I hear you. Look, either way, he's at least a very viable suspect. I've got someone to point at. I'll have to take a look at that alibi, those guitar lessons."

"Okay, but what about the Pete problem?" Joel asked. "I mean, is Archie Novotny the guy behind Smith?"

It was hard to imagine. Archie Novotny was an out-of-work union painter working part-time at Home Depot. We'd have to confirm all of this, but if it was true, he didn't have the resources to use a guy like Smith. "This guy hates Griffin Perlini, no question," I said. "I could see him committing the murder. But I just don't see this thing with Smith."

"Then you still have a problem."

Yeah, thanks. I drove back to my office building, parked underground in Shauna Tasker's space, and headed briefly back up to my office. I walked out of my office at about seven-thirty and headed over to my parking space to drive my car home. The Buick tailed me at an appropriate distance.

They didn't know I'd left the building this afternoon, I decided. They thought I'd been in my office until I walked to my car and drove home just now. I would be free to move about, when necessary, without their knowledge. It was one of the few advantages I had.

Among many disadvantages. Lightner was right: Even if I could put the murder of Griffin Perlini on Archie Novotny, I still had to find Smith. I still had to figure out who he was working for.

The smart money said Smith was representing the family of one of Griffin Perlini's victims. But it wasn't the Drurys, and I didn't think it was Archie Novotny. And beyond that, I couldn't name another victim of Griffin Perlini's sexual crimes.

How could I find this family?

SMITH DROVE to see his client, Carlo. His dealings with Jason Kolarich had been disappointing, though not entirely unexpected. Kolarich was a contrarian, a trait which had probably served him well in his life but was utterly unhelpful for present purposes.

No deal, Kolarich had said. But surely he didn't mean it. Surely, he'd be willing to play ball if it meant coming to the aid of his only remaining family, his brother.

Before getting out of his car, Smith popped a pill, something for his stomach the doctor had prescribed. He'd had recurrences of the problem over time, but now, with this thing with Carlo, his stomach was in full revolt. He'd been through a lot with Carlo over the years, had guided him through a number of tough times, but this thing—this was unique. It was unique because they had so much to lose, and because Jason Kolarich was unpredictable.

At Carlo's door, Smith was led into a large room where Carlo sat, stroking the hair of his daughter, Marisa. Smith stood at the threshold, not wanting to intrude, uncomfortable as he heard the soft moans and sobs of Marisa. Carlo, he thought, would not want Smith to encroach on this moment. Carlo was fiercely protective of his family, particularly of Marisa, who was *slow*—the term Carlo always preferred, a gentler term than *retarded*, which probably was closer to the truth. All the time Smith had known the family, he'd never known exactly how Marisa had been diagnosed. She was fairly functional, physically capable as well, but she was still a child intellectually and emotionally. All in all, a sweet woman who just needed some help to get along.

Smith still remembered vividly everything from way back when—God, it was well over twenty years ago now. Marisa had been a complete wreck. Carlo had gone so far as to move Marisa out of the house, away from the city, to another home he purchased downstate. Carlo's wife had recently passed, so he spent nearly all of his time downstate with Marisa for several years. A tough stretch for the entire family.

But they had bounced back. In her mid-fifties now, Marisa and her daughter, Patricia, now lived next door to Carlo in a house he'd purchased for them. He kept them close and provided for them in every way, but now everything was slowly coming undone. It was hard enough for a woman with Marisa's disabilities that she had to cope with a daughter who was growing sicker by the day, but now everything that happened back then was returning to the fore.

Still caressing his daughter's soft brown hair, Carlo turned one eye to Smith. Carlo nodded and whispered into Marisa's ear. He kissed her on the cheek and left the couch.

He moved past Smith in silence; Smith followed him down the hall to his study. Smith felt his pulse race.

"Give me something good," he said, after he closed the door.

Smith delivered it straight and concise. It would only anger Carlo more if he let it out tidbit by tidbit. "The lawyer understands his brother's vulnerability," said Smith. "I think he'll work with us now."

"You think. Okay, you *think*." Carlo gathered his shoulders, growing introverted. He scratched his arm absently.

"How's Patricia?" Smith asked.

Carlo shook his head. The news was obviously not good. "And you saw Marisa in there," he said. "She's a mess. I don't even know what to tell her."

Smith nodded. Carlo had a lot on his plate right now.

"My family needs me right now. You understand that."

"Yes, I do."

"This trial with this guy, Cutler. This can't be a problem for me.

I've got enough problems right now. You understand I'm counting on you."

"I do, Carlo. I'll make it right."

"I know you will." Carlo's eyes bored into his lawyer. "I know you will."

29

PETE HAD ACTUALLY cooked dinner when I got home, chicken pan-fried and sliced up for fajitas with sautéed peppers and onions, corn tortillas, and refried beans. "I have to do *something*," he said to me. "I'm going crazy here."

I was surprised at my hunger and I downed three fajitas in the space of five minutes. I had a beer, as did Pete, which I thought was not his first of the day. Afterward, we went into the family room with fresh bottles.

"Talked to Dan today," said Pete, referring to his boss. Pete's job *du jour* was a sales gig, selling medical products to retail outlets. It seemed like a pretty easy job to me, selling aspirin to a grocery store, but apparently the bigger issue was getting preferable product placement in the stores. Anyway, Pete was suited for sales, that personal touch, a dose of charm, and I'd hoped this might be the right career move for him.

"I told him," Pete said.

"You *told* him—about the arrest?"

He shrugged. "What, I'm gonna be sick for six months? He'd find out, anyway."

"No, he wouldn't, Pete. You don't have to tell him un—"

Pete gave me a sour smile and finished my sentence. "Unless I'm convicted," he said.

"You're not going to be convicted."

Pete pushed his hair back, sighed, looked up at the ceiling.

"You're not going to be convicted, Pete."

Pete nodded, but it was a sarcastic gesture. A cop had arrested him at a crime scene with a mountain of cocaine and a crate full of stolen fire-arms. His defense was that the whole thing was a coincidence, a misunderstanding. He wasn't liking his chances at trial.

I had to tell him the story. He had to know how this whole thing came to be. "This is my fault," I said. "You were set up, like you said. But you were set up because of me."

I ran through the whole thing for him, told him about Smith, his interest in my defense of Sammy Cutler, his proposed trade—I do what he wants and he fixes everything with Pete's case. My brother listened with rapt interest, but where I was expecting him to haul off and take a swing at me or something, instead he seemed, of all things, to be somewhat relieved. I had underestimated how much he was beating himself up over this arrest, how embarrassed he was to have to turn to me. In some way, circumstances notwithstanding, my role in this affair exonerated him. This wasn't a fuck-up entirely of his own making.

He'd always seen himself that way—the lesser of the two Kolarich boys. The one without the physical ability, without the drive. The one who took his father's abuse, not avoided it. The one who couldn't hold down a job, who partied too much and even got pinched a couple of times by the law, making it harder still to secure quality employment—a cycle I had seen firsthand as a prosecutor and defender of the lower ranks of society.

"I'll make this right," I said. "I'm going to figure out who's behind all this. Shit." I finished off my beer and wiggled the empty bottle. "I've got three weeks, little brother. Three weeks to figure all this shit out."

"Saving the world. That's my brother." Pete drained his beer and fetched some fresh ones for us. He handed me one and dropped back on the couch. "You know, Jason, they couldn't have done this to me without some help. Some help from me. Nobody made me go score some blow that night. Maybe you should be pissed at me for making your life more difficult. Maybe Sammy should be pissed at me, too."

I shook my head.

"Give me some credit, Jason. That's all I'm saying. For Christ's sake."

"Okay, okay. Just shut up already," I said. I worked on the beer, feeling the gentle buzz of intoxication. "You're giving me a fucking headache."

My brother stared at me, then said, "Not the first one I gave you."

"No, definitely not."

"Let me ask you something," he said.

"Shoot."

"You still going to the cemetery every day?"

"What, does everyone know about that?" I looked at my brother, who broke into laughter. I did, too. It felt nice, the release of tension.

"Let's go out," he said. "I'm sick of being cooped up."

He didn't have to twist my arm. We headed out to Lacy's, another of the trendy places with dim lighting and minimalist décor, ear-thumping music, and a healthy bevy of available women. Pete was in his element, and though I realized that this was the setting that typically enabled his drug use, I appreciated the skip in Pete's stride, the first time he'd seemed up since his arrest. And I was relatively confident that he was clean. I had found some opportunity, each day that Pete had been staying with me, to take an unauthorized inventory of his room, finding no evidence of drug use.

By midnight, the place was crawling with people, a vast majority of whom were in their twenties, making me a senior citizen and Pete, five years my junior, the coveted "older man" but not quite so aged that he looked out of place. Over these last months since Talia's death, when I've joined Pete and/or Shauna for a night out, I've played the bystander. These kinds of places, you start together with the person you came with, but if you're on the make like Pete, pretty soon it becomes a free-for-all. We started at the bar, where I took a double vodka, Pete a Tanqueray and tonic, and scoped out the place. It took all of five minutes before Pete had identified a group of women. He tried to get me to ride along, but he seemed to recognize that I wasn't going to bite, so he went off on his own while I hung back at the bar and people-watched.

The energy level at these places always brought back football to me, game days, the crowd stirring with excitement, stretching out electrified limbs before the coin toss, teammates slamming shoulder pads and pumping each other up. I'd always chosen solitude; I turned inward, searched for calm and focus, before a game.

The stereo speakers overhead were blaring a woman's voice, keeping pace with a staccato electronic drumbeat. *Wanting you, needing you, long-*

ing for you, she sang. Appropriate for the setting, but the lyrics and the alcohol returned me to Talia. Pete had touched on something earlier—I hadn't visited the cemetery in the last few days. I supposed that this represented some sign of progress. But I didn't like to think of such things. Progress suggested the future, a step along a longer path, and it was still difficult for me to think beyond the current day. It was hard to imagine a lifetime of these feelings, harder still to imagine that they would dissipate with time. *Dissipate*, I decided, was the wrong word. *Recede* made more sense. They'd go into hiding, ready to return on a moment's prodding.

I loved Talia. I missed her so much it still caused physical pain. I could never have her again, not even a single moment of her hair tickling my face, the smell of her perfume beneath her ear, the scrunched-up face she made when I rehashed a corny joke from my collection. Wanting her, needing her, longing for her. It would recede, yes. The pain would subside. Life would go on, and sometimes it would be good—I knew that. But it would never be as good as it could have been. It would always be just part of a life, not the whole package. It would always be the qualifier that defined me. Good athlete, good lawyer, good guy—but had that tragedy with his wife and daughter, never really got it back together.

Pete was entertaining five women sitting in a booth near a segregated area that I could best describe as a dance floor, because people were bouncing around like kangaroos on morphine. The women, I had to concede, were attractive in that trashy nightclub sense of the word. Pete seemed to be making some progress when he excused himself. He was heading to the bathroom, obviously, and I considered an objection. I wanted to pat him down for drugs, to follow him into the john, to make sure he didn't make a drug deal while my back was turned. I did none of those things because he was enjoying himself, and he was entitled to do so without me coming down on him.

But after about ten minutes passed and my brother still hadn't reappeared, I suddenly felt the need to inquire. A gathering storm of concern began to rise within me, and I quickened my pace, heading to the back of the bar and taking the stairs down to the ground level.

"Like a fight or something," one woman said to another, taking the stairs up from the bathroom.

"Were they bouncers?"

"I don't know."

I jogged toward the bathroom. "Pete," I said when I walked in, looking around at two empty urinals and a stall that was vacant. "Pete!"

I spun around, locating an exit down a hallway. Two men were loitering, talking to each other, noting me as I ran toward the door. Whatever was happening, I was reasonably sure these two were guarding that door, but I didn't have the luxury to inquire. I blew past them, feeling them move behind me. I pushed open the door into darkness, cool air, sounds of violent struggle.

I felt a *whump* across my chest, a heavy blow that took my breath. I fell against a brick wall and shrunk to the pavement. A moment later, light came from the exit door again, and I felt a sharp kick to my ribs.

"Just a reminder, Jason," the man said. I leaned forward, but I hadn't caught my breath yet. As several men scurried down the alleyway, I scanned through the darkness and saw a figure slumped on the ground. I could hear him moving frantically, the sound of fabric scraping against pavement.

"Pete," I managed, and my eyes adjusted somewhat to the darkness. Pete was rolled over on his side, pulling up his pants. "Pete."

I crawled over to him.

"They didn't do anything," he said. "They didn't do anything." He got his pants back up to his waist. "They didn't do anything," he insisted. He was humiliated, terrified, trying to put up a brave front to no avail.

"What—" I caught my breath, inhaled fully twice.

"A reminder," he spat. "What it'll be like—inside."

I put a hand on Pete, as he covered his face with his hands, lying in the fetal position, his chest heaving.

30

MY BROTHER AND I went straight home. I set the house
alarm and left on the lights on both levels of my town house. Pete
drank a little more to settle his nerves. Eventually, the terror of the alley
receded, replaced with a growing sense of dread for what lay before him
in the coming weeks and months. By three A.M., his eyes were crested
with dark circles. I coerced him to get some sleep. I don't know if he was
able to do so. As for me, sleep came episodically, twenty-minute pops
abruptly terminated by unidentifiable screams between my ears.

It wasn't panic. I was experiencing the same pregame sensation of utter
calm, focus, a sense of purpose. I knew then, if I hadn't already, that Smith
and company had no intention of holding up their end of the bargain—
their promise that if I saved Sammy, they'd save Pete. Their subtle coer-
cive methods had devolved into crude, tortuous gestures, an unveiled
threat from a prison gangbanger and then an outright attack in an alley.
These were people who settled their problems with violence. Even if I
won the case for Sammy, Smith and friends would evaluate their position, identify Pete and me as liabilities, and presumably kill us.

I had a few things going for me. First, I was Sammy's lawyer. For the
time being, at least, Smith apparently needed me. Second, for a reason I
couldn't yet pinpoint, time was on my side. Smith demanded that the
case go to trial within the next three weeks, without additional continuances or delays, so it was a pressure point I could manipulate.

Third, they needed Pete, too, to serve as the leverage against me. They had no problem roughing him up to punch my buttons, but they couldn't kill him, not yet. Still, for the time being, secure as he might have been from a violent death, Pete was still a sitting duck for Smith's thugs. I had to get him out of Dodge. I had to hide him.

It was for the best, anyway, that Pete get lost for a while. I didn't want him around for what might come next. I wondered about that for a long time, as I sat on my bed, waiting for the sun to come up, fatigue sweeping over me like a heavy coat, my eyes losing focus but the churning of my stomach preventing any attempt at sleep: What was I capable of doing?

SAMMY SEEMED TIRED, more than usual, when I visited him the following morning. Rare was the inmate who looked well-rested, but Sammy, I assumed, had done a great deal of thinking about his sister since the discovery of the bodies behind Hardigan Elementary School. Nor did it help that he was less than three weeks from a murder trial that could put him in prison for the rest of his life.

Despite his obvious sleep deprivation, Sammy listened attentively as I laid out the entire story about Smith, and what had followed with Pete. He was alternatively concerned and puzzled, two traits I had in great quantities myself these days. "Pete," he mumbled. "Pete."

I was running short on time, and I'd hoped that Sammy knew more than he was letting on about Smith. I was disappointed.

"Man, I don't know that guy Smith," he said when I finished. "He shows up, offers me 'the best lawyer money can buy'—I figured the same as you, Koke. He was working for someone who that asshole hurt. Some victim. Y'know, sympathetic to what I was going through. Wanting to offer help. I mean, yeah, it was kinda weird that he didn't want to give me their names, but, y'know, under the circumstances—a lot of people like to stay anonymous when it comes to, y'know—"

He was right. Sex abuse victims don't advertise on billboards. That might be all it was with Smith. But it sure felt like more. "These guys are hiding something," I said. "Something they're afraid I'll find. Sammy, I think—" I gathered my thoughts a moment. "Sam, look—I never ask a client if he's guilty. I dance around it, because most of my clients are guilty, and if I know that, I can't put them on the stand to testify they didn't do it. Right?"

Sammy was listening intently. He nodded slowly.

"Right," I continued. "But I'm sitting here thinking, Smith is working for someone who killed Griffin Perlini. Maybe they feel for you, maybe they want you to beat the rap, but their main concern is that they don't want me out there trying to find new suspects, because they're afraid I'll find *them*."

Sammy didn't answer. He'd given me ample reason to think he killed Griffin Perlini, though he hadn't come out and said it. But he'd also been the one to mention that I should consider other victims of Perlini's crimes. *Look at other people he hurt*, he'd suggested, the first time we talked strategy.

"Should I be looking for Griffin Perlini's killer, Sammy?"

Sammy looked away, turned his head. He hadn't shaved for a while, and a thickening red beard was forming. "I don't get this stuff with Smith," he said. "Doing all that shit to Pete and all. But there's one guy, I think—a good guy, but I could see. . . ."

Was Sammy proclaiming his innocence?

"The name," I said, but I thought I already knew it. I just didn't want to be the one to say it first.

"Archie," he said. "Guy named Archie Novotny. His daughter—Jody—was one of the victims."

I hadn't told Sammy of my visit to Novotny. "Why him?" I asked.

Sammy shook his head slowly. "He took the thing with Jody real hard. And he seems like the kind of guy who might have it in him."

"He's close enough to matching the description," I noted.

"Oh, you've met him."

"I did, Sammy. And I managed a peek in his coat closet. Guess who owns a brown leather bomber jacket and a green stocking cap?"

"No shit? Wow." Sammy fell back in his chair, new animation. "You think Archie did it? For real?"

I felt an uneasy heat to my face, a weight on my shoulders. "Sammy," I confessed, "I thought *you* did it."

He showed a brief hint of a smile. I wasn't sure what to make of this.

"Novotny says he has an alibi," I said. "He says he was at a guitar lesson. I'm checking it out."

Sammy thought about that. "Maybe it's a cover. Yeah, shit." He looked at me. "But that don't explain Smith."

I agreed. "I suppose Novotny could be the guy using Smith. It's just hard to imagine. The guy's a laid-off painter for the electric utility. Where's he get the money to hire a guy like Smith, and a bunch of goons to scare the shit out of my brother?"

"Don't make sense."

It didn't make sense. But at least I was making progress. I had a more than plausible suspect in Archie Novotny. Now, I would need to find a way to punch some holes in the eyewitness testimony placing Sammy at the scene of the shooting. I'd left one message with each of the witnesses already. On my drive from the detention center, I called each of them again, leaving them my office, home, and cell phone numbers.

When I got to my office, I amended my witness list in Sammy's case to include Archie Novotny and put it on the fax machine to the prosecutor, Lester Mapp. I'd have preferred to spring the witness on Mapp, but judges take a dim view of such things, and maybe—just maybe—if I convinced Mapp that Novotny was the guy, he'd walk Sammy.

Next, I did an Internet search for hotels in nearby suburbs and booked a room for Pete in a town just outside the city boundaries. Now I'd just have to make sure Pete got there without anyone noticing. He needed to fly under the radar for the time being.

Joel Lightner called me on my cell phone and gave some information I'd requested. He had found J.D.—John Dixon, Pete's supplier who escaped arrest when Pete got pinched.

"You want me to put a tail on him?" he asked.

"Not just yet, Joel. Thanks. I'll let you know."

"I'm worried about you, kid. Play it smart."

I smiled. Lightner had a pretty good head on his shoulders. "Always," I told him. "Always."

31

SUNDAY PRACTICE at State is usually the easiest of the week—film of the previous day's game, then a brief, no-contact workout in sweats and helmets, no pads. But today will not be your finest day. They are on you, the seniors, the team captains, before you make it to your locker.

What's this disappearing act you pulled yesterday? Tony Karmeier, a massive offensive tackle and four-year starter, is breathing heavily into the side of your face. Apparently Tony—and by the looks of it, the rest of the team—didn't look kindly on you walking off the football field yesterday, after the referee ejected you, and driving home. *You want to forget that scholarship and go back to being a loser?*

You don't answer. You open your locker and remove your helmet. Your right hand is still sore from the number you did on Jack, your father, last night.

Give me a fucking answer, Kolarich.

I'm thinking, you say.

He shoves you, and when a six-six, three-hundred-fifty-pound lineman pushes you, you fly sideways, landing on the floor.

We're a team. We play as a team. We don't have any room for this superstar crap. Are you a team player or a superstar?

You slowly get up and recover your helmet, still spinning on the floor. You feel your internal reservoir refilling with the hot venom from last night, the assault on your father. It felt good, you have to admit, better than it should have. Your hand balls into a fist and releases. You look again at the team captain, Karmeier, a physical mountain, mean as a snake, and you realize how much you hate him, how much you hate all of them.

Don't ever try that again, you tell him.

Or what? Karmeier moves forward, held back by some of the others gathering around the spectacle. *No, he's a big boy. I think he's threatening me. Are you threatening me, Kolarich?*

Your fist closes and releases. Close and release. You want him to do it, you realize. You began to feel it last night, with Jack in the parking lot, and now the momentum builds into a free fall: You are letting yourself go backward. You're a loser. A pretender. You don't deserve all of this, a free ride at State, all the acclamation. You're never going to make it. You'll become like him.

Since the day you got here, you think it's all about you. I'm so tired of your tough-guy bullshit.

You feel a smile on your face. *Come here and say that,* you tell him.

Oh, you're gonna square off on me? he says, approaching you. *You wanna—*

It happens in an instant, a release so satisfying, one-two, a right and a left like lightning from your fists, the second punch producing a sickening crunch as this heap of a man crumbles to the floor. You are on fire, breathing heavily, watching him writhe on the floor in agony, his hands on his face. You part the spectators, shaking your left hand, wondering if you broke it, sure that you broke Tony Karmeier's jaw. You use your right hand to push open the locker room door, never to return.

I CALLED PETE before I left work and checked that he had packed his bag. When I got home, I drove my car into the garage and closed the garage door. Pete came out through the kitchen door with the clothes he'd brought from his house following the arrest—and some of my wardrobe as well—in a bag, which he threw in the trunk. Pete was wearing a leather jacket and a blue baseball cap.

We waited a few minutes before leaving, so the whole thing wouldn't look too strange, so no one would wonder why I pulled into the garage, closed the door, only to leave again right away. I backed out the car and drove away from my house. The tail, today a blue Chevy sedan, followed my car from a safe distance. We drove to the Supermax movie theater about a mile away and bought two tickets to a sequel about a wisecracking treasure hunter who seems to wear tuxedos a lot and, for a history nerd, shows tremendous composure under pressure.

Pete, in his leather jacket and blue baseball cap, bag slung over his shoulder, was silent as we walked toward the movie theater. We found Shauna Tasker where we said we'd meet, in the back row of the theater, so I could see anyone walking in.

"Hey there, fellas." Tasker was in her typical contrarian mood. More important, she was wearing a leather jacket and blue baseball cap, identical to Pete. I checked my watch. In ten minutes, a cab would be pulling up on the street behind the theater. From the exit on the right of the big screen, Pete could walk to the cab in about ten steps.

"You have your money?" I whispered to my brother, as I kept my eyes on every person who walked into the theater. Pete couldn't access an ATM machine without the possibility of someone inquiring. I'd taken out a couple thousand dollars in cash for him.

"I'm good," he said. "I'll pay you back." Pete was doing his best to wear a brave face. He'd been shaken up pretty bad by those guys in the alley. It was more humiliating than physically painful. He had a lot of worries right now.

"I know you will."

He nodded. The lights dimmed. Animated popcorn boxes and sodas told us to turn off our cell phones and keep quiet.

"When you're in the cab, you'll text me," I said. "You'll be fine, Pete."

"I'm worried about *you*, brother."

We looked at each other. I battled myself all over again, questioning myself, wondering if this was the right move. I was tempted to keep Pete close to me, but this felt like the better play. He'd be in an anonymous little suburban hotel, ordering room service for food and not showing his face much. It should work out.

"I gotta say this, Pete."

"No, you don't. I'm clean, Jase. I'll be fine."

I gripped his hand. Emotion strangled my throat.

"I better go." Pete squeezed my hand and got up. I watched him intently as he walked down the aisle and out the exit door.

"He'll be fine, Jason." This assurance from Shauna. "And you're covering my ticket, right?"

"Shut up." I opened my cell phone and waited for the text message. It arrived, not two minutes later. *I'm in. Can I put porn movies on your credit card?*

I laughed, a brief moment of levity. Then I said a silent prayer for the only real family member I had left in this world.

When the movie was over, Mother Nature helped out with a rain storm. I used the weather as an excuse to get the car and pull up in front of the theater for Shauna, playing the role of Pete. All she had to do was keep her head down and pop into the car with the bag he had brought. There was not much of a chance that our surveillance could have made a distinction between my brother and my law partner. The identical leather jacket and blue baseball cap would be more than enough, as long as she kept her head down.

"I'm starting to feel like James Bond," Shauna said. It was twice now she'd helped me fake out our tail, first lending me the car, now switching up with Pete and spending the night at my house.

We hung out in my living room for a while, though it was late and Shauna had an early day tomorrow. It felt like old times, back at State. After I was kicked off the football team for the misunderstanding I had with one of the team captains, I moved off-campus, into a five-bedroom house, which sounds nice until you factor in that eight of us lived there. Shauna was one of those people. We used to kill plenty of late nights, drinking the cheapest beer we could possibly find—how bad could it be if it was "Milwaukee's Best"?—listening to REM albums, debating whether *Automatic for the People* was an interesting diversion for the band or a complete sell-out, discussing the merits of the Reagan Revolution, listing celebrities we'd sleep with—anything and everything. Easier times.

In another sense, it felt odd, maybe wrong, having a woman in this house for an overnight stay, the slightest hint of sexual overtone even if it was just Shauna. This was Talia's house. It always would be.

Shauna stretched her arms over her head and yawned. The movement, however innocuous, brought back a memory from high school, the short interval when we were more than friends. Her eyes linked with mine and I blinked away, feeling like I'd been caught in the act of something forbidden but enjoying it nonetheless. It wouldn't last, it wouldn't make sense, not with Shauna, but it had felt more like a lifetime than four months since I'd experienced the sensation. I was still alive. I still could feel.

Shauna excused herself to bed, breaking the tension and leaving me to wonder whether it was mutual. But I had other things to consider at this moment.

I went to my own room and sat up on the bed, thinking things through. At midnight, I turned off the light. The darkness felt appropriate. I sat on my bed in the blackness, trying to focus a mind running wild. It was like trying to corral a bunch of roaches scattering from light. Outside the rain was rattling the window and drumming on the roof. I thought about where Pete was right now. I had to trust that he would be safe, because the alternative was unbearable.

When I was a prosecutor, I was assigned a badge, which I had to surrender upon my resignation from the county attorney's office. But about three years in, I'd lost my badge and had to get a new one. Law enforcement offices do not have a sense of humor about losing badges, their use in the wrong hands, naturally, being problematic. The office reserved the right to dock a week's pay upon the first loss of a badge and my supervisor, looking to make an example out of me, took full advantage of that punishment. It was about two months later that I found my original badge. The proper protocol, obviously, was to bring it in, but I didn't. I didn't precisely recall why, but it might have had something to do with losing that week's pay and figuring I'd earned the right to keep it. Shame on me, then. Good for me, now.

In the darkness of my bedroom, I pocketed the badge and my revolver. Shauna, at my request, had parked her car the block over for my use tonight. But I had a thought. I called an audible. I decided to use my own car. First, because I wanted to see what would happen, if my tail was pulling a round-the-clock shift. And second, because I didn't want it to be Shauna's car I was driving, should things go wrong.

I backed my car out of the garage, taking care to look both ways for not only pedestrians but surveillance. I continued to look forward and in the rearview as I slowly drove down the street. I didn't see any lights on any cars. For good measure, once I turned south onto the adjoining street, I pulled over, turned off the car, and killed the lights. I waited for five minutes. No one was following me. That meant something. There was a limit to Smith's resources.

I drove for forty-five minutes on mostly empty streets and the highway, as the rain pelted my windshield. Rain always made me feel lonely, despairing, but this early morning it seemed to heighten my sense of isolation, allowing me to focus.

The place was on the far west side, a neighborhood that seemed to be on the way up, based on the stores that were being built on the main arteries. It was an apartment building. That was all I knew. I parked near the building and went through the first door, open. To my left in the small threshold were six mailboxes with tiny buzzers above them. Five of the mailboxes had makeshift nameplates. One was empty. I figured the empty one was the one I wanted. But that didn't tell me which of the rooms inside this building was his.

And that didn't get me through the locked, automated door separating the entryway from the rest of the building.

I went back to my car and drove on, turning right and then making another quick turn down the alley. Behind the apartment building, six parking spaces had been drawn out diagonally. Five spaces were taken, one empty. I checked the license plates against the one I was looking for. The car wasn't there.

Good. I kept the car running but got out and checked the rear entrance to the building, which was covered by a beaten-up awning. The door was locked. Nearby, next to the closest parked car, there was an overfilled garbage Dumpster that, I decided, would be the best I could do.

I moved my car back to its original parking space, not far from the front entrance of the building. Then I jogged back around to the alley in back and considered my options with the garbage Dumpster. It was closer to the door than the cars, which helped, but there was about ten, fifteen feet to cover between the Dumpster and the door. Not ideal but I could give myself some help.

I looked through the Dumpster, not particularly excited about getting my hands dirty. I fished out a McDonald's bag and found some food. I removed an uneaten part of a cheeseburger and placed it right by the door, separating burger from bun to make it a messy scene. I sprinkled a few fries as well, to balance the meal.

Then I removed the small jar of Carmex I had brought. Rather than rub my finger over it for use on my lips, I dug into it with my hand and liberally applied it to the handle of the back door, feeling like a sculptor as I ensured that every last bit of the oily lotion covered that handle.

Then I waited. It was tempting to stand under the awning to stay dry, but that would expose me. So I hunched behind the garbage Dumpster, helpless from the rain, which found its way under my collar and completely soaked my hair. Oh, Talia, if you could see me now.

Counting on the fact that I'd hear a car coming, I listened as best I could through the rain. Every few minutes, I got up and stretched out to stay limber.

It happened a solid hour later, which is what I would have expected but couldn't know for certain. By the time I heard the tires crunching along the uneven pavement, the unhealthy engine spitting and sputtering, I was soaking wet and probably in the appropriate mood.

I reached into my jacket pocket and removed a ski mask, which was wet but not nearly as soaked as everything else I wore. I threw it on and listened as the car painfully turned into the lot, backed up, and pulled into the diagonal spot. I opened my cell phone and dialed the numbers, but did not push "send." The car door opened and I steeled myself, cell phone in hand. Footsteps, but he hadn't appeared yet. I heard the trunk pop open. A moment passed, as he presumably pulled up the board over the spare tire and removed the stash, but I couldn't hear any of it with the rain still going strong.

I hit "send" as he came into my line of vision, only a few feet from the front door, facing away from me. Then I hit "mute" on my cell phone.

"What the fuck," he said, as he saw the food lying right before the back door, abruptly halting a jog as he fled the rain. I heard his phone ring. He reached to his belt for the phone, unaware that the person calling him was ten feet to his left.

He looked at the face of the cell phone, presumably checking for caller ID. Then he opened the cell phone and said, "Yeah?" As he did so, continuing to speak into the phone—"Hello? Hel-*lo*?"—he spread out his left leg to try to move the food from his immediate path.

I had the oiled-up door handle for additional help but I didn't need it. This was the moment, while he was preoccupied and off-balance with his leg out and one hand holding a phone to his ear.

The white noise of the rain rattling off the pavement helped mute my sprint. I closed the distance before he became aware of me. I treated him like a defensive back on a crack-back, though I wasn't worried about being flagged for an illegal block.

He was a lightweight, and he didn't see me coming. He flew off his feet into the brick wall on the other side of the door, his cell phone flying, his head smacking hard against the bricks with a sickening sound. The thought flashed through my mind, I had hit him too hard, but the noise escaping his throat, a combination of shock and pain, told me he was in sufficient condition.

By the time he knew which way was up, I had pulled my revolver and introduced it to his nose, as my other hand gripped his hair.

"I've been looking for you, J.D.," I said.

32

JOHN DIXON took a minute to respond. His head had met the brick wall hard. His right upper cheek was scraped, and his ear was bloody. The angle at which he had landed placed him beyond the awning's protection, so that the rain was attacking his face. I thought it added a little something to the overall atmosphere, and my clothes were already stuck to my body, so what did I mind?

He blinked his eyes rapidly, fighting rain and probably a concussion. Presumably nausea, too, and the last posture you want when you're going to vomit is lying flat on your back with someone sitting on your chest and pinning your arms down with his knees.

All things considered, the hour of three A.M. was not shaping up to be J.D.'s finest of this virgin day.

"Just take—take it already," he managed. He couldn't really focus on me, looking straight into a downpour as he was, and he was probably schooled enough to know not to spend too much time staring at the face of his attacker, not when that attacker was armed. In my time as a prosecutor, I found that many victims made a point of avoiding the eyes of their attackers, not wanting to be able to identify them, hoping that it would make them less of a threat to the assailant and increasing their chances of survival.

I got as close to his face as circumstances allowed, adding some body weight to the force of the revolver pressing into his nose. "I don't want your fucking dope, J.D."

"The fuck did you find me?"

That had been surprisingly easy. I figured that a drug dealer who's already had to leave his day job wouldn't stop his late-night occupation, no matter how well he was being paid to lay low. He'd want the cash and he wouldn't want his customers to find new suppliers in his absence. So I figured he'd be using that cell phone of his, the number to which I got from Pete. Then it was a small matter of having my high-tech private investigator, Joel Lightner, "ping" the cell phone, triangulating the signals sent off by the phone while in use, to pinpoint a location.

But I didn't feel the need to share this with Mr. Dixon. Better I remained something of a mystery to him. Instead, I emphasized the gun, jammed into his nostril. "I'm supposed to kill you," I said. "But I'm having second thoughts."

"Why you—why you gonna kill me?" he pleaded. "Why you gonna do *that*?" The downpour made it hard for him to talk, spurting out words as rain assaulted his mouth. Breathing was no small chore, either. This was like a cheap imitation of waterboarding. I'd have to remember to vote Republican next time.

"You think he's gonna let you live?" I said. "You're a witness, asshole. You're a liability."

"Man, I don't know nothin', man." He shook his head furiously, side to side, as best he could with my tight grip on his hair. "Don't even know the guy's *name*."

I didn't know who he was talking about. I was bluffing.

"Tell me everything you *do* know," I said evenly. "Fast, J.D."

"Man, the guy says—guy says deliver the kid to Mace."

"Yeah? What's in it for you?"

J.D. seemed reluctant to answer. Gentle encouragement was in order, and J.D. already had a gash on the right cheek, so a little symmetry seemed appropriate, courtesy of the butt of my revolver. He let out a noise that was drowned out by the rain. "That's me being nice, J.D.," I said. "What was in it for you?"

He took some time to recover. It's hard to take a blow when you can't move your head or arms to absorb the impact. Finally, he said, "They let me *live. That's* what was in it for me."

"Threw you some, too?"

"Maybe. A dime, a dime," he elaborated, when I raised my gun again. "They gave me ten thousand and told me, they won't come back. I just had to deliver the kid, is all."

"What kid?" Here I showed how clever I am, pretending not to know of Pete, thus hopefully concealing my identity should J.D. get around to pondering such things later.

"Pete."

"Pete who?"

He coughed out a mouthful of rain. "Pete Kolarich," he said. "Okay?"

I considered popping him one, but it didn't seem like a good idea to leave this guy's face in a pulp. J.D. seemed on board with that sentiment and, instead of trying my patience, kept going. "That's all I know, man. They said take him to Mace. Be ready to run."

Right. They knew Pete would get picked up by the police—that was the whole point—but they didn't want J.D. on an arrest report.

"Tell me about the cop," I said, again bluffing.

"The cop?" He moaned as his eyes filled with rainwater. "What cop? Man, I got out before the cops."

My gut said he was telling the truth. That didn't mean that Detective DePrizio was clean, only that if the detective was in on this thing, J.D. hadn't been informed.

"So who made you do this, J.D.? Describe them."

"Four white guys, is all. Four big, bad-ass white dudes. Same as you, man, they jumped me like that."

Not Smith. But that made sense. Someone else would handle the wet work, not Smith. I assumed these four thugs were the same ones who jumped Pete in the alley.

"Where's Mace?" I asked. The way J.D. was telling it, he might not have known Mace at all before this encounter. But I said it like I knew otherwise.

"Man, you want no part a that dude."

"Oh, but I do." I reminded him of the gun in his nostril.

"Guy's Tenth Street. C'mon now, man."

"His full name, J.D."

He seemed to be thinking about it. It could be, he was weighing some options, too. But I thought he was really trying to come up with the name.

"Mason's the last name," he finally answered. "I think Marcus?"

Marcus Mason. Finally, I had the name of Mace.

"Man, why they wanna kill me? I did like they said."

I shook my head. "They wanted me to test you, to see if you'd break," I said. "If you did, I was supposed to kill you."

"Oh, now, listen—"

"*You* listen, shithead. I'm not going to waste a bullet on your ass. I'll tell 'em you held up under questioning. And you—you pretend this never happened."

"Never happened," he readily agreed.

"If I were you," I told him, "I'd sit tight like they said. You run, J.D., they'll wonder why. And you know I'll find you." I let go of his hair. The rain had subsided to a light shower, but too late for John Dixon. His clothes were plastered against his body. He had twin bruises on his cheeks and a bloody ear.

"Businessman can't run no business no more," he complained, sitting up, wincing, taking inventory of the damage.

"Yeah, what's the world coming to?" I stuffed the gun in the back of my pants. "Get out of the business," I suggested. "Stick to the mail room job." I nodded to him, started to walk away, then turned back and kicked him hard in the ribs. That was for Pete. J.D. had gotten off light, all things considered. It remained to be seen how Marcus Mason would fare.

33

I LEFT THE HOUSE Wednesday morning alone. A Chrysler sedan followed me from a comfortable length. After I left, Shauna Tasker, who had spent the night at my place, left out the back door and walked to her car, parked on the street over. She'd known that I might be taking a spin with her car last night, but I told her I hadn't, after all, without elaborating. She probably knew I'd gone somewhere last night, but she didn't ask, and I didn't tell.

What did I have to show for last night, other than a cold? At least I had locked down that Smith hadn't been bluffing—he'd been behind Pete's arrest. It had gone down like I would have expected. They put a little scare into J.D. and stuffed some money in his pocket, and he made sure that when Pete came to find him to buy some powder, he'd be in the company of Mr. Marcus Mason.

Smith had money, and he had, at least, a small gang of people. Four white guys, J.D. had said. Probably the same four guys who had jumped Pete. Probably the same four guys who, as a team, were keeping tabs on me.

I caught myself nodding off at a stoplight. I hadn't slept in two days. I'd been relying on anxiety to prop me up. My vision was spotty and my hands were shaky. I asked myself for the umpteenth time whether I could handle what I was doing. But I kept coming back to two things: one, I had no choice, I had to represent Sammy; and two, I still had a generally over-confident opinion of my courtroom skills. A good trial lawyer thinks he can convince a jury that day is actually night, that up is really down. A good defense attorney adds in a general ability to confuse a situation, to smear the canvas, because he only has to get reasonable doubt.

I decided to place a call to Joel Lightner to keep me alert. I was probably the first driver in history to talk on a cell phone to improve his driving. "Our friend 'Mace' is Marcus Mason," I told Joel. "He's Tenth Street."

"Huh." Lightner gave off a disapproving grunt. The Tenth Street Crew was a pretty rough bunch, even by gang standards. They were particularly sensitive about loose tongues.

"Give me a location on this gentleman," I requested.

Lightner went quiet.

"Hello?" I asked.

"How 'bout I talk to this guy?" Lightner said.

"No, I'm good. Address and record would be fine." Marcus Mason wouldn't be hard to find. He probably had a sheet as long as the Magna Carta. "You find anything on that apartment where J.D. is staying?" I asked, in part to change the subject.

"Nothing much," Joel said. "He paid cash for one month."

"*He* paid?"

"Yeah, sorry."

Too bad. I guess I couldn't expect that Smith would write this landlord a personal check. These guys seemed relatively apt at covering their tracks.

"What about Archie Novotny?" I asked.

"We're watching him. Nothing interesting so far. He works at Home Depot and it looks like he's doing work on his house. Doing it himself. I don't know how to connect him to Smith, Jason. Because I don't know who the hell Smith is."

"Sure."

"I don't see anything in Novotny's background, at least so far, that suggests mob involvement or anything like that. This guy's an unemployed union painter who sits home at night and either watches TV or plays his guitar. He owns a small house and an old Chevy, and he doesn't have much money in the bank."

"Okay, well, keep at it." I had trouble picturing it, too. It was hard to see Archie Novotny connected to Smith and company.

When I got to my office, I made my third phone call to the prosecution's eyewitnesses on the night of Perlini's murder—the elderly couple who ID'd Sammy running past them on the sidewalk, and Perlini's neighbor. These people were stiff-arming me, a common problem for defense attorneys. You refuse to talk to a prosecutor, it's obstruction of justice. You refuse to talk to a defense lawyer, nobody cares.

Don't worry about the witnesses, Smith had instructed me. But I wasn't going to take his word for anything. I needed to visit them. I just had to make sure Smith didn't know I was doing it.

Marie buzzed me and told me that while I was on the phone, I'd received a call from Detective Vic Carruthers, who had investigated Audrey's murder back in the day. Initially, I'd hoped to prove that Perlini killed Audrey and then find some way to get that evidence before the jury, for no other reason than to make the jury hate the victim. But now I had another suspect—Archie Novotny—whose motive would be based on Perlini's molestation of Novotny's daughter. Now, the jury would know what kind of a guy Griffin Perlini was without my having to prove anything about Audrey. Besides, once I pointed the finger at Novotny, based on Perlini's molestation of his daughter, the prosecution would probably feel compelled to introduce evidence about Audrey to show *Sammy's* motive. With any luck, the jury would hear all kinds of ugly things about Griffin Perlini and decide that nobody should go to prison for his murder.

Maybe Carruthers was calling for his file back. I hadn't had much of a chance to look through it, and now I probably wouldn't need it at all.

"Detective, it's Jason Kolarich."

"Yeah, Jason. Thought I owed you an update."

"I appreciate that."

"I wish I had more to tell you. There wasn't much of anything in the graves. I'd hoped that Perlini left a memento, some souvenir or something, but he didn't. The girls were buried naked, so I can't even look back at clothing to match it up with something we know Audrey used to wear—if we could even do that."

"Bottom line," I summarized, "we have to wait for DNA testing."

"Yeah. I'm on these guys to put a move on it, but you know how these things go. It could be months before we have an answer. So your guy

Sammy, he'll have to put off his trial for, I don't know, maybe another year."

That was obviously out of the question, but I didn't care so much anymore. And Sammy had waited twenty-seven years for definitive proof that Perlini had murdered Audrey. He could wait one more.

"Only thing I can tell you," Carruthers added, "is we have a preliminary take on the age of these girls. They're all about the age of Audrey at the time. We can't be precise, you understand."

I grew up thinking that I couldn't fathom how difficult it must have been for Sammy's parents to lose a child in such a violent way. I had a new perspective now. The imagery produced by this conversation, which I struggled to stifle, was not of Audrey but of my daughter, Emily, strapped in her car seat, struggling for air underwater.

I stared at the motion I had drafted in Sammy's case—the motion for expedited DNA testing of the bodies discovered behind the grade school or, in the alternative, a continuance of the trial until DNA testing could be completed. I didn't need this anymore. I could use Archie Novotny's motive to tell the jury that Griffin Perlini was a pedophile. But filing this motion would certainly provoke Smith. Should I do it? It made me think of my brother. I dialed him on the cell phone.

"Bored as hell," he said.

"Bored is good. I like bored." I missed bored.

"How's it coming?"

"Working on it," I said. "Getting there."

I hung up and reviewed the motion. It was ready to go.

"Marie," I said into the intercom, "let's file this motion in *Cutler* today."

I'd be getting Smith's attention very soon.

34

LESTER MAPP'S OFFICE was on the sixth floor, above most of the courtrooms in the newly refurbished courthouse. He was given one of the plum, cushy spaces, by which I mean that he had walls and even a door. The place hadn't really changed since I'd left—torn-up carpets, cheap artwork, drab paint, low-grade furniture.

He swiveled around in his chair and nodded to me. He had an earpiece that must have corresponded to a cell phone. He waved me to a chair.

"Sure thing," he said, but his attention had turned to me. He was appraising his adversary and, I assumed, was probably feeling good about where things stood. It only took a glance in the mirror this morning to see the purple bags under my hazy eyes.

"Sure thing. We'll follow up. I've got someone here." Mapp reached to his waist, presumably killing his cell phone. "Jason Kolarich," he said, in a tone that suggested parental disapproval. "You've been the busy bee."

I didn't answer. Condescension is not high on my list of quality attributes. I'd prefer that he just call me an asshole.

"Archie—Archie . . ." He fished around his desk, which looked like a model of cleanliness and order compared to mine. "Archie Novotny," he said, seizing on the document I had faxed him. "Archie Novotny is the man who killed Griffin Perlini!"

He still hadn't asked me a question. I settled into my seat and looked around his office.

"Judge won't let that in," he informed me. "A back door to get in Perlini's pedophilia? C'mon, Counsel."

I forced a smile, the kind I reserve for people whose teeth I'd like to kick in.

"No, you can forget about that," he went on. "But listen, Counsel. With the headlines about Perlini and all—I've got a little room here. This was obviously a premeditated act with the equivalent of a confession, a store vid that puts him at the scene, I mean—"

"Lester," I interrupted. "Did you bring me here to tell me how shitty my case is? Or to offer me a deal?"

He watched me for a moment, then broke into a patented smile. This guy was like silk. "Murder two, twenty years. A gift. You go tell your friends you played me like a fiddle."

The way he presented it, you'd think balloons and streamers were about to fall from the ceiling. "Involuntary," I countered. "Time served." Involuntary manslaughter is the only murder charge that gives the judge the discretion to drop the sentence down to no prison time at all or, in the case of Sammy, who'd already spent almost a year inside, to time served.

"Time served. Time served." Mapp chuckled. He let a hand play out in the air, as if conducting a silent orchestra. "I could think about voluntary. I *might* be able to give you fifteen. Christmas comes early for Sammy Cutler."

I could see that the discovery of the bodies behind the elementary school—and the subsequent headlines—had had the intended effect. The county attorney's office was not thrilled to be coming down hard on a man who avenged his sister's murder. They couldn't give him a pass, nor condone vigilantism, but they wanted a quiet resolution where they didn't play the heavy.

"Let me give that some serious thought, Lester." I looked up at the ceiling. "Involuntary, time served."

The prosecutor's smile went away, but not without a fight. "Jury isn't going to know that Perlini was a pedophile," he said. "Or what he *allegedly* did to Cutler's sister."

"You're starting to sound like a defense attorney, Lester." The prosecutor was referring to the judge's pretrial ruling, excluding evidence of Perlini's criminal sexual history. If Sammy would have agreed to plead diminished capacity, this would be a no-brainer. But with Sammy saying he didn't do it, the victim's criminal past was irrelevant.

Then again, I wasn't so sure Sammy *did* kill Perlini. I was beginning to like Archie Novotny.

"Involuntary and three," I said. If Sammy could play nice and get a day for a day, and with credit for time served, he'd have about six more months inside. He could do that, I thought. Another variable was Smith. This would certainly satisfy his need for an expedited resolution, and I wouldn't be turning over any rocks he wanted to stay covered.

Mapp made a whole show of rolling his neck, moaning, warming himself up to a grandiose display of generosity on this, Sammy's early Christmas. The only thing missing from his car-salesman act was telling me that "they've never done this before," but that he "liked me."

What's it gonna take to put you in a plea bargain today?

"I'd have to go upstairs on this one," he began. "Voluntary and twelve. If I could even sell that for a premeditated murder—"

"With the equivalent of a confession, right?" I poised my hands on the arms of my chair, elbows out, ready to get up and go.

"Now, you're *not* going to tell me you won't take that one back," he said. "Twelve years?"

"You don't have twelve years, Lester. You said you'd have to take it upstairs."

He watched me again. He thought he was intimidating me with that direct stare. A lot of prosecutors think that. I probably did, too.

I pushed myself out of the chair. "Next time bring roses," I said.

My adversary switched tacks, bursting into a premeditated laugh and wagging his finger at me. "Kolarich, Kolarich, Kolarich. 'Next time bring roses.' That's good, that's good. Listen, Counsel. See about that twelve years, and I will, too. Maybe—maybe even think about ten."

Interesting. If I had ten years on the table now, I could probably knock it down to eight, maybe even six or seven if the judge would help me out, and that wasn't such a bad deal. I still wanted to know more about my case, but I had the prosecutor moving in the right direction. It wasn't much, but compared to the rest of the last week or so, things were looking up.

35

I NEVER LIKED POLICE STATIONS, even when I was a prosecutor. It reminded me of a fraternity house, only the members of this particular fraternity had sidearms and batons and the authority to search, seize, detain, and arrest. I never really had much time for the individual cops, either, only that was probably due more to the disdain I had for them growing up than anything else. Aside from the few cops that were outright wrong—on the take, corrupt—there were plenty of corner-cutters in the bunch, guys and gals who were sure the ends justified the means, who remembered a knock-and-announce that never was, who kicked the drugs into plain view after finding them under the mattress, who had an extremely generous interpretation of a voluntary confession. But then again, I didn't have to go through a door not knowing what was awaiting me. I didn't have to pat down a suspect, wondering whether there was a needle in his pocket infected with the AIDS virus. I didn't have to wonder, every shift, whether this was going to be the day. And I didn't have a healthy sector of the populace that resented me without understanding all the shit I had to put up with.

In the end, I played the whole thing to a draw. Cops were like any other group of people—some were okay, others weren't. On which side did Detective Denny DePrizio fall?

I leaned against my car, playing over my conversation with Lester Mapp earlier today, watching plainclothes and uniforms march in and out of the stationhouse as dusk settled over the city. A few of the cops had arrestees, the lot of whom submitted quietly save for a homeless guy, who was calling them "traitors" and mentioning, I'm pretty sure, Herbert Hoover, though my money said he meant J. Edgar.

I saw DePrizio pop out of his sedan as the sun was falling behind him. A partner, another white guy, got out of the passenger seat and said something to DePrizio that made him laugh. All in all, he seemed like a pretty affable guy for a cop, but in my mind that just made it less likely he was trustworthy. I prefer assholes. At least they tell you what they think.

I somehow caught DePrizio's eye, probably an eye well-trained to spot, in his peripheral vision, someone standing and staring at him. He did a double-take, then stopped, pointed at himself, and raised his eyebrows. I nodded. So did he. So now we had both nodded. I guess that meant that I had to come to him, which was probably the proper hierarchical order of things, but that didn't mean I liked it.

DePrizio cast off his partner and took a few steps toward me. "Counsel," he said, more of a question. I wasn't sure if he was having trouble placing me or just wanted me to think so.

"Jason Kolarich," I said, slowly extending my hand, because you always avoid quick movements with cops. "Representing Pete Kolarich."

"Kolarich." Again, take your pick—tapping the memory bank or pretending.

"Clean-cut white boy," I said. "Steady employment, no priors except petty possession who suddenly transformed himself into a major drug kingpin and gunrunner."

"Oh, the one who's innocent." He snapped his fingers.

I didn't smile. Neither did he. Denny DePrizio, in his white dress shirt open at the collar, brown sport coat and jeans, a youthful face and a full head of sandy hair, could have played the lead on a television show about cops. His eyes, dark and deep-set, were the only feature that suggested his age.

"You got something for me? I'm freezing out here."

I followed him into the station, which was in the midst of rush hour on the ground floor. Upstairs, the detective's squad room was more sedate, witnesses speaking softly to detectives, others typing on old computers, the smell of burned coffee and cheap cologne hanging heavily.

I pulled up a chair to his desk, and he planted himself behind it. "You want coffee or anything?"

I shook my head. "You had a web that night," I said. "Your CI snared someone and my brother was in the wrong place, wrong time."

He seemed amused. "That a fact?"

"Yeah. The guy you wanted got away, by the way. If you had audio, you already know that. If anyone was running guns and buying in bulk, it was that guy. My brother, he was just looking for a score—some powder. It was his bad luck that his supplier was into something ambitious just at that moment."

"The whole thing was a coincidence. A misunderstanding." DePrizio made a show of looking around his desk. "I think I've got a hankie here somewhere."

"Yeah? Well, I've got a half-dozen witnesses who'll say they were out with Pete, he left to go pick up some blow, and he never came back. I mean, come on, Detective. You know who your CI was bringing in, right? It wasn't my brother."

DePrizio leaned into me. "This CI—this guy must be the single most confidential 'confidential informant' I've ever had. Because even *I* didn't know about him."

He was denying that Marcus Mason—"Mace"—was his CI. "Then help me out," I said, playing along.

He fell back in his chair and studied me. "You think if this was a spiderweb, someone would've gotten away? What am I, a rookie?"

I didn't have an answer. I waited him out.

"I used to work the warehouse district, back when it was only warehouses," he said. "Drugs and whores, right? Maybe I got to know a tavern owner or two. So I'm over at Poppy's enjoying a couple refreshments with some pals. I walk out a little past, maybe half-past midnight, give or take. I see some asshole meandering around that building, used to be the old Lanier's Amusement Supply place. Abandoned now, like a lotta stuff around there. Getting ready for the wrecking ball, word is. So this loser, anyway, he doesn't look like the Avon lady, right? I mean, I worked patrol there and I did a stint in narcotics. I know these fleabags. I fucking *know* 'em."

I nodded. He was saying he spotted J.D. heading toward the entrance to the warehouse, where he was to meet Mace—Marcus Mason.

"So I called it in," DePrizio continued. "Possible 401 in progress, request assistance. Then I see your boy, driving right up to the damn place—and he pops in. So I'm a curious guy, right? I go take a peek." He shook his head. "Problem is, one of 'em looked like they got spooked—rattled. I had to go in and freeze it. So I did." He waved a hand. "Maybe five minutes later, a patrol has my back. So yeah, one asshole got away, two assholes got collared."

"What happened to the other guy you collared?" I asked, referring to Marcus Mason without letting on that I knew anything about him. "He wasn't in lockup."

A look of recognition crossed DePrizio's face. "Oh, so *that's* why you're thinking he was my CI. No, this guy was one of the Tenth Street Crew. And we already had a few of those in lockup that night. We didn't need to turn that jail cell into a reunion."

That was true. One of the T-Streeters, Cameron, watched over Pete that night.

"Plus, I figured, I put your preppy little brother in with that guy—well, he'd see your brother as a witness against him. Might not have been such a fun night for your boy. I sent the T-Streeter over to the one-five"—the neighboring precinct—"to cool his jets. You should thank me, Counselor."

I didn't thank him. I was watching him, looking for a crack in the armor. I was alternatively enraged and despairing. The detective's story was entirely believable. I struggled for a minute, not hiding my distress, dropping my shoulders, blowing out air, shaking my head.

Then I took another look at Detective Denny DePrizio, who was observing me with some interest. So much of this was going with your gut, trusting your instincts. I had a plan. It was the whole reason I'd made this trip today, but still I found myself second-guessing it. I thought again about the story DePrizio had laid out, sized him up, and made a decision that I hoped I wouldn't regret.

I decided to test DePrizio.

"I think my brother was set up," I told him.

36

DEPRIZIO WATCHED ME closely as I laid out my story—the part, at least, I was willing to share with him. When I was done, he shook his head slowly. "You're telling me there's a guy who's extorting you. He wants you to perform a legal service for him, but you don't want to do it."

"Correct."

"So this guy, he set your brother up for this bust. If you don't do what he wants, your brother goes to jail."

"Right again."

"But you don't know this guy's name."

"I don't."

"All you can tell me is he's five-ten, maybe two hundred, graying hair, maybe fifty, fifty-five. Which describes about two or three million people in this city."

"Best I can do."

"What's the nature of this legal service the mystery man wants you to perform?"

"I can't say," I told him. "Attorney-client privilege."

DePrizio was silent a moment, like he was awaiting a punch line, before letting out a small burst that was akin to a laugh. "And you expect me to believe all of this."

"Actually, I don't. But I'm hoping you'll keep an open mind."

DePrizio moaned, seemingly conflicted between openly rejecting a far-fetched story and showing me some courtesy. *Seemingly,* I say, because the more he played along with me, the clearer it became that Detective Denny DePrizio was full of shit. He was Smith's partner, part of the entire plan to frame my brother, and I had to tread carefully here.

Luckily, nobody was fuller of shit than me, so I kept going. "I can stand in your shoes, Detective. People lie to you every day. You get so you don't believe anything. But I figure you for a guy who still cares about the job. I mean, how many cops would check out that warehouse when they're off-duty past midnight, when they've got a couple of pops in them, when they're on shift the next morning—how many would say fuck it and walk away? But you didn't. The job still matters to you."

It was hard to say this with a straight face, but I thought I sold it. DePrizio studied me, and slowly nodded. "You sure know how to sweet-talk a fella."

I opened my hands. "This guy has me boxed in. I don't have the resources to take on this guy. I don't have private investigators or even associates to help me. I just need to know who this guy is."

That point was an important one. I needed to show him that I wasn't a threat to him or Smith.

The detective made a big show of doubt, rubbing his face, shaking the head, an Oscar-worthy performance. What he was really doing was thinking hard about this unexpected development. He'd performed a task for Smith and probably thought his job was done. *What now?* he was wondering. *Do I tell this lawyer to take a hike, or do I use him?*

My guess, he'd come to the conclusion, very quickly, that he and Smith would benefit if I took him into my confidence. Keep your enemies closer, and all that.

"Look," he said, "I'm not saying I believe you, Kolarich. Right? But even if I did, what could I do?"

Well done. Inching closer to me, but feigning reluctance.

I needed to reel him all the way in.

"I don't know." I shrugged my shoulders. "Like you said, three million people fit his description. It's not like I have a picture of him." I tapped my hand on the desk. "Forget it. You're probably the wrong guy to ask, anyway. You're the arresting officer. I can't ask you to work against your own case. I'll find some other cop—"

He raised a hand. The mention of *some other cop* was my ace. The last thing DePrizio and Smith wanted was for me to start sobbing to another cop about all of this.

"No," he said. "It's my case. If there's something wrong with it, it's my problem."

I got out of my chair. "I appreciate that. If I think of anything, maybe I'll—I don't know."

"Well, hang on here," he said. "I'm not saying there's anything to this. But you seem like a pretty straight-up guy here, Mr. Kolarich. If I can help you find this guy, maybe I'll see what it's all about. Maybe it affects your brother's case, maybe not. But I'll listen."

Good. I'd reeled him in. It's always more fun when the person you're playing thinks he's playing you.

"Well, there might be one thing," I said, "but we'd have to be discreet."

37

"TEN YEARS. TEN YEARS." Sammy Cutler played the idea over in his head. "Out in five, hopefully. Already got one in. So—four more."

"I can get you better," I said. "They don't want the publicity, now that Griffin Perlini's notorious. It puts the county attorney in an uncomfortable spot, having to prosecute his killer, especially when that guy was avenging his sister's death."

Sammy nodded along.

"Allegedly," I added.

"Well, I ain't doing four more here."

"I can get you a better deal. But we'd be dumb to rule it out entirely, Sam."

He wasn't inclined to fight me. "What about Archie Novotny?"

"Haven't checked out his alibi yet for the night of the murder—the guitar lesson. I will. Meantime, we've been looking all over him and not finding much of anything."

"Right." Sammy fiddled with the smoldering cigarette between his fingers. "Been thinking more 'bout that. I could see it. I could see Archie doing this."

I couldn't decide if this was an innocent man talking, or a man trying to see things through the eyes of a jury. I was also beginning to doubt my perception. I was bone tired. I'd managed about four hours last night, but the previous forty-eight hours of sleep deprivation were taking their toll. Sometimes a few hours' sleep is worse than none.

"Novotny fits your general description," I said. "Put the green stocking cap on him so you can't account for the difference in hair color—he's got about the same build. He could work. I could sell that to a jury, I think. But that's not the problem, Sam. You know what the problem is?"

He nodded. "My car."

He was right. Before I ask questions of a client, I like to give him the lay of the land, so he's clear on what the prosecution knows and what they don't know. It's always nice to demonstrate the wiggle room before giving the client the chance to wiggle.

I started with the obvious. "The convenience store down the street—its security camera is posted in the back corner of the store and points toward the register. It also happens to catch a little bit outside the store. Your car is parked right outside the store, just enough so the camera can catch the back end of your car—and the license plate. The vid is clear on it being your license plate, so we're stuck with that, right?"

He nodded.

"It doesn't capture who got into the car because that part of the car is out of the camera's range. So it's your car, Sammy, but they can't say who drove it there or who drove it away."

"Well, yeah, but . . ."

I was giving him the wiggle room here, but he seemed content to sit still.

"It was me," said Sammy.

I deflated. "Then we have some 'splainin' to do. That's a pretty big coincidence."

"Not really."

"Why not really?"

"They got that one store video? From that night? That's it?"

"Correct." I didn't get where this was going. "Just the one."

Sammy stubbed out his cigarette and blew out the remnants of smoke. He didn't look well. The sleep deprivation didn't help, but it was more than that. He had a heavy drinker's complexion, a smoker's wrinkles, a natural frown. He'd lived hard.

"About a week before he died," said Sammy, "I saw him. I saw the fuckin' guy."

"You saw Perlini—"

"I was in the grocery store where he worked, at the checkout, and some manager or something starts calling out for 'Griffin.' I tell ya, Koke, I heard that name and I—I just froze. We were kids and all, but man, I knew it was him, soon as I laid eyes on him. Soon as I fuckin' laid eyes on him." He lit up another cigarette silently before continuing. "So I waited 'til his shift ended and I followed the guy. I followed him to those apartments. I knew where he lived. And I tell ya, I thought about it every night. Every night for a week, I drove over by his place and I thought about Audrey, and what he did to her, and I wondered if I had the stones to do it—to kill that scumbag."

Sammy's story would not be found in the *Guinness Book of World Records* under "all-time greatest alibis." *I was there, contemplating murdering Perlini, when someone else did it.* And it was a hell of a coincidence. The week Sammy sees Griffin Perlini in a grocery store and begins to stalk him is the same week that Perlini takes a bullet between the eyes?

"So that night," I said, "you drove over there and thought about killing him?"

"Yeah."

"Did you get out of your car?"

He shook his head, no.

"If you did, Sammy—if you liked to walk while you think, instead of sitting in the car—it might explain why those eyewitnesses saw you. Like, you were standing somewhere around the building, you heard a gunshot, you started running, and that's when that nice elderly couple saw you. We'd have some kind of explanation—not the greatest one, but—"

"No, not the greatest one. I'd have to explain why I was hanging out, doing my thinking, right by his damn building. No, I was in the car the whole time. Camera can't say different."

Sammy had had a long time to think about this. This was his story and, apparently, he was sticking with it.

"Huge coincidence," I said.

He shrugged. "Life is full of 'em, right?"

Wrong. But we didn't have much to play with here. They had his damn car on video, parking at 8:34 P.M. and leaving at 9:08 P.M.—which happened to be the precise window of time in which Griffin Perlini was murdered.

My good friend Smith had suggested that we tag-team on an explanation for Sammy that night. I thought Sammy might be willing to go along with something, if we could drum something up, but how do you explain why you drove across town, parked there for only half an hour—the precise half hour in which the murder happened—and left?

But I let it go for now. If Smith and I could come up with a better alibi—and dollars to doughnuts said Smith was working on it—I could always try it out on Sammy.

As I was heading back to my car, my cell phone rang. The caller ID was blocked.

"Mr. Kolarich, it's Jim Stewart."

"Thanks for getting back," I said. His parents must have been awfully big fans of the actor, because, I mean, come on, you give a kid a name like that, he's gotta deal with the comments his entire life, the crappy impressions—*Ah, ah, say, now, ah, ah*—and Christmastime must have been hell with that damn movie playing every other minute.

"Your message mentioned Lightner? You work with Joel?"

"Yeah, he gave me your name. Said you were stand-up."

He laughed. "He probably said I was a good-for-nothin' drunk."

"That came up, too."

"Right, right. Anyway," he said, "sounds like we should meet?"

I looked up and down the street for my tail, which at the moment I couldn't see.

"You got some time for me this afternoon?" I asked.

"HONEY, I'M HOME!" I call out, something out of a '50s sitcom, a standing joke with my wife. It's a not-so-hectic week for me at the office. They don't come often so I try to make them count.

"Daddy!" Emily hears the door. She comes bounding down the stairs as I open my arms.

"Hey, princess!" I say, in that soothing voice I reserve for my daughter. We go through the usual routine, kisses, tickling, gleeful squealing. As

Emily and I climb the stairs, I hold Emily upside down to her nonprotesting protest.

I find Talia in the bedroom, just having walked out of the master bath, wiping at her eyes. She smiles at me but there's something besides innocuous happiness to her look.

"Hey, babe." I set down Emily and fix on my wife. There is something equivocal in her expression, not necessarily good or bad, but important. My eyes find their way to the bed, to an open box, a thin strip of paper next to it, a set of folded instructions.

"Oh." My eyes shoot back to meet hers. We've talked about it in a serious but casual way, serious in that she knew I meant it, casual in that we hadn't been formally trying.

"Is it—are you—?" I move around the bed and take her hands in mine. "We're gonna have a—?"

My forehead touches hers, an instant connection of body heat. She can no longer restrain her emotions. "This is what you want, right?" she whispers.

I wrap my arms around her. "Of course this is what I want, babe. *Of course* it is." I turn to Emily, who seems to understand that she is being left out of a secret. "C'mere, sweetheart," I say. I crouch down and lift my daughter into the air. "How'd you like a baby brother or sister, Em?"

I LEFT THE cemetery a little after one, a surge of bitterness gripping me, the mixing of anger with the ubiquitous anguish. I resented Talia. I wanted to close the book on what happened. I wanted to pretend that I'd never met her, we'd never had Emily. But the book, I knew, would never close. I'd just flip back to the beginning, or the middle, when I reached the end.

I wanted to understand it. I really did. I wanted to believe that there was a God, and He had a plan, and this was all a good thing in some way, but there was no way that a beautiful young woman and our precious, innocent child dying violent deaths could possibly be for the greater good.

The sky was debating another rainfall, and the temperatures had fallen. Midwestern October always does this, flip-flopping between extended

summer and early winter, occasionally giving us the autumn we desperately prefer.

"If you hate me," I said, looking upward, "then I hate you back."

I drove on, conscious of a black SUV a few cars back. These guys really
didn't have to switch cars every day. The fact that they did so told me that
they were trying to maintain a surreptitious cover. They thought I wasn't
aware of them. That, in and of itself, told me something. These guys were
serious customers but they weren't pros, at least not in the cloak-and-
dagger business.

I deviated from my normal destination and had to think a little bit
about the proper route to St. John's. It was the parish Talia and I had chosen, among many on the north side. It was hard to wave your arm in the
city without hitting a Catholic church, but we settled pretty quickly on
St. J's, as most people called it. Talia liked it because of the choir. I preferred it because I liked Father Ben, a younger guy with a good sense of
humor and a self-deprecating style. Catholicism, twenty-first-century
style.

None of them had the feel of our parish growing up in Leland Park, St.
Peter's. St. Pete's looked like it had barely survived an aerial bombing in
World War II and hadn't felt the need for an update in the interim. The
priest at St. Pete's preached his homilies like he was Moses descending
from the mountain following his one-on-one with the burning bush.

But Father Ben, he was okay in my book, as okay as I could feel about
a man of God today. When I walked into St. J's, I found him coming up
the stairs from the meeting rooms downstairs. I avoided looking to the
right, to the sanctuary itself, to the altar where Emily was baptized at
three months.

"Jason, it's good to see you." Father Ben was in a white shirt and dark
trousers. His flyaway hair wasn't in its usual order. It always seemed weird
to see a priest out of uniform. I let him work me over a minute. I'd
expected some gentle chiding for my lack of attendance since the funerals
but didn't receive it. We covered how I was doing, then talked a little football.

When the small talk subsided, he seemed to struggle with what would
come next. I preempted him by saying, "Thanks for your help today,
Father." *And for not asking me why,* I didn't add.

He gave a heavy sigh and surprised me by putting his hand on my shoulder. I raised my hand because I didn't want to hear whatever he might say. "Please, don't," I said, drawing away.

"Okay, okay. No homilies today. But can I just say one thing?"

I could hardly deny him.

"He didn't leave you, Jason. Don't leave Him."

I nodded slowly, a bitter smile creeping forth. "Or what?"

"I'm sorry?"

"Or what, Father? What's He going to take from me, He hasn't already taken?"

Father Ben deflated. His eyes searched me for something, I wasn't sure what. I tapped my watch. "I gotta do this," I said. "Thanks again for your help."

I took the stairs down to the meeting room. Jim Stewart, it turned out, didn't look anything like his namesake, the actor. This guy was short and stout and dour, a military crew cut, a guy who seemed like he didn't have a lot of friends. In his line of work, he probably didn't.

I thought of one of the actor's best roles, *Mr. Smith Goes to Washington*. I thought I might like a sequel. Maybe *Smith Goes to Prison*.

Or *Smith Goes to the Morgue*.

"I've got a problem," I told Jim Stewart. "I need your help."

38

THE ITALIAN DELI and coffee shop about two blocks from the criminal courts has been a fixture since long before I was a prosecutor. The proprietors, two Sicilian immigrants now in their sixties, are there every day chatting up the customers and telling stories about how things used to be in the city, before the federal government starting sticking its nose into the cesspool of local government, pinching aldermen, exposing bogus city contracts, generally bringing sunlight into areas of public works where shade used to predominate.

It's mostly a hangout for the lawyers who populate the criminal courts, though cops like to hit the place as well—the exorbitant price of the coffee and pastries notwithstanding. Detective Denny DePrizio was at the counter, as expected, at ten-thirty sharp this fine Friday morning.

We made eye contact as I walked in with the briefcase Smith had given me, still filled with the ten thousand dollars. I'd been followed, as always, by Smith's men but they kept their usual distance. I doubted they'd check on me unless there was a particular reason to do so, and I wasn't planning on sticking around for long.

In any event, if I was right, Smith and DePrizio were working together on this, and Smith already knew about this meeting.

DePrizio was at the counter, enjoying some coffee with his jacket thrown over the seat next to him. I moved next to him but didn't acknowledge him. I set the briefcase on the footstep of the counter next to his feet and leaned in, ordering a large coffee, black, to go.

"That's the briefcase?" he asked.

I nodded. "The only thing I have that Smith touched. You think there'll be any prints on it?"

"Hard to say," DePrizio answered. "Not likely but we'll know in a few days."

That was the time frame I figured. There is typically a pretty long line for fingerprint runs.

"Thanks for keeping this discreet," I said. "I don't know if I'm being followed, but you never know. Okay if I call you in a couple of days?"

"Sure, Kolarich." He didn't hide his opinion of my paranoia. It had been my idea, the surreptitious drop-off, but he'd been a sport about it.

I took my coffee, stuffed a dollar into the coffee cup for tips, and walked away, the briefcase of money at DePrizio's feet. I didn't take a deep breath until I was back in my car.

MARIE BUZZED ME in my office at about eleven. *"Mr. Smith calling."*

I felt a stirring in my chest, as I did every time I heard from him. We hadn't spoken for a while now, but he'd sent me a few messages in the interim—a friendly conversation with gang-banger inmate Arrelius Jackson, plus his henchmen mugging Pete in an alley outside a bar.

"Just wanted to check in on you, Jason. How are things? How's your brother?"

I forced a smile on my face and counted to ten.

"Have you been keeping up your end of the deal?" he went on.

"Memory serves, Smith, I said we didn't *have* a deal."

"Well, I've kept up my end. I have a suspect for you."

"The black-guy-fleeing-the-scene?"

"The very one. You'll need to see if your witness—his name escapes me—"

"Tommy Butcher," I said.

"Right, Butcher. You'll need to see if Butcher might be able to identify our suspect as possibly the man he saw fleeing the apartment building that night."

"But he *wasn't* the man he saw that night."

"Well, now, Jason, I'm sure you can be persuasive. This was a man he saw at a quick glance, and cross-racial identification is notoriously suspect."

"You mean, to a white guy, all black guys look alike? That's not very politically correct of you, Smith."

But then again, Tommy Butcher wasn't exactly politically correct, either. Butcher had been sympathetic to my plight, and if I told him that I had a legitimate suspect, he might be willing to "recall" that the person I pointed out to him was, in fact, the guy he saw.

This conversation I was having violated the letter and spirit of pretty much every ethics provision of the lawyer's code. But at the moment, I didn't have much of a choice, and the truth was, if this could help Sammy, I'd be willing to consider it, regardless of the source.

"Is this suspect—what's his name?"

"Ken Sanders."

"Okay, this guy Sanders—is he going to be cooperative? How's this going to work?"

Smith said, "He's obviously not going to admit to anything. But he won't be able to deny that he was in that building. Mr. Sanders has friends in the building he was visiting that night."

The building where Griffin Perlini lived, and died, was a subsidized-housing facility that contained, among others, many recently released cons looking to get back on their feet. It made me think that Ken Sanders might have been visiting some such gentlemen, which further made me suspect that Sanders, himself, had a sheet.

"That is correct," Smith confirmed. "In a nutshell, drugs and violence, but no murder. A full background was stuffed into your mailbox at your house in the past hour."

He enjoyed letting me know that he knew where I lived. It was a convenient way for him to deliver me something without showing himself or his men.

"Is this guy affiliated?" I asked.

"Is he—what?"

"In a gang, Smith. Is Ken Sanders in a gang?"

"No."

So Smith actually found a guy willing to be fingered by the defense as a suspect in a murder? He must have put a lot of money into Ken Sanders's hands.

Smith told me how to get in touch with the aforementioned Mr. Sanders but told me there was another reason for the call. I told him I was all ears.

"I see on the docket entry for the *Cutler* matter that there is a contested motion for next Tuesday? A defense motion?"

The county courts have recently discovered that we are in a new century, and lots of people use something called the Internet. If you have the docket number of a case, you can access the history of the case, with a data entry for every document filed since the case began. When one of the attorneys files a motion, the docket entry will identify the movant— the defense or the prosecution—as well as designating it "contested" or "agreed." So Smith could see online that the defense filed a contested motion, but he wouldn't know the content of that motion or its subject matter.

"I'm moving for expedited DNA testing of the bodies discovered behind that school," I explained. "Or, in the alternative, a continuance of the trial until DNA testing can be completed."

Smith was silent. I wondered, for a moment, if his phone had cut out.

"I can only assume you're joking."

"You can if you want, Smith. But I wouldn't."

"No way, Jason. That's completely unacceptable. Wasn't I clear about the terms of our agreement? There will be no—"

"Was I not clear that we don't *have* an agreement?"

"You will forget about those bodies and focus on Mr. Cutler's acquittal. If you don't, your brother will go away for ten years, Kolarich. And they will not be pleasant years. We will make it our highest priority to ensure that. I assume I don't need to draw you a picture. You've had a preview, yes?"

Smith's voice was shaking with anger—but, I thought, fear as well. I was really hitting a nerve here, a pressure point, to throw his words back at him. Why did he care so much about a delay of the trial? It didn't make sense.

Forget about those bodies, he'd said. That, after all, had been what prompted Smith to exert pressure on me by framing Pete—it was after they'd dug up the bodies behind the school.

Was I on the wrong track here? Was Smith hiding his real fear? I'd been operating on the possibility that Smith's people had killed Griffin Perlini, and they didn't want me nosing around and discovering that. Was I off base? Maybe Smith wasn't protecting someone who killed Griffin Perlini.

Maybe he was protecting someone who had killed those girls buried behind the school.

Someone who had killed Sammy's sister, Audrey.

"You will withdraw that motion or you'll be sorry," Smith warned.

"Drop the case against Pete, Smith. Make it happen. Or I go forward with the motion."

"You can't win this game, Kolarich. Neither can Pete." The phone line went dead.

I hung up the phone and pushed myself out of my chair on weak legs, contemplating this new idea. Was Griffin Perlini innocent of Audrey's murder? Had someone else killed Audrey, along with those other girls— someone who had accumulated enough wealth over the years to be able to finance an operation now to make sure that Griffin Perlini's murder did not reopen an inquiry into those murders?

I couldn't deny the possibility. It would explain Smith's desperation.

I went to the files in the corner of my office that Detective Carruthers had given me, files from Audrey's case back in the day. I'd neglected them, because I thought they didn't matter anymore. But maybe they mattered more than anything. I found the name I was looking for, looked through the lawyer's directory until I found a phone number, and made the call.

"Jason Kolarich for Reggie Lionel," I said.

39

ABOUT AN HOUR LATER, I found myself in the law firm of Guidry, Rogers, Lionel and Freeman. They were in one of the nice skyscrapers downtown, which seemed odd for a criminal defense firm, but they probably got a good deal on rent with the market being what it is.

"Reggie Lionel," I told the young kid manning reception. He was playing with some contraption that allowed you to watch a video and make a phone call and do your taxes all in one. The digital divide wasn't limited to the wealthy and the poor; it was age-based, too. By the time I'd said hello to this punk, he could have taken my photo, posted it on the Internet, stolen my credit card information, and learned what I had for breakfast.

"Third office down," said the kid, who wasn't inclined to escort me.

I knocked on the door, which was already open. Reggie Lionel was wearing an orange sweater and staring, through thick glasses, at a document. His eyes rose without his head of snowy hair moving an inch.

"Jason Kolarich," I said.

"Come in," he bellowed. I took a seat in an uncomfortable chair. Reggie Lionel was an old-timer by now, mid-sixties probably, which meant he'd gone through law school when black people were not exactly welcome. He'd jumped hurdles I'd never seen.

"Rare day off from court," he said, flipping the document onto a cluttered desk. Criminal defense attorneys like Reggie Lionel work on volume, which means they spend almost every day in court. He looked me over. "We co-counsel?"

"No, nothing like that." He figured I was jumping into some multiple-defendant case where we each represented one of the doers. "I've got a name from the past for you. A client from the late seventies, early eighties. Griffin Perlini."

His eyes rose up, his lips parted. I wondered if, before the recent news of Perlini's gravesite of victims had splashed all across the front page, Reggie Lionel would even remember the man he defended from a police inquiry well over twenty years ago. Maybe, maybe not, but the name had clearly been front and center recently, so he nodded with recognition.

I wondered what he thought about that, learning that his client might have been responsible for such terrible deeds, wondering if maybe his successful defense of Perlini had allowed the predator to kill and molest other young girls. That, in the end, is one of the great unspoken dilemmas facing a criminal defense attorney who represents the lowest of the low—you don't want to lose, but you wonder if you really want to win.

But hey, even I can see that everyone needs a lawyer. Guys like Reggie, they have to have a pretty healthy view of the Bill of Rights to plod forth on behalf of the dregs of society.

"Sex offender," he said.

"They liked him for a crime on the south side, Leland Park neighborhood," I reminded him. "A young girl named Audrey Cutler."

He closed his eyes and nodded. "Didn't stick, though. Didn't have eyes."

True enough. I wondered if he knew that those "eyes," Mrs. Thomas, had thought that Griffin Perlini was wrong for the murder. That, upon reflection, is what Mrs. Thomas had been saying to me when I visited her at the assisted living center. She didn't think Griffin Perlini was the person she saw running from the Cutler's home that night.

"Didn't have a little girl, either," he added.

No, they didn't have Audrey, not then, but the discovery of the bodies behind Hardigan Elementary School would change that soon enough.

"Griffin Perlini is dead," I said. "I assume you've heard."

His eyes narrowed. Yes, clearly, he'd read that article as well in the

Watch's coverage, or on television. But dead or not, Griffin Perlini had been his client, and if he thought there was any chance of a case being made against Perlini, even posthumously, he'd clam up.

"I've got the guy they like for his murder," I said.

"The girl's brother. Right. Sam, I think." Lionel's mouth ran around that idea, seemingly ending up with approval. These guys hold their noses and do their jobs, but they probably don't mind when rough justice comes the way of their scumbag clients. I doubted that Reggie Lionel had lit a candle for Griffin Perlini following his murder.

"I want to prove that Perlini killed that little girl. Audrey Cutler," I added.

"Audrey." He nodded. "Yes. Audrey." He gave me an ironic smile. "Way it works usually, the defense attorney's supposed to defend his client, not implicate him."

"Yeah, that rings a bell," I answered, a little too abruptly for someone looking for a favor. "Look, I just want to know if I'm barking up the right tree. I mean, the cops homed in on your guy Perlini in a heartbeat, given his background. And you remember, he had photographs of little girls, including Audrey, all over that coach house."

He kept nodding with me, but he wasn't talking.

"And you were smart enough to keep a lid on your client."

Still nodding, now smiling as well. I thought the details were coming back to him, if they hadn't already.

"So the cops focused on him immediately, and he wasn't talking. I'm envisioning the possibility here, Reggie, that maybe they got the wrong guy."

"Been known to happen."

Only one of us was enjoying this. But I had to play this his way, because a black man making it through a legal career defending criminals did not get where he was by taking people's shit. "Look, I'm not asking you to divulge confidences. How about you stop me if I make a relevant point?"

He chuckled to himself. He didn't think much of me, and he didn't mind displaying that sentiment.

"Audrey Cutler was my neighbor," I said. "A really sweet little girl. I have some reason to believe that maybe Griffin Perlini didn't kill her. If he didn't, I need to find out who did. She deserves some justice, don't you think?"

"Justice. Justice." He lost his smile. He had a weathered face that had seen a lot more than I had, and he didn't betray very much. I sensed that he had a profound sense of justice himself. I just didn't know what it looked like, and I hoped I never would.

"In the not-so-distant past," he said, "a prosecutor who went by the name of Jason Kolarich convicted a man named Walter Tucker for first-degree murder."

I thought about that a moment. "A shopping mall," I recalled. "A Tenth Street ticket." Walter Tucker, for his initiation into the Tenth Street Crew, had shot a teenager outside a shopping mall for committing the crime of trying to leave the gang.

"I knew the family," he said. "Good people."

I didn't answer. This wasn't a game I could win.

"You remember George Ryder handled the defense. He offered involuntary and twenty. But Jason Kolarich turned it down and went to trial with one pair of eyes and a shaky gun."

And I won. But I knew his thoughts without him saying them: *A white boy ID's a colored kid, of course the jury's going to convict.* I heard it all the time. And I wasn't sure I disagreed, not all the time, at least. But I didn't prosecute a case if I wasn't sure the guy was guilty. It made life simple for me.

"George said you were fair, though. Tough as hell but fair." He brought a fist to his mouth and let out a nasty cough. It seemed to move him off topic. "Okay, Jason Kolarich, tell me their theory. Those smart cops out there in Area Two with the missing girl, Audrey Cutler."

I felt like a student now, but okay, I'd play along. "Perlini nabbed Audrey Cutler from her bedroom, a snatch and run. He went to his house or his car, had his fun with her, killed her, and disposed of the body."

He leaned back in his chair and cupped his hands behind his head. "Snatch and run. Snatch," he repeated, "and *run.*"

His emphasis on that last word finally triggered it in my mind, finally scratched that mental itch. My body went cold. I felt my hand rise up to hood my eyes.

"Ah," said Lionel. "Did the cops do their homework, Jason Kolarich?"

A moan escaped my throat. No, in fact, they hadn't.

"But you did, right, Counselor?"

Yes, I did. But then, my homework was over twenty years later, and after Griffin Perlini was dead. So when I'd had the conversation with Griffin Perlini's mother, Griffin was not facing a first-degree murder charge, when everyone shuts their mouths and prays that the police can't put one and one together and get two. In fact, when Mrs. Perlini had told me that Griffin had torn the anterior cruciate ligament behind his knee a few years earlier—before Audrey's abduction—it was nothing more than an introduction to a story.

"Griffin had a torn ACL," I said. "He couldn't run."

"No more than I could do a triple axle off the high dive," said Reggie Lionel.

40

I WALKED BACK from Reggie Lionel's office in a trance, every assumption I'd made in the case now turned upside down. I'd had teammates who had torn their ACLs and, while it was not a universal rule, it was typically the case that a full tear of the ACL, unless surgically repaired, left you able to walk but *unable* to run. Perlini's mother had told me that they didn't have the money for surgical repair. The police, when investigating Perlini for Audrey's abduction, surely didn't put him through wind sprints. They'd have no reason to know of his inability to run. Reggie Lionel, wisely, had held his client back from revealing this fact to the police, because there was always time to do it, and most likely that time would have been in a courtroom, while he stood trial.

Lionel, back then, had played it smart. Wait out the cops, see if they can put something together, hold back your trump card in case you need it. He just never needed it, because the cops couldn't pin the rap on his client.

Mrs. Thomas had described the man running as very fast. It was impossible to imagine that Griffin Perlini could have pulled that off.

Griffin Perlini didn't kill Audrey. The notorious Mr. Smith's client, I was now sure, did.

Smith wasn't worried so much about delay as he was about me figuring out this very fact. He hadn't jumped to attention until the bodies were discovered. *That* was their concern. *That* was when they framed Pete to get control over me.

It was not lost on me that this revelation did some violence to my attempt to free Sammy Cutler. I'd hoped to show the jury that Sammy killed the man who killed his sister. If the jury knew that Perlini didn't kill Audrey, Sammy's murder looked a lot less justifiable.

But I couldn't let this go. I might not be able to solve this crime in a short time frame, but I would solve it. I would find Smith and I would find his client. I would find Audrey's killer.

Smith. I'd taken a gamble and filed the motion for expedited DNA testing—or a delay of Sammy's trial until testing could be completed—to rattle the tree, to force Smith's hand, to see if it might prompt him to make a move that would expose himself to me. He would have a counter, I knew, some effort to tighten the noose, but I was getting to the end of the line and I had no good leads on Smith, or his client, with less than three weeks to go until Sammy's trial.

If I was right that Smith and company were covering up Audrey's murder, and perhaps multiple child murders, the clock was ticking loudly for Pete and me. Once Sammy's trial was over, and they had no use for me, they'd come after both of us to cover their tracks. I had seventeen days to solve this thing before there would be a contract out on both of our heads.

What else could I do? I had forced Smith into a corner now by asking the court for DNA testing. I was trying out a plan on Detective Denny DePrizio, though it probably wasn't going to help Sammy. What else could I do?

Solve Sammy's case, for starters. I had two leads on alternative suspects now. Smith had given me Ken Sanders, the black-guy-fleeing-the-scene. And I had to follow up on the alibi of another potential suspect, Archie Novotny, who claimed he was at a guitar lesson on the night Griffin Perlini was murdered.

THE MUSIC EMPORIUM, located on 39th and Greenway, was a relic in this day and age, full of rows of albums and CDs in an era where nobody had a turntable anymore and most young people were buying music online. It was a cramped, musty, dark place with music posters for wallpaper, where the only conditions of employment seemed to be wearing your hair past your shoulders and sporting hallucinogenic imagery on your T-shirt.

I actually appreciated the place. We've become too impersonal nowadays, buying and reading everything through a computer. I still liked to hold a newspaper in my hand. I still preferred flipping through CDs in a store. I did so while I waited, going through some old Smiths music. This place had a pretty good collection. I bought a used copy of *Strangeways, Here We Come* because I'd lost mine, and a CD single of "The Queen Is Dead," which I still thought was their best song.

"Morrissey. Good taste."

I turned around as the clerk was ringing up my purchase to find the guy who I assumed was Nick Trillo. Archie Novotny had given me his name; this was his guitar teacher who could vouch for him. I hadn't formed a predictive image of the man in my mind, but in hindsight, he was about what I should have expected. He was skinny to a fault but with a minor paunch, a scatter-patch goatee, gray hair pulled back into a long ponytail.

"You, too," I said, nodding to his T-shirt, which was the cover art for *That What Is Not*, by Public Image Ltd., the band Johnny Lydon formed after the Sex Pistols, though I liked PiL's early stuff a lot better. "You know a better song than 'Acid Drops'?"

"Nah." His face lit up. "Nah, man, I don't." He hit my arm with the back of his hand. I had won him over. This ponytailed hippie and the yuppie in a serious coat and tie united in their appreciation of an early pioneer of punk rock.

"You needed me for something?"

"Yeah, yeah. Can we find a place to talk?"

"Sure, man, yeah. Here." I followed him through the store to a door that had a piece of paper on it that read: HEY! IF YOU'RE NOT AN EMPLOYEE, WHAT ARE YOU THINKING? TURN AROUND AND BUY SOMETHING. It made me like the place even more.

He led me to a room where, presumably, he taught guitar lessons. The walls were lined with some of the finest guitars ever made—a Les Paul, a Stratocaster, a Flying V. Otherwise, there was nothing more than two stools in the middle of the room and a lone guitar, standing upright in a pedestal, that apparently was the one Nick Trillo played when he taught lessons. I made a point of commenting on the classics on the walls to further soften any ice that might have formed. I was a lawyer, after all. People clutch up around me all the time.

"Did Archie tell you I'd be calling?" I asked.

"Yeah, he said something about some dates. He said to give you whatever you wanted."

That was helpful. This guy Trillo didn't need to know which side I was on—that is, that I was on the *opposite* side of Archie Novotny. Maybe he thought I was Archie's lawyer. If so, I would choose my words carefully, walking a fine line to let him believe that without actually lying.

"September 21, 2006," I said.

"Whoa."

"A Thursday night," I added. "Do you know if he took a lesson that night?"

"Well, yeah, Thursday night's when he's always had lessons. But that's like, over a year ago, man. Far as I know, yeah, he did."

I didn't want to be the inquisitor. I had to play this gently. "My only fear here," I said, "is that someone else might ask the same question, and they won't take your word for it. They'll want records. They'll want proof." I leaned into him. "I'll tell you what my real concern is here, Nick." This is where I hoped our bonding would pay off. "My real concern is that Archie and I give them the wrong answer. I just want the truth. If we say he was here and he wasn't, then we'll be in trouble. Or vice versa. If we say he wasn't here and he was, then, y'know, it looks like we're lying. I couldn't care less what the answer is, but it has to be verifiable."

Nick Trillo seemed troubled by all of this. "Is this, like, something really serious?"

I showed him my hand. "Not as long we tell the truth. We just have to make absolutely sure it's the truth, either way. Archie figured you might have some records that could verify whether he was here or not."

I wasn't being entirely forthright with the gentleman, but in the end, I was just asking for the truth. That, as much as anything, would be what he'd remember. The minor details of what I was saying would get lost.

"Are you, like, one of these criminal lawyers?"

I shrugged. "I do a lot of things. Like divorces, for example."

"Oh, okay." He seemed relieved. "So this is like a divorce fight or something?"

I smiled at him. "I don't think Archie would want me to answer that, Nick."

Rather slippery of me, admittedly. The guitar instructor thought about it a moment and, my guess, decided that this was a divorce where Archie Novotny's whereabouts on a particular night were in question. Probably an allegation of adultery. Maybe he hadn't thought it through, but either way, he was making me for Archie's advocate and he seemed to want to help.

"So," I said, "do you guys have any records of attendance?"

He thought about it, blowing out a deep sigh. "Well, y'know, I'll sometimes jot something down but—I mean, I wouldn't keep it. No, it's more like I just remember—well, I'll tell you what. We could see how much he paid. Yeah, I could do that. Hang on."

Nick Trillo left the room, leaving me with the guitars on the wall. I should have been a rock star. Other than the fact that I couldn't play an instrument, couldn't sing, wasn't all that attractive, and lacked the gift of lyrical composition, I think I could have.

"Here, okay." Trillo carried a hefty file box into the room and placed it on the floor, as there was no place else to put it. He sat on the floor and opened it up. "Month of September," he said. I looked over his shoulder at the files, which were tabbed by months of the year for the year 2006. He grabbed the tab labeled "9/06" and pulled it back to reveal a few dozen sheets of paper. On each one was a photocopy of a check.

"Twenty-five bucks a lesson," he said. "They usually pay that day."

"By check?"

"Boss's rule," he said. "One of the instructors who used to be here, he wasn't so honest with the cash thing. Boss says it's gotta be a check or credit card."

Good for me.

"September 7," Trillo said, showing me a photocopy of a check written by Archie Novotny in the amount of twenty-five dollars.

He kept leafing through the pages. "Here. September 14."

I didn't care about September 7 or 14. I cared about September 21, 2006.

Trillo ran through the pages. I was playing defense, praying for the absence of a record. I held my breath as he kept leafing, by my estimate a little longer than he should have, proportionately. I watched the dates on the photocopied checks, felt my heart skip a beat as the dates passed September 21, but that assumed that the checks were in perfect chronological order.

"Okay. This is weird." Trillo held up a photocopied check from Archie Novotny, dated September 28, in the amount of fifty dollars. "He paid for two lessons on the twenty-eighth."

Which would have included the twenty-first. But my eyes fixed on the memo line of that check, in which the handwritten words "I insist!" were written.

I felt my knees go weak, the adrenaline flow with a vengeance. I thought I understood this, but I wanted to get Trillo on the same page with me. " 'I insist,' " I said.

"Huh. 'I insist.' Yeah."

"What does that mean? What was he insisting on?"

Trillo thought about it. I decided to help him along.

"So he didn't write you a check on the twenty-first, and then he wrote you a check for the following week with the words 'I insist!' on it."

" 'I insist.' 'I—.' Oh." Nick Trillo looked up at me, shaking the paper. "I remember this. Yeah. *Yeah*." He got up from the floor and pointed at me. "He missed a lesson. He missed a lesson and I told him he didn't have to pay for it, but he insisted, 'cause he hadn't called ahead to cancel it. He said, fair was fair."

I tried to remain calm, though I wanted to wrap my arms around his bony frame. "He missed the lesson on the twenty-first but insisted on paying for it."

"Yeah." Trillo nodded with excitement. "Yeah. Must have been the twenty-first. He'd paid for every other one. Yeah, I remember, I told him not to worry but he said, well—"

"He insisted."

"Right. He insisted." Trillo looked at the paper and chuckled. "I feel like a detective or something. You want copies of this stuff?"

"If it's not too much trouble," I answered. And if it was, I would personally take them to a Kinko's and make copies myself.

Trillo left for a few moments, returning with fresh copies of each of Archie Novotny's checks for September—twenty-five dollars for September 7, twenty-five dollars for September 14, and fifty dollars for September 28.

"Good thing we checked," he said.

Indeed it was—good for me, at least. Not so good for Archie Novotny. Mr. Novotny, it seemed clear, missed his guitar lesson on the night that Griffin Perlini was murdered. Then, if he was even thinking this diabolically, he tried to cover his tracks by paying for it anyway.

"Hey, if it's not a problem," I said, "I'll come back tomorrow with an affidavit—a legal document describing what we discussed. That okay with you?"

"Yeah, that's great." He was still excited about our little adventure in puzzle-solving. Sooner or later, he'd become less excited when he realized that I was not serving Archie Novotny's interests. But the truth was the truth, and I'd lock him down with the affidavit, in any event.

I left the Music Emporium with some steam in my stride. I had Archie Novotny. I had motive, opportunity, and an attempt to manufacture an alibi. I tried to imagine the look on the face of Lester Mapp, the prosecutor, when he saw this.

"Sammy," I said to no one, "we might just win this case."

41

YOU KILLED ME, JASON.

I awoke with a start, my eyes stinging from the sweat, the echo of Talia's voice lingering between my ears. The dream was always a little different, but always she was dead, visiting me, a vision within a dream, appearing out of nowhere but somehow I knew she was coming, and I knew she was right.

I tossed the pillow, soaked in sweat, to the foot of the bed and stared up at the ceiling.

"Happy birthday," I said. Talia was born on October 13, 1972, in a small town outside New York City, where her father was opening a Kmart. It had been his job, moving across the country as new stores opened. Talia lived in ten cities growing up, attended three different high schools, a nomadic life that taught her an adaptive personality but left her longing for permanency as an adult. She'd made me promise, before Emily was born, that we'd stay in one place, that Emily would stay in one school system.

I thought of her parents, Nelson and Ginny, what today would mean for them. I considered calling them, but we hadn't spoken since the funeral. They hadn't placed blame per se, but they'd noted to me, coolly enough, *You were supposed to go with them.* I'd already beaten them to the punch.

That's what you do—you play it out, isolating any single moment that could have altered the chain of events, turning every one of those moments into blame. I should have told Talia, all along, that I was still on trial, that it was unrealistic to expect that I could break away for the weekend at her parents' place. I should have told her about Ernesto Ramirez, the ex–Latin Lord who could blow open the case against Senator Almundo.

She'd have left earlier in the day. She'd have left during daylight, making that turn along the road before it was dark. Had I not strung her along into the early evening, she'd have left that morning. Talia and Emily would still be alive.

I got out of bed and went to the bathroom, vomiting until there was nothing but dry retching. I got a glass of water downstairs and sat in the family room, dark and chilly, as the morning sun filtered through the blinds.

Time passed. I didn't spend it in the way one might expect—lighting a candle, looking over photos. In fact, I spent several hours on the couch drifting in and out of sleep filled with vivid dreams of Talia: The first time we slept together in college, cautious and awkward; an ice-cream cone she threw in my face along the lake one summer afternoon; smiling through tears as she told me she was pregnant; the delivery room, Talia's remarkable cool during eleven hours of labor; my dumbfounded fascination as the nurse put the scissors in my hand to cut the umbilical cord. Each time I popped awake, fresh sweat covering my forehead and my heart racing.

As I stumbled to the bathroom, I passed a clock that told me it was just past two in the afternoon, which reminded me that I had work to do today, that today could not be all about mourning. My cell phone rang and I scrambled around the living room to find it. It was under the couch, though I couldn't recall how that happened.

"Hello?" I managed, my voice sounding like a poor facsimile of my normal speech.

"Hey." It was Pete. "Wanted to see how you're doing."

"Not the best day."

"No, I know. You wanna—you wanna grab dinner or something? Probably a good day that you could use some company."

True, but I couldn't run the risk of being seen with my brother. He had to stay secluded or Smith could sink his teeth into him.

"The day will come and go," Pete said. "Tomorrow will be better, Jase."

I took a shower in scalding water and threw on a sweater and jeans. Neither Sammy nor Pete could afford the luxury of my wallowing in self-pity. Sammy's trial started in sixteen days, and while I had a few pieces of a defense, I hadn't yet decided how to make them fit together.

ACCORDING TO THE FILE Smith had delivered to my house, Ken Sanders had a pretty long sheet of violence and drugs. He'd been in and out of the joint and now worked as a dishwasher at a Greek diner on the west side.

I ordered some coffee at the counter and waited for him to come out. I'd seen a glimpse of him back in the kitchen—what looked like him, at least, compared to a mug shot—and I felt like I knew this guy already. I'd prosecuted this guy, a hundred times over, a guy on a treadmill of crime, having not much of a chance at anything promising once out of prison, so he returns to what he knows best: to criminal activity out of necessity, to drugs out of despair. One of the downsides of prosecution is you get so overwhelmed by these individual tragedies that you wall it off, you focus on the crime and not on the person, leaving you wondering how much sense any of this makes, whether you're making any meaningful difference at all.

He came out about twenty minutes later and dropped across from me in the booth, reeking of fried foods, his white top wet at the sleeves and stained with various colors.

Kenny Sanders, my black-guy-fleeing-the-scene, looked all of his thirty-eight years and then some, a few scars along his long forehead, blemishes on the cheeks, a scrawny neck that bore a small tattoo resembling some kind of weapon. He had ex-con written all over him—the beaten-down expression, the submissive stoop in his shoulders.

"I'm Jason Kolarich," I said, though he already knew that. "You were expecting me?"

"Okay," he said, nodding compliantly but not making eye contact.

"You talked to our friend?"

"Didn't talk to nobody, boss."

Right. That would be the story, obviously. "You were at that apartment building on the night of September 21, 2006?"

"Okay."

"Can you tell me who you were with?" I already had that information, too, courtesy of our mutual friend Smith.

"Jax and Clay," said Sanders.

"Jackson Moore and Jimmy Clay?"

"Right, okay." Still nodding.

"And they'll say you left them about nine-thirty that night?"

"Okay."

Leaving Sanders with sufficient time to attempt a robbery of, say, a guy who lived two floors up named Griffin Perlini, a mousy little guy who'd be an easy mark, though something might have gone wrong, see, and instead he ended up popping the guy between the eyes. That would be my story to the jury, of course. Kenny Sanders wouldn't go quite that far, I assumed. Whatever deal he cut with Smith, however much Smith was paying him for this little charade, Kenny Sanders would not flat-out admit to murder—certainly not to one he did not commit. No, the way I figured it, he'd allow himself to be the object of suspicion but nothing more.

"Do you deny you left your friends at nine-thirty that night?"

"Not sayin', okay."

Right. "Did you leave your friends on the second floor of that building, head up two flights to Griffin Perlini's apartment?"

"Not sayin'."

"Did you attempt to rob him?"

"Not sayin'."

"And when he struggled, did you shoot him between the eyes?"

"Not sayin'." He shook his head. "No sir, not sayin'."

"Did you then run out of the building?"

"Not sayin'."

"Were you wearing a leather bomber jacket and green stocking cap? Not saying," I answered for him.

"Not sayin'," he agreed.

Smith had worked this out with Kenny Sanders just right. There would be provers—Jax and Clay—to put him in that building at the time of the murder, and to have him leave at nine-thirty, which is the approximate window of time that would allow him to go upstairs, kill Perlini in an aborted robbery, and run out of the building.

But Kenny wouldn't testify to any of that, and he'd take Five on all the hard questions. The jury would hear the invocation of the Fifth Amendment so many times that they'd be repeating it in their sleep. The prosecutor, Lester Mapp, might try to give Kenny immunity to compel his testimony, but Kenny here would just deny everything, and I, the great defense lawyer, would play up the grant of immunity, which typically tells people that someone is guilty of something. If Mapp took the route of immunity, I'd shove it so far up his ass he'd be tasting it for dinner.

Sanders pulled up his sleeve and scratched the dry skin on his arm. This man had been malnourished his entire life, from the baloney-on-white in the local lockups to the inedible garbage that is prison food. This guy started with nothing and would end up that way.

"This is ridiculous," I said.

"No." For the first time, Kenny Sanders eyeballed me. "No, sir."

He needed this, he was saying. He was being rewarded handsomely for giving himself up as a scapegoat. I could follow my conscience and my preppy-white-boy guilt, but Kenny wanted the payday.

"Please," he said, eyes averted again, nodding insistently. "Please, sir."

And in the end, Kenny Sanders wouldn't go down for this. The prosecution had their sights set on Sammy. No, the only thing stopping me was my ethical constraints, and I'd already checked those at the door.

"Okay." I slipped him my card. "The prosecution's going to want to talk to you," I said. "That will happen soon. You'll probably be testifying even before trial."

"Okay, yeah. Good, okay."

"I—have to take this picture," I said. He knew I'd need to do this.

I had a digital camera I'd given to Talia two Christmases ago. She was the photographer in the family, but I wasn't completely useless. I snapped Kenny's photo and stopped at a drugstore on the way home to get the picture developed with copies. When I had it in my hand, I made the call to Tommy Butcher, my only eyewitness.

"I need you to look at something," I told him.

42

I FOUND TOMMY BUTCHER at the work site in Deemer Park where Butcher Construction was erecting a new facility for the city park district. I don't recall what previously existed, what had been torn down, but the replacement building was a massive structure, big enough to house indoor tennis courts. First time we met, Butcher had explained to me that his company was a few weeks behind schedule with the project. Apparently that was still the case, if working full-boat on a weekend was any indication.

Men on scaffolding were working on the building's facade, while others moved in and out of the building through an opening that, one day, would house double doors. Tommy Butcher was surveying their work while he spoke on a walkie-talkie. I caught his eye and he looked away casually, then did a double-take to return to me. He waved to me as he tried to get off his radio. "Okay, Russ, write up the change order and we can decide later. You gotta make a record with these fuckin' guys, understand me? Now, this isn't coming from the old man. The old man isn't working this. It's coming from *me*." He clipped the radio to his belt and gestured in the direction of the building. "These people are gonna be the death of me," he said.

"The park district?"

He nodded. "Everything's our fault with these guys. These guys write up the worst specs you've ever seen, but we're supposed to read everyone's minds. Every time we talk, we gotta make our record with those people."

"Sounds like someone who's afraid of a lawsuit."

He looked at me. "Oh, they'll sue us. That's a given. It's just a question of how much we can get back in a counterclaim."

So much of the business world is like this now. Litigation is just another cost of doing business, no different than payroll and insurance and bribes to city inspectors. "So, Mr. Butcher—"

"Tommy."

"Tommy, I have a photo for you to look at."

He drew back. "No fuckin' foolin'? You found this guy?"

I struggled with that—or pretended to. "I'd rather not, uh, put ideas in your head."

The message was clear enough. "You found him," he repeated.

"Can you just take a look?"

Butcher glanced around before he leaned into me. "Mr. Kolarich, I saw this guy a year ago, runnin' past me. Right? Understand?"

"Tom—"

"Listen, I saw a guy. I told you that. A black guy. That's the God's honest. You tell me you did some digging, you found the guy, I say great. You tellin' me you got your man? Then it's the guy I saw. You tell me it's not your man, then it can't be the guy I saw. Right?"

I deflated. I couldn't believe I was even having this conversation. The process was being turned on its head. Usually, Kenny Sanders would be a legitimate suspect only if Tommy Butcher saw him that night. Here, Tommy Butcher saw him only if he's a legitimate suspect. There are some cops, and maybe some prosecutors, who did it this way. I was never one of those guys. I wore that pride like a badge.

"Hey, look," he continued, raising his hands, "you got a client who did right by his sister, sounds to me like. Guy killed his sister, so he kills that guy. Me, I might do the same thing. But if it's me on trial, and there was a black guy barreling out of that building with a gun in his belt, I'd want someone to step up and say so. So I'll say so. Believe me, I got a hell of lot better things to be doin' than goin' to court. But I'll do it, if you found the guy."

The wind was whipping up, dropping the temperatures to near freezing. I thought of Talia. I thought of Sammy. And Audrey. I thought about justice and fairness and how rules we put forth to guide a criminal justice system don't always get it right. There was something larger at play here, a higher ethic. If Sammy killed Griffin Perlini, he didn't deserve to spend his life in prison. And if he didn't do it, he sure as hell didn't deserve a single day inside. No rule of law could alter that truth.

"I found the guy," I said. "But you didn't hear me say that." I handed him a copy of the photo of Kenny Sanders.

He took the photo and didn't even look at it. "Okay, then. I didn't hear you say that."

I told him to keep the photo, which was a subtle direction for him to study it, to commit details to memory. I told him the prosecution would fight his testimony hard and probably try to exclude it prior to trial. Then I left him to his construction project, retreating to my car, safe from the wind. I drove off, secure in the knowledge that I now had two legitimate suspects, Kenny Sanders and Archie Novotny. Each of them was a plausible alternative to Sammy Cutler as the killer of Griffin Perlini. I was disavowing everything I was taught about my profession, crossing virtually every moral boundary, mocking every canon of ethics I had once held sacred. I had fabricated evidence, put words into witnesses' mouths beyond any typical lawyerly cajoling, and I felt absolutely nothing. No regret. No self-doubt. Just the realization that I was now a lawyer in name only, a man hiding behind a title. I would focus on winning and ignore what I had willingly lost.

"HAPPY BIRTHDAY TO YOU, happy birthday to you."

Talia sits patiently at the table, wearing that sweet smile and a party hat we have forced her to don for the celebration. I've acquiesced in letting Emily carry the cake, dominated by lit candles, from the kitchen to the dinner table. Talia's parents join in the singing, her mother holding our infant daughter, Justine. Her parents have glasses of wine in front of them, but not for Talia, who is just beginning to show with our third child, a boy.

"Mommy, how old are you?" Emily asks, taking a seat like a big girl at the table.

"Old enough, honey." She laughs in her self-deprecating way.

"You don't get any more birthdays," says Talia's mother, Ginny. "Because that means *I* get older, too!" Little Justine, in her lap, begins to whine. She is shaping up to be a carbon copy of Talia.

I am cutting the cake, screwing it up as usual, as Justine is handed over the table to Talia. I pause a moment to watch them, mother, daughter, granddaughter, the shared olive complexion and dark Italian features.

When her parents have left and the children are in bed, I take Talia in my arms and drink in the smell of her shampoo, the silky skin of her neck, the dark, watery eyes that always seem to project multiple colors, the forming lump in her belly. My heartbeat pounds against my chest, against her body joined to mine, and it feels like *I love you* doesn't even begin to cover it.

I BREATHED a sigh of relief when the clock passed midnight, as if there were something magical about the passing of a minute or hour. Sammy's trial was only two weeks away, and I had many things to do. I had to disclose to the prosecution the additional evidence about Archie Novotny—the photocopies of the checks he wrote to Music Emporium. I had to disclose Kenny Sanders and Tommy Butcher's positive identification of Sanders. I still had to reach the prosecution's eyewitnesses—Griffin Perlini's neighbor and the elderly couple on the street who ID'd Sammy as the killer.

I had to find Smith and the people he represented, because they would probably try to kill Pete and me once Sammy's case was over.

Two days from now—Tuesday—I would appear in court to argue for the expedited DNA testing of the girls found behind that school, or otherwise a delay in the trial. Smith hadn't been shy about voicing his objection, and I was still hoping he might back down on Pete—call off his witnesses and let Pete off the hook in exchange for my dropping that motion. Or maybe Smith would make a wrong move and somehow expose himself. It wasn't much more than a long shot, but it was all I had.

Other than Denny DePrizio, that is. Another long shot.

Question marks. I had plenty of them. And I was running out of time.

43

SMITH FINGERED A BREADSTICK, considering it but unable to bring himself to eat. The private room in Locallo's was dark but warm, a comfortable setting, and the rigatoni was the best he'd ever had in the city, but his appetite eluded him this evening. He replayed the entire course of events leading up to today, wondering if he could identify a particular misstep on his part. The only misstep, he decided, was in underestimating Jason Kolarich.

"The fuckin' guy knows how to play poker," he said. "That motion he filed for the DNA testing and to delay the trial. He knows he's hit a nerve. He's trying to force our hand."

"He's desperate."

"Yeah, but so the fuck are we," Smith said. He drained his Scotch and felt worse for doing so. "The question is, does he know *why* we're desperate?"

"No."

"You don't know that. You *hope* that." Smith looked squarely at Detective Denny DePrizio.

"I'm telling you," said DePrizio. "He doesn't know which way is up. He's desperate, but he doesn't have a clue. He basically told me he was waving the white flag. He said you had him boxed in. He said he had no way of finding you, unless you accidentally left your fingerprints on that briefcase or the cash inside."

Smith didn't know his adversary sufficiently. That had been his problem all along. Jason Kolarich hadn't been his choice; he was Sammy Cutler's pick. And Kolarich was proving to be more difficult to manipulate than he'd thought.

"That guy's a stubborn prick." Smith looked at DePrizio. "I don't think we have a choice now. Do we? I think he's going forward with that motion in court. The judge is going to move the trial date and let him do DNA testing. With all the publicity after those bodies were found? Of course she will. We don't have a choice."

"He's bluffing," DePrizio said. "He's taking a free shot at getting you to let his brother off the hook. He won't go through with it." DePrizio scooped up a healthy fork full of linguine and shoved it into his mouth.

Smith pushed away the plate of rigatoni, which now revolted him. "Goddammit. This wasn't supposed to happen like this. All that asshole had to do was follow instructions and we'd be fine. *Now* look at us. Look what we're thinking about doing here. This was never supposed to happen." He looked over at DePrizio, who was dishing more food into his mouth. "Denny, I'm real glad this isn't spoiling your appetite."

DePrizio shrugged. "Hey, nobody asked *me* if this was a good idea." He swallowed and wiped his mouth. "This whole thing, from day one, was pretty much a clusterfuck, right?"

That didn't make Smith feel any better. He reached for another stomach pill and washed it down with water. "What other choice did we have? You tell me, Denny. What the hell else were we supposed to do? This is the only thing we could do."

"Okay, it was the only thing you could do." DePrizio poured himself some more wine. "I mean, I get you. You want to control the outcome of this trial and keep the spotlight off Carlo. So you do what we do, right? You throw some money at him. Only that didn't work, he still does whatever he wants. So then you apply pressure. That's how it works. Only you got this lawyer who isn't being real compliant." He took a healthy drink of the Merlot, a nice bottle from 1994. "So yeah, I think you're right, you don't have much of a choice now. You gotta up the pressure. You gotta move on that brother of his."

Smith had always regarded DePrizio as something of a lightweight—a valuable asset, given his position, but not the brightest bulb. Still, Smith wanted some validation for his idea. He needed to hear that someone agreed with him.

Because Smith, himself, was out on a limb. This was a very quiet operation. Carlo turned to Smith not only because of their long-standing relationship, but because he wasn't telling Smith anything he didn't already know. They'd borrowed a handful of guys to do the heavy lifting, but those guys didn't know shit. No, in the end, it was Smith and Carlo, and Carlo, with his sick granddaughter and his daughter in pieces over it, was in no position to decide on details.

This was all on Smith, and it wasn't going so well.

"Look at it this way," DePrizio added, helping himself to Smith's rigatoni. "When this trial was over, you were gonna do it, anyway, right? You were gonna move on the lawyer and his brother. Am I wrong?"

Smith looked away. He hadn't shared those kinds of details with the detective. DePrizio served a limited role here. Still, Denny was right. After Sammy Cutler's trial, it was inevitable that Carlo would want the garbage collected. Jason and Pete Kolarich could not remain as threats.

Smith found himself warming to the decision. DePrizio had said it correctly. They'd have to come for Pete Kolarich sooner or later—sooner, in all likelihood, once Cutler's trial was over. They wouldn't be doing anything they hadn't already planned on doing. They'd just be moving up the timetable.

Smith watched DePrizio devour the remainder of his rigatoni. "Jesus, Denny. It's like you don't have a care in the world here."

"I don't." The detective sat back and patted his stomach. "Because I did my part. What can blow back on me? Anyone says I pinched that kid on a bogus charge, I say prove it. I say I caught him in the act. Who's gonna say I didn't? Now you, my friend, that's another story."

"The hell is *that* supposed to mean?"

DePrizio poised the glass of wine at his mouth. "Not for nothin', but maybe you should start thinking about what happens if this doesn't turn out so well. You think Carlo's gonna remember how good a friend you've been?"

Smith made a face. "You're out of line, Denny. You're drunk." But the thought, of course, had been on Smith's mind. And things were about to escalate. It was one thing to set up the idiot brother on a drug and guns charge. All that took was DePrizio and some money thrown at Pete's drug supplier, who wouldn't be able to identify Smith because he'd never laid eyes on him. So far, Smith had remained invisible. Insulated. He wouldn't be meeting with Kolarich face-to-face any longer, and he was calling him from an untraceable phone. He was clean. So far.

But now, the men he had borrowed would be doing more than scaring Pete Kolarich in an alley outside a bar or surveilling Jason Kolarich around town. Now, if Smith went through with it, they were talking about major felonies. It would be messy. And there would be no turning back.

"Keep an eye on Jason Kolarich," Smith told DePrizio. "Use all that charm of yours to keep him close to you. Where's that briefcase with the money?"

"In the trunk of my car."

"In the trunk of your car. Well, obviously, the briefcase comes back without any traceable prints. But offer to help Kolarich. Keep him close."

"I can do that." DePrizio enjoyed the wine. It annoyed Smith, the detective's calm in the face of this. But then, DePrizio didn't have to over-see this operation. He didn't have to answer to Carlo if this whole thing went south.

Smith wiped his forehead with the napkin. "I have no choice," he said.

44

I WOKE UP MONDAY MORNING with heavy eyes. I'd slept only in fits. Part of me had expected Smith's boys to come after me. Smith, clearly, was considering his next move, and I'd expected that he might move by coming after me in the middle of the night.

I reached for my cell phone and called Pete at the hotel where he was holed up.

"Bored to tears," he told me.

"Bored is good," I told him, again.

I showered, got dressed, and went to the garage. I took care in doing so, to the point of peeking beneath the car and into the backseat before getting in.

I backed the car out of my driveway and checked the rearview mirror as I drove to the office. Strange. Traffic was as plentiful as ever but I didn't sense that anyone was tracking me. Maybe they were getting better at it. Maybe they were sure I'd be heading straight to the office and felt no need to watch me until I arrived there. Maybe.

I had the same feeling when I pulled into the parking garage—nobody following me. I ran through the same calculus, the possibility that I just couldn't see them. Weird.

When I got to the office, I found a message from Lester Mapp, the ACA prosecuting Sammy. I hadn't gotten back to him about a possible plea deal, hoping to show strength in my silence. I figured he could wait a little longer. First, I wanted him to know about Kenny Sanders—that I had a positive ID on the black-guy-fleeing-the-scene from Tommy Butcher. I drafted the disclosure to the prosecution, announcing Sanders as a new witness and the ID from Butcher. I also disclosed the new information regarding Archie Novotny—his absence from his guitar lesson on the night of the murder. I had Marie fax the whole thing to Lester Mapp and imagined the look on his face when he received it.

I made a couple more phone calls to the eyewitnesses from the night of the murder—not Tommy Butcher, but the ones the prosecution would call—once again leaving a voice mail for them. I had been officially stiff-armed by these witnesses and needed to pay them a visit myself or go to the judge for some assistance. It occurred to me that Smith might have something to do with their reluctance.

I worked through lunch, reviewing reports, taking notes, beginning the outline of my closing argument at trial. You always start with the closing argument, your wish list of what you want to be able to say at the end of the trial—and then you work backward to make sure that you'll be able to do so.

At one o'clock, I received another call from Lester Mapp. This time, I took it.

"You must be joking, Counsel," he said.

"Good day to you, too, sir. I'm just sitting here trying to decide whether I should call Archie Novotny or Ken Sanders first. Who would you choose, if you were me?"

There was a pause, then an unhappy chuckle from the prosecutor. "The convenient Negro rears his head. I suspect you'll be shooting for an all-white jury, too? I'm moving to bar. This guy shows up a year after the murder with a story about an African American suspect, and then lo and behold, you find *that* guy, too?"

It sounded like Lester Mapp wasn't having a good day.

"This Thursday," he said. "I got a two o'clock from the judge. I'll have a motion to bar on file by tomorrow. I'll send you some fun information on Mr. Butcher, too. Your star witness isn't such a star."

That didn't sound so good, but I didn't want to let on to being concerned.

"Two o'clock, this Thursday," he said. "You'll have my motion to bar by tomorrow."

"I'll count the hours."

I put in a call to Tommy Butcher's office at Butcher Construction. I left a message with the date and time for this coming Thursday. I'd already warned him of this possibility. The prosecution was right to take a free shot before trial to exclude the testimony—before the jury could hear Tommy Butcher identify Ken Sanders. I was sure that Lester Mapp would put Butcher through the paces. I reached for the phone to call Kenny Sanders, to notify him of the same thing, when the intercom buzzed.

"*Detective DePrizio?*" Marie said.

I took a breath and punched the button. "This is Jason Kolarich."

"Denny DePrizio. Got some bad news for you, Counselor."

In the background noise behind DePrizio, I heard sounds of automobile traffic, a horn honking, an engine revving. DePrizio was calling from a pay phone somewhere. I didn't think there *were* any pay phones these days.

"Oh, shit," I said. "Don't tell me."

"Nothing, my friend. The briefcase, the money—all clean."

"Dammit."

"Y'know, if what you're telling me is on the up-and-up, then these guys would be too smart to leave a print, anyway. Right?"

I sighed. "I guess so. It was a shot in the dark, I guess."

"Yeah, well, listen. I'm beginning to feel like I'm being bullshitted here. And I don't like being bullshitted."

DePrizio was pretty good at this. He actually sounded like a good cop trying to look into something for me.

"It's not—I'm not—" I let out a low moan. "I guess I can't really expect you to believe me."

A long pause. "Well, listen—you show me something, I'll look at it. I'm not too interested in wild-goose chases, right? But you give me something real, I'll look at it. Fair enough?"

"Fair enough. Shit."

"In the meantime, I got a briefcase with ten thousand bucks?"

"Give it to charity," I said. "I don't want that guy's money."

He laughed. "You gotta take this money back, Mr. Kolarich."

"How about I get back to you on that? I'm tied up for the next couple of days. I need to be careful about meeting with you."

"Still the black helicopters following you?" He was pretty clear on his opinion of my paranoia. "Call me," he said, laughing.

"I will," I said. "And when I do, I'll have something tangible for you."

I left the office and went to my car. I needed to talk to those eyewitnesses the prosecution had identified and I was done waiting for them to return my calls.

I was on my way to the highway when my cell phone buzzed, a single bleep, indicating a text message. I picked up the phone and watched the graphic on the screen, the back of an envelope appearing, within which the words, "Message from Pete."

I hit the "read" button and read the words of the text message:

> J: I have to get out of town. I feel like I'm trapped. I'll never beat the charges and I can't go to prison. I am not cut out for it. I hope you understand. I can't tell you where I'm going but I will try to get in touch with you soon. I'm sorry. Pete

I struggled to keep my focus on the road, reading and rereading the message. I clicked it off and dialed Pete's cell phone. Wherever he was, he had his cell phone close.

"Answer the phone!" I yelled. The call rang into voice mail. I hung up and typed a text message of my own, in reply to him: "Tell me where you are."

I hit "send" as I sped down the highway. I held the cell phone in front of me, in the event Pete would respond with another text. The text message was optimal from the sender's perspective because it avoided a conversation. And it was anonymous. It didn't have to be Pete making the communication. It was just Pete's phone.

I called the number of the hotel where he was staying, asked for his room, and got nothing but a half-dozen rings and then a voice mail. "Dammit," I said into the phone. I redialed the hotel and this time asked for any information on Pete Kolarich. The front desk had nothing in the system to indicate that Pete had checked out.

But I knew that he had.

45

I DROVE TO THE HOTEL, with the dawning realization that Pete wouldn't be there, that I had made a fundamental mistake, that Smith's goons could have found him any number of ways, including the same way I found Pete's supplier, J.D.—by triangulating his cell phone calls.

They even had a plausible cover for the abduction. Pete was facing a stiff prison sentence, and the text message made sense on a superficial level. He was running. He couldn't handle prison. Hell, I'd made it easy for them. Pete had taken a leave from his job and he was hiding in a hotel, having cut off contact with everyone. He had already isolated himself. Nobody would wonder where he was, why he hadn't shown up for work. Nobody would notice his absence.

I had underestimated Smith. I had miscalculated his desperation. I had backed Smith and his friends into a corner, and now they had my brother. They had taken a step that was irreversible. Until now, they could remain fairly anonymous, working behind the scenes to frame my brother on drug and gun charges. And they could reverse it. The same people who helped frame my brother could recant, or disappear. But abducting Pete? There was no retreating from that.

I'd long suspected that once Sammy's trial was over, Pete and I would have bull's-eyes on our chests. Smith and company would come after us. I'd hoped to wrap up everything before then to prevent it from happening.

But now they'd taken the first step down that road. They had my brother, and they'd use him for leverage against me—to drop the motion for DNA testing, to follow their game plan for the trial, to do whatever they wanted—but they'd never let Pete go now.

I left the hotel, having talked the management into letting me look briefly in his room, confirming, by the presence of his suitcase, his toiletries, that Pete had not willingly checked out of the hotel.

My body went cold. I drove in silence back to my office, where I expected to receive the call. I knew Smith would freeze me for a while, let my fear and imagination get the better of me. I turned to the stack of files in the corner of my office, devoted to the investigation into Audrey Cutler from way back when. If there had been any doubt that Smith's mysterious client had murdered Audrey and those other girls, there wasn't anymore.

I read through everything I could in the file, forcing out images of Pete and what they might be doing to him. When my intercom buzzed, I jumped from my seated position on the floor, revealing the extent of my nerves.

"Mr. Smith for you on 4407."

I punched the button and didn't speak.

"Your brother's alive," Smith said. "Whether he stays that way is up to you."

I didn't answer.

"Drop that motion. Forget about DNA testing or delays. Use the guy we gave you—Sanders—and stick to the goddamn script."

I took a deep breath, then another, before answering, the same answer I gave to Father Ben recently. "Or what?" I asked.

"What do you mean, 'or what?' You know what."

"My brother might as well be dead already. You'll never let him go."

"You have to trust that we will," he said. "What's the alternative?"

I could do this. If there was one thing I learned from my childhood, it was how to act tough when I was scared. This guy had my brother and me by the balls, but I could keep my voice strong, I could play the hardass. I had no other choice.

"The alternative is that I make you pay, Smith, starting tomorrow. The judge is going to allow my request for DNA testing. We both know that."

He paused. I had him thinking.

"Let Pete go right now," I said, "and I drop that DNA request. It's your only option."

"Hey, asshole, I'm the one with the options. You know what I have to do to keep my guys from tearing your brother from limb to limb right now? They want to take a razor blade to the guy."

I closed my eyes, shutting out the images. I felt like I was spinning out of control, full-throttle panic, just at the time that I had to *retain* control. My body began to shake uncontrollably. My brother was in their hands, and there was nothing I could do. I wanted to capitulate right there, cry uncle, offer to drop the DNA and go along with whatever they wanted, as long as they let Pete go. But what I had said to Smith was true—they'd never let him go. Not now. My game of poker had backfired.

"They're telling me, starting tomorrow, it's one finger a day, every day, until they're satisfied that you've fallen in line. I can't stop this, Jason. Only you can."

Time passed, what felt like an hour, though it was only a matter of minutes. We were both silent, save for our labored breathing. I wasn't the only one who was scared. I could hear it in Smith's voice. We'd taken this game too far, beyond the point of return. Neither of us was having fun.

"Okay, Smith, this is a one-time-only offer," I said. "Are you listening?"

I knew that he was. He was a wounded animal, just like me. No matter how much he had me over a barrel, it was clear that I had him by the shorthairs, too.

"My hearing is tomorrow at one P.M. That gives you a short window of time to do as I say. I want signed affidavits from the people who helped pinch Pete on that arrest. I know one of them is his supplier, J.D. I don't know who the other guy is."

I did know, of course—it was Marcus Mason, the notorious "Mace." Joel Lightner had delivered me a rather voluminous file on that gentleman. But I didn't need to share that with Smith.

"J.D., and the other guy," I continued. "They will swear in their affidavits that Pete was only there to make a small purchase of powder cocaine.

He wasn't a drug dealer, and he wasn't a gunrunner. He was in the wrong place at the wrong time. They will deliver those signed affidavits to the detective who arrested Pete, a guy by the name of Denny DePrizio. I think he works a regular day shift, so he shouldn't be hard to find."

He didn't need to know that I had connected DePrizio with him. Maybe he'd figured it out already, but I wasn't going to tell him. I needed to be as much of a question mark to him as he was to me.

"No chance," Smith said.

"You have my brother," I said. "And you're not letting him go until the trial is over, if ever. You've got the leverage on me, Smith. You win. But if you really mean what you say about letting him go when this is over, and clearing him of the charges—well, then, you have to do part of that now. Clear the charges now, show me that you're serious. And then I'll drop that request for the DNA testing. If that hasn't happened by one o'clock tomorrow, then I go forward with that motion."

"No deal," Smith said. He must have enjoyed that, throwing my oft-repeated line back at me.

"Then I have to assume you're just going to kill Pete, anyway. I have nothing left to lose. That's DePrizio, D-E-P-R-I-Z-I-O. He better have affidavits in his hand before my one o'clock hearing. You know me well enough to know I'm not bluffing, Smith."

I hung up the phone and held my breath. I fought it as best I could, any thought of what might happen to Pete. I couldn't rule out, much less control, anything they might do to Pete to make his stay with them less enjoyable. If I showed weakness, it would only get worse for him. They had to see me as a forceful adversary. It was the only way to get Pete back.

Unless, between now and the trial, I could figure out who killed Audrey Cutler.

I SAT ON MY BED, watching the clock approach midnight, pondering everything, using my abilities at cross-examination to punch holes in my plan. There were plenty of flaws, but I was satisfied that I was doing all I could do. The best thing I had going for me was the element of surprise. They didn't know me. They thought they did. It would have to be enough.

Just after midnight—thirteen hours before my hearing on the DNA testing before the judge—I turned off the bedroom light, leaving my entire town house in darkness.

46

JUST PAST THREE in the morning, two men—two of Smith's men—approached the town house from the rear. The front made no sense; it was too well-lit and on a fairly busy street. The rear, on the other hand, worked well for their purposes. The town house was backed up to an alley, a locked gate separating the alley from a small garden area consisting of a circular patio with the ubiquitous barbecue grill, table, and chairs.

The gate lock had to be picked, but that was not an overly difficult chore. Once past the lock, the two men slowly moved through the garden area toward the town house. One of the men, the bigger of the two, looked through the back-door window into the kitchen, searching for the house alarm. The alarm had a green light on it, meaning it was disarmed.

"It's not armed," he said to his partner. He readied his tension wrench and hooking pick to get through the back-door lock. "We spend all that time getting the combo to the alarm from his idiot brother and Kolarich doesn't even set the damn thing."

"Someone should tell these yuppies there's crime in this city," said the other, quietly.

"I'll make a note of it," I said, swinging my baseball bat at the bigger guy first, just as he'd turned, connecting square across the nose. The second guy was reaching for his weapon. I kicked out at his knee, the heel of my foot hitting the side of his kneecap, causing a painful buckling of his leg before he fell. Once he was on the ground, I used the butt of the baseball bat, two sharp blows into his face, knocking his head against the stone patio. The bigger guy hadn't had time to recover—he was stunned, crumpled awkwardly on the two concrete stairs leading up to the back door, blood gushing from his nose. "Where's my brother?" I asked him.

"Fuck . . . you," he said through his hands.

I swung the bat with all my might, with all the rage that had festered, into his kneecap, then into his chest. I didn't want to kill these guys, nor did I want retrograde amnesia. They needed to get word to Smith, with the one phone call they'd be allowed.

"Tell me where he is or I crush your skull."

At that moment, a light went on in the town house next door. We were making enough noise to wake the neighbors. It didn't look like I was going to get the answers I needed. I'd miscalculated, yet again. I should have let them come into my house and jumped them there, instead of huddling in the corner of my back patio awaiting them. My thought had been that I was safer outside, where I could run, I could yell for help, if these guys got the better of me. But if I'd chosen inside to make my move, I probably could have spent more time with them. I could have extracted the information I needed. Another mistake.

Figuring that my neighbors would be doing so shortly, I pulled out my cell phone and called 911, giving the dispatcher my address and telling them about two men trying to break into my house. Then I put the phone back in my pocket and surveyed my attackers.

They were suffering badly. The bigger guy's nose was shattered and bleeding uncontrollably and the blow to his chest had left him struggling for air. The second guy was stunned from the blows to his face followed by the immediate contact with the patio, forming a one-two punch that left him unable to discern up from down, dark from light, such that he didn't even seem to notice that his knee was dislocated.

I went back to the first guy. "Try again, Igor," I said, poising the bat over my shoulder. "One last chance. Where's my brother?"

"Your brother's . . . gonna fucking die." He managed something in the realm of a chuckle. I hit him across the chest with everything I had. He didn't take it well.

"You, Einstein." I stood over the second guy, who was barely conscious. "Where's my brother?"

I'd hoped that his dazed state might serve as truth serum, but he was unable to respond. I tried a couple more times with the bigger guy, alternating my watch from one to the other—they were armed, after all, and I had to be sure they wouldn't reach for their weapons. I decided not to disarm them because I wanted the cops to find them that way.

The bad thing about living in a nice neighborhood—normally a good thing—is that the cops come quickly. It was less than ten minutes later that two uniforms approached from the alley, coming through the same gate that Smith's buddies had entered.

A flashlight shone on my face. I was holding up my driver's license. "I'm the owner of the house," I said. "I called you. My name is Jason Kolarich. These guys are armed," I added, "but at the moment, not dangerous."

The cops, guns drawn, were not in the mood for levity, but it didn't take them long to get matters settled. My mentioning that I used to be an ACA, worked felony review out of Area Four, handled Judge Weiss's courtroom, all that good stuff, helped them considerably. I was, after all, the owner of the house, and the two guys lying wounded and weary, with guns stuffed in their pants, looked like they'd come off the set of *The Sopranos*.

I'd figured that Smith's final play before tomorrow's court hearing would be to mess me up, or maybe even detain me briefly—anything to keep me from attending that hearing. It's what I would have done, if I were them. But then, if I were them, I might have considered the possibility that my adversary might anticipate that very move, and might be lying in wait in the corner of his back patio with a baseball bat.

The goons were arrested on attempted aggravated burglary and suspicion of unlawful weapons charges. They were taken to the station house for processing and detention. I sat at the desk of a lieutenant and gave my statement. He gave me the names of my attackers and mentioned that each of them had encountered more than one brush with the law in the past, which suggested that their bond might be set pretty high when their arraignment came.

"These guys had handcuffs and rope," the lieutenant told me. "Didn't look like they were looking for a smash-and-grab. It looked more like a kidnapping, in fact."

I expressed my utter shock at the possibility. "Why me?" I asked.

"I was going to ask you that."

"Never heard of these guys, Lieutenant. Nino Ramsey and John Tunicci? I don't have a clue."

"You said you're a criminal defense lawyer. You ever represent any organized crime?"

"No."

"Okay. Okay." The cop thought about that. "These guys, they're nothing but a couple of thugs. Enforcer types. They freelance from time to time, but they usually run with the Capparelli family."

He was talking about old-school mafia, Rico Capparelli's crew. Rico, last I recalled, was serving out the rest of his life in a maximum-security federal pen. It stood out, more than anything, for the prosecutorial joke. The old man went down for federal racketeering charges—Rico was pinched on RICO.

Was I up against organized crime? It could mean so many different things nowadays, that phrase. As much as the feds had curtailed their influence, they hadn't so much cured the world of crime as simply forced these scumbags to scatter into subgroups—less "organized," maybe, but still criminals. It didn't narrow my focus much at all.

But at least I had two of these guys out of the picture for a short time. I was confident now that I was up against a small band of people working for Smith—four people, to be exact. Two of them, presumably, had been baby-sitting Pete while the other two came for me. Now, for a time, at least, they had lost half their manpower.

When I left the police station, as the sun was rising, I drove to a hotel. I had several changes of clothes in the trunk of my car along with toiletries. I had no intention of going home, or going anywhere that Smith might expect me to go, until that court hearing at one o'clock today. Smith would not have another chance to come at me.

I knew I had to get some sleep. I knew it, but I couldn't force it. I stretched out on the rickety bed and closed my eyes, trying to focus myself into calm. I woke with a start, the bedside clock telling me it was just past nine o'clock. I took a shower, dressed in my suit, reupped with the hotel for another night, and drove to the criminal courthouse, where I would present my motion in about three hours. I figured that Smith might make one last run at me, but he wouldn't count on me showing up three hours early to court.

Once inside the courthouse and past the metal detectors, I called Joel Lightner and gave him the names of my would-be attackers, Nino Ramsey and John Tunicci. "Enforcers, I think," I told him. "Apparently, they run with the Capparellis."

"The Capparellis? What the hell have you gotten into, Jason?"

"I wish I knew. Anyway—they're my best lead. My guess is, they're freelancing for someone, I just don't know who. Hoping my prized investigator can help me with that?"

"I'll do my best," Joel promised. "Hey, did you get in touch with Jimmy Stewart?"

"I think he prefers 'Jim.'"

"That's why I call him 'Jimmy.'"

"Yeah, I met with him. He says you're a drunk and a womanizer."

"I'll sue."

"Truth is an absolute defense, Joel. Gotta run."

"Say, Jason. Do you know what the hell you're doing?"

I didn't have an answer so I punched out.

I made my way up to the courtroom where my motion would be heard later today. The courtroom was empty. I walked around to the judge's chambers and found her clerk in the anteroom. "Does the judge have any free time tomorrow?" I asked. "I might need to continue something I have up today."

The judge had a few openings, though I didn't take them, not yet. I loitered in the hallway for a few minutes, checking my watch.

At eleven-thirty, my cell phone rang.

47

I STOOD AGAINST the all-glass south wall of the building to maximize the reception on the cell phone. As I looked over the city's southwest side, the industrial yards and beaten-down residential neighborhoods, I opened the humming phone.

"Kolarich." Smith didn't sound so upbeat.

"Having a bad morning, Smith?"

He paused, showing his appropriate disdain. "The affidavit has been prepared."

"Affidavit? Singular?"

"Marcus Mason is the man who was picked up with your brother."

Mace. I knew this already, but he didn't know that I knew.

"The affidavit will meet with your liking."

"I want an original delivered to my office and a copy to Detective DePrizio."

"We found this detective and delivered it to his attention. You didn't say anything about a copy to your office."

"I'm saying it now. Make it happen. Listen, Smith. You call me in exactly half an hour—high noon—and my assistant better have seen that affidavit by then."

"Listen—"

"Half an hour," I said, closing the cell phone.

I returned to the judge's clerk and canceled today's 1:00 P.M. hearing.

Then I called the prosecutor, Lester Mapp, and broke the news to him. He didn't seem to care much about the hearing but said he wanted to continue our "previous discussions," meaning a plea deal, though I put him off.

At ten minutes to noon, I called my assistant, Marie.

"Just got it," she said. "Let's see. 'Affidavit of Marcus Mason.'" She read the contents to me. "'My name is Marcus Mason. I have personal knowledge of all matters stated herein. I have a relationship as an undercover informant with Detective Dennis DePrizio. I was working with Detective DePrizio on an operation involving the sale of a substantial quantity of firearms and rock cocaine. The plan had been that a man who called himself "J.D." and I would meet on Saturday, October 6, 2007, at an abandoned warehouse previously owned by Lanier's Amusement Supply Company, on the 3300 block of West Summerset. However, on Friday, October 5, 2007, near the hour of midnight, I received a call from "J.D." in which he insisted that we make the purchase immediately. I had no choice but to agree. I immediately contacted Detective DePrizio at his home. As far as I could tell, Detective DePrizio had been asleep. Then I drove to the old Lanier's warehouse to meet with "J.D."

"'Before Detective DePrizio arrived, "J.D." arrived at the warehouse and we began to discuss the terms of the purchase. He informed me that he had received a telephone call from someone who would be arriving, not to purchase the rock cocaine or the firearms, but for an unrelated reason that had nothing to do with me or the transaction. He told me this person's name was "Pete." He asked that I not mention anything about our transaction.

"'This gentleman, who introduced himself as "Pete," arrived shortly thereafter. He was Caucasian, approximately five foot nine, approximately one hundred sixty pounds. He asked "J.D." if everything was okay. He seemed concerned and asked "J.D." what was taking place. "J.D." told him it was nothing that concerned him and he shouldn't ask questions. "Pete" seemed suspicious and said that he was going to leave.

"'At that moment, Detective DePrizio entered the warehouse and announced his presence. "J.D." was not apprehended. I assume that he escaped to the rear entrance. "Pete" was arrested along with me. "Pete" did not appear to have any idea what was taking place between "J.D." and

me. I have no reason to believe, and do not believe, that "Pete" had anything to do with the transaction involving the rock cocaine or the firearms.' That's it, Jason," said Marie. "It's signed by Marcus Mason and
notarized."

It was like a song with the most beautiful lyrics I'd ever heard. It
absolved Pete of all wrongdoing—not even a minor drug charge. Smith's
desperation was evident.

"Scan that affidavit into the computer and e-mail it to me, to Shauna,
to yourself, okay?" I didn't want to run the risk that a paper copy would
get "lost" after I'd made this deal with Smith. My cell phone buzzed, indicating another call. "Gotta run, Marie."

The new call was Smith, five minutes early. "You got what you wanted,"
he said.

"I got most of what I wanted, Smith. What I really want is those charges
against my brother dropped."

"There is no way your brother could be prosecuted with that affidavit
out there. But I can't make those charges disappear. That wasn't our deal.
You said all I had to do was produce that affidavit by today—"

"Yeah, don't you hate it when the other side doesn't play fair? So shut
up and listen to me, Smith. I'm going to reach out to that detective, and
he better have that affidavit in his hand. And it better be enough to convince him to drop the charges."

"*I* can't control what that detective—"

"I said shut up, didn't I? So shut up. If DePrizio has the affidavit, I'll
withdraw the motion for now. But you and I both know that I can renew
that motion. And if the prosecution doesn't want to drop the charges
against Pete, then I *will* renew that motion. For your sake, you better
hope DePrizio buys this affidavit and can sell it to the prosecutors."

"That affidavit—"

"That affidavit," I said, "could be explained away later by some kind of
bullshit. Mason could say I put a gun to his head and made him sign it.
I'm not taking any chances, Smith. So I guess you better pray."

I hung up the phone and paced the halls, forcing myself to bide my
time. Twelve-fifteen. Twelve-thirty. I made the call.

"Detective DePrizio, please," I told the receptionist.

A moment later, he answered. "DePrizio."

"This is Jason Kolarich, Detective."

"Kolarich. Kolarich. Just the guy I wanted to talk to. Guess what I'm looking at?"

"Probably the same thing I just got in my office."

"Yeah? Like you don't know anything about this?"

I didn't respond to that. He was just doing this for show, anyway. He was part of the game. And my brain was too frayed to get creative with him.

"Okay, so maybe Mason *was* my CI," he said. "We had a sting set up but it's like the affidavit said, this scumbag J.D. called an audible. It started early and I barely got there in time. I just talked to Mason and I guess you were right—your brother was in the wrong place, wrong time."

Sure, whatever. I didn't see where I could add anything to the conversation. The ball was rolling down the hill and the best thing I could do was to simply get out of the way.

DePrizio sighed. "I guess your brother's owed an apology."

My brother was owed a lot more from this scumbag of a cop, but I just said, "No apology necessary. A dismissal of the charges would be fine. I want the charges dropped within twenty-four hours or we'll sue."

DePrizio groaned. "Let me see what I can do. Personally, I think it's the least we can do for your brother."

I rested my head against the glass wall, looking down at the passersby, lawyers and clients scurrying to court. My brother, Pete, wouldn't have court to worry about anymore. He would walk completely from these charges. I took a moment to celebrate, to savor this victory in the battle.

Because that's all it was—one small battle in a larger war. They had my brother, and they had no intention of ever letting him go. Whatever else they might tell me, as soon as Sammy's trial was over, they'd kill him and then come looking for me. The trial started in thirteen days, and once it began, I'd be too tied up to find Pete.

I had thirteen days to find my brother. The only way I knew how was to locate Smith. And the only lead I had on Smith was the murder of Audrey Cutler. I was now sure that Smith's client had been behind that murder. I had less than two weeks to solve a cold case.

"I'll find you, little brother," I promised.

48

I'D JUST RETURNED to my law office when Smith called again. "You withdrew the motion, I trust," he said.

"I withdrew it, yes," I said into my cell phone. "Now, we have to set a few more ground rules, Smith."

"I still have your brother. Let's not forget that." Smith seemed calmer now, trying to reassert control. I'd spooked him good with the threat of that DNA motion, but he was getting his groove back.

"I want to hear from Pete every day. I want him to read that day's headline from the *Watch*. And I want you to send me a photo every day that shows me that you aren't hurting him."

"If I think it's to our advantage to let you hear his voice, I'll do that," he said. "If not, I won't. But don't forget what I said, Jason. You've pissed these guys off beyond belief, and they have a pincushion named Pete Kolarich to take out their frustrations. Do not fuck around, son. Not one inch off course. You keep your nose clean, they won't hurt him any further."

Further. My stomach sank.

"Oh, yeah," he said, picking up on my hesitation. "You didn't think your little stunt would go unpunished, did you?"

"Tell me what you did to him."

"It's nothing that would prevent him from fully functioning, if things go as we all hope."

"Smith, you tell me—"

"Let's focus on the future, Jason. Beginning with two days from now, this coming Thursday. The prosecution is contesting the testimony of Mr. Butcher."

I struggled to control my emotions. He knew he was stinging me with his mention of what he did to my brother. But I had to keep the upper hand here. I made myself believe that he was bluffing, anything to stifle the images flooding my brain.

He was correct that this Thursday, the prosecution would be asking the court to bar the testimony of Tommy Butcher's identification of Kenny Sanders as the black-guy-fleeing-the-scene. I'd told Butcher that this might happen—it's what I would do, if I were the prosecutor—and I had agreed to the hearing this Thursday. I hadn't yet seen the prosecution's written motion, but yesterday, Lester Mapp had promised it was forthcoming. He told me yesterday he'd file it today, and I recalled a particularly disturbing comment—*Your star witness isn't such a star.*

I went to the county Web site to pull up the notice of the motion. There it was, the line for "Contested Motion—Prosecution," followed by, "Hearing—10/18/08, 9:30 A.M."

"This will be a critical moment," he said. "Mr. Sanders is crucial to this case. The jury must know that Mr. Butcher identified him as fleeing the scene. Don't fuck this up, Jason."

Your star witness isn't such a star. "We'll beat the motion," I predicted, hoping they weren't famous last words. "But Smith, if you want me to beat that motion, you won't be sending any more goons like Nino and Johnny after me, will you?"

He didn't answer.

"How are they doing, anyway?" I asked. "Last I saw, they'd taken some pretty good beatings."

"Enjoy that, Kolarich. Have a good laugh. Because your brother certainly didn't."

With that, the line went dead.

AFTER TALKING TO SMITH, I put in a call to Kenny Sanders at the restaurant where he worked. The first time I did so, the phone was eventually hung up. I tried again and the second time was a charm.

"It's Jason Kolarich, Mr. Sanders. The lawyer."

"Yeah, okay."

"You have to be in court this Thursday," I said. "The prosecution is going to fight this evidence."

"Gonna fight, okay. Yeah, okay."

"Have you received a subpoena from them?"

"Haven't got nothin'. No, sir. Didn't know 'bout it."

"Well, you will get a subpoena, probably today. You have to be there. Can you do that?" I gave him the time and location.

"So what do I gotta do?" he asked.

"Probably nothing except show up. But just in case, we should go over your testimony again before the hearing."

I made some arrangements with Sanders to talk again.

Marie walked in with a copy of Lester Mapp's motion to bar the testimony of Thomas Butcher, which would be heard in two days, along with a notice of the issuance of a subpoena to Butcher to attend the hearing. There was no subpoena issued to Kenny Sanders, though. That was interesting. The prosecutor didn't want to question Sanders, only Butcher.

The motion to bar Butcher's testimony was rather brief, but attached to it was the criminal history of Tommy Butcher. Butcher, it seemed, did not have a spotless record. He'd pleaded guilty to submitting fraudulent bid documents for a public construction job in 1982, for which he'd spent five months at a Club Fed. Then, in 1990, he pleaded to lying to federal prosecutors in an investigation into payroll-tax fraud and received a year and a day in a federal penitentiary.

Not just crimes, but crimes of dishonesty. I'd have vastly preferred a good old-fashioned assault and battery. Butcher had twice pleaded to what, in essence, was lying under oath.

Mr. Butcher's history of perjury, together with his suspiciously last-minute identification of a man approximately one year after the occurrence, takes this matter beyond the traditional balancing of probity versus prejudice to a preliminary issue of the inherent unreliability of Mr. Butcher's testimony. Lester Mapp was laying it on pretty thick, but he had to. He had to convince Judge Poker that the testimony was so wholly unreliable that the jury shouldn't ever hear it in the first place. It was always a problem for me that Butcher had come forward over a year after the trial, and now we were going to ask a jury to believe that he could remember a man—Kenny Sanders—who he'd seen for all of a few seconds as Sanders ran past him on his way out of the apartment building.

I put in a call to Tommy Butcher but got his voice mail. He had to know that his criminal history would be a part of this, but he hadn't mentioned anything to me. Maybe a layperson doesn't think about such things. Butcher struck me as someone who probably wouldn't feel a whole lot of remorse for his prior actions, and maybe the whole thing hadn't occurred to him.

My cell phone rang. It was about to die and I plugged it into the cord.

"Jason, it's Denny DePrizio. I've got some good news for you."

I didn't speak.

"You said you'd be willing to waive any right to sue over this thing?"

"Yes," I said.

"Then we can get this thing wrapped up tomorrow, like you wanted."

"Good." I listened to him as he gave me the details.

"You okay, Kolarich? You sound funny. Different."

"I'm fine."

I was anything but fine. But at least I would get Pete's case dropped. A fresh start for him, if he could make it out of this whole thing in one piece.

49

PEOPLE VERSUS PETER KOLARICH, Case Number 08 CR 67782."

"Good morning, Your Honor, Jason Kolarich for the defendant."

Judge Bonarides raised his tired eyes to me. "The defendant is not present?"

"He's not, Your Honor."

"Well, I suppose under the circumstances," the judge said. "Counsel?" The judge looked at the prosecutor, a young woman named Elizabeth Morrow.

"Motion State S-O-L, Your Honor," she said. The prosecution, on its own motion, was asking that the charges against my brother be stricken with leave to reinstate.

Judge Bonarides cast another glance in my direction. He was probably wondering how some fairly significant drug-and-gun charges were being dropped straight out, without a plea deal. Himself a former public defender, he presumably had a narrow view of the prosecution's willingness to forgive and forget. Their willingness, in this case, stemmed from my signing of a different sort of agreement only minutes earlier—my agreement not to sue the county for false arrest or wrongful prosecution. But that fell outside the purview of a criminal courts judge, and no one would ever know about it.

Or maybe the judge recognized me. He came out of the same west-side

area that produced Senator Almundo. There was a good deal of resentment in the west-side Latino community over Hector's prosecution, with
claims of selective prosecution based on race, resentment that became
justified after the feds lost the case. As one of Hector's defenders, I had a
few fans in that community.

"The defendant answers ready for trial," I said, which started the clock
on their time to refile the charges. But this was all just a formality. The
drugs-and-guns charges were officially dead. And whatever curiosity
Judge Bonarides might have, in the end, another case was disappearing
from his docket, and he wouldn't break out a hanky over it.

The judge was on to the next case only moments later. I shook the
prosecutor's hand. "Thank you," I said.

"Don't thank me. The cop and the CI went south."

It wasn't the most gracious acceptance, but I didn't care. I'd at least
closed one chapter of the book. Pete didn't have a criminal case to worry
about. Now he only had the small matter of staying alive.

As I walked out of the courtroom, I caught the eye of Jim Stewart, who
was sitting in the corner of the courtroom, dressed in a sweater and a
baseball cap over his crew cut. I acknowledged him and he nodded back.
I thought I even caught the hint of a smile cross his sober face.

I MET TOMMY BUTCHER at the construction site where I last
found him, directing traffic and conversing with people who appeared to
be from the park district, the owners of the building he was constructing.
He was tired and ornery by the time he made time for me. We found a
spot at a table that had been set up inside the half-constructed building
for the workers to eat lunch.

"Oh. Right," he said, after I laid out for him a detailed recitation of his
criminal background.

"You forgot to mention it."

"I forgot, period. What's the point? I still saw a colored guy running
from that building. Nothin' I did back in the day changes that."

I sighed.

"Look, I got better things to do, Mr. Kolarich. I don't need this shit."

"No—"

"I'm tryin' to come forward here and tell what I saw. Someone's gonna turn me into a crook for sayin' so, maybe I'll take a pass on the whole thing. Get me?"

"I get you." I raised a hand. "Look, I need you. My client needs you. I'm just saying, we need to be prepared for this. They're going to go after you—"

"Everybody and their fuckin' brother fudged bid apps back then," he said, his face fully colored in anger. "I put down a subcontractor as minority-owned when they weren't. So what? Then in 'ninety, yeah, I'm paying some people in cash under the table so Uncle fuckin' Sam doesn't bleed me dry. Maybe I don't volunteer that info when the G comes around. So now, suddenly, I *didn't* see a brother runnin' out of that building that night?"

"See, this is precisely why I'm here, Tom. This is precisely how the prosecution's going to want you to react. You just be forthright with your explanations, admit to whatever you admitted in terms of plea bargains, and act like it's all behind you. Don't fight with them. The judge is going to believe you if you keep your cool."

"Keep my cool," he said, shaking his head. "This sounds like it's gonna be a world of fuckin' fun. I'm startin' to get real glad I volunteered for this."

The attitude, Tommy, the attitude. This was going to take some serious work. This was going to take the afternoon. I'd have to beat him up so many times that he became immune to it, that he'd be ready for it when Lester Mapp came after him.

Because, at the end of the day, Tommy Butcher's identification of Ken Sanders was one of only two things I had going for me in the case against Sammy Cutler. That, and Archie Novotny. I couldn't deny that Sammy was parked just down the street from Perlini's apartment, and I couldn't deny that the window of time that his car was parked perfectly matched the time it would take Sammy to go to Perlini's apartment, kill him, return to the car, and drive away. I couldn't even speak to the witnesses who identified Sammy, all of whom were refusing to return my phone calls. And Sammy's would-be confession—where he blurted out

Griffin Perlini's name before anyone even mentioned why he was being questioned—didn't help, either.

No, all I had was two alternative suspects. I would give the jury Kenny Sanders, identified by Tommy Butcher as the black-guy-fleeing-the-scene, and I would give them Archie Novotny, who had motive and no alibi for the night of the murder. That was it. That was all I had. And Novotny would deny everything, of course. He would be an adverse witness.

Which made Tommy Butcher's identification of Kenny Sanders all the more crucial. These were the only witnesses who were on my side. I had to make sure that Tommy Butcher held up under an intense cross-examination by Lester Mapp.

"Let's take it from the top," I said.

MY CELL PHONE rang at my office near eight o'clock that evening. When I answered it, I heard Pete's voice.

"Jason, it's Pete. I'm doing—okay. The headline of the *Watch* is 'County Budget Assailed.' Take care of yourself, man."

The line went dead. It was a tape recording, not Pete's live voice. That was smart. They couldn't risk Pete blurting something out that would tell me where he was, or anything at all that might implicate them.

The cell rang again.

"Jason," Smith said. "Best of luck at that hearing tomorrow, with Mr. Butcher's testimony. A critical moment, obviously. Critical for Mr. Cutler. And critical for your brother. Y'know, I think these guys are almost hoping you'll screw up, so they can get to work on Pete."

He hung up before I could reply. I checked the county clerk's Web site to be sure of the time of tomorrow's hearing, a superstition of mine.

I called Kenny Sanders one more time to check in with him.

"Never did get one," he told me, referring to a subpoena from the prosecution.

"The prosecution didn't subpoena you? Or call you?"

"No, sir. Only reason I know 'bout it's 'cause of you tellin' me."

"Okay, well—show up anyway," I said. I hung up with him. Then I looked back at the county Web site again.

There it was, just below the line for "Contested Motion—Prosecution," without elaboration that it was the prosecution's motion to bar testimony. "Hearing—10/18/08, 9:30 A.M."

I picked up my cell phone again and dialed the number for Joel Lightner. "The name is Tommy Butcher," I said. "I need his background and more, Joel. Starting as soon as you can."

50

SAMMY WAS BROUGHT into the courtroom at a little after nine in the morning. The deputy removed his manacles and he took a seat next to me, wearing his prison jumpsuit. There was no jury, so no need to make him look more respectable in a suit.

Across from me, Lester Mapp was conferring with another attorney, a young woman. He carried that air of authority that accompanied his position. He wore it a little too proudly. I never felt comfortable with it, myself, the self-righteousness. The way I saw it, lots of people do lots of things they shouldn't, and the ones hauled into court are just the ones who got caught. Unless we could be more consistent in how we enforced the law, the air of superiority didn't fit.

I checked my watch for the fourth time when Tommy Butcher walked in. I'd told him to wear a suit, but the best he could do was a brown tweed sport coat, red tie, and slacks, which didn't seem to fit him too comfortably. I nodded to him but didn't approach, other than to make a calming gesture with my hands.

"All rise."

Judge Kathleen Poker walked into court with her typical no-nonsense approach and got right down to business, looking over her glasses at the courtroom. *"People versus Cutler,"* she said. "Show Mr. Mapp present for the People. Show Mr. Kolarich and the defendant present as well. Mr. Mapp?"

"Yes, Your Honor." Mapp rose and buttoned his impressive suit coat.

"I've read your motion. Do you have anything further?"

"We'd ask to call Thomas Butcher, Your Honor."

"Is Mr. Butcher present—okay, Mr. Butcher. Will you please come forward, sir?"

Witnesses come in all shapes and sizes, well-dressed and not, confident and meek, but you always want someone who seems comfortable, which means they're being honest. Butcher seemed to do well enough on first glance, walking slowly to the witness stand and swearing the oath given to him by the bailiff. He rolled his neck, showing his discomfort with a buttoned-up collar and tie. That part wasn't so good. Fidgeting was not on a lawyer's wish list for his client.

"Permission to treat as adverse," said Mapp. I didn't bother to object, because Butcher was a defense witness. Mapp was asking for the right to cross-examine, to ask leading questions.

"Your Honor, for the record, I assume we can stipulate that the offense under indictment—the murder of Griffin Perlini—took place on September 21, 2006."

"So stipulated," I said.

"Thank you, Counsel." Lester Mapp opened a file folder on the lectern between the prosecution and defense tables. "Mr. Butcher, good morning."

That was about as friendly as the prosecutor was going to get.

"You gave a statement to the police in regard to this crime on September 18 of 2007," he said. "Two-thousand-*seven*. Almost an entire year later."

"Yeah, that's right." Already, Butcher was getting his back up a bit, adjusting in his seat and setting his jaw. His eyes shot in my direction.

"On the date of this shooting—September 21, 2006—you were not aware of a shooting taking place."

"No. Not then, no."

"You heard about it later?"

"Right. I read about it in the paper."

"The *Watch*?"

"Yeah. Some article about the case."

"Do you recall when this was?"

"Not the exact date."

"Well, okay—but let's try it like this," Mapp said. "You came to the police on September 18 of this year. How many days before that date had you read the article?"

When I asked Butcher almost that precise question yesterday, he couldn't say. I went through the online archives of the *Watch* and found an article dated September 16 of this year, which was the Sunday edition. The article was a one-paragraph in the Metro Shorts about a firm trial date being set, including in the discussion that a shooting took place outside the Liberty Street Apartment Complex on the evening of September 21, 2006.

"The Sunday previous," said Butcher. "Something about it in the Metro section."

"Okay." Mapp was slightly disappointed. He obviously had done some research in this regard and was aware of that article. "And what made you come forward?"

"Well, it's like I told the cops. I'd seen this man running from the building with a gun in his pants. So I figured, maybe there was something to it."

"You remembered the date that well?" asked the prosecutor. "You remembered September 21, 2006, as the date that you saw this alleged man running from the building?"

"Well, not exactly like that. I mean, I had to think about it. But then I checked back and it was a Thursday that it happened, and I asked my brother Jake about it, and we both thought about it and figured that, yeah, it was the right date."

"All right, let's come back to that," Mapp said. I felt a flutter in my stomach. Sometimes lawyers change the topic because they're not making any inroads, and rather than cry uncle, they just act like they'll "come back to it." Other times, however, they're hoping to trap a witness by jumping from topic to topic, locking them down on one detail and then using that detail against them in another area.

"Tell the Court where you were," Mapp said. "Before this event, I mean."

"Downey's Pub is the name." Butcher looked at the judge. "Over on West Liberty, right about Liberty and Manning."

"Manning is the cross street," Mapp confirmed.

"Yeah."

"That's about four city blocks away from the Liberty Apartments, right?"

"Somethin' like that."

"Okay, and who was present with you at Downey's Pub?"

"Me and my brother."

"And why Downey's Pub?"

"Good place, I guess."

"You didn't go there for the décor, I take it."

Butcher smiled. "Downey's? No."

"Or for the nice neighborhood?"

"No, definitely not."

Not a good answer. I'd talked to Butcher about that.

"Kind of—kind of a rough neighborhood, wouldn't you say?"

"Kind of rough," Butcher agreed.

"But no particular reason for Downey's?"

I could have objected but didn't.

Butcher opened his hands. "I mean, what do you want?"

"I want to know why you were there. You live, what, about four miles from the place?"

"Yeah, so?"

Lester Mapp shrugged easily. He was handling this pretty well. "There's a tavern or two between your house and that bar, right?"

The judge smiled. Butcher chuckled. "One or three hundred," he said. "It's as good a place as any. Me and my brother, we used to go there a lot before we had wives."

Several people sprinkled in the gallery, a reporter or two and some court junkies, laughed. Judge Kathleen Poker did not.

"What was the occasion for going out that night?" Mapp asked.

"Now you *sound* like my wife," he answered.

More laughter, but the judge turned to Butcher and said, "Please answer the question."

Butcher nodded at her. "Okay, well, we was out, that's all. Me and my brother blow off some steam now and then. It had been a long week."

"Oh, it's not unusual?" Mapp asked it casually, but it was not a casual question.

"No. We go out a lot."

"How often? Once a week?"

"Could be."

"Twice a week?"

"Been known to happen."

"You didn't need a special occasion that night," Mapp said.

"No."

"And you didn't *have* a special occasion."

"No."

"So let's talk about that month last year. September of last year. How many times did you two go out drinking that month?"

"Oh, well, come on—I don't know. Who knows?"

No—that was not a good answer. You can't claim to remember a date certain, going back a year, but then act like you have no memory of other dates in that month.

"No idea," Mapp confirmed.

"No, I mean—I don't know."

"Fair enough. What were you drinking that night?"

"Probably whiskey."

"Probably? You're not sure?"

"It's what I usually drink."

"You don't have a specific memory."

"No. Not, like, specific."

"How many drinks?"

"I don't know. I mean, I was okay afterward, so not that much."

"But you don't recall."

"No."

"How long were you there?"

"Oh, probably a normal amount. Maybe couple hours, three hours maybe."

"You don't specifically recall?"

"No, but it wasn't, like, a marathon session."

Mapp smiled. "Okay. What was the weather like that night?"

Butcher cleared his throat. "Probably—I mean, pretty much normal."

"Cold? Rainy? Snowing?"

"No, I mean—pretty much normal, I guess. Not rainin' or nothin' like that."

"Okay. Oh, by the way—did you pay with a credit card? Or did your brother?"

Butcher and I had worked on his answer to this question.

"I don't know for certain, but I doubt it," he answered. "We usually pay cash."

"You usually pay cash? Why's that?"

"Keep it off the credit card bills," he said. "The wives, you know. No offense, Your Honor," he added, looking up at the judge.

The judge shook her head but smiled.

"So there's no record of this transaction?"

"There's a cash record."

"Okay, fine." The prosecutor had made his point, and it seemed like it wasn't lost on the judge. "A cash record. Okay. Did you eat there that night?"

"No."

"You just went there for some drinks?"

"Yeah."

"Alcoholic drinks? You're not saying you went there for fountain sodas?"

"No." Butcher chuckled again. "We didn't drink Pepsi."

"What time did you leave?"

"Maybe—maybe ten. About ten?"

"Was that early for you guys?"

"I don't know about early. I mean, the missus doesn't appreciate it, you stay out real late."

"You wanted to get home to your wife."

"Yeah."

"Did you guys drive together?"

"No."

"Okay, where'd you park your car?"

"A few blocks away."

"What direction from Downey's?"

"Well, west of it, 'cause that's the direction we were walking."

"Okay, where specifically?"

"I don't know, specifically."

"But to have passed the Liberty Apartments Complex, you'd have to walk four city blocks from Downey's Pub. So you were parked at least four city blocks away, right? A half mile away."

Butcher and I had worked on this answer extensively.

"Yeah, see, but that's on purpose," said Butcher. "That's what I do when I'm out. I give myself a walk after drinking. Straightens you out. Sobers you up. So yeah, I parked a way's away."

"But you don't know where, exactly."

"No."

"And the point was, you guys were drinking, so you wanted to give yourself a walk."

"That's it."

"Whiskey, I think you said."

"Probably."

"Probably. But definitely not soft drinks."

"No, definitely not."

Mapp paused, which probably meant a segue. "Now, Mr. Butcher, you have a criminal record, isn't that true?"

Butcher adjusted his position in the witness chair. "Yeah, it's true."

"You were convicted of submitting a false bid application on a public construction contract, isn't that the case?"

"Yeah."

"You were a project manager for Emerson Construction Company back in 1982," he said.

"Yeah, and in a bid application for an annex to a high school, we listed a subcontractor as a minority-owned business that, it turned out, was not minority owned."

"*We* listed. You mean, *you* listed."

"Well—yeah, I mean, I wasn't an owner at Emerson. This was before our family owned our own company. But yeah, I was the one who filled the thing out."

"And you knew, when you listed that subcontractor on your bid application—you knew that the sub was not a minority-owned company."

"Yeah, I did. It was wrong."

"And you signed an affidavit swearing to the truth of that statement."

"Right."

"So you lied under oath."

"I admitted to that. I was young and stupid."

"Were you young and stupid in 1990, too? Isn't that when you were convicted of obstruction of justice when you lied to an IRS inspector about payroll taxes?"

"Well, I don't know about young—but I was stupid."

"You knew that it was a crime to lie to a federal agent, didn't you?"

"I s'pose I did."

Mapp nodded. I was getting uneasy. He had something up his sleeve here.

"Before you were to find yourself in another legal—predicament, let's say—I'd just want to make sure you were clearly testifying to the truth here today."

"Objection," I said. "Argumentative."

"Let's move on," the judge said.

"Yes, Your Honor." Mapp did a slight bow. "Mr. Butcher, you're sure it was Downey's Pub you were at that night?"

"Yeah."

"You're sure you were drinking alcohol?"

"Yeah."

"And you're sure it was September 21, 2006?"

"Yeah. Why?" Butcher asked, a bit meekly. Suddenly, his brown tweed sport coat and buttoned collar seemed a little warm, a little uncomfortable, as Butcher rolled his neck and kept his eyes on the prosecutor.

"Why?" Mapp paused. "Because, Mr. Butcher, I'm just trying to figure out how Downey's Pub could have served alcohol on September 21, 2006, when Downey's Pub *didn't have a liquor license* on that date. When it wasn't even *open* on that date."

51

"OBJECTION." I got to my feet on shaky legs. Lester Mapp handed me a certified copy of an order handed down by the state's liquor control commission, which suspended the liquor license of Downey's Pub effective September 1, 2006, for the period of thirty days.

"Selling alcohol to a minor was the offense," said Mapp. "A third violation, warranting a one-month suspension. A one-month suspension that ran through the first week of October."

"Objection," I repeated. "This wasn't disclosed to the defense. This wasn't provided to me and it wasn't in the prosecution's written motion." What I was saying had merit, but it was like complaining that a life preserver hadn't been properly inflated to federal regulations. I was right, but I was still going to drown.

"I just got it today," said Mapp. "We're two weeks out from trial. This is just a hearing."

The judge shot the prosecutor a look. She didn't appreciate the grandstanding. She read from the document that Mapp handed her.

Unfair surprise, I wanted to say, but there was no cure for my ill. Mapp was right. I had almost two weeks before trial. And the document said what it said. Tommy Butcher couldn't have been at Downey's Pub on the evening of September 21, 2006, the night Griffin Perlini was murdered.

"Counsel," the judge said, waving the document at me. "I don't know—you're right, of course, that Mr. Mapp improperly sprang this on you. But that doesn't change what I'm reading here. Mr. Butcher." She turned to him. "Mr. Butcher, this is a serious development for you."

Butcher had already figured that out. He was white as a sheet. "Your Honor, best of my memory—I mean, maybe he was open anyway?"

"The front door of the establishment was locked on order of the Liquor Control Commission," Mapp said with confidence. He was clearly enjoying himself. "The state locks the front door with a padlock. They don't leave a key for the owner. The owner can go in the back door, but he's not allowed to open the place to the public—"

"I understand, Counsel. You've more than made your point."

I couldn't believe this was happening. One-half of my two-pronged attack was coming apart before my eyes.

"Mr. Butcher," the judge said. "I'm going to ask you a few questions, and you have the right to have a lawyer present if you wish."

Butcher didn't answer. His mouth parted, like he was a curious child.

"Would you like to consult with an attorney, Mr. Butcher?"

"No—no, Judge."

"All right, then. Do you have any personal stake in the outcome of this case?"

"Me? No."

"Do you have any relationship with the defendant, Mr. Cutler?"

"No."

"Or Mr. Kolarich, the attorney?"

"No, Judge." Butcher still looked like the guy who hadn't figured out the joke was on him. Maybe that's because the joke was on me. And Sammy.

"Fuck," Sammy mumbled.

"Judge, this can't be right," Butcher said. "Maybe—maybe—"

"All right, now." The judge resumed her position, facing the entire courtroom. "The Court will state for the record that it is inclined to believe that Mr. Butcher has made an inadvertent mistake and not an intentional lie. It would not be my decision ultimately, but I think the record should reflect my viewpoint." She looked at the prosecutor. "In light of Mr. Mapp's surprise evidence here, I think it would be imprudent for me to bar Mr. Butcher's testimony today. Maybe, Mr. Kolarich, you can find some way to resuscitate it. I will hear this motion to bar the testimony again, if necessary, the day of trial. But Mr. Kolarich, do not try my patience here. It seems abundantly clear to me that Mr. Butcher's testimony is mistaken, at best, and I absolutely will not allow his testimony unless you can give me an extraordinarily satisfactory explanation for why I should. Am I making myself clear?"

I managed to say, "Yes, Your Honor." In the space of five minutes, Tommy Butcher had been officially scratched off my witness list.

"And Mr. Mapp, this will not be the first time you spring evidence on the defense at a hearing before me. It will be the *last* time. Am I making *that* clear?"

"Of course, Your Honor."

The judge rose and left the bunch. I looked at Tommy Butcher, who was mumbling to himself, his eyes frantically darting about.

The deputy came over to escort Sammy back to detention.

"We still have Archie Novotny," I told him.

He looked at me with fear in his eyes. "I sure hope so, Koke," he said.

The deputy took Sammy away. I looked back at Tommy Butcher, his face ashen, sitting motionless in the witness stand.

"Voluntary and twelve." Lester Mapp, enjoying the upper hand, approached me. "And after today, you thank your lucky stars I haven't pulled that offer."

"You'd mentioned voluntary and ten." I did my best to sound confident, after having my lunch handed to me in court.

"I said think about ten years, and you didn't get back to me, and now you've lost the best thing you had going for you. You're lucky twelve is still on the table."

I found myself nodding as Lester Mapp left the courtroom. For the first time, I seriously considered a plea bargain. I was down to one witness, one alternative suspect—Archie Novotny, who would make for a decent suspect but who would deny any involvement. It was all I had.

Twelve years, out in six with good behavior. One year already served awaiting trial, leaving Sammy with five years more. Lester Mapp, albeit in his condescending way, had spoken the truth back in his office when we discussed a plea: This was a gift. Griffin Perlini had become a temporary media celebrity with the discovery of the dead girls, and the county attorney's office wasn't all that thrilled about prosecuting the man who avenged his sister's murder.

When the courtroom had completely emptied out, Tommy Butcher pushed himself out of the witness stand. He looked like he'd just received some really bad news from the doctor.

"What the hell just happened?" I asked him.

He shook his head slowly. "I don't know what coulda happened. I mean, I know what I saw. I mean, nothin' that happened here changes the fact that the guy—the guy you showed me the photograph of—that guy was there that night, right?"

It was true that I could still place Kenny Sanders at the Liberty Apartments on the night of the murder. But Sanders wasn't going to admit to anything beyond that. I needed Butcher's testimony to have him be not only *there*, but fleeing the building with a gun at around ten o'clock. After this court hearing today, it would be a tough sell to get the judge to allow Butcher's testimony at all, much less to get a jury to believe it. And without Butcher, all I had was Kenny Sanders admitting he was there that night but not admitting anything beyond that. I had nothing at all.

"Christ, it was a year ago," Butcher told me. "I *thought* it was Downey's. It must have been some place else. Lemme think on this and—"

"Forget it, Tom. It's over."

I was still numb from disbelief. What colossally shitty luck. The place gets its liquor license pulled?

"Tell me what I gotta do, Mr. Kolarich. Tell me how to fix this. I definitely saw a guy running out of that building. Tell me what I gotta do."

I closed up my briefcase and shook my head. "Pray," I said.

Butcher walked out, seemingly in a trance. I waited in the empty courtroom until he was long gone before I removed my cell phone. "Brown tweed jacket, red tie," I said to Joel Lightner. "Heavyset, balding. Give him about five minutes and he'll be outside."

52

L ET'S SAY EIGHT. Eight years, out in four, with one already served. That's three more years inside, Sam."

I'd caught up with Sammy in the holding cell in the courthouse before his transport back to the detention center. My client sat against the wall of the cell, dejected and bitter.

"They're at twelve now?" he asked.

"Say I get him to eight."

"After today?"

"Sammy—say I get him to eight," I said. "Let's pretend, okay? Could you do that?"

He played with the idea. It was never an easy thing to accept, obviously, but the whole point was considering the alternative.

"I have Archie Novotny," I said. "And they have your statements to them, which were pretty close to a confession, and they have your car at the scene, at the time of the murder, and they have eyewitnesses. Maybe— maybe I can shake those witnesses, Sammy. I haven't even been able to talk to them yet. I will. But nothing I do to them will change the fact that they picked you out of a lineup."

He didn't answer. It was as if he hadn't heard me.

"Could you do eight?" I asked again.

"After what that asshole did to my sister?" Sammy's head fell back against the cell wall.

"I don't think Griffin Perlini killed Audrey." I blurted it out without thinking. I hadn't necessarily planned on telling Sammy this fact any time soon. It really didn't change our case at all—in fact, it hurt it. But I thought it might help Sammy accept a prison sentence.

Sammy stared at me for a long time without speaking.

"Remember Mrs. Thomas, our neighbor?" I said. "She didn't think it was Perlini who ran off with Audrey. She thought Perlini was too small to fit the man she saw running off with Audrey. And that's not all, Sam. Here's the real problem: Perlini had a bum knee. He'd torn his ACL and never repaired it. He couldn't run, Sam. The guy who took Audrey was in an all-out sprint."

"Then—who?"

"Our friend Smith? I think he's shilling for the guy. I think his whole reason for being involved is to keep me from figuring out who really killed her and those other girls buried behind the school."

Sammy pushed himself up and began to pace the cell. I couldn't fathom the impact of this revelation. He'd spent his entire life on an assumption that, I was now telling him, was a lie.

"I—I killed a guy who didn't—who—?"

I killed a guy. He'd never said the words to me. So now we were even on the revelations. Sammy did, in fact, murder Griffin Perlini.

"You killed a guy who molested a bunch of young girls," I said. "Maybe he didn't kill any of them. I don't know. But don't turn him into a Boy Scout."

Sammy had nothing to say to that.

"Think about eight," I said, as the deputy approached to tell us it was time to wrap up.

I WENT BACK to the office and fell in my chair. I had a raging head-ache with no time for self-pity. I had to find the elderly couple who positively identified Sammy as the man running from the Liberty Apartments and pray that I could find some way to tear apart their testimony. I had to do whatever I could to make a stronger case against Archie Novotny, the only thing I had left in Sammy's defense. And then there was the small chore of solving Audrey Cutler's murder, finding the killer, and hopefully finding my brother along with them.

My cell phone rang. Dread filled my stomach.

"Kolarich," Smith said. "I need to know exactly how you intend to win this case after today's monumental fuck-up." His delivery, while intended to be threatening, was edged instead by tension. No doubt, he'd heard about the developments this morning.

I didn't have a good story about how I could win this case. My best bet was a plea bargain, and I thought I could get the prosecutor down to eight years. Lester Mapp was riding high after knocking out Tommy Butcher's testimony today, but in the end, the reason the county attorney's office wanted a plea had nothing to do with the strength of its case. It was public relations. Griffin Perlini had just been turned into a monster in the press, a headline story of a gravesite filled with dead girls, and the elected county prosecutor wasn't going to score a lot of points by coming down hard on the man who killed the killer. They wouldn't let Sammy walk, but they'd accept a quiet plea bargain that put this thing to rest.

That, I figured, was why Lester Mapp had filed this motion to bar Butcher's testimony pretrial. He could have waited until just before trial, handed me the evidence that skewered Tommy Butcher's testimony, and left my case in tatters. But he wanted me to see, up front, that my case wasn't as good as I'd thought, so I'd accept a plea deal.

"I have another suspect," I told Smith. "His name is Archie Novotny. His daughter was molested by Griffin Perlini. He feels like Perlini ruined his family. And he wasn't where he claims to have been on the night of the murder. He has an alibi—a guitar lesson—but I can prove that he wasn't at his guitar lesson that night. It's a fabricated alibi, Smith."

This was news to Smith. He didn't volunteer his opinion of my story. He just asked me to repeat the story, more than once, and tried to get his arms around the strength of the case.

"I don't suppose you can get Kenny Sanders to cop to the murder," I said.

"I tried. He was willing to place himself at the scene, but anything beyond that, there's no way. We needed Mr. Butcher to put the gun in his hand, running from the building. Without him, Ken Sanders is just a man who happened to be in the building."

That's what I figured. "Then we go with Archie Novotny," I said. "I can win that case."

"Losing is not an option, Jason. It's not an option for you or your brother."

Smith hung up the phone. I found my eyes trailing upward before I closed them.

53

CARLO BUTCHER SAT passively in the kitchen, his three children—Marisa, Jake, and Tommy—having joined him and Smith for
a late dinner. Nobody was eating. Marisa, though in her mid-fifties, still
reminded Smith of a child. She'd done quite well for her mental impair-
ments; she'd kept a home of her own—even if it was next door to Carlo's—and she'd done a fine job of raising her only daughter, Patricia. Still,
Carlo had propped her up her entire life, financially, emotionally, in every
way, and she was leaning heavily on him now. But there was only so much
Carlo could do. This wasn't a problem that could be solved with money
or influence. Marisa's daughter, Carlo's granddaughter, was sick. Marisa
spent every visiting hour at the hospital, as did Carlo, helpless, each of
them, as Patricia slowly declined.

Carlo looked terrible. Smith had been around when Carlo's wife had
passed away, but it was nothing compared to watching Carlo suffer along
with his daughter and granddaughter. Carlo had waged war his entire
life, from the city's northwest side, as a white kid in a predominantly
black public school, through a brief run in the Capparelli family before
he started into the construction trade at the lowest level, working as a
laborer and later a foreman, finally taking a chance and building from
scratch a construction company of his own, Butcher Construction, turning it into a multimillion-dollar enterprise.

He'd made compromises at every level, payoffs and side deals for pref-
erential treatment in contracting, political contributions, and off-the-
books cash payments, but Smith had always found Carlo well-grounded
by his family. He was a man of substantial means at this stage, in his mid-
seventies, but he never left this rather modest home, where he'd lived
with his wife. He drove a simple car, wore simple clothes, rarely took
vacation or time off, except to spend with his daughter and granddaughter. He'd worked hard to save for the time when he was no longer around
for Marisa and Patricia, stowing away millions in long-term securities
and investing heavily in life insurance.

Tommy pushed himself away from the table first, leaving the chicken
and rice virtually untouched. He walked down the hall to Carlo's office,
where he and Smith would break the news of today's events to Carlo.
Carlo would not take it well. He'd always been hard on Tommy, the oldest
of the three kids and not saddled with developmental disability, and
Tommy had not always lived up to his father's standards. There had been
the two scrapes with the law, meeting with Carlo's disapproval more for
their stupidity than their illegality.

But today—today was a disaster. It had been Tommy's responsibility,
visiting the scene of Griffin Perlini's murder, walking the neighborhood,
settling on Downey's Pub as the anchor of his story. In fairness, Smith
thought, how could Tommy have known that Downey's had had its liquor
license pulled during the month of September 2006? But these distinc-
tions would be lost on Carlo, in his distracted, even panicked state.
Tommy would endure his father's wrath.

"Jake, stay with your sister," Carlo said. Jake was the outcast in many
senses. He hadn't joined the family business. He'd done quite well in real
estate development and often partnered with his family's construction
company, but he'd largely kept his distance. He was different. He was his
mother's child. He hadn't been involved in any of the seamier tactics necessary to run a construction company relying on public-works contracts,
nor had he been involved in the most recent family project, other than
vouching for Tommy.

Smith followed Carlo, moving gingerly, into Carlo's office. Smith
closed the door behind him. Tommy was already seated, his leg crossed,

his foot wagging nervously. Smith, as was his usual practice with Carlo, got right to the matter of delivering the bad news. Carlo liked hearing bad news like he wanted to remove a bandage, as quickly as possible.

"Unbelievable," Carlo said, shaking his head slowly. It was more unnerving to witness a calm reaction from Carlo than to watch one of his patented eruptions. "This lawyer is good?"

It was a question he'd asked before, but he was certainly entitled to the comfort of repetition. "That seems to be the case," Smith said.

"Seems like he knows what he's doing," said Tommy cautiously, still reticent over his screw-up.

"He believes that his brother will die if he doesn't deliver?"

"Yes," Smith said.

Carlo poised his hands with a slight tremble, owing to his advancing age, perhaps, but Smith thought otherwise. "I don't—I don't know what to do. I don't."

Smith had never heard anything of the kind from Carlo. Carlo hadn't always made the right call, but decisiveness had never been a problem.

"What about Jimmy DePrizio's boy?" Carlo asked.

"Denny?"

"Right. Denny got any bright ideas?"

"Not recently." Smith shrugged. "I'll check in with him. He's supposed to be keeping an eye on Kolarich."

Carlo nodded, then sunk into a thought. "What if we kill the brother?" he asked. "Tell the lawyer he's next, if he doesn't deliver?"

Smith inclined his head. "I don't know, Boss. Jason Kolarich is hard to predict. But I think it wouldn't help."

"*You* think." Carlo focused on Smith. "How we doin' so far, on what *you* think?"

Smith didn't answer. There was no winning this argument. Carlo ran his hands over his bare forehead. He was showing his age, for the first time, his movements more tentative, the tremble in his hands.

"Maybe—maybe this is comeback," Carlo said. "For past wrongs." He dismissed the two men with a wave.

Smith and Tommy left the office. *I don't know what to do*, Carlo had said. But Smith thought otherwise. He thought that Carlo was beginning to warm to a decision that would affect all of them.

54

"HE WENT to the construction site, then to St. Agnes Hospital to visit someone, then to his father Carlo's home," said Joel Lightner.

I was driving, talking to Joel with my earpiece. I was done making phone calls to the eyewitnesses placing Sammy Cutler at the scene of the crime. I was going to make a personal visit.

"Why so suspicious of this guy, Jason? Wasn't he your witness?"

I probably should have figured on Tommy Butcher earlier on. A guy shows up a year after a murder and remembers something? I guess I wanted his testimony to be true so badly that I let myself believe the unbelievable.

"Smith knew all kinds of detail about the hearing involving Butcher's testimony," I explained. "But the county Web site didn't provide any details. And the guy Smith put up—Sanders—didn't know about it at all. So the only way Smith could have known was from Butcher himself. That, and his obvious lie about being at that bar on the night of the murder."

"You think he's the killer?"

"My gut would be no, though I don't know what a child killer looks like. But I'm going to find out."

"And how are you going to do that?"

"Powers of persuasion, Mr. Lightner. Keep an eye on Mr. Butcher, would you?"

"I will. Hey, what's cooking with Jimmy Stewart?"

"That's *Jim*, my friend. It's going fine, I think. Just trying to rattle the cage."

"Jimmy's good for that," said Joel. "I'll say that much."

"KOLARICH ISN'T TALKING to me." Denny DePrizio ripped a piece of bread from the loaf and dipped it into a plate of olive oil.

"Then talk to *him*," Smith said. "Make sure his priorities are straight."

DePrizio smirked. "He's got you by the balls, doesn't he?"

"That's funny to you," Smith said, as he saw a number of men in suits approaching their table. The leader of the four-man group was short and wide, with tightly cropped hair.

DePrizio looked up. The color drained from his face. Smith noticed that the front man, in fact all of the men, were wearing police shields on their belts.

DePrizio froze for a moment, then recovered, grabbing the bread again and focusing on the plate of olive oil. "Well, well," he said. "If it isn't Jimmy Stewart, king of the rats."

"Sorry to interrupt your lunch, Detective," said Stewart.

"And what can I do for the men of Internal Affairs on this fine day?"

"Take a ride with us."

DePrizio, in a flash of anger, threw down the chunk of bread. "Now, why would I do that, Lieutenant?"

Stewart looked over at Smith, debating whether to engage. "Not here," he said.

"Here." DePrizio wiped his hands on his napkin.

Stewart waited, then nodded. "Okay. You'll want to help explain how a guy named Peter Kolarich got dropped from a multiple-count narcotics and weapons beef only a few days after his arrest."

"Kolarich. Kolarich." DePrizio was struggling to keep the brave front. "They blur together, Jimmy."

"Let me see if I can help you out, *Denny*. This was the one where your CI had a sudden change of heart."

"It happens." DePrizio's level of enjoyment was quickly evaporating.

"Does it usually happen after someone delivers you a briefcase with ten thousand dollars in it? That usually happen, Denny?"

DePrizio didn't move. He didn't speak.

"How about we have a look in the trunk of your car, Denny? You think we'll find a briefcase like that? The one we have you on videotape receiving from Jason Kolarich at that coffee shop?"

DePrizio worked his jaw, trying to find words. "I want my delegate," he said.

"No problem, Denny. Not a problem at all," said Stewart. "But let's take a ride. We don't—we don't need a scene in front of this lunch crowd."

Denny DePrizio slowly pushed himself from the table. His planted smile quickly deteriorated into a scowl. His eyes flashed across Smith, who remained still.

GEORGE AND MILLIE Robeson lived two blocks north of the Liberty Apartments, where Griffin Perlini was murdered. The whole area was pretty much a dive: streets littered with garbage and broken-down automobiles, convenience stores with garish signs for cigarettes and lottery tickets and phone cards, competing gang graffiti advertising the reign of the Latin Lords and the Columbus Street Cannibals.

The apartment building where the Robesons lived was the exception to the rule, a well-kept, if humble exterior with a clean brown awning noting that the structure was a "residence for seniors," which in some cases might be an invitation for mayhem, but an armed doorman, who spent a lot of time in the gym, helped ensure a sense of security.

I introduced myself to the guy, showed him my bar card, and waited while he dialed a number on his phone and mispronounced my name. He mostly listened, then hung up the phone and stared at me, like I was supposed to say something.

"They don't want to talk to you," he finally said.

"They have to talk to me. Or I come back with a court order and a police officer, and I *make* them talk to me. Call them again, Lou," I said, noting his name tag. "Be a sport."

Lou wasn't in the sporting mood. He made a point of dropping his hands to his lap, telling me he was done debating with me. But he wasn't done.

"I'll make sure to come back when you're on duty," I said. "Interfering with an investigation. Witness tampering." I removed a small notepad from my breast pocket and slipped the pen out. "What's your last name, Lou? For the affidavit."

He waited a beat, to show me his resolve, before he dialed the number again. He turned away from me, but I didn't really need to hear what he was saying, anyway.

"Mr. Robeson'll be down," he told me.

"You're the best, Lou." I paced around the small foyer, decorated with a few pieces of decent furniture and some sports magazines on a round table. The elevators were behind a thick plate of glass and a secure door. One of the elevators chimed and a man walked out, a tall, thin African American with ivory-white hair, wearing a sweater, trousers, and a displeased expression.

He pushed open the secured door, enough for a conversation, but didn't walk through.

"Mr. Robeson." I approached the door.

"You're representing the guy on trial," he said, his voice matching his feeble frame.

"Yes, sir. I've tried to call—"

"I didn't see nothin', okay? Didn't see nothin'." The man's eyes were ablaze with fury, with pure hatred.

I paused. I wanted him to calm down. "Mr. Robeson, you told the police—"

"You stay away," he interrupted. "I said I didn't see nothin', now you stay away from us."

I drew back. "I've never spoken to you."

"*You* never did. *You* never did." The man directed a bony finger in my direction. "I fought for this country," he said. "I fought, y'hear? I didn't put my life on the line so's people could threaten good people who come forward and do the right thing."

Don't worry about the witnesses, Smith had cautioned me. His goons had reached this man and his wife.

"Someone threatened you," I said.

Robeson's eyes narrowed. "You oughta be ashamed. *Ashamed.* Now, I told you, my wife and me, we didn't see nothin'. Don't remember anything of the kind. You stay away."

Robeson let the security door close with a *click.* He kept mumbling angrily as he walked back into the elevator.

I turned back to the doorman, who looked like he wanted to draw his weapon on me.

"These are nice people," he said. "They don't hurt anybody. They just wanna be left alone. So *leave* them alone."

I didn't have a response. There was no sense trying to convince the Robesons that I wasn't the one who threatened them. There was nothing I could do but leave.

As I was walking to my car, my cell phone rang, the caller ID blocked. Smith, presumably.

"Kolarich, you've tested our patience. What did I tell you?"

I didn't know what he meant, but I had an idea. I figured it wouldn't take long before Lieutenant Jim Stewart and his boys at IAD would pick up DePrizio for questioning about the briefcase full of money I'd handed him.

It occurred to me that I might have made a big mistake. My plan had been to pinch DePrizio, make it look like he was extorting money from me, to help spring my brother from the criminal charges he faced. But that was before I'd managed to get Pete's charges dropped. And that was before they'd abducted Pete. The landscape had changed. Now, I was pissing off the very people who were holding my brother.

"I said no police, Jason. That includes Internal Affairs."

"I didn't sic the police on you, Smith," I said quickly. "Maybe on DePrizio, but not on you. Internal Affairs doesn't know about you. They've got DePrizio on false arrest and extortion."

"Go home," Smith said. "And then we'll talk."

"Why am I going home?"

"Because you've got mail," Smith said, before hanging up.

I broke about twenty different traffic laws on my way home, my imagination running wild. He was talking about Pete, I knew. He had something to show me.

I pulled up to my house just fifteen minutes after Smith's call. I slowly approached the front door of my town house, then the gold mailbox next to the front door, as if there were a bomb inside. Instead there was a series of junk mail and a large, unstamped envelope. I held my breath, opened it up, and removed an object wrapped in thick bubble wrap.

I ripped the first few layers off, until it was clear that it was holding a severed finger.

55

I TAPED BACK UP the bubble wrap holding the finger and put it in my freezer, not sure if there was any point to it, realizing that the odds of my ever seeing Pete again were dwindling. I was playing high-stakes poker, but it was my brother, not I, who was suffering the consequences.

"I didn't know they were going to kidnap you," I said aloud. "Jesus, Pete, I didn't know. I thought I was *helping* you."

I paced around my kitchen, trying to burn off the anxiety, slamming my fist into a cabinet, cursing and shouting, sweat breaking out on my face. They were torturing my brother because of my stupid one-upmanship.

Accomplishing absolutely nothing at home, I went back to my car and drove to the office, hardly able to keep my hands on the wheel. When my cell phone buzzed, I turned to it with venom in my heart.

"Kolarich," Smith said.

"Every finger he loses, Smith, I take two of yours."

"Who the hell do you think you're dealing with?" he hissed. "You think you can threaten us? You think we won't hit you back ten times harder? Are you finally getting the picture here, son?"

"I'm sorry," I said, silently cursing myself for the show of weakness but overcome with desperation. "I was just trying to protect him. Just please let him go. I learned my lesson. I'll—I'll make it right with DePrizio."

I knew I was giving Smith what he wanted, capitulation. Every synapse firing in my brain told me it was the wrong move, that I needed to keep the upper hand, but I couldn't fight back my fear. *Please let him go. Please let him go.*

"Make it right with DePrizio, period," he countered. "Every day that you don't, they'll cut something else off your brother. Oh, and I'm supposed to tell you—your brother screams like a goddamned girl."

I bit my tongue. He had me over a barrel, we both knew it, but I had something of my own. DePrizio was now a threat to Smith, a wild card. He could sing to Internal Affairs—give up Smith and his client to save his own ass. Smith couldn't be sure. He needed DePrizio cleared.

There was no good answer here. If I gave in, they'd probably kill Pete eventually, anyway. If I held out for leverage, left DePrizio hanging out to dry, they'd torture Pete in ways I couldn't even consider—but at least I'd still have a chance at getting him back.

That was it. No matter what it might mean for Pete in the interim, I had to get Pete away from them. I had to use whatever leverage I had remaining to get him free.

I took a deep breath and spit it out: "Not until you let Pete go." I hung up the phone, almost crushing it in my white-knuckled grip.

I made it to my office, fortunate to avoid an accident in my current state. I hadn't had a decent night's sleep in almost three weeks. My brain was foggy, my limbs like noodles, my emotions scattered. I had no gas left in the tank, and my job was only just starting.

"I'll find you," I said to nobody, to the air.

"Now you're talking to yourself?"

Shauna Tasker was standing at the threshold of my office doorway.

"God, Jason, you look like hell."

"Leave me alone," I said through my hands as I rubbed my face.

"No." Tasker walked in and surveyed my office. "No, I don't think I'm going to do that."

"Leave, Shauna. For your own good."

I meant it. Smith's people would come after me when Sammy's trial was over, and they'd kill Pete even before they got to me. If I'd had any doubt on that subject—and I didn't—their little present in my mailbox reinforced the point. They'd gone too far down the road with me and my brother. And I couldn't let Shauna Tasker become the third target.

"You look like you haven't slept in a month," she said. "You're running around like a crazed man, I see this affidavit from some guy named Marcus Mason talking about Pete and the drug bust—and you're playing the Lone Ranger, thinking you can solve all the world's problems by yourself. I don't know what's going on, Jason, but you need to let me help."

"Anything you do puts you in danger," I said. I looked up at her. "The truth is, Shauna, you might already *be* in danger."

"Then I'm already in danger. Why not go all in?"

I shook my head.

"Hire me," she tried. "Attorney-client. You got a dollar on you?"

I waved her off.

"Okay, *pro bono*, then." I didn't react to the joke, so she went on. "At least bounce this off me, Jason. I won't participate. But you have to talk to someone, my friend."

I let out an exhausted sigh.

"How's Pete? I take it, from that affidavit, that you got him off the charges?"

I shook my head, no. "Attorney-client?"

"C'mon, Kolarich. Spill it."

"They took him. They kidnapped him. I get Sammy off the charges, they say they'll let him go. If not, he's dead. Me, I figure he's dead, either way, if I don't find him."

Tasker stared at me like I'd just proposed marriage to her. After a while, she grabbed a chair and pulled it up. "Talk to me," she said. "Tell me everything."

LOCALLO'S HAD LONG been Smith's favorite Italian restaurant in the city, not owing to the owner, a longtime friend, but to the rigatoni, served with fresh mozzarella and sausage and red pepper. But Smith was beginning to associate heartburn with the place. Not a week ago, he'd dined here with DePrizio to discuss the chess move made by Jason Kolarich—the motion he'd filed in court requesting DNA testing of the dead bodies behind the elementary school.

Now he was back, once again responding to Jason Kolarich. This time, the meeting was even more surreptitious, not taking place in a private dining room but in the basement's wine cellar, before the place had even opened.

It served no purpose, Smith knew, to replay what could have been. The plan had never been simple—the underlying circumstances were anything but simple—but it was not the first time they'd tried to exert pressure on a reluctant target. Jason Kolarich had proved unwilling to follow instructions, so they'd decided on a course of action that typically worked. They'd hit him where it hurt. They'd set up his brother for an arrest that, no doubt, would have held up under scrutiny. DePrizio had done it before. It was what made a cop useful to people like Smith.

But Kolarich had fought back, and now Smith and Carlo—and DePrizio—found themselves in the unusual position of playing defense, not offense. The difference, he knew, was that this time, the people exerting the muscle were as vulnerable as the target. Carlo had as much to lose as Jason Kolarich.

Smith approached from the alley and let himself in through the back door, which the owner had left unlocked. He took the stairs down to the basement, where he found Denny DePrizio nervously pacing. The scent of vintage wine brought memories of heady times, of celebration, but nobody was breaking out the party hats now.

DePrizio was smoking a cigarette, something he'd quit years ago. He raised his arms at his side, as if asking a question. Smith's immediate reaction was to promote calm.

"Hold on, Denny—"

"The fuck am I supposed to do? IAD has me on tape, accepting a briefcase full of money from Kolarich. They're saying I set up the bust and held him up for ten thousand, then got the charges dropped when he paid—"

"I understand," said Smith. "What did you tell—"

"Nothing, is what I told them. I said it was bullshit. This is bullshit." DePrizio stubbed out the cigarette, angrily blowing out residual smoke. He directed a finger at Smith, started to speak but held back. He resumed his pacing, mumbling, "Fuck, fuck, fuck."

"Take it easy," Smith said.

"You gotta pop that motherfucker," said DePrizio. "You gotta do it or I will."

"We will, Denny. *We* will. But not until the trial is over. It'll be just over a week now, before the trial starts. And in the meantime, we're working on Kolarich to get him to recant his accusations against you."

DePrizio studied Smith. "How're you 'working on' him? The brother?"

"We're working on it, Denny. Believe me, we want this resolved just as—"

"Where is the brother? Where do you have him? I'll rip his fucking head off."

Smith held out his hands. "It's covered."

"And how's Kolarich gonna walk this one back?" he said. "How's he going to explain that him handing over that briefcase wasn't what it looks like?"

"It's covered," Smith repeated.

DePrizio stopped his pacing, standing next to a rack of wine. His eyes narrowed. His hands were trembling. *He's losing it*, Smith thought. *He's going to be a problem.*

"I'm not gonna be hung out to dry," DePrizio said.

"They haven't even charged you yet, Denny."

"They have my badge and gun. And they're *going* to charge me." He waved a hand. "You're telling me to do nothing."

"I'm telling you that *we'll* do something."

"When?"

"When we do something, that's when. We have his brother, Denny. He's not going to play around."

"I'm not either," said DePrizio. He slowly approached Smith, who braced himself. Up close, Smith could see it even more clearly, even in the dim setting. DePrizio's eyes were deeply set and fiery. He was coming unglued. "You tell Carlo, you tell anyone you need to tell. I'm not playing around, either." He drove a finger into Smith's chest before leaving the wine cellar.

56

SHAUNA SENT OUR ASSISTANT, Marie, for sandwiches and coffee. I felt a little better after a thick, salty roast beef sandwich and a healthy dose of Starbucks, and even better after unloading everything on Shauna.

"I'm desperate," I said. "I have to find Pete right now."

"*They're* desperate," Shauna countered. "I mean, Jason, 'desperate' doesn't begin to cover it. Kidnapping someone? They've dug themselves a pretty big hole here. Desperate? These guys have gone off the reservation."

"Covering up a series of child murders will do that to you."

Shauna nodded. "You think they killed Audrey and those other girls, and they'll stop at nothing to make sure you don't find that out."

"That's why they were so worried about the DNA test."

Shauna made a face. "But there's going to be a DNA test, anyway, right? I mean, that cop who investigated Audrey's murder back then—what was his name?"

"Carruthers."

"Carruthers is already doing a DNA test on those girls, isn't he? If nothing else, to try to determine their identities?"

Right. Shauna was right. "Okay," I said, playing along, feeling a bit of momentum. In my panicked, sleep-deprived state, had I missed something? "Then why was he so worried about the DNA test that I was going to ask for? A DNA test is a DNA test. Doesn't matter that I'm the one requesting it. Sooner or later, there's going to be one, period."

Shauna stared at the ceiling, deep in thought. "Delay," she said. "If that cop Carruthers does one, it doesn't affect Sammy's trial. It's a different investigation. Right? But if you ask for one in the context of Sammy's trial—"

"Then Sammy's trial is delayed. That's right. It comes back to delay. To timing." I felt like a door had opened, but I still couldn't see inside. "My assumption is, the longer I have this case, the more time I have to figure out who killed Audrey. So they want to rush me into the trial."

"And they want you to *win* the trial," she said.

I thought about that. "Yeah. They gave me Tommy Butcher. They gave me Kenny Sanders. They tried to scare off the eyewitness against Sammy." I nodded. "Yeah, I think they want Sammy to beat the rap."

Shauna shook her head. "Forget about what we think. Focus on what we *know*."

I shook out the cobwebs. I should have come to Shauna earlier. She was right. I was motoring around on no sleep, a fuzzy, scattered brain, with no help from anyone.

"What we *know*," I said, "is they want Sammy to win this case, and win it now."

"Right."

"We also know that Griffin Perlini didn't kill Audrey," I added. "He couldn't have. Smith's people are the killers, Shauna. I know it, sure as I'm sitting here."

Shauna dropped her hands on her knees. "Then that's how we find Pete. We find Audrey's killer."

I made a sound, a cross between a chuckle and a moan. "Yes, that small task. Solving a thirty-year-old case that the cops couldn't solve when the scent was fresh."

"Yeah, but we know something they didn't," Shauna offered. "We know Griffin Perlini didn't kill Audrey."

That was certainly a distinction. She was right—the police had jumped onto Griffin Perlini almost immediately and focused on him. He was a natural suspect, but it took their focus off any further investigation.

"But we don't have anything to go on," I said. "We don't have any witnesses. Sammy was a kid, like me. Sammy's mother died from kidney disease long ago. And Sammy's father left the house just a couple of weeks after Audrey was taken."

Shauna snapped to attention. "Say that last part again? About Sammy's father leaving?"

"He left—I mean, I think Mrs. Cutler threw him out."

"He left two weeks after?"

"You had to know the situation," I said, defensively, though I didn't know why I was being defensive. I'd always viewed this through the prism of a child's eyes. Maybe it was time that I approached it through the clinical eyes of an adult, of a skeptical attorney.

"He—I mean, look, he was always kind of a shitty father. He gambled and drank a lot with his buddies. He wasn't around much. He was out drinking the night Audrey was taken."

Shauna made a face. "Oh, *really.*"

"Yeah, I mean—I think Mrs. Cutler had just had enough. She blamed him for not being there at a time when Audrey needed him. I mean, she didn't *blame him* blame him. But I think it was just a microcosm of a bigger problem. She threw him out. I think—I think I saw him maybe a couple of times after that, but at some point he took off for good. When Sammy got sent to juvenile detention, when Sammy's mother died—he wasn't there for any of that. He was ancient history by then."

Shauna gathered the food wrappers and my empty coffee cup and tossed them in the garbage. "Well, Counselor, I'd say we have someone we should talk to. Do you know where this guy is?"

I didn't have the slightest idea. But I knew someone who might.

"I can't get in to see Sammy until tomorrow morning," I said.

"Then go home and get some sleep. You can't function like this, Jason. Tomorrow's another day."

"Tomorrow's another finger off of Pete's hand," I said. "Or a toe or an ear or—or—"

"You can't do this without sleep. Tell you what." Shauna hit my shoulder. "I'll go through these files and look for anything about Sammy's dear old dad. Any interviews, vital statistics, anything. I'll go through this whole thing tonight, and you get some sleep."

I rubbed my face, feeling my eyes sink as my eyelids shut.

"We'll touch base in the morning," said Shauna.

I got off the couch and grabbed her arm. I wanted to thank her, but it felt like an insufficient way to express the old emotions that welled up at that moment. Then again, I needed help—I'd needed help for over three weeks—and Shauna was coming to my rescue. I told myself that was it, nothing more, as I loosened my hold on her forearm. For her part, Shauna, other than looking down at my hand, didn't acknowledge anything, but even her stoicism suggested something. Neither of us spoke for a moment, and when I released her arm, I did so gently, my hand suspended as if it had committed a trespass.

"Go get some rest, Kolarich," she said, the flip use of my last name concluding whatever may have just transpired. As usual, Shauna was making the right call. I was in no condition, mentally or circumstantially, to do anything but head home.

The depth of sleep deprivation was sudden and heavy. Maybe it was the power of suggestion. Maybe it was a release of tension, having let Shauna in on the secret, knowing that I finally had some help in all of this. Either way, the walk to the elevator, then across the street to my car, felt like the Bataan Death March, cast in shadow, my movements awkward and timid. I made it home at an hour that I would typically be eating dinner, just getting started on an evening of isolation, shitty paperback novels, and insipid television sitcoms. I hit the pillow thinking of Pete, how I'd failed him, how I was getting some shut-eye as he faced another day of torture. But the guilt, however powerful, was no match for my exhaustion. I was asleep in minutes, leaving me with my dreams, with an insecure, troubled sibling fighting various demons of the human and inhuman kind, a wife and child struggling for air underwater, a young next-door neighbor being swept out of her bed in the midst of sleep, wondering where the scary monster would take her.

57

I AWOKE WITH A START, to the vanishing sensation of being electrocuted, only to find my cell phone still in my hand from last night, now buzzing. I'd slept like a rock. I hadn't moved all night. I was still in my clothes. The clock at my bedside read half past seven. I'd slept over ten straight hours.

"Today's the day," said Smith, when I answered the cell phone.

I was dazed, still coming out of a heavy fog.

"Today's the day you make things right with DePrizio," said Smith. "Or it's not a finger. It's an entire hand."

I sat up in bed, shaking out the cobwebs. "Denny's gonna rat you out," I said.

"Something you don't want," he countered. "What do you think will happen to your brother *then*? You think we'll let him live?"

I was still in recovery mode. I didn't have my wits about me. "Talk to me later today," I said. "Maybe I can make you happy."

"Yeah? You've thought about how you'll explain this away to the police?"

"I have some thoughts, yes."

"I'd like to hear them."

"I'm sure you would." I hung up the phone and got out of bed. I took a quick shower, dressed, and drove to see Sammy at the detention center.

"I'LL TAKE EIGHT." Sammy Cutler said these words the moment the sheriff's deputy left us alone in the all-glass interview room at the detention facility. His eyes were clear, his chin up. He'd been thinking about this, clearly, at great length since we spoke and seemed comfortable with the decision. "This guy Perlini, he was a bad guy. He did bad things. But he didn't kill Audrey. Right?"

"Right."

"So I can't walk away from what I did. I don't want a life sentence for killing this scumbag, but killing's killing, right? I shouldn't get off, either." He nodded. "I can do eight. Out in four, one already served, right?"

My first thought, I had to admit, was my brother, not Sammy. I could close this thing off right now. Smith's people would avoid a trial. He would get his certainty right away, no delay. I thought about my conversation with Shauna Tasker last night, parsing through all the information we had, distinguishing what we knew from what we thought:

They want Sammy to win this case, and win it now.

Was an eight-year plea enough of a "win"? I couldn't imagine why Smith would care about that. The case would be over. He'd have the conclusion, the certainty that he wanted. From Smith's standpoint, this should be a satisfactory resolution. And from Sammy's standpoint, it was acceptable as well.

From *my* standpoint, I still had a problem. I still had to assume that they'd kill Pete—and me—as soon as they didn't need me anymore.

"The prosecution has offered twelve," I said. "I can try for eight."

Sammy softly patted the table between us. "If it's twelve, it's twelve," he said. "I can do twelve, too." His fingers began to caress the table as he lost himself in his thoughts. I couldn't imagine what runs through your mind as you contemplate surrender, a long prison term.

"I told her," he started, and then his throat choked off. His eyes filled with tears. It was a long moment before he was able to continue. "I know it's funny but I still talk to her, Koke, y'know? She's still that little girl. Still that little kid following us around." He looked at me. "I told her last night, I fucked up again. My whole life, I fucked up everything I did, and then I see this guy in the grocery store, and I think to myself, here's your first chance to do something right. To do something for Audrey. And I couldn't even do *that* right. I killed the wrong guy."

"I'll find the right guy, Sammy. I promise. I promise you that."

He nodded; then a partial smile broke out on his face before evaporating. "Koke, if it was me with the talent, I'd have done the same as you. I'd have gotten out of our sorry-ass neighborhood quick as I could and not looked back."

I drew back. Something I hadn't expected. "But if the roles were reversed," I said, "would I have taken the fall on the drug charge and let you walk?"

"Course you woulda. *Course* you woulda. They already had me. What was the point a makin' you go down, too?"

Maybe. I didn't know. I wouldn't ever know. All I could do was go forward, the advice I'd received so many times over the last four months, since the death of my wife and daughter. Go forward. Do better. Keep motoring until the day your ticket is punched.

"You still pray?" he asked me.

"Do I—no, I don't." I shook my head. "No."

"It helps." He took a deep breath. "I mean, we was kids, we just went 'cause our moms made us go. But, y'know, I've been gettin' back to it since I've been inside. I mean, before, I was inside for drugs or such, and I never really saw why I had to be locked up for messing up my own life. But since this thing—since I killed somebody—I been talkin' to Him. You kinda work things out that way."

I packed up my stuff and signaled to the guard. "We should quit while we're ahead," I said. "Let me see what I can do about this plea. We'll get you the hell out of this place in a couple of years and get you back on track. Okay, my friend?"

Sammy lifted his manacled hand and shook mine. "Okay, Koke."

AS I DROVE back to my law firm, the cell phone buzzed, the caller ID blocked.

"Any progress?" Smith asked. "You told me you might have something that makes me happy. You should really want to make me happy right now, Kolarich, because my friends are just itching to keep going on your brother."

I took the ramp onto the highway to head back to the city's commercial district. "I can end this whole thing for you," I said. "A plea bargain. I have the structure of it already in place."

"You have—a plea bargain?"

"Sammy cops for a reduced sentence, and I promise not to come looking for you if you let my brother go. No hard feelings, is how I see it. You get this thing over, which is what you want, no delays, and I pretend the whole thing never happened. And the *reason* I pretend the whole thing never happened," I added, because Smith would need convincing on this point, "is that I know you could always come after Pete and me again. So we call a truce."

I knew that I would never rest until I found Smith, until I found Audrey's killer, but it was the best sales job I could give Smith.

"Tell me about the plea bargain," said Smith.

"Eight years."

"Oh, no—"

"With good time, out in four, and he's already served—"

"No. No, absolutely not. You can't do that, Kolarich. You can't do that!"

He was on the verge of panic. I didn't understand.

"Why the hell do you care how long he serves, if it's okay with him?" I tried to process this information, as I tried to control my frustration. "What's the diff—"

"An acquittal," said Smith. "*Acquittal.* Do I need to spell that word for you? You cut a deal with the prosecution, Jason, and your brother will be dead five minutes later."

They want Sammy to win this case, and win it now.

"And if I don't hear, in the next few hours, that you've found a way to clear DePrizio of that charge, your brother won't be right-handed any more."

The phone line cut out. I coaxed the accelerator, weaving through traffic as my car picked up speed, on my way to my office, until I saw an endless row of brake lights. Something up ahead, an accident or construction, had brought traffic to a standstill.

58

H E WON'T DO IT. Kolarich won't save DePrizio's ass." Carlo
Butcher stood in his bathrobe, a cup of morning coffee in his hand,
looking out his back window at the half-acre in his backyard. "If he did,
he wouldn't do it in a way that we could trust."

"We have his brother," said Smith. He'd called Kolarich only moments
ago from his car and had now arrived at Carlo's house to inform him of
recent developments.

Carlo turned momentarily, gave Smith a look of disgust, before looking back out the window. "You keep telling me, 'We have his brother.' Look
how much that's gotten us. He's shoving this thing right up our ass."

It was true. Smith, himself, was beginning to doubt the plan. The only
thing he could think of was to make Kolarich recant his accusations, find
some way to conjure up an innocent explanation for the handing over of
the briefcase to DePrizio. But Carlo was right. Kolarich wouldn't do it, at
least not in a way satisfactory to them.

He wondered about Carlo. He, ultimately, was calling the shots and
had always willingly done so. Now, he was being quiet, keeping his decisions to himself.

"Y'know, Jimmy DePrizio and I—Jimmy was like a kid brother. He
used to follow me around when I did my rounds. I'd let him hold my
money for me. Christ, he'd guard it like it was Fort Knox, that kid."

"I remember Jimmy," Smith said. Denny DePrizio's father had died five years ago.

"His boy, Denny—you got any special feelings about him?"

Carlo looked back at Smith. Smith made an equivocal face—the reaction, Smith knew, that Carlo wanted. He'd already made the decision, and Smith wasn't going to get in the way.

Carlo's eyes broke from Smith's, and then he slowly nodded. "Okay, then." He looked back into Smith's eyes, and that was it.

It wasn't the first time that losses had to be cut, and in this instance, it was the only decision Carlo could make. DePrizio was an even larger threat to them now than Kolarich. DePrizio could take down everyone—not just Carlo but Tommy and Smith, and the other men whom Butcher had borrowed from the Capparelli family for this venture.

"This lawyer," said Carlo, stuffing his hands in the pockets of his bathrobe. "He's getting close." He looked back at Smith again. "Isn't he?"

"We don't know that, Carlo. This could still work." Smith wanted to believe it as much as he wanted Carlo to believe it. But he knew there was plenty of reason to doubt it now, and he could see the same opinion washed across Carlo's face.

Carlo drank the last coffee from his cup. "Well, all right, then." He looked at Smith. "I had a pretty good run."

"Carlo—"

Carlo put a hand on Smith's shoulder. "Always do right by your family." He raised his index finger. "Most important thing. *Only* thing, at the end." Carlo moved past Smith into the living room, where he settled into a chair with a groan.

"Carlo," Smith said, more gently.

Carlo shook his head, his way of indicating he wasn't in the mood for debate. "What happened back then," he said. "It was on me. Not you, not Tommy, not Jake, not Marisa. Me. Understand?"

Smith, in his near-panic condition, felt some relief with Carlo's words. He was telling Smith, this wouldn't blow back on him. Carlo wouldn't let him take the fall.

"Carlo, this can still work," Smith insisted. "Kolarich could win at trial.

It could happen. Why not wait, at least? We take out DePrizio now, yes, agreed, his time has come, but not Kolarich—"

"And in the meantime?" said Carlo. "In the next couple of weeks before the trial even starts, this lawyer figures it out himself? Then what? Then it's everybody. Everybody. This way," he said, pointing to himself, "it's only me. We do this on my terms. That's the decision. Collect the garbage. DePrizio, the lawyer, and his brother." He raised his eyebrows to Smith. "And that's final. We clear?"

Smith paused, then nodded. "DePrizio, the lawyer, and his brother," he confirmed.

"Start with the lawyer," Carlo said. "And do it now."

IT TOOK ME TWO HOURS, with the overturned truck on the highway, to get back downtown. When I returned to my office, I found a stack of papers on my chair, compiled neatly with binder clips and tabs. Shauna had performed admirably, going through the old files on Audrey Cutler's case to find any information relating to Sammy's father.

"Oh, hey." Shauna popped her head into my office. "I gotta run to court. There's a Social Security number there, and a little information on what Sammy's dad was doing that night that Audrey was taken. Not much, I'm afraid. But the Social might help."

"Thanks, Shauna. Really." I leafed through everything briefly, still troubled by the conversation I'd just had with Smith. I was missing something. I knew it.

I called Joel Lightner. "Same story with Tommy Butcher," he told me. "He goes home, he goes to his father Carlo's house, the hospital, the job site—"

"That's fine, Joel. Here, I have a Social Security number I need you to track down, okay?" I read it to him.

"I suppose you need this fast, like you need everything else fast."

"Faster," I said. I placed the papers down and separated them. I focused on a portion of the investigator's notes that summarized an interview with Sammy's father after Audrey's abduction:

Mr. Cutler indicated that at the time of the incident, approx. 2:00 A.M., he was at McGilly's Tavern, 2602 South Marks in

Travis Heights. Mr. Cutler indicated he was at the tavern with Daniel Caldwell, Rick Eisler, and Rusty Norris. Mr. Cutler indicated that he was a union plumber who had recently completed work on the library addition at Mansbury College and that Caldwell, Eisler, and Norris were laborers with Emerson Construction Company, the general contractor on the project. Caldwell, Eisler, and Norris confirmed that Mr. Cutler was with them until approx. 3:00 A.M. at that establishment.

It took me a second before it took hold, the reference to Emerson Construction. When I was quizzing Tommy Butcher about his prior criminal history—the false bid application he'd filed—I hadn't focused on the company for which he was working at the time. But Lester Mapp had mentioned it in his cross-examination of Butcher at the hearing. Butcher, back in 1982, had worked for Emerson Construction Company. I'd been so caught up in the possibility of losing that hearing that I hadn't focused.

I recalled it, then, the celebration picnic held by the construction company following the successful completion of the Mansbury library project, which I had attended with Sammy's family. It had been my last vivid memory of Audrey, scampering across the grassy park, holding the candy in her hands. *Emerson M&M's*, we tried to get her to say, laughing when she couldn't navigate the tongue-twister. *Emoson-ems.*

I remembered Sammy's mother, so content that day, trying to contain her hair blowing in the wind. A good moment, for her, her loser husband notwithstanding, as she watched her children run and play. As I thought about it, I realized that it was my last good memory not only of Audrey but of Mrs. Cutler, too—before the loss of her daughter sapped her spirit, before a terminal disease claimed her life.

They want Sammy to win this case, and win it now.

"Oh my God," I said. I sprung up from my chair and let the whole thing wash over me, every little piece finally fall into place.

Then I ran for my car.

59

I RAN FROM THE ELEVATOR out of the building, across the street to the parking garage. I turned over the whole thing in my mind, gaining speed as it became clearer and clearer to me. I didn't bother with the elevator, taking the stairs two at a time up to the third floor. I clicked the remote to unlock my car but it didn't beep back to me. I opened the car door, threw the key in the ignition, and suddenly realized why the car hadn't responded to my remote.

The car had already been opened.

An arm strangled me from behind, from the left, pinning my head to the headrest. The butt of a gun sunk into my right temple.

"Don't fuckin' breathe."

My mind raced, considering my options, but with the gun to my head, there were no options that would prevent the gun from discharging into my brain.

"Is this Nino, Johnny, or one of the other stooges?" I asked.

"Oh, that was my brother you cold-cocked, Kolarich. I'm the one who sliced off your brother's finger. If you hadn't heard, he cries like a little girl. I just want you to be real clear, Kolarich. Your brother's next on my list, and I'm gonna enjoy it."

An image of Pete at age thirteen, watching me catch the football at a high school practice. I remember the look in his eyes, the admiration, and how much it meant to me, wondering if I ever conveyed to him how *much* it meant to me. The first time I met Talia, my heart doing a leap as her eyes swept across mine, the subtle smile that told me so much about her, that made me want her love. And my little angel, my beautiful Emily, her tiny hands opening and closing, her unfocused eyes dancing, swelling me with an indescribable love.

I closed my eyes as I heard the *click* of the trigger.

Then I opened them again.

"Shit!"

I shot up my right arm, gripping my attacker's wrist and forcing the gun butt upward. He'd lost his left-arm grip around my throat now, leaving me with the advantage of being in the front seat, both arms going for the misfired gun, while my attacker was forced to reach over from the backseat.

It was no contest, but he wouldn't let go. I grabbed for the gun and his wrist with both hands and used my weight to fall forward into the front passenger seat, taking his arm with me. It was hard to tell what I'd done to my attacker—the sounds of bones snapping and joints ripping left me with a guess that I'd broken his arm horribly and dislocated his collarbone. The garbled cries of my attacker confirmed that his arm had ended up in a position where no arm had been built to go.

I had the gun now, which had misfired once and could go off for any or no reason at this point, so I put it on the floorboard of my car. Then I turned to my attacker, his head between the car seats, his broken arm dangling helplessly. "You scream like a girl, too," I said. I popped him a couple times around the nose—once or twice, or it could have eight or ten—until his eyes seemed firmly closed. I went around to the passenger side of the car and dragged his prone body out of my car.

I removed his cell phone, wallet, and keys as souvenirs. Just to make it that much harder for him, I removed his shoes, too, and dropped them down to the next ramp level of the parking garage. I would have loved to stick around and interrogate him, but that wasn't necessary anymore. I knew where I needed to go.

I started my car, backed out of the spot, and drove down the ramp and out of the building. When I got outside into traffic, I looked back down at the backfiring gun, then up at the sky.

———

I PARKED IN THE GARAGE of St. Agnes Hospital and walked up toward the front entrance of the building. Several smokers lingered at the hospital's front doors, some in scrubs or white uniforms, and a few others presumably visiting someone here. I held my breath and passed through them. I got to reception, signed in, and asked for directions. As I was fastening my visitor tag to my jacket and approaching the elevators, my cell phone buzzed. But I soon realized that it wasn't my cell phone. It was the cell phone I had taken off the man who jumped me in my car.

I paused, looked at a caller ID that was blocked, and opened up the cell phone. I couldn't do much of an impression of the man who attacked me, so I chose a whisper. "Yeah?" I said, keeping it short to make it harder to discern a difference.

"Is it done?" It was Smith's voice.

I thought for a moment, then said, "Call back in two minutes." Then I jumped in the elevator and hit the button for six.

I got out on six and looked around. The sixth floor of St. Agnes Hospital was the intensive care unit. Visitation was restricted, according to the signs everywhere. I walked up to the receptionist and said I was here to visit the Butcher patient.

"Your name?"

I thought about that for a moment. I had the driver's license of the guy who'd just jumped me in my car—Nick Ramsey—but I was done playing games.

"Jason Kolarich," I said.

SMITH SAT IN THE CHAIR outside Patricia's room, waiting out the two minutes. He couldn't tell if Nick had succeeded, or if he was still lying in wait for Kolarich. He'd just received a call from one of the other men, who had reported successfully on Denny DePrizio. DePrizio had been taken easily, a bullet through the forehead upon walking into his garage.

Kolarich, hopefully, would be just as easy.

An orderly approached the room and stepped inside. "You have a visitor," the young man said to Carlo and Carlo's daughter, Marisa.

"Who?" he heard Carlo say.

"Jason Kola—Kola-something?"

Smith's head whipped around. He popped out of his chair and walked into the room. "Who?" Smith asked. "Jason Kolarich?"

"I think so, yeah."

"Wait. Wait just a second." Smith moved back into the hallway and dialed the cell phone number again for Nick Ramsey.

"Hello, Smith."

Smith felt his stomach sink. "Where are you?"

"I think you know where I am, Smith. And judging from your reaction, I know where you are."

"I don't know what you mean."

"Either you let me in, or I bring the police. You have exactly one minute to decide."

The phone cut out. Smith's heart was rattling against his chest. He walked back into the hospital room. Carlo sat passively in a chair by the window. "Marisa, sweetheart," Carlo said. "You and Raymond, go take a walk, would you? Would you do that? I need to speak with someone."

"No," Smith said.

Carlo dropped his chin and stared at Smith. He cupped his hand and motioned Smith over. He pushed himself out of the chair and whispered into Smith's ear. "Marisa can't see this. Get her out of the hospital and take her home. And keep your phone nearby. I will take care of this."

Carlo pushed Smith away and turned to his daughter, Marisa. "Come here, sweetie," he said. Marisa looked terrible. She wasn't sleeping at night, worrying about her daughter, who lay in the bed clinging to life. It was tough enough to cope for someone with all their faculties, but Marisa's disabilities, her mild retardation, left her wholly unequipped for this.

Carlo cupped his hand around Marisa's chin. "Marisa, you know how much I love you, don't you?"

"I know, Daddy."

Carlo kissed her cheek and held her for a long time. He stroked her hair and whispered into her ear. "Now, Raymond is going to take you home for a little while. I'll stay and watch Patricia, don't you worry. Run along now, sweetheart."

Marisa picked up her bag. She went over to the bed, stroked Patricia's hair, kissed her forehead, and whispered something to her. Smith took her arm and looked back at Carlo. Carlo nodded and turned to the orderly.

"You can show Mr. Kolarich in," Carlo said to the orderly.

I STAYED ON HIGH ALERT as I was walked down a corridor filled with customary hospital smells, soft voices and moans, laughter at the nurses' desk. It was hard to imagine anyone jumping out at me under the circumstances, but I'd just survived someone putting a gun to my head and pulling the trigger, so I figured I had used up all my good luck for the day.

"Right here, sir." The orderly pointed to a room that was designated by the tag PATRICIA BUTCHER. I looked in before I entered. An older man, probably in his seventies, was sitting in a chair by a window. Sun streamed in and hit the floor near his feet.

"Carlo," I gathered.

"I've heard a lot about you, son."

"All of it good, I hope." The private bathroom was to my left, Carlo straight forward. "Let my brother go."

He nodded. "I will. Give me your phone and it will be done."

I remained motionless at the threshold of the room.

"Well? Aren't you going to come in?"

I took a deep breath and entered the room, past the bathroom, and saw the patient lying in the bed. Tubes passed from her wrist to a device that looked like an ATM machine on a diet. Her chest lightly rose and fell. The coloring of her skin was closer to yellow than to human flesh.

"This is my granddaughter," he said. "She can't hear us."

I started to walk over to her but froze in place. Her hair was matted against her head. She was breathing with assistance. It felt inappropriate to stare at her, but I couldn't take my eyes off her.

"Her name is Patricia," said Carlo.

I rested my hand on the post at the foot of the bed. So much adrenaline flowed through my body, I almost couldn't get the words out.

"Her name," I said, "is Audrey."

60

"THANK YOU, RAYMOND." Carlo handed me back the cell phone. "Your brother is on his way."

I closed the door to the room and placed a chair against it. I wasn't expecting an ambush but I wasn't going to make assumptions.

"Good," I said. "Now give me one reason why I shouldn't kill you."

"I only *have* one. Because you're not a killer. And you don't want to become one. Trust an old man on that." Carlo, still seated, rested his head against the wall.

"She was the best thing to ever happen to Marisa," he continued. "The best thing to ever happen to *us*. My only regret is that my wife, Patricia, never knew her. We named her after my wife."

"That's very touching, Carlo."

He shook his head but didn't look at me. "Marisa, my daughter—do you know about her? She's as beautiful a creature as God ever put on this earth, I'll tell you that, Jason. But she's a little slow. They used to say 'retarded.' Now they say 'developmentally disabled.' I say 'slow.' Just a little slow, is all. A good mother. A loving mother. She just needs some help, is all.

"Well, it's not easy being in that condition. She wanted to have a life. She wanted boyfriends, you know, everything a young woman wants. And she wanted to have a child of her own. Especially after Marisa's mother—my Patricia—died. She became so fixated on it. She had to have a child. She *had* to. I guess she thought it was some way to cope with the loss of her mother."

"Circle of life."

"That's just it. Yeah. Circle of life." He sighed. "But try telling an adoption agency that you're a single, mentally retarded woman. *Try* telling them that. Jason, do you have any idea what it's like to see your daughter in so much—" Carlo's eyes fixed on me. "Well, now I guess you do have some idea, don't you?"

"Let's leave me out of this," I said. "I think you're getting to the part where you decided to kidnap Audrey for Marisa."

Carlo inclined his head. "She saw the girl at that picnic. She followed her around, watching her. I wasn't aware at the time. But she was fixated. She kept talking about Audrey, Audrey, that kind of thing." He shook his head. "And this man, Frank Cutler, he was no kind of a good man. He was a drunk, is what he was. Half the time, he showed up to the job in the bag. The other half, he didn't show at all."

"Hold up," I said. "You're justifying this?"

He stared at me, a whisper of a smile across his face. "It's what you do. You justify. You tell yourself that you can give this girl a better life than she'd have with a loser for a father. Yes, you justify."

"You made sure he was away from the house the night you took her. You had some of your people keep him out and drunk at a bar."

"Yes. That's true. But they didn't know about this," Carlo said. "This was all my idea. All my doing."

"You took her? You were the one who took her from her bed?"

"Yes," he answered.

I didn't believe it. But I couldn't prove otherwise. At this point, there was no way I could prove whether it was Carlo, one of his sons, or even his daughter who pulled Audrey Cutler out of her room. But it was very clear that Carlo, the patriarch, was going to take the fall for everyone else.

"I told the family she was adopted," he went on. "My daughter? Bless her heart, but how would she know different?"

"And your boys?"

"Your father tells you something, you believe it."

I looked again at Audrey, hooked up to tubes and machines. "She got her mother's genes," I said, recalling similar machines hooked up to Mary Cutler while she was on her deathbed. "Her kidneys are failing."

"She's dying. The donor lists won't cut it. It's a genetic thing. She needs her brother's kidney. And she needs it fast."

But by the time they found her brother, Sammy, he was under arrest for the murder of Griffin Perlini. They couldn't very well waltz into the Department of Corrections and announce themselves. It would be copping to kidnapping.

Correction: They *could* have done that. But they didn't want to get caught.

So they needed Sammy to beat the rap—and to do so quickly. Carlo sent his boy Tommy to tell the police that he saw a black man fleeing the murder scene. Keeping it in the family, of course, because this kind of a secret was too sacred.

Then they sent Smith to offer Sammy the best legal representation money could buy. When he insisted on me, they had no choice. And then I started getting creative. I helped find a burial site of young girls, among other things, and Carlo and Smith began to worry that I was going to drag this case out. They knew I'd want DNA testing on those bodies to confirm that one of them was Audrey, and even though that test would obviously come out negative, there would be a delay of the trial. A delay that could cost Audrey—Patricia—her life. That's when they started lowering the boom on me, using Pete.

Stick to the script, they told me, after they'd pinched Pete in that drug bust. Sure. Don't get creative, in other words. Don't worry about the witnesses against Sammy. Don't cause a delay. Don't do much of anything, in fact, while they went to work on the case, offering Tommy's perjured testimony, finding Kenny Sanders as a fall guy, strong-arming the witnesses against Sammy.

"Out of curiosity," I said. "How did you expect this to play out? You get Sammy off the charges, and then you just tell him, 'By the way, your long-lost sister is still alive, and could she please have one of your kidneys?'"

"You say these things as if there were many options. But there were no options." He looked at me. "What would we have done? I don't know. Offer him money for his kidney and for his silence, I guess. Would we have killed him afterward? You want me to tell you that wasn't a possibility? I don't know." He shook his head. "None of that mattered until we got him out of jail."

That stood to reason, which is to say, there was no reason. From his perspective, his only hope, short of confessing, was to get Sammy free and then think of something.

"You need to know, Jason," Carlo said, wagging an insistent finger at me. "You need to know, this girl has been loved every day of her life. She was given everything, but most of all our—our love," he managed, choking out the words. "Extreme actions. We took extreme actions, yes. But it was a matter of life and death. I would rip"—he grabbed at his midsection—"I would rip every organ out of my body to save her. So would my boys. We would do anything."

"Everything but confess to a crime. This could have been all over months ago."

"Yes. I admit it. I'll confess now. Call the police. Have an officer come to this room."

"I'm going to do just that." I opened my cell phone, searched through the directory, and made the call. "Detective Carruthers," I said. "Jason Kolarich. You won't have to keep that photo of Audrey Cutler any more."

I gave a little taste of the details and signed off.

"You tried to kill me today," I said to Carlo. I thought it deserved mention.

He nodded. "I knew it was over. I was ready to go to the cops. I just wanted to protect the rest of my family. This was my doing. It should be me who pays. Me. Just me." Carlo rose from the chair with some effort and approached me. He took my arm as he began to lose composure, his body trembling, tears falling. "I beg you, Jason. I beg you. The brother— he'll hate me. He'll hate all of us. He has every right to. But please, son— *please* convince the brother to donate a kidney."

MY BROTHER ARRIVED at the hospital at almost the same time as the police. He showed up without an escort, having been dropped off at the hospital with instructions to head to the sixth floor. His left hand was bandaged where he'd lost the finger and he looked like absolute hell, but he was relatively intact and the sense of relief was all over his face.

My brother and I weren't much for hugging over the years, but we had a long embrace and then I checked him over, with one arm over his shoulder. "I'm okay," he insisted. "Other than the finger, they didn't lay a glove on me. They pretty much ignored me, actually."

I patted his chest. "A braver man than I."

Police officers were streaming in now. Carlo had left Audrey's room and was being questioned by Carruthers and other cops in an empty room down the hall. The whole thing was turning into a madhouse.

"Let's get lost," I suggested. Pete needed to have his hand examined—at least we were in the right place for that. But mostly I wanted to usher Pete away from this scene, from the entire affair, as quickly as I could. And once we broke away, there was another stop I wanted to make, too.

61

HIS NAME WASN'T SMITH. It was Raymond Hertzberg, an attorney in private practice who specialized in transactional work, an interesting way to describe what he did. His clients were a who's who of shady characters—some whose names and photographs would be found on flow charts in the FBI offices, and many who didn't quite rise to the level of mafia but had some connection or another with organized crime.

He was at his office until well after ten o'clock. He stuffed a number of documents into his old suitcase and carried an additional gym bag for the overload. A long trip was in the making, some place sunny with favorable extradition laws.

He had a firearm, which he typically didn't carry, stuffed into his suit pocket. Just a few hours now and he'd be on his way, hopefully just to be sure everything had settled in a manner favorable to him. Otherwise, perhaps a permanent stay.

He trusted Carlo as much as anyone that ever lived. He knew Carlo wouldn't give him up. But that didn't guarantee Smith wouldn't be exposed, least of all to Jason Kolarich.

He took one last look around his office space, wondering if he'd ever see it again. Then he awkwardly navigated the front door of the suite, putting down his suitcase, unlocking the door and pushing it open, then picking up the suitcase again and pushing the heavy door with his shoulder.

The door pushed back, crashing him against the door frame, once, twice, a third time, taking the wind from him. His suitcase fell, dumping over, papers scattering everywhere. A final time, the door crashing against his forehead and knocking the back of his head into the frame, a one-two combination that left him seeing stars as he shrunk to the ground.

"Hi, Smith." Jason Kolarich's foot connected with Smith's jaw, knocking Smith sideways to the floor. Smith rolled over and looked up at Kolarich. "I'm not going to kill you," said Kolarich, "unless you go for that gun."

"He was an old friend," Smith managed, fighting the searing pain in his jaw. "He was just trying to help his daughter."

"I've heard the story, thanks." Kolarich dropped a document onto Smith's chest. "You've been served, Smith," he said. "Or should I say Raymond?"

Smith tried to sit up, taking the document in both hands. He caught a caption, *Peter Kolarich and Samuel Cutler versus Raymond Hertzberg.*

"We're suing you," Kolarich said.

"Suing—?" Smith managed to get into a seated position and looked at the document. In his confusion and pain, he began to feel a stream of relief, as well.

"My brother is suing you for the tort of unlawful restraint, Smith. Sammy's suing for intentional infliction of emotional distress. I think that's an understatement, myself."

Smith leafed through the five-page document.

"It's quite vague, I admit," said Kolarich. "Probably wouldn't survive a motion to dismiss. I could always amend it and put in all sorts of details. But I'm not going to do that."

"And—why—why aren't you going to do that?"

"Because after I file it tomorrow, I'm going to voluntarily dismiss it."

Smith shook his head in confusion, causing further pain to his jaw.

"You and me, we're going to settle the lawsuit. Right here, right now. I'm thinking a million dollars for each of them, Smith. Think real hard before you answer."

Smith touched his jaw. It was broken, he thought. He understood what Kolarich was doing. He was getting a sorry-for-your-troubles payoff from Smith but giving it cover—the settling of a lawsuit. Smith would officially be paying this money not as extortion but to settle a lawsuit out of court. And both Pete Kolarich and Sammy Cutler would collect a million dollars in tax-free compensatory damages.

"A million apiece is reasonable," Smith said.

"I think so, too. Sign at the dotted line, please." He threw a second document at Smith, a settlement and release of all claims, in which Smith was agreeing to pay these sums to Peter Kolarich and Samuel Cutler. Smith caught the pen that Kolarich tossed him and signed the document.

"Terrific." Kolarich folded the document into his jacket pocket. "Looks like you might be planning a trip? Go ahead. Bon voyage. Personally, I hope you leave and never come back. But understand, Smith, I'll have a judgment that I can enforce against you. I'll attach every asset you have in this state, thanks to this settlement, whether you live here or in Barbados. Oh, and one last thing."

Kolarich threw a third document at Smith, who gathered it and read it. It was a sworn affidavit from Jason Kolarich, detailing virtually everything that had happened since Smith first visited his office. "That affidavit," said Kolarich, "is in my safe-deposit box, in my e-mail, in my lawyer's e-mail, you name it. Anything happens to me or my brother or Sammy, this affidavit goes to the police. But you stay away from us, Smith, and we stay away from you." He took another step toward Smith, who winced. "I don't want my brother to have to think about you ever again."

"The feeling—the feeling is mutual," Smith managed.

Kolarich surveyed the scene. "Well, Raymond, I wish I could say it's been a pleasure."

"It will be a pleasure—for this to be over," Smith said. He touched his jaw again, feeling light-headed. He felt himself swooning, losing consciousness, but fought it. He gathered himself together and looked back at the door. Jason Kolarich was gone.

62

SAMMY WALKED THROUGH the corridor tentatively, a coat thrown over his wrists to hide the handcuffs, people watching him carefully as he passed. He was a celebrity. His story had been splashed everywhere. He was unaccustomed to such notoriety and had responded with silence, refusing requests for interviews and making no comment whatsoever. Still, someone had leaked today's visit and the media had swarmed outside the hospital today. St. Agnes had made special arrangements for his arrival, escorting him from the Department of Corrections van to a private doctor's elevator bank to the sixth floor.

Sammy, the two armed deputies, and I stopped outside the room. The deputies uncuffed him, per an earlier agreement reached between the Department of Corrections and me. Sammy looked back at me, as if seeking advice.

"She's your sister, Sammy," I said.

He nodded and looked at the door. "Come with me, Koke?"

I followed him into the room as he came upon her. He stood, motionless, for what felt like a lifetime. He didn't speak, either. What he was seeing was a very, very sick woman who didn't have long to live. Dialysis was keeping her alive but not for long.

But he was also seeing his sister, for the first time in twenty-eight years.

He pulled up a chair and sat, his trembling hands in his lap. "Hi," he said awkwardly, unsure of himself. Then he leaned closer to her ear. "Hi, Patricia."

I winced. Sammy was calling his sister by the name she'd known almost her entire life, the one given to her by the Butchers. If she survived the kidney transplant, she'd have plenty of time to learn the story. For now, she was Patricia.

"I don't know if you can hear me," he said. "This probably doesn't make sense to you, but I've missed you. I've thought about you—"

It came at once, the emotion, closing off his throat. His chest spasmed. Tears began to streak down his face. He touched her hand and then took it in his, stroking it. "You're gonna be—you're gonna be okay now," he whispered. "You're gonna be okay now."

"TIME SERVED," I said. "First of all, he didn't do it. Second of all, let's let this poor guy be with his sister."

Judge Kathleen Poker, sitting in her high-backed leather chair in chambers, was receptive to my plea, particularly in light of recent media interest in the case. Sammy was being bathed in a sympathetic light, and no one was feeling sorry for a child predator who had killed four children and molested countless others. That had been another benefit of the media intensity over the last week and a half—the state police had expedited the DNA testing and confirmed that Griffin Perlini had raped each of the four girls found buried behind Hardigan Elementary School.

I had a child killer for a victim and an aggrieved man recently reunited with his abducted sister for a defendant.

The judge made a steeple with her hands, touching them to her lips. "Yes, I notice there was no diminished-capacity defense. Your client maintains he didn't do it?"

"Yes, Your Honor. In fact, we think we know who did. We named him on the witness list. Archie Novotny. His daughter was molested by Griffin Perlini. He has the same jacket, and the same green stocking cap, that witnesses confirmed the killer was wearing. And he has no alibi for that night."

The judge's eyes shifted to Lester Mapp, the prosecutor. "Judge, look.

We don't want to bury this guy. We don't—we don't need that. But we can't give this guy a pass, either."

"And what about this Novotny person?" the judge asked.

Mapp let out a sigh. "We haven't been able to speak with him yet, Judge. He won't talk to us."

The judge looked at the prosecutor with curiosity. "That's called obstruction, isn't it?"

"Not if you're taking Five," I interjected.

"Ah." The judge nodded. "He's invoked his rights."

"Yeah, that should play out well at trial," I noted.

"We think we'll be giving him immunity, Judge." Lester Mapp was generally displeased with the state of affairs and, of late, no doubt, with his assignment to this case in the first place.

"He thinks," I said. "He thinks he'll give Novotny immunity. He says he thinks because he's not sure that Novotny didn't commit this crime, and he wants to be careful what he wishes for."

"I understand, I understand." The judge raised a hand. "Mr. Mapp, where is the state on a plea?"

"We offered ten, Judge."

She thought about that. "Mr. Kolarich, can I assume you'll be asking for an instruction on involuntary?"

"I certainly will, Judge." When a defendant is charged with a crime like first-degree murder, a defendant can ask that the jury be instructed on a lesser-included offense, which here would include involuntary manslaughter. It's up to the judge, but if the court believes that the evidence warrants a finding on a lesser-included offense, she can give that option to the jury.

The nice thing about involuntary manslaughter is that the judge can impose a sentence down to probation. Everyone in the room knew what she was doing. She was telling Lester Mapp that she could drop the sentence well below the ten years he was seeking.

"Give us a minute, Counsel," the judge said to me. It was common for judges to conduct pretrials with each lawyer separately, provided all sides agreed to such ex parte communications.

I went into the courtroom and sat. In the last couple of weeks, I had slowly recovered sleep. I hadn't done any legal work except for Sammy. I'd spent a lot of time with my brother, whose newly buffered bank account, courtesy of Raymond "Smith" Hertzberg, had given him the freedom to decide to return to school for a master's degree.

Sammy was going under tomorrow for the kidney transplant. He'd left me with the same instructions as he had earlier. He could take a twelve-year sentence, he'd prefer eight. So I was going a little off the reservation here, but I didn't see what interest of justice was served by putting Sammy Cutler behind bars for several years. The way I saw it, Griffin Perlini probably would have returned to his old ways had Sammy not performed a community service by shooting him.

About twenty minutes later, Lester Mapp passed the torch to me. He sat in the courtroom as I returned to the judge's chambers.

"Involuntary and four years," said the judge. "Your client already has one in. He's looking at about another year."

Half of which would be spent at a halfway house on his way out of the system. God bless the severely overcrowded state prison system.

"I have authority for three," I said, taking my best shot.

"No, four's the best you're going to do." She threw up her hands. "Four it is, Mr. Kolarich. Take it or leave it."

I thought about Sammy's willingness to take twelve. I thought about our scapegoat, Archie Novotny. I thought about all the ways this could go south. I was relatively sure that I didn't want the prosecution to take a long, hard look at Novotny.

"We'll take four," I said.

63

I THOUGHT WE TALKED about eight," Sammy said from his hospital bed.

"We did. But you have remarkably able counsel. I got you four." I pointed to the door. "I can go back and offer to double it, if you'd like."

Sammy smiled and laughed. "No, four sounds pretty good."

Sammy was in pre-op, getting ready for tomorrow's transplant surgery.

"Hey, just to ask," he said. "You think we would've won the case?"

I made a face. "I would've used Archie Novotny to make sure the jury knew that the dead guy was a child molester. It was possible, right there, that they'd acquit. But other than that, I don't know, Sammy. They had a strong case." I paused, then added, "I don't think Archie Novotny would've held up under scrutiny."

Sammy didn't look at me. "What do you mean?"

"I mean, he was pretty clever, but maybe too clever by half. It was nice of him to leave the closet by his front door open when I came to visit, and even nicer of him to have that bomber jacket and green stocking cap prominently displayed for me."

Sammy didn't answer.

"Nicer still," I added, "that the murder happened on a Thursday night, when Archie would normally have a guitar lesson which he conspicuously missed. I mean, he even went so far as to write a note on his check to the guitar instructor, in case anyone might forget that he missed his lesson on that fateful night."

Sammy shook his head, fighting a smile. A shade of rose colored his cheeks.

"Let me guess," I continued. "If we went to trial, Archie would have pleaded the Fifth, leaving me to shit all over him in front of the jury and getting us a long way toward reasonable doubt. And if the prosecutor gave him immunity, Novotny would have grudgingly admitted that he missed his guitar lesson that night but he'd say he didn't remember where he was that night. He'd deny murdering Perlini, but it wouldn't have been a convincing denial. Right so far?"

Sammy brought a hand to his flushed face.

"And say the shit really hit the fan. Say the prosecutors decided to charge *him* with murder. I'd imagine that Archie had an out. One that he could say he 'forgot,' given that it was over a year ago—but push comes to shove, Archie had an alibi. Didn't he?"

Sammy paused, then spoke through his hand. "He went to the emergency room that night, complaining of chest pains."

"Ah, I like that," I said. "Nothing the prosecutors would ever think to look for. But he could always play that card. The hospital would have documented a check-in time, all sorts of testing, and a check-out time. An iron-clad alibi, in his back pocket, if he needed it."

"Archie's a good guy," Sammy said. "Perlini really fucked with his family's life."

"So the deal was, you'd kill Perlini, and Novotny would play the alternate suspect."

That was the reason, all along, that Sammy hadn't wanted to plead temporary insanity or a similar defense. He didn't want to admit to killing Perlini because he knew he could point to Archie. It had been Sammy, after all, who had referred me to other victims of Perlini as possible suspects. Novotny's daughter was a documented victim, one of the two who had sent Perlini to prison for molestation.

"Smart," I said, "but maybe too smart. Conspiracy to commit, Sammy. You guys could've both gone down for that. You knew that, right? That's one of the reasons you wanted to cut a deal. You decided, end of the day, you didn't want to risk Archie."

He nodded. "That was part of it, yeah. But like I told you—when you told me Perlini didn't kill Audrey, I felt like maybe I should pay a price."

Sammy, I decided, had paid plenty. Maybe the sentence he'd serve would be slightly out of proportion to the crime he'd committed, but all things considered, I didn't think the world was terribly out of balance as a result.

I looked around the room. "You ready for tomorrow?"

"Yeah." He nodded. "It feels good, y'know? I'm helping her. I get to do something positive. A guy like me, I don't get to do a whole lot of good."

"Call it a second chance, then." I patted his arm. "I'll be here when you wake up," I promised. "And when Audrey wakes up."

"Yeah." He lit up at the mention of her name. "She don't even know me, Koke. She's got a whole family now."

Such as it was. She'd only be seeing the man she thought of as her grandfather, Carlo, during visiting hours at Marymount Penitentiary. Carlo hadn't been formally sentenced, but I was pretty sure his term would be tantamount to life for a seventy-three-year-old man. Her "mother," Marisa Butcher, had received a complete pass from law enforcement, who'd never be able to prove that a mildly retarded woman was behind a plot to kidnap Audrey. In fact, I don't believe she played any role in it whatsoever, and I'd found her to be a sweet, gentle woman. She'd been on quite the roller coaster recently, losing her father to prison but gaining a kidney donor for her desperate "daughter."

Tommy, Audrey's "uncle," was a different story. Regardless of what he knew about Audrey twenty-eight years ago—he claimed total ignorance, naturally—it was pretty obvious that he was clued into the truth recently, given his role in Sammy's murder trial. Prosecutors were taking a hard look at him for perjury from his testimony at Sammy's hearing. Given his obvious self-interest in the outcome of Sammy's case, it seemed like one whale of a coincidence that he happened by the Liberty Apartments on the night of Griffin Perlini's murder and spotted a black man fleeing the scene, particularly when he clearly was not at Downey's Pub drinking liquor that night, as he'd said. I figured the odds were good that he'd take a fall on that one. Which meant that Tommy's brother, Jake, who had provided corroboration for Tommy, might get hit with an obstruction charge himself.

So all was not warm and fuzzy in the Butcher household. Audrey, if she awoke tomorrow with a new, healthy kidney, would find herself down a grandfather and possibly two uncles, and with a hell of a revelation about her entire family.

But she'd have Sammy.

"Audrey knows you," I told him. "And she *will* know you." I put on my coat and walked to the door.

"Hey."

I turned back around.

"I'm not the only one who got a second chance."

It was true. Not many people can say they dodged a bullet and mean it, literally. Guns misfire. It happens. Should I accept that as an element of some grand plan, an act of divine intervention? I couldn't just turn off a lifetime of cynicism, nor could I accept that compromise—my life for Talia's and Emily's.

THE AIR OUTSIDE had grown chilly. I lifted my chin to the November sky, letting the wind curl inside my jacket. *This is it,* I thought. Life 2.0. As bizarre and sometimes terrifying as October had been, it was better than the four months preceding it. I'd been pulled out of my funk— against my will, but pulled out no less. I'd probably look back on that span of time and summarize it as grief bookended by twin traumas, though the second one had a pretty happy ending, all things considered.

But that meant that the worst of that grief—not the dull ache but the pulse-pounding, nightmare-inducing, breath-whisking horror—was over. And this was the truth: I was more frightened now than I'd ever been during the four months after my family died; more scared than I was at any time while Sammy, Pete, and even I faced life-threatening challenges. I knew how to mourn; that, in many ways, was easy. But this part—moving on, starting fresh, the beginning of the rest of my life— this, I didn't know how to do. This didn't make sense. Put a smile on my face, earn a living, have some laughs with Shauna and Pete, smell the occasional flower—and pretend that all of it means something?

Pretend. That, I realized, I could do. Hide behind a confident swagger, a screw-it-all attitude, the occasional sarcastic zinger. Hide behind that facade while I wait for the road to materialize before me.

Because I wanted to see that road. I wanted to go on. I wanted it to get better. I wanted to have a reason.

"I'll try," I said. "That's all I can promise." I pulled up my collar and started for my car.

ACKNOWLEDGMENTS

As always, I am indebted to others in the writing of this novel: Dan Collins, for his patient explanations when it comes to matters regarding law enforcement; Dr. Ronald Wright, to whom I always turn for help on forensic sciences; Jim Jann, for brainstorming on plot and tweaks on characters and atmosphere.

Larry Kirshbaum and Susanna Einstein, my brilliant agents, helped mold the initial plot into something much more meaningful. You guys are the best. Rachel Holtzman—my eternal gratitude for all of your macro- and micro-comments that added so much depth to the novel; best of luck in future endeavors.

Michael Barson, Summer Smith—everyone at Putnam who tries to make me look good. Not a small chore. My thanks to you as always.

Thank you to Ivan Held, Neil Nyren, and Leslie Gelbman for your enthusiasm and support. I greatly value your trust and encouragement. I realize how lucky I am.

And to Susan, my best friend, the love of my life, my oxygen. You make it all worthwhile.